the

awkward

age

the

awkward

age

Francesca Segal

RIVERHEAD BOOKS

New York

2017

RIVERHEAD BOOKS
An imprint of Penguin Random House LLC
375 Hudson Street
New York, New York 10014

Excerpt from "Poem for a Daughter" from *Poems 1955–2005*
by Anne Stevenson (Bloodaxe Books, 2005).

Library of Congress Cataloging-in-Publication Data

Names: Segal, Francesca, 1980- author.
Title: The awkward age : a novel / Francesca Segal.
Description: New York : Riverhead Books, 2017.
Identifiers: LCCN 2016048993| ISBN 9780399576454 (hardcover) |
ISBN 9780399576478 (ebook)
Subjects: LCSH: Domestic fiction. | BISAC: FICTION /
Family Life. | FICTION / Coming of Age. | FICTION /
Literary. | GSAFD: Bildungsromans.
Classification: LCC PS3619.E374 A97 2017 |
DDC 813/.6—dc23
LC record available at
https://lccn.loc.gov/2016048993
p.   cm.

Printed in the United States of America
1   3   5   7   9   10   8   6   4   2

Book design by Meighan Cavanaugh

For GMA

Why does a mother need a daughter?
Heart's needle, hostage to fortune,
freedom's end. Yet nothing's more perfect
than that bleating, razor-shaped cry
that delivers a mother to her baby.
The bloodcord snaps that held
their sphere together. The child,
tiny and alone, creates the mother.

A woman's life is her own
until it is taken away
by a first, particular cry.
Then she is not alone
but a part of the premises
of everything there is:
a time, a tribe, a war.

—ANNE STEVENSON, "POEM FOR A DAUGHTER"

part one

1.

THE TEENAGERS WOULD FUCK IT UP. CERTAINLY THEY ALWAYS tried; it was the only impulse Gwen and Nathan had in common, besides their hostility toward one another. This morning the thought of waking her daughter filled Julia with a particular foreboding, despite her own excitement about the weekend.

They were all going to America, to James's hometown, which Julia had imagined since meeting him. They had given one another their futures but she was greedy for his past, too; she would never know him young, but knowing Boston seemed the next best thing, a way to make up the impossible, inconceivable deficit of all the wasted days spent not loving him, before they'd met. She wanted to see the places that had mattered; to visit Harvard, where James had turned his tassel, had become a doctor, a husband, a father; had grown from unknown boy into the cherished man who now lay beside her, breathing steadily, facedown in his pillow, in their bed, on the top floor of what was now their home, a narrow Victorian terraced house in Gospel Oak, north London. She was looking forward to Boston. On the other hand, this holiday meant three intensive days with Nathan, who would no doubt take every opportunity to needle her with casual reminiscence about the halcyon days during which his father had been married to his mother. Meanwhile Julia's own daughter, Gwen, would be dependably more difficult. Such had been the way.

James stirred, smiled sleepily up at Julia, and hooked an arm round her waist. He drew her back to the horizontal, and began to mumble into her hair. A muscled thigh fell over hers, hot and marble-heavy, and she was pinioned.

"The cab's in an hour, we've got to get the kids up. I have to do the dog."

He shook his head, without opening his eyes. "Send the kids without us, let's stay here. It'd serve them right for being pains in the rear end."

On cue, a thudding bass began beneath them, too loud for the rest of the terrace at this or any hour. Nathan was awake. Impossible to rouse most mornings he was home from boarding school, it seemed he could spring up before daylight when Boston—and an escape from her house, Julia suspected—lay ahead of him. Predictably, dispiritingly, Gwen's voice now rose, shouting a sleep-slurred obscenity. At the sound of so many humans unexpectedly awake during his early shift, Mole began to bark with joy. The thump of tail on wooden boards was followed by a frantic scrabbling outside their bedroom door. "Shut *up!*" they then heard, and the dog and the rest of Gwen's complaint were drowned out when Nathan turned up the volume.

"When will they start to be nice to each other?"

James had tipped forward and was fishing on the floor beside the bed for last night's T-shirt, bare buttocks in the air. "Probably never," he said cheerily, from this position. "But we can get rid of them soon. College. The army. Sell them into service." When this got no reply he sat up again and said more gently, "Give it time, it hasn't been very long. It's a big change for both of them."

"Saskia's been civilized. Why is your daughter an angel when mine is being such a nightmare?"

"Saskia doesn't have to live here," James pointed out. He was squinting at his watch. "Cab's in an hour and twenty. Have I got time for a run? I'll take the dog."

He was out of bed, flexing and yawning, and Julia paused to look at him. It was extraordinary that this man now shared her bed. He was broad chested, solid, beautiful. At fifty-five he was still mostly blonde. He was tall, and square in the way that only Americans are square—as if raised, corn-fed and free-range, on strong sunshine and red meat and the earnest and deliberate pursuit of happiness. Her English imagination placed him in dungarees on a tractor, a piece of straw between white teeth, or tugging on the brim of his cap as he swaggered up to bat on a sun-bleached baseball diamond, a mixing of metaphors inspired mostly by her admiration for his height, and his shoulders. This visit to America would begin to set her imagery straight, and that he was, in reality, a Jewish obstetrician from a working-class neighborhood of Boston would remain a delightful incongruity. In surgical scrubs he looked outsized and vaguely alarming. He saved women's lives. He saved Julia, every day.

When they met she had been raising Gwen alone for five years, with the volatile intensity of hostages long held together. He had come to Julia for piano lessons and she had found, over time, that her weeks began to shape themselves around his classes. He had an easy charm and made her laugh. With a series of caveats she eventually agreed to coffee, ostensibly to discuss his musical progress (which was poor, if dogged). On their first date, timed to coincide with Gwen's Geography field trip to study glaciated landscapes around Keswick, Julia had sat, prim and awkward and resistant, had spoken little but had drunk a great deal of red wine, and had eventually launched herself upon James in the taxi home with an alarming and volcanic hunger, and had spoken her first honest, unguarded words to him, hungover and ashamed the next morning. This was an English first date, as she remembered it. To James, its speed affirmed his growing conviction that they were meant to be together. For they were meant to be together. He was all she'd never dared to want.

Until that time, Gwen had been absently polite when James arrived each week—just another of her mother's students traipsing to the first-floor music room with Chopin nocturnes and a mediocre hand span—but overnight had sworn him mortal enemy, blood-deep rival, her father's bitter adversary and her own. She had lost one parent, and would not yield her mother without a fight. Julia feared Gwen and feared for her, and had never before withstood her daughter's rages. But she had uncovered a new, accidental source of strength: she had fallen in love. Despite the obstacles, James brought sunshine and she had begun to believe, with his help, that her own happiness could start to heal her daughter. This new relationship was entirely different from her marriage, and for that she was grateful. It made it simpler, somehow, to find for James a chamber in a heart that had for so long been only Gwen's. James encouraged Julia to relax, to take him for granted, to believe that he was hers to grow old with, but she would not. Such wasteful complaisance would be unforgivable when their luck was too extraordinary. That their two fragile human hearts continued to beat each hour she knew to be a miracle. Joy was a passing alignment of stars, a flash of sun burning gold flames on water before the clouds came. Julia knew life to be a series of calamities. She waited for the piano to fall, the tornado to strike, and in the meantime her own pure happiness thrilled and frightened her. If only Gwen didn't hate him so much.

JULIA CAME DOWN to find both children already in the kitchen, still in pajamas, still deftly, stubbornly ignoring each other. Nathan stood spooning porridge into his mouth before the open fridge door, staring into its cavern with steady interest, as if watching television. He had not yet styled his hair, which meant a lengthy tenure in the bathroom lay ahead. It stood electrified in thick dark tufts above his dark brows, and his milky complexion was slightly roughened by excessive unnecessary optimistic shaving. Julia had not yet grown accustomed to the boy's minute interest in and attention to his own appearance, which far outstripped her daughter's daily maintenance. The other day she had come upon him sprawled on the sofa while his girlfriend, Valentina, iced and plucked his eyebrows. He had waved in lordly greeting, unembarrassed.

Gwen lay extended on the tiled floor beside Mole, stroking one of the Labrador's black silky ears and whispering apologies for the upcoming disturbance. Mole yawned hugely in reply, black wax lips contracted, long pink tongue extended and curling upward. Gwen took this to be the end of the conversation and stood up. She was taller than her mother, taller even than Nathan. She had the alien, angular proportions of a fashion model, Julia knew, and desperately hoped the idea would never occur to her. In any case, Gwen moved not with grace but with clumsy, gangling awkwardness. It would be charitable to believe that she had yet to learn her own proportions, that she'd simply grown too quickly, but she had been almost six foot tall since she was thirteen—three years, now—and still she bumped into walls, and tripped over invisible objects, and banged her knees beneath tables. Today she had piled her exuberant red curls on her head and skewered the fat knot with a striped black-and-yellow pencil. She bent to brush her knees, vigorously. Her glasses slipped down her nose and she pushed them back up with her knuckle.

"Must you?"

"Must I what?"

"Darling, you're getting dog hair all over the kitchen."

Gwen gave a last swipe at her pajama bottoms. "It's not my fault he sheds. Oh! So listen, I found my black jeans, they were—duh, duh duh!—in my school bag. The mystery is solved."

Behind her Nathan had begun to whistle "Yankee Doodle," softly, out of tune. Julia carried the kettle to the sink, fantasizing about coffee and silence. "Good morning, Nathan," she said, in his direction. Then to Gwen, remembering, "Have you got the dog stuff together for Grandpa?"

Gwen nodded toward the door. "There. He said just bring food and tablets, he'd use his own bowls."

Nathan was still gazing into the fridge. Misty cold expensive air reached Julia. Eventually he extracted a basket of raspberries, which he then began to plop one by one into the saucepan of remaining porridge bubbling over on the hob. Julia averted her eyes. She had stayed up late last night, cleaning the kitchen.

"Oatmeal?" he offered, extending the saucepan toward her.

"No, thank you."

"I might have some," said Gwen, freed by her mother's presence to speak to him directly. "But you're meant to wash raspberries, they're covered in stuff."

"I wouldn't take undue risks in that case," said Nathan, tipping the mess into his own bowl. He scraped the pan then set it, empty and encrusted, back on the hob. Their methods varied but on balance the children were equally rude to one another, and James had told Julia he thought they could be safely left to duke it out between themselves. Privately, she was inclined to blame Nathan, who goaded.

Julia sipped scalding coffee and went through her list again. The windows had been done; she had taken out the rubbish but there would be more generated by the children; something needed to be done about the heating. James would happily do it all when he returned, but she had grown used to running her household alone, and could not bring herself to tempt fate by depending upon him. They were really leaving, and it would soon become clear whether this idea of a family trip had been foolhardy or inspired.

Nathan took out a chopping board and announced his intention to make a vegetable omelet, following this with the news that he had never attempted an omelet before, but how hard, after all, could it be? It was important to travel on a good, square meal. He was back in the fridge, taking out eggs, butter, milk, tomatoes, several zucchini, and the whole cheese drawer, which Julia knew from experience was almost impossible to get back onto its plastic runners once it had been removed. Had James been here he would have put a robust and efficient kibosh on this plan as Nathan was unlikely to starve between Gospel Oak and Terminal Five, and had not yet finished packing. But James was not yet back from his jog, and Julia had so far avoided disciplining or even advising his son. She looked at her watch. The morning was slipping from her grasp, and they still had to drop the dog with Philip.

2

ALL THIS COHABITATION WAS NEW. THE HOUSE IN QUEEN'S Crescent had been home to Julia Alden since before Gwen's birth. She and Daniel had bought it when she was heavily pregnant, moon-faced and cumbrous as she unpacked boxes and helped Daniel to paint the baby's room in pale willow and stronger mint greens. The room would become a grassy landscape against which their tiny, red-faced, orange-haired daughter would resemble a furious, insomniac leprechaun, demanding and bewitching in equal measure. When Daniel died five years ago, succumbing in six months to the efficient liver cancer he had long before managed to beat with such misleading ease, Julia could not bring herself to move. Queen's Crescent was where he was, or wasn't, and his palpable absence had been all that she and Gwen had of him. She was no longer on speaking terms with her own bitter and disappointed mother but Daniel's parents, Philip and Iris, had helped her with the practicalities. How they felt about this latest development was an uncertainty that made her anxious; asked directly, they were unfailingly elegant and generous. Iris Alden had for some time been suggesting, hinting, commanding that Julia ought to "move on." It was unhealthy for Julia and Gwen to live in such intense and inward symbiosis, Iris had reproved her daughter-in-law, and each now needed a man around, for different, equally valid reasons. But "moving on" was abstract, where "moving in" was concrete, deliberate, and unavoidable. Julia had first met James through Philip Alden, who had befriended him at an obstetric conference. This ought to have eased her conscience, but didn't. Philip had recommended her to James as a piano teacher, not a life partner. When she found the time Julia worried for her in-laws, in between worrying about everything else.

Along with five suitcases, several crates of expensive red wine, twelve cardboard boxes of books (many of which proved to be the U.S. paperback editions of novels already in the house), an elaborate sound system with large, freestanding speakers, and a cherished American coffee maker, James Fuller and his son, Nathan, had arrived one afternoon in the balmy golden light and warmth of early September, and for the eleven weeks since then, the household had been black with tension and thunder. Gwen was constitutionally incapable of concealing her loathing and distress; Nathan, a year older and slightly more socially sophisticated, was equally unhappy but would not admit it. To Julia he was obsequious and detectably patronizing.

Alone with Gwen he mostly ignored or bullied her, idly, correcting her grammar or mocking the blog she kept, on which she re-created key scenes from her week with miniature plasticine figures staged in elaborate shoebox sets. James was represented by a Lego figure of Darth Vader, black-helmeted, sinister, wreaking destruction. Nathan appeared in clay, always hand in hand with his girlfriend, Valentina, a polished and imperious little sprite who stayed over whenever he was home for the weekend from boarding school. Gwen had made Valentina beautiful, had faithfully rendered the girl's silky blonde hair and prominent bust, but she always made the couple's clothes match, and put them both in sunglasses, even inside, even at night. This was a clever and irreproachable way of making them look slightly ludicrous. Julia, Philip, and Iris made frequent use of this blog to gauge Gwen's mood. Once upbeat and sunny, it was now unfailingly despairing, since her mother had fallen in love with Darth Vader.

"I JUST WANTED TO SAY *bon voyage*, darling."

Julia wedged the phone between ear and shoulder and continued to do battle with the zip of her luggage. Poised and unflappable, unfailingly judgmental of those who were neither, Iris had an unerring instinct for Julia's most chaotic moments.

"Thank you. The *voyage* part might be a bit stressful, we're late already, nobody's downstairs. You'd think we were preparing to go away for a month."

"Under the circumstances three days may come to feel like a month. Have you and Thing planned anything *à deux* while you're there? A little breathing space?"

"No, I don't think it's possible this time. It doesn't seem fair to the kids."

After a heavy silence Iris observed, "Traveling with babies can be so wearying."

"Iris"—Julia tried once more and the zip slid effortlessly up to its hilt, several fine threads of her favorite wool scarf snared halfway down between its teeth. She lowered her voice to a whisper: "I took on board what you said. I'm trying not to infantilize her, but there will be a lot happening for her——"

"There will be a lot happening for you, too. Last time I checked you were meant to be having some fun."

"We will."

"Well do, please. No martyrdom while you're there, it would be very unfashionable, Americans don't believe in it. Channel the national spirit. Be plucky and aspiring."

Julia promised to try. Neither of these characteristics came easily to her, though they were the twin peaks dominating Iris's own natural territory. Julia poured the remains of the milk down the sink, scanning the surfaces for anything else that might turn into a disaster in three days of neglect. When the doorbell rang she was squeezing a perfunctory spray of kitchen cleaner onto the hob where light splashes of Nathan's porridge had already set, hard as concrete. Iris was now describing her own most recent trip to America, and a production of *Indian Ink* on Broadway. Julia of all people really ought to get tickets to the BSO, and Thing loves music, too, doesn't he? Couldn't they sneak off to the Symphony Hall? Didn't Julia think she might deserve it?

"Oh, God, sorry. Cab's outside, I'd better go. Oh, wait! Iris?"

"Yes, I'm still here."

"Are you sure Philip can handle the dog? I know how much he loves him, but Mole's just so big . . ."

"Philip Alden will be just fine, it's good for his knees to walk. He's always threatening to rescue some abandoned scrap from the pound, you know how dotty he is about anything with four legs. They'll be two *alte Kackers* together."

Julia bit her lip. An image arose of the dog bolting after an insouciant London squirrel, pulling slow-moving Philip to the pavement and thence to broken ribs, pneumonia, death. She suppressed this. Mole had not bolted for many years, and his cataracts occluded large items of furniture, so he was unlikely to spot squirrels. His arthritis rivaled Philip's own.

Julia turned her attention to the thermostat. It had a holiday setting, she was certain of it. She pressed buttons, experimental, pessimistic. Iris interpreted her silence, and responded.

"You want me to say I'll take him if it doesn't work out. Julia, that animal reeks. In fifty years I've never let a stinking beast into my beloved house."

"Only if something goes wrong? If Philip seems tired?"

"Nothing will go wrong, but yes, if it makes you feel better, I'll take him should it seem necessary. Now go, and have a lovely time. Don't let the ex-wife intimidate you. Remember she's ex for a reason."

James had come in and was miming his intention of taking her bag out to the idling taxi.

"Mmm. I can't really discuss that right now."

"How subtle you are, darling, a veritable Enigma code. *Bon voyage.* And *bonne chance.* And for the love of God have some fun."

"Thank you. Lots of love, Iris, thank you."

From upstairs Gwen shouted, "Is that Granny? Can I speak?"

"The cab's here! Sorry, Iris, one sec, Gwen's yelling at me." Mother and daughter met in the hall, where Gwen, still shoeless, was extending her hand for the phone. Her hair was in a fat and sopping plait from which a halo of drying curls escaped, glinting copper and gold; she held three packets of polymer modeling clay in white, cherry red, and peacock blue. Nathan thundered down the stairs, flung open the hall cupboard, and began throwing out items, like a dog turning up garden dirt. A pile of hats and gloves and scarves grew behind him.

"Mum, are these 'gels or liquids,' d'you think? Can I carry them on the plane?"

"Please put some shoes on. Iris, sorry, I'll call you when I'm back." As she was speaking she heard Nathan, his head deep between coats, muttering, "I think it ought to be fairly clear they're not liquids, given that they're solid." It was going to be a long weekend. "Found my scarf!" Nathan added, in triumph, and disappeared outside to the waiting car.

Gwen put a sharp little chin on her mother's shoulder and bellowed, "I'll call you from the airport, Granny! Love you!" as she handed her deafened mother the plastic-wrapped clay and then slid off down the hall in search of her sneakers while Julia poked in hopeless uncertainty at the thermostat. It read ++ENTER SUMMER MODE?++. That would have to do.

In her kitchen in Parliament Hill, Iris poured herself a second cup of coffee and dialed Philip Alden. Someone in the family had to listen to sense.

WHEN THE PHONE RANG, Philip had been napping. Since his eightieth birthday sleep had been an evasive and unsatisfying business and he now rose each morning at five a.m., unable to bear the racing of his mind while trapped in stiff and supine immobility. Better to be in physical motion, however tentative and ponderous. By now—just after eight a.m.—he could sometimes manage forty winks in a chair.

His basement flat was touched by brief morning sun, thick yellow beams that poured in through high windows and showed, briefly, the motes of dust that swarmed and rolled in dense clouds around the battered furniture. Otherwise the living room was murky, illuminated only by a pair of fringed, tangerine silk bedside lamps that had been re-homed on the large and middle-sized segments of a nest of laminate tables on either side of the sofa, a low-backed cube upholstered in threadbare, milk-chocolate velvet that had been the proud centerpiece of the Aldens' living room in the seventies. An Anglepoise stood beneath the bookshelves, raised off the floor only marginally by four hardback copies of the *Physicians' Handbook of Obstetric Intensive Care, VI Edition*, edited by Philip. Last summer Gwen had taken quilting lessons in a Kentish Town church hall, and her only quilt now lay across her grandfather's knees, a garish herringbone of purple and mustard cotton stuffed with a sheet of thin foam. *"I love you, Grandpa"* was embroidered in its center, surrounded by glittering, cross-stitched hearts pierced by glittering, cross-stitched arrows. In his lap a print-out of a short story by Stefan Zweig, e-mailed to him by Iris with instructions to analyze it so they could disagree about its intention.

By the time Iris had swept into his life Philip was a confirmed bachelor of thirty-six, a new consultant in the Obstetrics and Gynaecology department of University College Hospital, his limited spare time spent overseeing a clinical study of the use of forceps in persistent occiput posterior births. Iris was interviewing physicians for a feature on the first anniversary of the Pill. She had whisked Philip to the Pillars of Hercules, fed him whiskey, made him laugh. She had sharp gray eyes and glossy hair, carbon black, that slipped like satin through his fingers. She was furious, vivid, fearless, young. He had awoken, and learned happiness. Iris had brought a wonder and confusion that had thrilled and dizzied him, but he had never trusted that it could be his, lifelong.

When after three decades their marriage had finally ended, when Iris had decided that Philip ought no longer to ignore her long-standing affair with Giles Porter, her section editor, Philip had acquiesced without great protest. He bought a modest basement flat on Greencroft Gardens, off the Finchley Road. It was a return, in some senses, to a familiar routine. He knew life to be quiet, to be a serious and solitary business. His late son's family, as well as his friendship with Iris, were precious beyond measure and more than he had ever hoped for, or expected.

Iris remained in the house in Parliament Hill, with Giles. The three had maintained a cordial relationship, and Philip had still, on occasion, come for dinner, or cocktail parties, or for drinks on the terrace of the garden he had planted. It was Iris and Giles who had started to argue almost as soon as they had begun to live together, and three years later Giles retired permanently to his house in France after which the fighting had stopped, aided by the civilizing separation of the Channel. When Giles had died not long after his move to Provence (a maddeningly predictable heart attack, Philip felt, after years of taking dogged, perverse pleasure compounding atherosclerosis with bacon sandwiches and unfiltered cigarettes), Philip had been genuinely saddened, and sorry. If Iris had had other relationships since then, they were not discussed, and though he visited Iris often, Philip had seen no evidence.

MANY NIGHTS ON CALL had trained him; the phone would be at his ear, the other hand dutifully taking dictation of a patient's name, her complication, the state of the baby, before the fog had fully lifted. He sounded awake, professional.

"Iris?"

"Gwen is still bullying the American. And I have a bad feeling about this Boston business."

Philip considered. "Surely not bullying."

"She barely speaks in his presence, and she still won't touch his cooking, or even Julia's cooking if he's served it to her. And now apparently she pretends she hasn't understood anything he's said because of his accent. That part is rather ingenious, actually, but it can't go on. And they're meant to be going for a jolly weekend jaunt with the insufferable son."

"I really don't think James can be bullied. He trained under Steingold at Harvard, after all."

"But she can't get a taste for it. These early days matter."

"He's got teenagers of his own, he must know she's having a hard time. He's a very nice man, Iris. I liked him long before—before all this."

"Yes, well. I'm not interested in him," said Iris, primly. This was an outrageous lie. Iris was consumed with curiosity about James Fuller and his family. "I'm interested in Gwen's happiness, and she can't be allowed to behave so badly he finds her intolerable. People have long memories for that sort of thing. And now they're going to be piled on top of one another, and this evening they'll be fresh off the plane and going to Give Thanks at his ex-wife's house. It's a thoroughly bizarre expedition. If they wanted a romantic break, then Julia and Thing should be off frolicking in a country hotel somewhere, not forcing their warring children to pretend to be civilized."

"I think he wants to show her a little of Boston."

"Yes, well, that's one thing, but showing her the ex-wife is quite another. Why do they have to see her?"

"She's Nathan and Saskia's mother. And they're apparently on very good terms."

"It's distinctly odd," Iris declared, with finality. Neither alluded to their own long years of devoted and easy friendship, risen as it was from the ashes of their intermittently tempestuous marriage. It had long been agreed that they were the exception. Instead, Iris moved swiftly to the purpose of her call. "I want Gwen to come to the Puccini with us next week, not that her taste for melodrama needs encouragement. I plan to stage a subtle intervention."

"Your interventions are never subtle. Will you ask her, or shall I?"

"You'll ask her. They're en route to you as we speak, to deliver the slavering beast. Now listen, I know you adore that creature but if Mole wears you out, stick him in a taxi to me. And don't invite. Insist." She rang off.

3.

IT WAS JAMES WHO KNOCKED ON THE DOOR OF GWEN'S HOTEL
room and announced they were ready to go. She presumed it had also
been James earlier, tapping a maddening military tattoo on the inter-
connecting wall, which she had ignored. The fight, for the moment,
had gone out of her, but she would not join in with the pretense that
they were all together on some sort of fun-filled summer camp. So far
there was nothing sunny about being here—needles of icy rain had
stabbed their faces on the short dash from the airport terminal to the
taxi, and the early evening sky was not promising. Nathan's com-
plaints about London weather did not, on first sight of Boston, make
any sense whatsoever.

Gwen stepped into the hallway, where thin floral carpets met
elaborately paneled, dark green walls, and pulled the door shut, not
quite a slam. Julia stood behind James looking apologetic and, on second glance, unexpectedly stylish. While getting rid of James was her
own, ultimate goal, nonetheless Gwen did not want her mother bested
by the mysterious Pamela. She knew James's ex-wife was English

(James obviously had a fetish)—this did not stop her from picturing her as American, and therefore sophisticated. Nathan had once hinted that his parents had divorced due to an unmanageable excess of sexual chemistry, and that he would not be surprised if in the future James and Pamela were reconciled. Gwen had not shared this threatening information but had protected Julia from it, and acted on her behalf. She felt a twist of guilt and tenderness for her mother, who seemed vulnerable without her layers and folds of cocooning wool and denim and ancient, sensible silk vests. Instead she was in a black silk shirt with a wide, soft collar, and a black wool pencil skirt that almost, but not entirely, revealed her knees.

Julia had a neat, wiry figure and a clear, very pale complexion. Everything about her was pale—her veins showed grass-green through translucent skin, her eyes were palest blue, and her eyebrows and lashes were almost invisible, a defect that she had long ago given up bothering to correct. Her thick hair was a forgiving ash blonde, the right shade to camouflage, for the moment, the streaks of gray that had appeared by stealth over the last few years. She wore it too long, because she rarely felt strong enough to argue with her hairdresser about highlights and layers, and the other age-appropriate measures he wished her to take, and so avoided going as much as possible. Once employed only for actual hiking, her ancient boots had, somewhere along the way, been appropriated for daily wear, practical both for arch support and for indicating, as clearly as a sign hung in a shop window, that she had closed for business. At forty-six she had known her romantic life was over, and to dress as if she hoped otherwise felt pathetic, and unseemly. Then James.

Julia found herself attired to do battle. Her legs, so long concealed beneath thick, bobbled tights, or shapeless trousers, or sometimes a practical layering of both, were now required to compete. They must look not only amazing, Gwen had decreed, but more amazing than Pamela's, and as neither of them knew what Pamela looked like, they could not know how high the bar was set. Gwen had insisted that they go shopping, and had folded herself cross-legged on the floor of the small changing room in Whistles on Hampstead High Street, hunched over her phone, tapping, looking up only to issue brief, strongly worded and—Julia had to concede—accurate assessments of various garments. Of the outfit they had eventually chosen Gwen had pronounced, "With heels it will make your calves look amazing. Shoes next," and had marched her mother up the road to Hobbs. This was the closest Gwen had come to supporting the relationship, and it had at first moved Julia and then seduced her into a *folie à deux* of anxiety. "You have to wear the heels we got, it's what they're for!" Gwen had screeched when Julia, having second thoughts, had begun to pack a pair of black, lace-up flats, rubber-soled and sensible. "Those are like nun shoes. You have to be sexy!" Gwen almost always addressed her mother in the imperative but had seemed even more urgent than usual, and this anxiety was contagious.

It was five p.m. on Thanksgiving and the hotel had not been able to find them a taxi. They could wait an hour for the hotel minibus to return from dropping guests in Belmont, the concierge said, otherwise they could walk. James had reached a pitch of vigorous, impenetrable enthusiasm. "It's so close, we oughta walk!" he boomed, commanding the attention of the entire lobby. "You guys don't mind, right? Mad dogs and Englishmen." His nerves were out of character and Julia, who in any case had no idea how far they were going, felt she must acquiesce. Even Gwen, who did not usually miss an opportunity to cross him, said nothing. She merely tugged the hood of her sweater out from beneath the collar of her coat, pulled it tight around her face, and followed him out into the blustery street.

It was a brief window of respite in a day of near-relentless, pounding rain, and the uneven sidewalks had become a hazard of icy gullies and slick, mulched leaves. Julia watched Gwen's long form bent against the wind, trudging obediently after James toward this odd, modern encounter. Her uncharacteristic compliance made Julia's heart hurt. She wanted to scoop up her gangling child and bustle her into the warmth of a taxi or better yet, back into the comforts of the hotel, where they could have a quiet dinner, and then commune with the wondrous, vacuous numina of American cable television. In the lobby's adjoining restaurant she'd seen aproned waiters ferrying huge Cobb salads; thick, chargrilled burgers heaped with fat-sheened onion rings; and black skillets of steaming macaroni and cheese. Gwen would love these dishes. Julia wanted to pore over the menu with her daughter, to order absurd portions that they could never finish, to compare them with their English imitations—to be, in short, a mother and daughter exploring the New World. It was her own first trip to America, after all, as well as Gwen's. Julia was filled with sudden regret for the holidays they hadn't taken in their years alone together and realized, with an unexpected pang, that she might have missed that chance, now that she had James. Ahead, James's and Gwen's figures retreated down the dark street. Badly dressed for the weather, Julia was given no choice but to follow.

They hurried along streets of South End brownstones, their broad, steep front steps intermittently decorated with fall paraphernalia. On one, a small scarecrow in overalls and a straw hat slumped drunk-enly on a hay bail, rain-battered and sodden. Several stoops displayed a series of knobbly, unadorned pumpkins and squashes, lined like Russian dolls on one side of the front door. Fairy lights trailed like ivy around spade-headed railings. It was, indeed, a short walk, but the wind felt arctic, already beginning to freeze a thickening crust onto the black surface of the puddles.

Moments away from Pamela's house came the minor calamity. In England there is no weather with the muscle to warp and weft brick pavements into roller coaster humps and valleys; Julia, used to mild, English puddles polite enough to plunge only half an inch, stepped off the curb and into a pool that engulfed her up to the ankle in a slurry of filthy, iced water. She screamed with shock.

James had been charging ahead, describing buildings and restau-rants, encouraging a moderately responsive Gwen to tell him of the various gifts she planned to buy her grandparents. He hurried back to Julia looking shamefaced.

"God, I'm so sorry, we should have waited for the van. I'm a putz. I'm nervous. This suddenly seems insane, I've lost my mind dragging you both to Pamela's. We could have taken the kids and all gone to Mexico for Thanksgiving instead of— Did you hurt yourself? Can I carry you the rest of the way? Should we ditch it and go for Chinese food?"

Julia shook her head. Her right foot was burning with the cold, and pain radiated up through her marrow. She kicked several times, and then began to limp onward, leaning on James's arm. The shoes that Gwen had pressed upon her, undeniably flattering, horribly expensive soft gray suede, were ruined beyond repair, and even immediate use.

Julia felt the right one loosen and slacken with every sodden step she took. She had lost all feeling in her toes, a welcome relief from the burning. It began to rain.

On the doorstep, Julia prepared for Pamela, carefully arranging her face into an expression of openness and enthusiasm, but it was an older man who opened the door. He was extending a hand to shake James's when he was pushed aside, rather violently, by a large woman wearing voluminous, autumnal robes. Pamela—blonde, buxom, a whirl of loose wraps and silken items and alarming glimpses of flesh through folds of draped fabric, came upon them. She wore Thai fisherman's trousers in raw plum silk, huge and flowing and tied in an elaborate bow at the waist, and a silk vest in bright tangerine. The sleeves were so deeply cut that when she raised her arms the side of her torso was visible almost to the waist, as well as the fold of a rather pendulous breast. A raw amethyst buried in silver hung on a formidable chain around her neck. Every surface, and she had many, was glistening faintly—the jewels, the raw silk, the loose blonde hair. Her face and décolletage shimmered faintly with sweat. Gwen, who had felt violent hatred for several people in recent months, took an instant, vehement loathing to Pamela. Her hair was too long for an old lady. She ought to have worn a bra.

Julia found herself clutched to Pamela's bosom and was immediately and unexpectedly distressed by the image of James, in earlier days, enjoying the comforts of precisely this musky declivity. The amethyst was pressed painfully into her clavicle. Pamela looked very young, the extra weight she carried smoothing and plumping her face into girlishness. She did not look like the mother of teenagers. Julia felt conscious of her rain-frizzed hair and of her sopping, painful foot.

"Sister!" Pamela cried, releasing Julia and holding her out at arm's length, as if she were a garment under consideration at a market stand.

"Not sister," said Gwen involuntarily, louder than she'd intended, and saw a tired expression cross her mother's face. Pamela rounded on her, beaming. "We're all sisters in the same fight, lovely girl. Gwendolen." Gwen in her turn was embraced by Pamela, rescued by her height from the same suffocation as her mother. Over the top of Pamela's head she tried to catch Julia's eye, but caught only James's; he smiled, looking rather manic.

"Julia needs dry footwear," he told Pamela, who freed Gwen and spun round, silks flying, and bent over Julia's feet. Julia was afforded a clear view down the front of her shirt, beyond the swinging crystal.

"Boston's brutal. It's brutal. It took us two winters—you remember, two long winters?—to get it, really. You have to be dressed like Shackleton to survive. I did a whole winter the first year with a coat from Marks and Sparks, I nearly died, I was so unhappy and I kept begging James to go back to miserable old England with me, or transfer to Stanford or anywhere. And then he came home one day with a fur hat, and I thought, well, I might just about survive. Fur, I know," she addressed the gray-haired man who had let them in. "You'd have been shocked to know me then. But those creatures died so I could live. I still have that hat, I was going to give it to Saskia but perhaps I should bury it. Take those impractical things off immediately," she commanded. Several other guests were visible through the open door of the living room and Julia was aware that people to whom she had not been introduced were now looking on with curiosity. "James, you didn't tell her! Boston's not a town for pretty little heels. Come upstairs, there's no rush at all, everything's out. We were far too many to sit down, I've flung together a buffet. Start, people! Go, start!"

Julia was now in stockinged feet in the hallway and Pamela held her shoes captive, suspending them by their ankle straps like a pair of shot birds. "Come up here, lovely lady," she commanded, surging up the stairs, holding Julia by the wrist. "I'll introduce you once you're sorted out. Jamesy, just man the bar till we get back."

4.

GWEN STUCK CLOSE TO SASKIA, WHO HAD AMBLED DOWNSTAIRS moments after Julia's kidnapping. This meant remaining regrettably close to James, who had not seen his daughter since the summer, though they spoke, as far as Gwen could tell, nine million times a day. She ate sugar-coated peanuts, crossly, and waited for her mother. She had been promised family time in America; obviously she had misunderstood Julia's definition of family.

"I missed you. Let me see you."

"Same as when you saw me on Skype yesterday." Saskia pulled away from her father's bear hug and gave a lazy twirl, and then a slow dipped curtsey. She tucked her long loose hair ineffectually behind her ears, and it fell forward over her face again.

"You look beautiful, kiddo, you really do. Did your mom book your Christmas flights?"

"Not sure, I'll ask her. Is that sorted? Am I definitely coming?"

"You're coming. Tell me if Pamela hasn't and I'll do it, I need my girl back home with me for a few weeks. I tell you something, your

brother's a pain in my ass. Enough with all this college and independence bullshit, come home already. How are you? How was the drive
back? How did the paper go, did you turn it in on time in the end?"

Saskia rested her head on James's shoulder and smiled mildly. "So
many questions." She yawned, as if merely hearing them had exhausted her. "I told you stuff."

"Tell me more stuff about stuff. Tell me about the term paper."

Gwen gave her studied attention to a bowl of potato chips on the
mantelpiece, between a photograph of small Saskia and smaller Nathan on bicycle and tricycle respectively, and a burnished ebony statue
of what looked like, but surely could not be, a vagina. She hoped James
would take his revolting display of paternal concern elsewhere, but he
had noticed her turn away and took his arm from his daughter's shoulders and drew Gwen back into the conversation. "If you're looking
for some impressive small talk, that guy," he whispered, raising a
blonde eyebrow toward the far wall where a round, white-haired man
in frameless spectacles sipped a large tumbler of whiskey and studied
Pamela's straining bookshelves, "holds a gastroenterology chair at
MIT. He's the world's leading expert in flatulence. Seriously. Enjoy."
He then strode off, promising to return with sodas.

Gwen had liked Saskia from the beginning, the single ray of pale
sunshine to penetrate the bank of black cloud that James had cast
upon their former life, and was slightly in awe of her calm and serenity in the face of life-altering family developments. Saskia was three
years older, a solid girl with unkempt dark blonde hair, broad shoulders, and a bust (an unimaginable asset to Gwen, who hoped that her
own might burgeon into noteworthiness when she reached seventeen).
An entirely different creature from rangy, high-strung flame-haired
Gwen, she moved in languid slow motion. Her detachment was radi-

cal, and thrilling. It wasn't that she didn't notice what her parents did but that, having noticed, she then returned, unfazed, to the concerns and interests of her own life. Gwen, in the active process of collecting characteristics with which to furnish her future adult self, coveted this one in particular. For as long as she could remember, her mother had seemed in constant danger of error or accidental self-harm, and only Gwen's anxious vigilance and interference could stave off certain disaster. Wasn't this evening, coming to James's ex-wife's Thanksgiving, evidence of Julia's poor judgment? Gwen ought to have put a stop to it.

"It's awesome you're here." Saskia put a plump arm around Gwen's waist and squeezed.

"Is it not superweird for your mum, having my mum here?"

"No way, Pamela loves having the house full of randoms, and FYI you are not the most random of randoms here. I think she dated that professor of farting. She's *beyond* that you guys are visiting. How's it been?"

"Weird. Whatevs. The same. Mum and your dad obsessed with each other, it's ongoing. It's beyond foul."

"It's such a weird thing to study. Like, I think I'm going to study gas?"

Gwen gave an indistinct reply and returned to what preoccupied her. "They're literally *obsessed*."

Saskia shrugged. "But if they're happy together . . ."

"Also your brother hates me," Gwen went on with her gloomy update, "and Valentina hates me, and whenever they're back at weekends she's like, *there*, all the time, flicking her hair around and being evil. It's like a hate-fest, they officially hate me."

Nathan came up behind them, startling Gwen, who felt her cheeks flush. He was in skinny, faded jeans, gray suede sneakers, and a large, bright purple hooded sweatshirt, bearing the same brand name across its oversized pockets as the black one she herself wore, which displeased her. He was gallingly attractive despite a painful-looking spot on his forehead, for which Gwen did not judge him, as she fought her own sebaceous battles. Unlike his sister's, which sounded enviably American, Nathan's accent hovered diplomatically mid-Atlantic, tending East or West depending on the company and his mood. To Gwen, this suggested fickleness, and a more general unreliability. A large set of neon-green padded headphones was slung around his neck, like a DJ, off-duty. He was always disconcertingly sure of himself. "It's true," he said, and as she watched he hung his head briefly on one side and passed a loving hand through his dark hair to encourage its wave. "Officially. I filed paperwork to make it legal just this week. I officially hate you."

"Shut *up.*"

"Aww, guys." Saskia put an arm around each of them and drew them into a group hug. Both had to bend down to her height. "Be friends! Feel the love!"

"I feel it." Nathan dropped his head, overcome with the evangelist's fervor. "I feel it. All is healed. Sas, listen," he whispered, now that they were close enough to confide, "don't leave me alone with Wentworth again, he's seriously dry."

His phone began to ring, and he broke free of the huddle. "*Amore mia.*" There was a long pause, then, "Yes, can I call you later—you're right, I'm sorry, you're up very late. Can we Skype tomorrow? I know, I said I was sorry—" He stopped, grasping a fistful of hair, holding it back from his forehead. A few moments later he murmured, "I love you, *cara mia*. Saskia and Gwen send love. *A domani.*"

"Hiatus continues," he told his sister in an entirely different tone, putting away the phone.

"What, you've broken up, you mean?" Gwen demanded. She was surprised. A recognized fact of teenage life was that relationships would end, and whether they lasted days or years did not change this expectation. Yet Nathan and Valentina had seemed exempt, their union entirely established, and unalterable. Like adults. Valentina had talked openly about their wedding, had once even been heard to say that their first daughter would be called Fabia. This development was extremely interesting. "Why were you calling her *cara blara* if she's not your girlfriend?"

"It's only a hiatus." Nathan sounded irritable. He moved Gwen aside two steps to check his appearance in the antique mirror behind her. "She wanted us to stay at your mom's house for the weekend while you all came here, which is classic Valentina insanity as obviously I'm going to visit my mother and sister for Thanksgiving. I'm taking some time to reconsider."

"It didn't sound like you were on a hiatus. And we didn't send love."

"I would have," Saskia protested, mildly.

"We're not just going to stop talking after two and a half years."

"So basically you just decided not to see each other this weekend when you couldn't see each other anyway because you were on opposite sides of the Pacific. How radical." She felt pleased by her appropriation of what she felt was his own, airy manner. "And you literally spend more time looking at yourself than I do."

Nathan made a final, invisible adjustment. "I'm not sure that's anything to boast about. And it's the Atlantic, but don't let the details bog you down. Come, let's get food."

"It was raining," said Gwen, crossly, trying to tame the frizzing corkscrews that she saw had escaped from her ponytail. Admired and envied by older women, her hair was disobedient, far too thick and wiry, and an appallingly bright color, but to master it and make it serve her would take a patience she lacked. Together with her height it made her obtrusive, and to be obtrusive at sixteen was the unhappiest of states. Nathan had departed in the direction of the buffet table and beside her in the mirror she saw Saskia shaking her head, looking sorrowful.

"You two are so mean to each other!"

"He's mean to me."

Saskia held out a bundle of plastic cutlery wrapped in a paper napkin printed with prancing turkeys. "Poor Valentina. It will be a major deal if they break up."

"She's had a lucky escape, if you ask me," muttered Gwen, but when she noticed Saskia's crestfallen expression she apologized and resolved to save her abuse of Nathan for private moments with her mother, or her grandparents, or her friend Katy who simultaneously fancied Nathan and hated him, and therefore made a satisfyingly insatiable audience. They discussed him at length.

GWEN WAS DISTRESSED to see Julia descending the stairs bare legged, and in sagging purple mohair bedsocks. She abandoned her plate on a sideboard and rushed over.

"Mum! You look so weird."

"It's all she gave me, darling, I couldn't get out of it."

"Take them off!"

"I took my shoes off, too, to be companionable," said Pamela, appearing behind Julia with a flourish, her hand extended to clasp and squeeze Gwen's. Gwen looked down to see naked white feet, the toenails vermillion, a toe ring in black-stained silver shaped like a serpent and wrapped, sinuously, around the second toe.

It was the first sight of this toe ring that led Julia to understand that James had sold to her a picture of family harmony that was not wholly accurate, or possible. She and Pamela would not, she saw, be friends. Pamela did not seem the kind of woman who was a successful friend to other women, whatever proclamations she might make about sisterhood. It was unimaginable, and indeed now was not at all the time to be imagining that James had married and had his children with this expansive, threatening person.

"I love that you're with us," Pamela whispered, as if Julia had been at death's door and had rallied bravely to attend her party. She linked her arm through Julia's and squeezed, like a confiding schoolgirl. James, who had been across the room helping himself to one of the many untouched M&S mince pies that Pamela had requested he ferry from London, hurried over to Julia's other side and took her fingers. Julia felt for an odd moment as if they were parents leading her toward an altar, possibly marital, possibly sacrificial. Pamela summoned over the man who had let them in.

"I'm going to introduce you to everyone. This is Wentworth."

"Wentworth Hale." He nodded and offered a hand to Julia for the second time, doffing an imaginary cap to Pamela. Behind one ear he'd tucked a hand-rolled cigarette, and a small white badge pinned to the breast of his leather waistcoat read STAMP OUT REALITY. His gray ponytail was held back with a thick blue elastic band that looked as if it had once held together a bunch of asparagus.

"Wentworth is fighting the good fight with us, he's on our board at the clinic and he's done fantastic advocacy work for us, I've never known anyone make better use of their retirement, I can't even tell you. He campaigned and wrote letters for us when it looked like our local admissions privileges were under threat—he'll tell you all about it and I'll make some drinks. Gwen," Pamela called, "would you like a G&T?"

"I'm sixteen," Gwen replied rather frostily, and then seeing a way to avoid Nathan at the buffet table added with marginally more warmth, "I'll make them though, if you want."

"Thank you, lovely girl, that would be marvelous. Limes in the Minton."

THOUGH PAMELA HAD not grown up with Thanksgiving, as a hostess she had nonetheless managed to capture its essence: a day on which hardworking Americans are required to spend upward of five hours on a freeway (one way) in order to eat turkey, very late, in the twilit company of family members avoided the rest of the year. With no nearby relatives of her own, Pamela ensured a little friction by populating her parties with ill-assorted friends, colleagues, and acquaintances from yoga who had in common only that each could think of nowhere better to go. Julia and James's journey from the hotel had been nothing compared to those of a recently divorced speech and language therapist who had driven from Amherst past three accidents and a two-mile lane closure, and a professor of pediatric oncology who'd been on an unsuccessful date with Pamela several months earlier, who had been on I-95 since eight a.m. and now, slightly sickened by a large Dunkin' Donuts pumpkin latte and a bag of powdered donut holes, was mutely nursing a Calvados and wishing he'd stayed at home. The most cheerful guests were twin toddlers currently chasing one another with peacock feathers, overdue for a collapse into sticky, corn syrup tears.

Julia did as expected. She ate dry, lukewarm slices of turkey breast—cruelty-free, Pamela assured her. She tasted sweet potatoes topped with blackened marshmallows, as cloying as imagined, and far more delicious. She compared gelatinous tinned cranberry sauce to Pamela's glossy homemade rendering and dutifully admired the latter (the recipe handed down through James's family). She sipped lukewarm too-sweet apple cider in which sharp shards of cinnamon bark bobbed, and in which there was regrettably no alcohol. She met midwives and doulas, a hypnobirthing expert and a drunken, florid acupuncturist. She listened while Pamela described to a widening circle of listeners the day that James, as a young resident, had stitched up a new mother with such assiduity that he had closed off her urethra and had then had to call her back into the operating room to confess and remove three stitches. Julia saw that this anecdote was intended to make James look foolish and that it succeeded, noting its effect upon James himself: a rigid tension in his jaw. "Who really needs to pee, right?" He shrugged, as if telling a deprecating story himself, but it was clear he was not happy.

Though this visit had been his own initiative, James had seemed frantic to leave almost as soon as they arrived. Julia now understood that he and Pamela were friends only on the telephone or by text message, and in the reassuring narrative he told himself about the end of his marriage. They were amicable when the Atlantic lay hugely between them, but in person were irritable and competitive. James evidently found his ex-wife aggravating, but was too much a gentleman to say it. What he did say, coming up behind Julia, slipping his hands around her waist and speaking low and urgently was, "I need to leave ten minutes ago." She squeezed his forearm and promised to find Gwen. The visit had been instructive, and Julia was now glad they'd come.

She was scanning the room when she felt her phone vibrating and glanced down to see that it was Philip. It was, Julia calculated, quarter past one in the morning in London. Philip had never called her after half past nine.

"Are you okay?"

"Yes, *maidele*, please don't worry, I'm fine. Have you got a minute, though?"

"Of course." She went up the winding staircase and closed herself in a spare bedroom, next door to Pamela's own boudoir where earlier, among gauzy scarves and crumpled piles of silky garments, she had been forced into Pamela's socks. Here hung the guests' damp coats on a cloakroom rail, and behind it various items necessary for attending home births. Three cylinders of oxygen were aligned against one wall, and beside these was a tower of loose plastic packets of absorbent pads. A stack of bedpans stood on the bedside table. The large bed was made up with a crocheted blanket in shades of sage and umber and orange. Julia sat down, only to roll sideways. A waterbed, she realized, righting herself and feeling a liquid, undulating wave lift and fall beneath her. She stood up again feeling tricked, and slightly foolish.

"There's nothing for you to worry about, but I just wanted to let you know that Mole hasn't been very well, he's with the vet now and they're taking good care of him."

"Now? It's late, how did you get him there? What happened?"

"I took him in a little while ago but I wanted to stay and see what they said. He's dehydrated, primarily, so they've put him on fluids and they'll see what's what overnight."

"Poor Mole. Poor you, I'm sorry."

"By the time I left him just now he was wagging his tail; dehydration does make one miserable. He looked better in half an hour. I wouldn't have bothered you, only I thought you might have spoken to Iris and worried."

"Thank you. I'm so sorry it's kept you up. Are you okay? You must be exhausted."

"Right as rain. How is it?"

Julia stepped out into the hallway and peered over the banister to judge, swiftly, whether anyone could hear. Closed in the spare room once again she said, "Pamela is quite a big personality, shall we say. I don't really think she's your cup of tea; she's written a book about orgasm in childbirth."

"God help us," said Philip, with a chuckle that turned, almost instantly, into a cough. "As if birthing mothers don't have enough to worry about."

"She's signed a copy for you."

"I look forward to it. How's my granddaughter?"

"Good, I think. The girls get on so well." This was her own favorite reassurance. She sat down again, gingerly, on the waterbed. "I should probably go back, I'm lurking in a spare room with all her medical equipment." She peered into a bag that lay open by her feet and saw a package of empty syringes and pink-tipped needles in sachets; glass bottles; and tubes. She picked up a tiny vial that contained a coarse white powder and shook it, speculatively, and then returned it. "I'd much rather hide in here talking to you, it's so lovely to hear your voice. Are you really not worried? Should I say something to Gwen? She'd be devastated if something happened to him."

There was a long pause. "He is twelve, you know." Philip said this very gently. "But don't think about it now. Iris and I will go and see old Mole in the morning."

Julia waited a moment before descending. Gwen had been very little when Daniel had come home with a puppy, and his decision had taken Julia by surprise as in those days they had still been trying for another baby. Perhaps he'd guessed it might take longer than they'd hoped; at that stage he could not have imagined that it would never happen. With hindsight, she thought, tiredly, he had probably been trying to force to a close that fraught and unlovely chapter of their marriage. In the early years Gwen had fawned over Mole, dressing him in hats and outfits and trying to draw him into her games, with mixed success. Later her enthusiasm had waned; for years he had seemed part of the furniture and had been, in truth, Daniel's dog, for it had been Daniel who'd walked and fed him, groomed him and planned their weekends for his amusement, choosing pubs that were dog-friendly and walks that Mole might favor. He took after his father (Philip had almost become a vet, before choosing medical school). But after Daniel had died, Gwen had turned back to Mole. They both had, Julia realized, and had each focused deliberate love and energy upon him as a proxy for Daniel himself. The warmth of the dog's rough fur had soothed her; at night when he lay next to her on the sofa Julia sought out the quick, steady gallop of his heart beneath her hand. She and Gwen had often agreed about Mole's wisdom, an impression that had deepened since the coarse fur around his eyes had turned from black to ashy gray. Mole's mortality, like Philip's, like Iris's, like her own, in fact, was just one more item on an extensive list of impossible, uncontrollable anxieties. They would all have to go on living because they simply had to, for Gwen.

She knew that Iris and Philip thought she'd coddled Gwen, that Julia failed to admonish small rudenesses, that she reflexively lifted responsibilities off Gwen's shoulders. But why deny any wish so easy to grant? Julia had never minded what they had for supper; so easy to let the little girl decide. Why care about report cards, or place emphasis on schoolwork that frustrated or upset her when to build her own miniature refuge in clay brought a smile to her face, and connected her to an online world when she had been so lonely in the real one? All adult life lay ahead in which to do laundry and pick up crumpled jeans, to learn—as Julia's own mother had never allowed her to forget—about the Sisyphean battle against entropy and chaos that was maintaining a household. What innocent liberty it was, to believe that a water glass left empty on a bedside table would appear, clean, back in the kitchen cupboard. So little magic remained for her. And so Mole could not be ill because Gwen would be unhappy, and Julia could not bear for her daughter to be unhappy again. Committed pessimism was supposed to offer this single, ultimate benefit—that one could never be sideswiped by sadness. It was only now that she realized her vigilance had slipped. She had stopped—so foolish!—she had entirely ceased worrying about the dog. And now look.

5.

NATHAN WAS STAYING WITH SASKIA AND THEIR MOTHER; BACK
at the hotel Gwen announced with greedy satisfaction that she was
going to watch sitcoms and eat candy in the bath. James took Julia toward the river. It was still very cold but the sky was clear and he
needed, more than anything, for Julia to see and understand the
beauty in this fine, proud city. He had grown up in a spare, rented
apartment on the top floor of a Dorchester triple-decker. Later a schol-
arship spirited him across the river, and he spent four years at Harvard
as an undergraduate, followed by many more at the Medical School
and then a residency and fellowship at Beth Israel. The deep, turgid
black of the Charles River stirred his soul; in the words of the anthem
bawled in the happy heat of Fenway Park, he loved that dirty water. He
would play her the song, he thought, when they got back to the hotel.
Holding her hand, he felt like a boy, making a gift to her of every place
he'd been happy. He wanted each site blessed by her gaze. He wanted
her to see that he would always give her all he had.

"I understand why Pamela wanted to come back," Julia said, leaning on the railings. They had walked to Harvard Bridge and stood looking down into blackness, halfway between the boathouses and jewel-bright polished cupolas of Cambridge and, on their other side, solid, honest Boston. There was a sharp wind coming in off the water and Julia pulled her collar up higher until only her eyes were visible. She had been quiet for some time and he had been waiting, patiently, to discover what it was she had on her mind. After a moment she added, "You didn't want to move back when she did?"

He pulled her to him. In his arms she felt slight, even beneath the insulating layers of her winter coat. They had had similar conversations before, but it felt different in Boston. Here he heard the unspoken questions and understood her earlier silence. *Will you leave London? Will you leave me?*

"You look cold," he said, gently. "Are you?"

"A bit."

He began to lead her back toward Storrow Drive. "Here, take my scarf. Let's go and have Manhattans in the lobby. Or something warm, maybe Irish coffee. You know, I do really love this town. But I love London also, and now London has you, which makes it the only place I'd ever want to be. I'm not going anywhere. You're my home," he added, and smiled to himself at his unconscious appropriation of another lyric from Boston's defiant punk theme song. But he meant it.

"Thank you. I know, I think. Sorry. I suddenly saw just a glimpse into your life here, before we met, and I got jealous. Of a city. You had a whole life before I knew you, and I missed it." Their gloved fingers were interlaced and she squeezed his hand.

"Truly, the only life I want is what's ahead, with you. It was all

practice, before." After a moment he added, "Pamela is . . . an experience." He felt that Julia had been graceful in the face of Pamela's as-
sault. Once that theatricality and confidence had captivated him but
this weekend, seeing the two women side by side, he had found his
ex-wife more than usually enervating.

He had been a fourth-year medical student when they met and Pamela had intrigued him, British and bosomy, full of sexual and intel-
lectual confidence. They had taken Urogynecology together and she
had challenged a famously irascible surgeon day after day, asking
questions that infuriated him, immune to his loathing while better-
liked students were regularly reduced to tears. James had found himself in her busy and unmade bed, where he stayed for the rest of
medical school. They had been, in that way at least, a good match.

In adulthood they were not well suited. He had felt perpetually
unsettled; she, increasingly defensive and competitive as he relied less
and less on bolstering infusions of her own self-belief. She had exhausted him, and they had irritated one another. The divorce, they
agreed—sometimes amicably, at other times in the throes of an accidental, old, appalling fight—had been the best choice they'd made
together.

Now he was fifty-five and truly in love, deeply in love, for the first
time in his life. Tonight, above all, he was grateful Julia had trusted
him and come to Boston. She had the generosity to see that to keep his
family on civil terms was so very important to him. He pulled her
closer to him as they walked. He felt expansive with love for her.

"She's very attractive. I was a bit intimidated."

"You're so beautiful, Julia; that's crazy. Please don't be intimidated
by anything at all; she's a friend now but we got divorced for a rea-

son." He tried not to speak ill of his children's mother but this statement was not disloyal to anyone, and was true.

"Why did you get married?"

He considered. He had told Julia a great deal about the separation, but had talked little about what had come before. In general
he did not spend a great deal of time in retrospection. "I was . . ." he
considered "overpowered" and then said, "over*whelmed* by her. She
was—is—brimming with confidence and social ease, and I wanted
both of those things. She sort of . . . kicked me up the ass, I think. I
wasn't superyoung but I was still pretty immature. I'd never really
known anyone like that before. She was kind of the British equiva-
lent of the Waspy girls who would never look at me. Except she
looked at me."

"And then?"

"And then I grew up, a little slowly I guess, and once I was more
mature or self-assured, we began to fight. We outgrew each other."
He had talked enough, and so returned to the far happier present.
"And now I'm with you, which is exactly where I should be."

They had turned into the pedestrian mall at the heart of Com-
monwealth Avenue and walked in silence for a while beneath the can-
opy of yellow elms looming black in the darkness. Before them drifts
of fallen leaves lifted and skittered in the sharp wind.

"What did Philip say about the dog?"

"It's so hard to tell; he wouldn't want to worry me but it didn't
sound good. I feel so awful he has to deal with it."

James stopped and faced her, and took both her hands. He had
been thinking for some time about how he could help. He watched
her struggle with her guilt for distressing him, and for introducing a

note of sadness into this first, small vacation. He could see she was anxious.

"Listen to me," he said, gently. "When we get back to the hotel I'll look online for the best vet in London. I'll find the guy who looks after the corgis, just tell me how to help. Your people will be my people. And your dog, my dog."

6.

THE NIGHT BEFORE THEY HAD NOT SEEN BOSTON AT HER BEST, but early the next day she welcomed them, awash with pale yellow sunshine beneath a blue sky, the air crisp, the light dazzling. On the broad black silence of the Charles the rowers rowed; along the esplanade the runners ran, in hats and earmuffs, in fleece and gloves and clouds of their own quick breath. The greedy stasis of Thanksgiving was behind them; busy Bostonians had returned to river life.

"Oh em gee"—Gwen bounded off the bus, scarf flying, and calling backward to Saskia—"this is unbelievable." James had taken Julia and the girls to Cambridge to lead them through the leaf-strewn paths beneath the ivy-clad red brick of his glorious alma mater, but Gwen's praise was in fact for a fire hydrant. She fell upon it with a cry of joy, a delightful reunion with this old friend known only from the quaint, unreal America she inhabited on television. She photographed it, and then crouched down beside it for Saskia to capture her looking at it. She measured its solid contours with her gloved hands. She would make one for the blog, she told them all. She giggled at the sign that offered instruction in case of SNOW EMERGENCY and asked her mother to take another picture of her with Saskia beneath it.

"Nathan's just getting off the T, he'll be here shortly. I'm not sure the Widener can compete after a hydrant and a sign. But there may be other signs in Harvard Yard. 'No Smoking. Fire Exit.' That sort of thing."

Julia watched Gwen with anxious interest but Gwen merely grinned. "Fire hydrants are cool. I like Americana."

Not rude, Julia noted, just conversational. Progress.

James led them toward a small ice cream shop. In the doorway Saskia paused, and she now gently poked her father's shoulder.

"I'm leaving, Dad. I'm meeting people for lunch."

"We're people. We're people right here. Three people, who all live in England and who pine for you across the ocean . . ."

She patted his head mildly. "Bye, Dad."

"Have you got cash? Scarf? Batphone? Call me if you need a ride from anywhere."

"You don't have a car in this country, but thanks." Saskia turned to Gwen. "When you go into Harvard Yard, don't let him or Nathan tell you to rub John Harvard's toe; the students pee on it. Kay, bye. Get the black raspberry."

NATHAN WAS LATE, and they ordered without him. Gwen held out her cone of black raspberry to James, tentative, casual. James took it, tasted, considered with head cocked to one side, reviewed it favorably, returned it. He offered Gwen his own malted white chocolate. They agreed to swap and Julia watched in a state of rigid disbelief and fascination, breath held, as if willing a paused and watchful wild animal to approach a tidbit held on offered palm. This would have been unthinkable in London. It was Nathan's absence, surely, or it was Boston, or it was the alignment of the planets. In her pocket her phone vibrated, and she excused herself from the table, handing Gwen her untouched frozen yogurt and stepping out into the noise and chill of Massachusetts Avenue.

"I'm so sorry, *maidele*," Philip said, when Julia answered. She stood in the cold, numbed. "It wasn't right. We couldn't let him suffer."

A hope extinguished. Each change had come like this. Gwen's first day at secondary school. The rapid and murderous blight that afflicted the blowsy, salmon-pink roses that had always climbed their garden wall, flourishing over the years despite total ignorance and neglect. The transformation of their family's beloved local curry house into a fluorescent-lit, linoleum-floored nail bar. Each wave swept Daniel further from his little girl, a stronger tide even than the accumulated minutes since she had last seen his face. And Julia could do nothing but stand on the shore and watch, hopelessly, as he receded, alone with the wounded little girl he left behind. Gwen's longing for her father was why Julia would not get a new car, nor replace—of all the things about which to be sentimental—the unreliable microwave. Gwen had asked her not to. Through the glass she watched Gwen talking, gesticulating, eating the ice cream James had given her, opening up to him, possibly for the first time. And now she would have to be told and would suffer. It was on this duty that Julia fixed as she turned her face away from her family and into the biting wind, permitting herself only a short, silent weep before she returned to the café.

7.

JAMES WAS AN OPTIMIST. HE WAS DETERMINED THAT EVEN-
tually Gwen would love him and, though at present it was challenging to imagine, that one day he would also love Gwen. There was no
question that Gwendolen could be extremely trying and that Julia's
guilty permissiveness had not helped. She would be a less demanding
child and, more important, would show greater fortitude, he thought,
had she not been raised in such a spirit of compensatory contrition
and apology. But they were family now and the only way to proceed
was with positivity. Falling for her mother did not entitle him to a
role in Gwen's upbringing, and he would keep his opinions to himself.
Primum non nocere. And one did not need to be her parent to see that
she was absolutely devastated about the dog. Julia had led her gently
to the bathroom for privacy. They had been gone some time.

When they returned Gwen was even more hunched than usual,
folded in upon herself as if she carried something fragile clutched to
her chest. Her eyes were red-rimmed but she was composed, and she

pulled her jacket tighter and huddled into the cocooning woolen mask of her scarf. Julia put her arm around her daughter and kissed her forehead, stroking back her red hair. At the last minute James decided to offer no eulogy, wagering—correctly—that Gwen would not like him to besmirch Mole's memory. Instead he squeezed her shoulder and she'd given him a brief, wan smile. They gathered up their belongings to go.

As they were pushing back their chairs Nathan loped up, drinking from a stainless steel travel mug that James immediately identified as Pamela's. The ghosts of a dozen arguments rose from that mug like unwelcome genies—disputes about paper coffee cups "choking our landfills," about disposable nappies and the reuse of plastic bags, and a particularly hysterical exchange about the "poisonous and inhumane" chicken nuggets James had bought for Saskia on a visit to Sea World that had really been, he was convinced, about the fact that at that stage they had not had sex for almost three months. All their disagreements echoed in that mug; the petty, ludicrous, deathly serious battlegrounds of discordant—and subsequently divorced— parenting. He considered they were mature and cordial, and yet he knew she would be working hard to undermine many of his choices this weekend. He couldn't blame her—he would begin his own exorcism at the airport by treating everyone to McDonald's.

"Well, hello to all of you," said Nathan, looking between them, perplexed. "What an overwhelmingly enthusiastic welcome."

"We're a bit sad, that's all," said Julia, squeezing Gwen's arm. "Gwen's grandpa phoned this morning and we heard the news that Mole died."

Nathan exhaled through his teeth. "Christ, you scared me, I

thought something awful had happened. Well, look on the bright side"—he grinned and raised his coffee to Gwen in a partial toast— "at least you won't have to clear up shit in the kitchen anymore."

James had sensed this comment long before Nathan's arrival, he realized, had felt it in the air like coming rainfall, yet nonetheless he was momentarily floored by his son's misjudgment. He turned, but before he could address Gwen she was already outside and crossing back through the speeding traffic of Massachusetts Avenue. The lights were not with her and for one heart-stopping moment she had looked—he hoped Julia hadn't seen—the wrong way to check for on-coming cars. Julia stood and went after her daughter. With a hand on the doorframe she paused and looked back, addressing Nathan. "That was utterly uncalled for. That was crass and unkind." She then departed, breaking into a run.

And now Gwen would need to be pieced back together all over again, James thought, frustrated. Why couldn't Nathan keep his mouth shut? Why was Gwen so maddeningly thin-skinned?

Nathan began to stir Julia's tub of melting frozen yogurt, looking sullen. "She's so hypersensitive."

"Well, there's no concerns about sensitivity with you."

"I was only joking, she's like a three-year-old, running off all the time and throwing tantrums."

James had been about to protest this accusation, but then conceded: "I know, she does. But can I explain something? I don't entirely blame you because I know you were trying to be funny and probably wanted to make everyone feel better. But we've come into a family that's very different from ours—"

"—too right."

"Right," insisted James, earnestly, refusing to be drawn at this moment by the temptation of disparaging collusion, "but you've also got to understand that this is about her father. I don't want to ask you to imagine but can you just for a moment, imagine what that must be like to lose your dad? She misses him all the time. And it's been just the two of them for all those years, and it absolutely does not excuse her behavior in other circumstances, I agree, and Gwen can be difficult, but that dog was her father's. He bought that dog and trained that dog, and probably spent a lot of time with Gwen and the dog, and she's probably thinking about her father today and feeling like she's lost a connection to him. She's really hurting. You have to think of things in context."

"I'm sorry. I was kidding."

James paused. His son had been, he felt, consistently mature and accommodating in the face of seismic family change. The divorce had been hard on both children, and Pamela moving back the following year had been a second loss. Now their little threesome had been disrupted: Saskia was back in America, they'd sold their flat in Kilburn, and moved in with two relative strangers. His own low-level guilt reminded him that his kids had not had it easy, either. They were beautifully mannered, which hid their sadness, but the squeaky wheel shouldn't always get the grease.

"I think you're doing a fantastic job. I'm so proud of you and your sister. This hasn't been straightforward, and you've both made it so easy for me."

"Unlike some people?" Nathan prompted.

"It's not a competition."

"But if it was," said Nathan, putting Pamela's thermos cup on the floor between his feet where James resisted the urge to kick it, "we would win, right?"

There was no one to hear him; it was a relief, in that moment, to admit aloud that he preferred his own children. Of course he did, who wouldn't? It was tiring to pretend otherwise, the only lie he'd told or would ever tell Julia. She was the first woman with whom he could be entirely honest and with whom he felt entirely himself. Yet it had not been honest to say—*your daughter is a bonus!* He wanted it to be true and tried to make it true by saying it, but Nathan, too, deserved some rare time alone with his father. "I mean it, though. No one asks for a new sibling and a stepmother at seventeen. Let's walk, I can't sit here anymore. We were meant to be doing all the Cambridge sights this morning; will you come with your old dad for a nostalgic walk around Harvard Yard? And then let's go down to Eliot House, I'll give you the James Fuller undergrad tour. First, I'll show you where I never managed to make out with girls in the stacks."

"Dad, no."

"No?"

"Just no."

THEY ENTERED THE YARD beneath the Porcellian's carved stone boar head, hoisted blank-eyed and openmouthed above McKean Gate. The freshman dorms on either side seemed empty, with most of their inmates home for the first time since their arrival at Harvard, returned for Thanksgiving to condescend to younger siblings, to have clothes laundered and stomachs filled, to oversleep in crisp new Harvard-branded sweatshirts and pajama bottoms and H-logoed nonslip bed socks, and to be bad-tempered with the parents they instantly resented for behaving as if nothing about them had changed.

Stripped of undergraduates, only tourists remained in Harvard

Yard. The centers of the segmented lawns were still green but their edges were balding and muddied, roped off to recover from heavy rain and heavy footfall. James and Nathan rounded the looming gray flank of Widener, down a path slippery with a mulch of oak and elm leaves and then farther on, around the corner to the statue of a man who was not John Harvard, despite his label, slouched huge and complaisant beneath a vast flag that snapped and wavered in the wind like a mainsail. They waited, watching while a family from Germany took pictures of one another reaching up to rub the statue's polished bronze toe. Three blonde daughters, small, medium, and large, in matching green-and-pink–flowered anoraks and new Red Sox baseball caps took turns to strain upward for the top of the plinth. James offered to take their photograph together and they thanked him, handed him a huge-lensed camera, and posed, smiling and squinting only slightly in the sharp bright chill. After they'd gone, Nathan put an arm around his father's waist, tenderly protective.

"You and Mom are obsessed with talking to randoms."

"I know, our existence is excruciating. If you come here to college, I promise not to hang out and talk to students. Go rub his toe, it's good luck for applying."

"Dad. That last worked when I was about eight. So anyway, I've been meaning to ask you," Nathan changed the subject, casually, "before, you said 'stepmother,' but are you actually going to get married again?" He and Saskia did not agree, neither could they agree whether it mattered. Nathan refused to admit that a legal contract endowed a relationship with permanence, using their own parents' marriage as an example. But still, he felt, there would be an ineluctable shift. At present, whatever his father might believe, Nathan had neither stepmother nor stepsister.

"I don't think so," James admitted. "Julia doesn't want to, she's worried about Gwen. I think we're fine as we are. Come, let's walk to Longfellow's house."

"I've been a million times."

"Just to walk a bit."

"But you think of her as our stepmother now in any case."

"I can't think of alternative, unmarried terminology. We're in it for the long haul, marriage or not."

"'Cause you're happy," Nathan observed. In Harvard Square, a busker in a Santa hat and mauve-and-yellow-striped fingerless gloves was playing "Feliz Navidad" on the accordion. The wind picked up, and without thinking Nathan handed Pamela's travel mug to his father and thrust his hands into his pockets, happily unencumbered. James was reminded of his son as a much smaller child, absentmindedly passing him the smeared wrapper of a candy bar or the fuchsia-stained stick of a Popsicle, or even his chewing gum, plopped into an open palm without thought so Nathan could race off ahead. No running with gum had been one of James's few rules. Pamela, for ecological reasons, had vetoed gum under all circumstances.

"Yes. I'm happy. Is that okay?"

"I suppose we can overcome our childish amazement that parents are people and allow you to have, shock horror, a life of your own. You can pay for our therapy later, if you like. Even Mom said you seem good together. She said you need someone unchallenging at this stage in your life."

"Did she. Come on," said James, firmly. "We're going this way."

They passed the Coop, where the Harvard insignia crept like a pox across towels and bed linen and cufflinks and jewelry and soft toys and toothbrushes and commemorative pewter and glassware. There were Harvard bottle openers and Ping-Pong balls, baby bibs and pencil cases. They stopped to admire these wares, James offered to buy his son an Ivy League chocolate bar and tried, and failed, to imagine his own father in such a place. "'S'tempting fate," Nathan told him solemnly. "Buy me one when I get in."

"When you get in you can have the engraved champagne flutes."

"Thanks, Dad. Smile," Nathan commanded, leaning backward, inclining his head toward James's shoulder and extending his arm to take their picture. He seemed pleased with the results, zooming and cropping until it was just the two of them smiling, the burgundy and white VERITAS banner prominent behind them. As they walked on Nathan captured them in various locations: Nathan making bunny ears behind his father outside the freshly painted cream-yellow clapboard of Longfellow's house. Sipping hot chocolate together outside Peet's Coffee. Both grinning with shy pride, arm in arm outside the closed gates of Eliot House. James's children both documented their own lives obsessively. Where did all these photos go? When he asked for copies they laughed at him.

"You know, you guys aren't little kids, and you and Gwen will both go to college in the next few years," said James, returning to the subject so he could conclude and move on to more congenial topics. The thought of Nathan leaving—possibly coming here, across the Atlantic—created a strange sad pressure in his chest. "Let's cross and walk by the river awhile. I don't think you should have to pretend you're siblings. But just—flatmates, maybe, all of us. Friends. It might take the pressure off."

"Yeah, maybe. Look, cool picture of us."

"Great picture, send it to me. I don't know why I say that, you never do. Will you make it up with her?"

"I promise. And with Julia, too. But may I just say, in the privacy of this conversation, that I'm not completely gutted about the future lack of giant elderly dog shit in the kitchen."

"Nathan."

"Okay, okay." He grinned at his father, wide-eyed and deliberately, disarmingly, devastatingly winsome. "Should we buy them another dog? What about a Siberian husky?"

8.

IT WAS ONLY TEN P.M., BUT THEY WERE ALL SUBDUED AND weary and Gwen, in particular, was longing for the day to end. Mole's absence was unthinkable, and so she would not think it. In the television's narcotic company she could stave off the truth, just for tonight, but the fragile membrane of her shield required solitude and so she had refused her mother's offer to stay with her, dismissing her almost frantically at the door of her hotel room. Until only a few months earlier Julia would not have offered to stay like a polite, concerned acquaintance but would simply have been there, holding her hand while they sat together, absorbed in a flickering, inauthentic reality and safe, warm silence. One being. In this manner they had staved off grief before. Offered, Gwen could not accept. And she did not want James to think her a baby, tempting though it was to separate them and be spared the nauseating and insistent image of their not-quite marital king-size bed.

There was a rap on Gwen's door and she opened it to see Nathan, bundled up in his coat, a woolen beanie pulled down low over his eyes. She went to close it, and he thrust his foot out to stop her.

"Wait," he whispered, loudly. "Just wait. One second."

Her pajama top was an old cotton tank top of her father's, and was almost certainly see-through. She crossed her arms firmly across her unimpressive chest and stared down at the chipping blue polish on her toenails. She became aware that her pajama bottoms had ridden up, but she could not release her arms to adjust them for fear of exposing a breast. The shorts were puce, printed with a motif of repeating black mustaches and a less regular, overlaid pattern of bright lilac bleach-stains, and were not for public viewing. She hunched, awkwardly, and did not reply. He would not have the satisfaction of seeing her upset.

"I'm sorry. I mean it. I know you think I'm a dick—" Nathan began. Gwen began to speak and he continued hurriedly, "I know, I know, what I should say is I know I *was* a dick." He took a step and she began to protest again, but he did not come farther into the room, merely reached for the door handle and began turning it slowly, back and forth, inspecting the mechanism. "We never even had a goldfish or a hamster or anything, because Pamela thinks that animals shouldn't be enslaved to human needs, not that I'm saying Mole was enslaved; I'm just saying my mother's a little eccentric, which I'm guessing hasn't escaped your notice this weekend, but I just didn't think. Your mom got mad, which I totally deserved, and my dad said that Mole was your father's dog, and I didn't know that, either. I'm not making excuses but—I, I just wanted to say that I can't imagine how sad it must be for you today."

Gwen nodded, fiercely. She turned aside in order to wipe her face with the back of her hand, noticing as she looked back that Nathan, too, wore an expression of genuine distress. He cleared his throat and repeated, more steadily, "Anyway. I just wanted to notify you that the jury have returned a unanimous verdict of Dickhood, and sentenced me accordingly."

"It's okay," Gwen said, because it was expected. But now that he was here she could not help herself from inviting him to annul the other words that had hurt so much this morning. She wanted them not repented but somehow actually un-said. "Did you really not like him at all?"

Nathan missed this prompt. His sister was rarely angry with him and when she was forgave him in silence and without discussion. Valentina specialized in spectacular tantrums, in canceled or aggressively terminated phone calls, and on the infrequent occasion she knew herself to be in the wrong she would ring repeatedly until he picked up, imperiously demanding his forgiveness. These fights had not equipped him with a sophisticated understanding of how to nurture, or comfort. All he'd learned so far was to reassure women of their beauty and of their value to himself, neither of which seemed useful in this circumstance. In later years, in adulthood, he would have understood that he was meant to declare that Mole had been extraordinary and precious not only to Gwen but to humanity; had been the sweetest-tempered animal, the most intuitive, that there would never be another like him. Grief can be petty and voracious; it craves repeated assurance of the worthiness, the unique value of its subject. He would learn. At seventeen he did not understand the cue, and simply said, "I don't really know about dogs."

"He wasn't like other dogs," Gwen said, let down, and started to cry again.

"Come and sit on the roof and have a drink, I've got whiskey, and they've got hot apple cider downstairs at the bar. It's only ten. If you get dressed, I can get one and make us hot toddies," Nathan offered, anxious to distract her, reaching into a capacious pocket to produce a hipflask. He wanted her to feel better, and to know that he had been forgiven. He was keen to win back Julia's approbation in order to deserve his father's.

"It's late. What is it? I don't really drink. And I only like Malibu."

"That's probably because it's the only thing you've ever tried," said Nathan, reasonably. "Whiskey's medicinal. It's why I picked it, it's reviving. Saint Bernards delivered it in the Alps. Or maybe that was brandy. Anyway." Would this canine reference be enticing, or insensitive? "Come up. Five minutes?"

She nodded her assent and elbowed the door closed, careful not to unclamp her arms from across her chest.

TEN MINUTES LATER they reunited on the roof beside a deep, square swimming pool. This had been drained for the winter, though the small round lights embedded into its walls still shone, filling the pool with overlapping rings of cold, turquoise light. A drift of tiny leaves had collected on the blue-tiled bottom.

The chaise longues were stacked and shackled beneath tarpaulins for the winter, so Gwen and Nathan sat on the concrete lip of the deep end, cold seeping through coats and jeans. It was impossible to remain there and they both stood up almost immediately, casting around for alternatives. Nathan noticed a panel of switches by the elevator and began pressing them in turn, and eventually a large heater came on above the door. Gwen found two small aluminum coffee tables, icy to the touch and beaded with moisture from the damp air, and dragged these into the doorway where they could sit shielded from the wind and warmed, fractionally, by the buzzing fan. That morning James had presented her and Saskia each with a pair of yellow, faux-fur ear-muffs, and she clamped hers tighter over her ears.

Gwen's few, tentative experiments with rum and pineapple juice had been uneventful. She had always mixed her own drinks at parties and, cautious about quantities, had used the tiny plastic screw cap of the lemonade bottle as her measure. She watched Nathan pouring long slugs of toffee-colored liquid into two white paper cups of hot apple juice. Far below, in the street, an ambulance wailed.

Her first sip made her cough. "It's burning," she said, recovering herself, but immediately tried again. "It's so grim, how can people drink this?"

Nathan made a show of taking a swig straight from the hipflask. "It is rather smoky, it takes time to acquire a taste for it. I took it from a decanter in my mother's house. The current man likes Scotch malts, apparently."

"Is that Wentworth guy her boyfriend?" Gwen asked. Something in Nathan's careful enunciation of "Scotch malts," a spitting quality, caught her attention.

"Who knows. My mother is quite liberal with her favors."

Gwen giggled, shocked.

"I speak only the truth. Boyfriend, who knows? But I mean," Nathan continued, forcing an unsuccessful innuendo, "he keeps his *whiskey* at her *house*."

"Won't your mum notice you took it?"

"I didn't take it. I used it for its proper purpose. I decanted it."

Gwen's earmuffs were itching and she took them off, shaking out her hair. Nathan smiled.

"Those look absolutely ridiculous."

"Take it up with your dad; he bought them."

"Well, no one ever claimed he was a sartorial genius."

"What does 'sartorial' mean? Why do you speak like that?" she demanded, made bolder by the dark, and by this unexpectedly companionable transgression.

"You mean, with words? In sentences? It means 'about or to do with clothes.' It was the perfect word for the moment."

"You could have just said, 'No one ever claimed he knows about clothes.'"

"Orwell would admire your commitment to simplicity."

"I'm not simple!"

"I never said you were any such thing. You are quite complex, in fact. Like all women," he added, loftily.

She clamped the earmuffs back on, defiant.

"You look like a Fraggle with those things on your head."

"I never watched it. Didn't the main one have red hair?"

"Yes. How come you're actually wearing a gift my execrated father bought you?"

"I'm not even going to ask you what that word means." She shrugged, her hands in her pockets. "My ears were cold. And I'm trying to *adjust*, isn't that what we're meant to be doing? Adjusting to our new family. My mum wants me to be nice to him, so I'm trying to be nice to him."

"I wouldn't expend too much energy adjusting," Nathan said. He was typing on his phone as he spoke, and did not look up. "It'll last till it lasts, and then who knows."

Gwen fell silent. She had never—not once—considered the possibility of the relationship "not lasting." Adult relationships lasted forever or until someone died, which was precisely why James's appearance had been so devastating. The idea that it could just end and life could return to normal was thrilling. She and her mother could slip back into old, easy ways, the soft comfort of favorite jeans after this stiff, unnatural costume.

"Why d'you think it won't last?"

"I can think of a hundred reasons. First of all, I don't believe in marriage."

"They're not married!" cried Gwen, horrified.

"You are terribly literal. I don't believe in lifelong monogamous cohabitation, then."

"I don't think it matters if you believe in it, I think it matters if they believe in it."

"Well my father obviously doesn't either or he'd still be married to my mother."

Gwen considered this—it made James sound rather threatening. "Who broke up with who?"

"Whom. Who broke up with whom. In any case," Nathan said, easily, "it was never all that clear. I think it's one of those absurdly passionate can't-live-with, can't-live-without things. When Mom lived in London Dad was always randomly staying over. She'd have chucked some boyfriend or other and then on Sunday morning Dad would be there, all jolly and making pancakes and wearing some weird old clothes that he hadn't bothered packing when he moved out. It doesn't bear thinking about. People over forty should be forced into celibacy. It's so wrong."

"So why aren't they still married?"

"Oh, I'd not be surprised if they got back together properly at some point, when they're living in the same country again." And then, as if discussing his own children he added, with indulgent fondness, "I've given up second-guessing. Nothing with those two would surprise me. Don't look so freaked, it's not like he'd ever be unfaithful to your mother or anything. He's utterly besotted right now. I just don't believe anything lasts, that's all."

Gwen's fantasy scenarios of getting rid of James involved her mother listening to reason and evicting him. She did not like to think of Julia being abandoned for a seductress who lured him back with pancakes and a restoration of his former family life. Then she remembered Mole, and to her dismay she felt a lump begin to form in her throat.

Nathan glanced at her. "That girl Fraggle was quite hot. Red."

"Being ginger's awful," she said, crossly.

"Red was her name, I mean. Red hair's pretty." He moved the small table he was sitting on until it was immediately next to hers and reached out to lift a strand from her shoulder. Gwen thrust her hands deeper into her pockets. His face was very close to hers, inspecting a curl beneath the dull yellow light.

"Not bad," he said, and she felt his gaze, slightly unfocused, shift away from the lock of hair that lay in his gloved hand.

There followed a fraction of a second in which Gwen felt he might kiss her. And a fraction of a second later, she realized that she had misunderstood, but that this had been—just for one, painful instant—what she wanted. She felt herself flush. Nathan's face remained inches away from hers but he was still, with a show of great interest, studying the color of her hair. Then he looked up at her, but did not sit back.

"I like red," he said, quietly, so close that his breath tickled her lips. He was twirling the strand around his finger.

She looked back at him and thought—*I'm drunk. I am humiliat-*

ingly drunk, on two-thirds of a paper cup of lukewarm apple juice and whiskey. He is almost my stepbrother. And what if it's illegal? At that moment he lifted his hand to her cheek and drew her face toward him, and their lips met.

A border crossed. A new territory and uncharted anxieties. His tongue, unexpectedly firm, was in her mouth where it remained, probing her own. She did not know whether it was permissible to close her lips, briefly, now that they were parted, and wondered, too, when she might be able to pause for a moment in order to swallow. But if they paused, they would have to speak to one another and that, when it came, would be excruciating. Their heads were tilted to the right—was there a prearranged moment at which one was expected to rotate ninety degrees and incline the other way, left to left? Nathan did not seem to want to stop, nor appear to suffer any salivary concerns.

So this was it. And it had not happened in the dark, buttered-popcorn recesses of a cinema, or years before, beneath the rolling swell of disco lights on the dance floor of a bar mitzvah, to a soundtrack of a power ballad and the envious whoops and giggles of spectating friends. It had happened in America on an icy hotel rooftop, with a boy much more experienced than she, a little older, very much cooler, who might or might not have a girlfriend and to whom she might or might not be related. It was possible she had been, until tonight, the only sixteen-year-old in London who had not yet kissed a boy, but she already knew that this tale, when she recounted it to an envious Katy, would be worth the wait.

Nathan's hand was at the back of her neck, pulling her toward him with a new and surprising insistence. In a moment of tentative confidence she pulled away, swallowed furtively, and performed her revolution, right to left, her neck relieved of its increasing tension in the chill. After the successful execution of this move she started to relax. The racing of her mind began to slow, and she found herself thinking, with a flash of new triumph, that her mother, James, Katy, and Valentina would all be horrified, for different, precious, valid reasons.

9.

PHILIP HAD LOST HIS ANDREW-AND-FERGIE COMMEMORATIVE mug, one of the treasured possessions of his recent years. Gwen had accepted his attachment to this object without judgment. Julia was bemused, while Iris found it risible, and an embarrassment. Philip didn't mind. If they wished to believe he had lately become an ardent collector of royalist memorabilia, so be it. Iris need not have the family monopoly on caprice, and it was considerably less humiliating than the truth: that he was a man whose surgeon's hands had been seized by arthritis and who hoped—correctly, it turned out—that a two-handled mug would mean he could once again drink tea first thing in the morning. He had happened to mention that it was missing, and Gwen had raced over to help him hunt.

"Well, where did you last have it?" Gwen demanded, her hands planted on her hips. She had painted a butterfly on the back of her left hand and every now and then glanced down at her own handiwork with admiration. She spun on her heels in place, scanning the room, and her hair, in two fat braids, thumped against her back and chest as she turned. It was a pleasing sensation and she did this several times back and forth. "Can't we put some more light on?"

"It is on. It really doesn't matter, darling," Philip said, gesturing for her to sit down again. She peered around once more without moving and then flopped back on the sofa, pulling her phone out of the marsupial pouch of her sweater. "Let's find another one on eBay, I'll bid on a few to make sure. Oh! Maybe they've got Charles and Diana?"

"Later, later. It must be somewhere. Tell me how you are, first. How have you been?"

"I'm okay." Gwen shrugged, tucking her phone away again. "School's boring. You know."

"Your blog was very moving," Philip told her. "The portraits were beautiful. I don't know how you think of these things. Beautiful. You made your grandmother cry."

"Really?" Gwen brightened. "Is that possible?"

"It's possible. Not frequent, but it happens. You moved us both."

Gwen had depicted herself and Julia hand in hand in the Museum of Fine Arts in Boston, beneath a gallery of portraits of Mole, tiny, recognizable Old Masters in which an elderly black Labrador had replaced those old familiar faces. Mole, peacock-blue-and-gold robed in His Studio; an uncertain, white-turbaned Berber King Mole; Mole in the brass-buttoned, double-breasted uniform of the Arles postman.

The dog's final, rattling breath had slayed Philip, though he had remained calm and professional with the pretty, sorrowful young vet while she had wielded her terrible needle. He did not tell Gwen that when he had seen her portraits he had wept until fat tears had fallen onto his keyboard. When he had collected himself he had called Iris and they had agreed that their granddaughter was a genius. "*Memento mori,*" Iris had said, thoughtfully, and he had agreed, though these days he needed no such prompt.

Gwen was looking at him, her expression solemn. "I wanted to say—thank you *so much* for taking care of him. I'm glad he was with you. You're the only person—you are very soothing, you know, Grandpa. I'm sure Mole loved you."

"And I him. Thank you, *maidele.* I do promise you, I made the decision that felt moral."

"Oh, I know," Gwen said, with a decisive nod. "I'd have felt awful if you'd kept him suffering for me. It would have been so selfish. You're a dog person, I totally trust you. And a *doctor.*"

"You're anything but selfish."

"I dunno." Gwen drew her brows together in a frown. "I'm trying not to be but sometimes I just am, without realizing. I get upset about things and then that upsets Mum, and then I feel bad, but I never know it's happening till after it's happened, you know? Suddenly we're having a huge fight and I don't even know *how.* And then I can't talk to her properly because we're literally never alone. Ever. We used to get ten milliseconds in the car on the way to pottery, but now James comes with, and they go to the gym together during my lesson. The *gym.* I mean, Mum in the gym is so beyond ridiculous, it's so try-hard, it's only because James is obsessed with it. She doesn't even have leggings; she goes in, like, linen trousers. So we literally have to whisper in the bathroom or whatever, and I get upset and then she gets sad and worried and feels *torn,* and then I get upset she's upset. I'm not joking, I have to physically kidnap her to talk to her anymore." She had begun to look brooding. Philip saw his son's defiant dark eyes flash in his granddaughter's face.

"It sounds like you miss her. Have you talked about it?"

"Maybe a squillion times and she just says it's an 'adjustment period.' If I need to say something private, I message her now, but she's so rubbish-texting it's painful, I can see her across the room and she'll be spending five hours typing three words so it's actual parental abuse to make her do it. You text superquickly. You're amazing." She said this with some pride.

"I use voice recognition. It's why my punctuation is sometimes a bit strange."

"Punctuation's so not important, Grandpa," said Gwen loyally, and Philip, who wished to differ, held his tongue. Instead he asked, "And the rest of last weekend, apart from what must have been the very hard parts? How did you find Boston? Your mother says you get on well with James's daughter."

"Saskia's awesome, she's coming for Christmas I think, because her mother, you know Pamela? She's coming over, too, to visit her sister. She is a total and complete psycho. It literally scares me how mental she is. No wonder James is a total wet blanket, I think she ate his brain when they got married. She's like, terrifying."

Philip laughed and began to reach forward, painstakingly, for the lemon biscuits Gwen had made him, and she sprang forward and handed him the plate. "Terrifying in what sense?"

"She just throws herself around all the time, it's gross. Nathan is convinced it's because she's still in love with wimpy James, but I mean, good luck with that when he's clearly obsessed with Mum, which I said and he was like, I know, I know, *for now.*"

"So you and Nathan are friends now? That sounds like progress."

Gwen opened her mouth to speak and then clamped it shut with such sudden contraction that he heard the hollow *thock* of teeth closing together. "Not friends, he's lame. But we're stuck with each other, so everyone keeps saying."

10.

THEY HAD BEEN TO COLLECT GWEN FROM A VISIT TO HER grandfather's, and when Philip had appeared at the threshold to wave good-bye, Julia was moved by the warmth with which he'd greeted James.

The two men had met at a conference on neonatal health. Their rooms had been side by side in an isolated block at the far end of campus, and each morning, Philip had reported, the blond American next door had knocked and invited him to walk to breakfast. Together they had crossed the neat triangular slices of lawn that lay between redbrick faculty clusters, and in the refectory Philip would find them seats while James had lined up for their oily, lukewarm fried eggs. When the conference ended James had offered Philip a lift back to London, and over coffee in an M4 service station had mentioned that he was considering music lessons. There had been no music in his house growing up, he'd confided, only the low susurrations of financial anxiety and the dissonance of raised voices. Was it a foolish aspiration, in his fifties? Philip had carefully lowered his cup and felt in his breast pocket for a pen. A surgeon should take care of his fingers, he had counseled. James absolutely must learn to play the piano. He had pushed Julia's e-mail address into James's hands.

James was a terrible, determined pianist, combining exuberance with Julia's first true experience of a tin ear. He strode in tired from the hospital but in lessons seemed inexhaustible. He claimed to practice relentlessly, yet made no progress. He grinned, and swore, and hunched over to redouble his efforts. When a phrase defeated him he played it louder. He charmed her, but she knew he did not see her.

And then for his fourth or fifth lesson he'd arrived to find her stapling programs for her students' winter concert. The youngest, only five, would open with "When the Saints Go Marching In"; Susannah Gowers, who at twelve was the eldest, was rounding off the night with Mozart's Sonata No. 12 in F Major, K. 332. James had picked up a stiff white card.

"A recital."

"Yes."

"How many students playing?"

"All of them. Sixteen, in total."

He'd run his finger down the list, frowning. Bach, Brahms, Chopin, Mozart, Bach again. "When am I?"

She willed away the bubble of laughter rising in her throat. It was a four p.m. children's concert in a school hall, on a sticky Pearl River upright. There would be orange soda and pink wafers. There would be proud parents filming, most of whom themselves were younger than James Fuller.

"Don't worry at all, and definitely don't waste paper printing them again; you can just pencil it in. Perhaps I should perform the Schubert we've been working on? Or something new? I think you should decide what would work best for me. What about 'Für Elise'?" He was grave, respectful. He regarded her unblinking.

"I"—she was defeated into acquiescence by her own bitter disappointment; she had liked him, and he was deranged—"if you like," she said, weakly.

"Great." He sat down at the piano and began to murder the first few bars of the Fantasie. "And I've been thinking," he called over his shoulder, jaunty, like a music hall entertainer, "I'm going to sit for my grade three. I think I'm almost ready, what do you think?"

Julia had made a strangled noise, and it was then that James had laid his forehead against the music stand and begun to shake with silent laughter. He gasped out, "'Für Elise!'" and she caught up. He was not deranged. He was wonderful and foolish, and he had spectacular muscled shoulders, and she was smitten. Later that day he had called, between patients, and suggested coffee. She did not know whether the life-altering generosity of Philip's introduction had been deliberate, and she could never ask. The belief shimmered in and out of certainty. She wondered whether she would ever be able to sense if Philip found it painful or distasteful to see them together.

JULIA ENTERED THE KITCHEN to find Nathan and an apparently reinstated Valentina sitting at the table, playing cards. This weekend there had been no trace of her, an unprecedented period of serenity in the household. Under normal circumstances, if she wasn't at their dinner table, she was interrupting it with calls and text messages, and it had been a relief to be free of her pouting and huffing, her air of bored pretension. She batted sooty lashes at James, addressed Julia as if condescending to a member of household staff, and rarely deigned to speak to Gwen at all. Julia had felt cautiously hopeful that without her Nathan might be a nicer boy, and so it had proved. He had been more relaxed, able to act his age and to drop his air of world-wearied, supercilious cynicism. It could not be a coincidence that Gwen and Nathan had been getting on so much better. On Friday night the children had volunteered to go shopping together for supper, and later Nathan had sat with them watching at least ten minutes of one of Gwen's favored reality shows without once suggesting that the devoted followers of such programs must be lobotomized morons. James had heard from Pamela (who had heard from Saskia) that Nathan and Valentina had broken up. If true, this would have been radical, and auspicious. But now it was Sunday evening and here she was, barefoot and back in their kitchen.

It was Valentina's pointed look toward the refrigerator, accompanied by a stifled, fey little giggle, that first attracted Julia's attention to the blackboard on the back of the fridge door. When the fancy took her Gwen would write notes on this board, or practice her various calligraphies, or paint rainbows or self-portraits with chalk-dusted fingertips. Frequently she drew elaborate illustrations of the shopping list. "Grapes," Julia would write, and the next day a vine would climb and twine around the letters, heavy with misty bunches. If Julia reminded herself to pick up some cottage cheese, she might find a drawing of a thatched and rose-wrapped little chalet perched upon a wheel of generously perforated Emmenthal. Julia had always treasured these artworks, begun, like so much else, in the months after Daniel's death, another form of silent communication, and another small way in which they worked to make one another smile. Family traditions could go some way toward making two people feel like a family. Gwen's rendering of a winsome, smiling anchovy had remained in one corner for months.

Today, a new, tertiary commentary had appeared. In Julia's handwriting it said, "Olive oil, mushrooms, cheddar." James had written "Spuds," which Gwen had then rubbed out and replaced with a drawing of a potato. She had made her own additions to the list but several of these, "MAYONAISE" and "TOMATOS"—had since been amended in thick red chalk to their correct spelling by a third, unknown hand. A drawing of an anthropomorphized fish finger that had been there for days had been wiped away and in its place, in ornately serifed uppercase, the words, "5/7. TRY HARDER NEXT TIME."

Julia frowned at Nathan but from his face it seemed he, too, had only just noticed. Beside him she saw Valentina widen her eyes, and pout. She snapped a card down on the table and looked back at her hand with an expression of rather camp, exaggerated innocence, then raked her fingers through her long hair and pulled it forward over her shoulders, and stretched. "Hello, Julia," she said, sweetly.

James came in, unzipping his coat, and betraying no surprise at seeing Valentina in the kitchen, for which Julia admired him. She moved to get a damp cloth to wipe the blackboard, but at that moment Gwen appeared. She stopped short in the doorway, looking startled.

"I'm so sorry for your loss," Valentina cooed, with an exaggerated expression of regret.

Gwen appeared to struggle with a series of conflicting emotions but then said, rather stiffly, "I haven't lost anything."

"She means Mole," Nathan explained, looking embarrassed.

Gwen appeared not to hear him. "I haven't lost anything I actually *wanted*."

While this indecipherable exchange was taking place, Julia edged forward and tried to conceal the horrible, unsolicited little spelling test by standing in front of it. This drew everyone's attention.

Only Julia had a vantage place from which to see Gwen's expression of bewilderment collapse into raw new shame. Gwen opened the fridge, extracted an apple, then left, slamming the door only marginally harder than necessary. Her footfalls up the stairs receded. To follow would compound the humiliation, Julia felt, though she longed with a magnetic pull to go to her daughter. James glanced at her and then turned and ambled out again. "I'm going to do a little work," he said, as he left, "I'll see you guys."

Julia noticed, unmoved, that Nathan was glaring at Valentina. "It's late," she said, finally. "I'm going to start dinner. Do you two mind shifting to the living room?"

"Val's not staying for supper," said Nathan, smearing his hand over the scattered playing cards and pulling them toward him on the table with the satisfaction of a Vegas dealer. "Anyway, she's given up eating till next year. Nil by mouth till she's the size of the square root of minus one. Imaginary." He sounded blithe but looked guilty, Julia noted. In truth, she thought, it wasn't on to let him make fun of Valentina, either, and James would have pulled him up on it, but Julia did not feel inclined to defend her daughter's assailant. Policing all these delinquent and unrelated teenagers was tedious. She took two eggplants from the newly denuded refrigerator and began to chop them. Behind her she heard Valentina saying, "Forgive me for thinking we had major things to talk about," and then in a lower voice, "What? She won't actually care. They don't believe in stuff like spelling at her school, anyway, do they? It's too rigorous and constraining. Who needs to be able to spell when you can draw such a jolly, friendly little *fish finger*?"

Julia pulled open a lower drawer and clanged several saucepans on her hunt for the colander. If Nathan replied, she couldn't make it out, and the next she heard was Valentina adding, petulantly, "*E ho già detto che*, don't call me Val."

SO THAT, GWEN THOUGHT, was that. Shame twisted within her. Valentina might be odious but she, Gwen, was something far worse, for she was stupid. Whatever peculiar Bostonian wormhole had yawned open and deluded Nathan into finding her attractive had resealed, and the natural order of the universe had been restored.

All week she had been summoning the courage to message him at school to ask about Valentina—silent rehearsals of phrasing and rephrasing in which she tried to balance the desire to know with her more pressing wish not to seem invested in his answer. It had been a waste of energy. They were obviously back together, if indeed they had ever broken up.

But then why, why all the kissing? Alone in her room she flushed, reliving it. He'd been home from school for the weekend and since then they had kissed for nearly two cumulative hours, she had calculated, and all of it initiated by Nathan.

It was true that he had never attempted to approach her in the house, but this had surely been appropriate caution under highly unusual circumstances. If they were going to be boyfriend and girlfriend—and this had been her sustaining and most cherished fantasy from that first fraction of a second, on the roof in Boston—if they were going to be in a serious relationship, then a certain degree of tact would be required of both of them. She had planned it all out.

On Friday he'd already been kicking about in Belsize Park when she'd got off the bus from school, when he usually spent Friday nights at Westminster. They had walked home together through the nature reserve where he had turned and pulled her to him almost in the middle of a sentence, stumbling with her off the path and pressing her up against the broad, rough trunk of an old oak, and on the way out had even held her hand, their fingers interlaced until they'd emerged into the familiarity and exposure of Lawn Road.

And there had been other developments. When it first happened, the night of their return to London, she had fended off his hands as they'd snaked their way beneath her sweater. On Friday in Belsize Wood, she had waited a third and then a fourth beat before pushing him away. The cold of his fingertips had shocked her but there had been something else, too, and though it had begun to rain and the wintry, late-afternoon darkness had long fallen, she had felt a clenching low in her belly, a knot of sudden hunger, and had wanted to let him continue. Even to contemplate it was impossible—it thrilled her that a boy like Nathan would make these attempts but it was impossible to succumb to them. Her first kiss had been only a week ago; it was far too soon for anything further. In any case, she had privately resolved, his hands would go nowhere until he had clarified his position with Valentina. She would have told him of this stipulation had he asked.

It had become clear that Nathan was a two-timing weasel and a liar. Home was now officially and comprehensively unbearable—

there would be nowhere to which Gwen could escape except her own room, and even that would be no liberation if Valentina started staying over again. It was not only in the movies, she'd discovered, that headboards banged against walls with rhythmic and unequivocal insistence. Valentina had read Dante in Italian, she was not dyslexic, and she would definitely be accepted to read English at Merton, which was—Gwen had heard it discussed as a *fait accompli* so often she might scream—what she planned to do after graduating from Westminster. Not hoped. *Planned.* Gwen did not know who or what Dante was, though she knew it to be the name of a character on an American television drama. Alone in her room, her cheeks flamed. She wanted to open her new polymer modeling clay, a deep indigo that she'd hoped would be perfect for rendering denim, but Valentina's mere presence made her art feel foolish and for that she hated her more than anything. It was the anchor of her identity without which she was undifferentiated and unremarkable, and it was childish and pointless.

There was a cheery rap, and James's head appeared round the door.

"Your mom sent me psychic vibes that she wanted me to come and check you were okay. She'd have come herself but she's busy lacing arsenic into the dinner."

"Good. Tell her to make it a double dose for me."

"Not for you. But I think she's ready to dispatch our little visitor." James advanced a little into the room and opened the door wider behind him. He always did this when they were alone together, Gwen had noticed with exasperation, shuffling away on sofas and adopting modes of ostentatiously monkish propriety that he had no doubt learned from a book of pop psychology. *How Not to Make Your Stepdaughter Think You're a Perv, Volume I.* This was the first time he had ventured alone into her bedroom and so he must have been on high alert. He needn't have bothered. James did not have it in him to be anything so interesting as a pervert. Of all her objections that, thankfully, was not a concern. His self-conscious behavior merely drew attention to the idea that he could have been an incestuous pedophile, but wasn't. Still, if he was willing to insult Valentina, he could stay.

"Your son," Gwen said, with slightly wobbly scorn, "is a total douche."

"He has it in him," James conceded. "But I think that particular little nastiness was someone else's handiwork. I saw his face, I really think he hadn't seen. Do you want to come back down and show them that you're a bigger person?"

"Is that some kind of joke?" Gwen demanded, ever attuned to anything that could be construed a reference to her height. "You think I should like, stand on her, or something?"

James looked bewildered and then horrified, briefly. "No! I wouldn't make personal— No, no. Retake. Do you want to come back down and show them you are a *more mature person* than she?"

"I'm not. I'm a retard who can't spell." Gwen promptly burst into tears. James would never attempt to hug her unchaperoned, and she felt fleeting gratitude for this consideration before sinking back into the partial relief of misery and self-pity. And her mother hadn't even come up. She'd sent her new proxy, as if she and James were interchangeable. Gwen's companionship no longer necessary, her requirements no longer paramount. Gwen had no one. James sat down in the open doorway and pulled his knees up, awkwardly.

"You know, nowadays we have spellcheck," he mused. "I'd say on balance I'd rather be you."

Gwen shook her head, mute with unhappiness, but just then a message arrived.

> Sorry about V. She's mad because it's
> totally over, that was last talk. You're
> my girl? xxx

Gwen gave James an unsteady smile that broadened as she reread. She said he could go, thanks. She would be okay.

11.

CHRISTMAS HAD ALWAYS BEEN PRESUMED A POINT OF TENSION between Julia and Daniel but had been, in reality, quite the opposite. Before they'd married they had felt obligated to visit Julia's mother every year on the grounds, put forward by Julia's mother herself, that Daniel's parents were Jews and it was not "their day." "They can't have everything," she had said, dark and obscure. Julia had sat in shame and misery while her mother scorched a crown of turkey, refused Daniel's help with anything but taking the bins out, and instead sat, slashing deep scores into the bottoms of tough sprouts and alternately ignoring or interrogating him on the subject of his religious beliefs. Unearthing his agnosticism, layered on top of the already unacceptable Judaism, had been the final insult. They had gone one final time when Gwen was tiny, teething, battling an unfortunate coincidence of pinkeye and impetigo, not a celestial Christmas cherub but a blotched and irritable tyrant. Julia's mother had refused to hold the baby but instead had sat back, arms crossed defensively across her chest, and offered the bewildering adage that "a redhead aboard a ship brings bad luck," implying that both Gwen and Daniel might have had the same ill effect upon National Rail, opined that it had been wicked to take the child on a crowded train spreading all those germs, and had then gone on to suggest that they had done so only because Daniel (and wasn't it always the case with his sort?) was too tight-fisted to pay for the petrol. Julia had not repeated the mistake, preferring to visit alone, and at less charged points on the calendar. Christmas had offered too much tantalizing material, too many baubles of obvious conflict and star-points of attack.

Since Daniel had died, they had not visited. Julia had fought hard to forget that final conversation, to lock it away, sealed very tightly out of sight, in the dark, where it could no longer hurt her. Daniel would have dismissed it, would have laughed and told her to forgive, would have said that Hell didn't exist anyway so how could a fanciful evocation matter; he knew Julia didn't believe fairy stories, nor that he'd face lakes of fire or unquenchable flaming pits. But she could not forgive, and even to contemplate it burned like a betrayal. Gwen had never asked to go back, and the birthday cards she received, containing five pounds and the unvarying and unpunctuated message in blue Biro, MAY JESUS KEEP YOU FROM GRANDMOTHER, were never mentioned. Julia had embraced Daniel's family traditions with relief.

GOSPEL OAK: a pleasingly ecclesiastical name at Christmastime. The Queen's Crescent lights as scanty and ineffectual as a weak torch in daylight and lit not by a minor local celebrity but instead by whichever council-employed electrician has garlanded the lampposts in perfunctory and partially functioning strings of white bulbs. Stiff felt Santa hats and last year's Dairy Milk advent calendars appear on market stalls, adding to the usual array of tissue multipacks and plastic children's shoes and individual batteries on sale in a clear plastic washing-up bowl, the tartan-print vinyl shopping trolleys, nesting Tupperwares, and carousels of polyester headscarves. In December a regimental bank of small, potted poinsettias stand on proud display beside the usual buckets of wearily opening lilies. The market itself takes on a genial air and here, for the last ten years, Julia bought tinsel and wrapping paper and boxes of reliably cheap and unreliable fairy lights. She joined in with Christmas in the scrappy and defiant local style. And this year there was James, her family and his, around a single table. Thrilling. Terrifying.

He had set her free. Julia had never before considered retiring. Give up teaching for what? More hours of solitude? But James would retire in ten years, and was already full of ideas. He had a colleague supervising a training program for community midwives in Sierra Leone and he wanted to spend three months a year there, teaching. He'd always thought he'd move back to New England but now he talked of Sussex, "Lewes or some other absurdly beautiful British town," and learning to cook on an Aga, and walking together, if not by the icy western Atlantic, then on the quieter shores of the English Channel.

What did she want? She hardly knew, and she'd never dared consider. Growing up she'd wanted a mother who wasn't always angry; whose love did not feel conditional upon being unobtrusive, or upon the meek and tireless execution of chores. James's asking allowed her to wonder, and to fantasize. She would adore the opera at Verona, or to go to JazzFest in New Orleans, and wanted to walk with James along the northern Appalachian Trail he'd described to her so vividly. They would wake up together in Maine, and New Hampshire, and Vermont.

A new phase ahead, when their hours were freed only for one another. Whispered to James as they fell asleep, these wishes did not sound foolish. Instead, now, they sounded like plans. She no longer need dread the loneliness and silence of her daughter leaving home but instead could look forward to the new world that Gwen's growing up would enable. If they left London and moved to Lewes, she could buy a better piano. Gwen would visit—with a degree, a boyfriend, with stories, with laundry—and then return to her own life. James and Julia would have one another.

But in the meantime, all must coexist in closer quarters. And no doubt Gwen was dreading every moment of Christmas lunch today, Julia thought, swallowing the hard bead of guilt that had lodged in her throat. She would find time alone with her on Boxing Day. Maybe they could go for a long tramp on the Heath together as they had last year, and the year before. They no longer had Mole, but she hoped Gwen knew they still had each other.

UPSTAIRS, JAMES WAS FOLDING the laundry and examining his own sense of faint unease, probing it like a sore tooth. He had felt almost instantly at home in this house, he reflected, and had only realized it with hindsight, now that his sense of belonging was unexpectedly undermined. Each meeting with them had been characterized by generous goodwill and decorum, but Daniel's parents had not visited the house since he had moved in, and he was surprised by the degree of his own discomfort. He knew he was not a usurper. Nonetheless, he intended to remain upstairs until Iris and Philip had arrived to avoid the insensitive accident of welcoming them into a hallway that they knew better than he.

Since the divorce he and Pamela had managed to spend the holidays together in relatively amicable coalition. (Usually they gathered in Boston and once, less successfully, in Barbados—in the course of that week they had reunited intermittently for angry late-night sex, the pleasure of which had been entirely undermined by the magnificent violence of their daytime arguments. Afterward they'd agreed to celebrate chastely, and in Boston again.) He had readily agreed to host the Aldens for Christmas lunch, but this would be the first year that Nathan and Saskia would not have their parents together, and he knew, though they would not admit it, that they minded. Both had spoken to their mother several times already, and he'd overheard Nathan, in particular, sounding wistful and slightly guilty. Pamela had flown over with Saskia the day before and was having lunch with her own sister and extended clan in Sussex; the kids would join her on Boxing Day. They were shuttling, in the time-honored tradition of broken homes. It turned out they were not the rule's exception.

Nathan appeared, looking conspiratorial. Then he rearranged himself, cool and collected again and drawled, "They're here. Jeez, how boring. But at least now we can eat." He tossed the hair from his eyes and grinned, winsome, devilish, spearing James's heart with love, and then was gone again, footsteps thundering heavily down the stairs. James followed and joined them all in the hallway. Julia looked up and gave a quick nervous smile. He willed her to understand: they're yours, and I shall learn to cherish them as you do, or try. *I will love them*: another tender, necessary lie.

"Really, you're going to have to help us," Iris was saying, "I've booked tickets for the whole series and I'm just not sure that I can face them every week." She was shrugging off a black fur coat, silky, heavy, and Philip stood behind her attentively to receive it. Iris raised a leather-gloved hand to James in greeting. "I was just telling Julia I've booked a thousand and one tickets for a series at the Wigmore. You two are going to have to take a few off our hands; my ears were bigger than my stomach. Take the Borodin Quartet Shostakovich in February."

Philip had hung Iris's coat over the end of the banister and was slowly unwinding his own scarf. "I sometimes find Shostakovich rather exhausting," he mused. He took off his glasses slowly and began to polish them on the corner of his cardigan, smiling blindly toward James.

"Which is precisely why I am offloading him. I'm saving us Brahms and Liszt."

"Thank you," said Philip, humbly. Glasses replaced, he extended an unsteady hand to James. "*Chag sameach.* Thank you for having us."

"Right, exactly. Christmas *sameach.* Come in, come in." This invitation was just what he had intended not to say, and with nerves he had somehow said it twice. Come in, make yourselves at home. Too late. He stood back, allowing them past him and into the living room. Philip patted his arm.

From the kitchen came a loud clattering, and then Gwen skidded in, hair loose and flying. She threw joyous arms around her grandmother, who recoiled. "Darling, you reek of fish, get off me immediately!"

Gwen pushed a curl from her eyes with the back of her wrist, and then sniffed her hands. "Yuck. Sorry, I've been making smoked salmon rosettes. I should have rubbed lemon on them."

Saskia followed from the kitchen, and smiled vaguely around. "Hey," she said in general greeting, and then added, "Does that really work? Mine stink, too; I've been unwrapping. Gwen's cooking awesome stuff, come see."

"Gwen doesn't cook, she presents," Nathan amended.

"That's true. But I tell you something, my presentation is seriously *Off. The. Charts.* Granny, I've made a cream cheese snowman, he's in the fridge, he's got poppy seed hair and everything. There's not really cooking to do with Christmas bagels." She pirouetted on socked feet, landing rather heavily on her heels.

In the last weeks James had detected a thaw between Nathan and Gwen—not an alliance, for that would be too much to ask, but a truce, perhaps. Late at night, he and Julia whispered about it with cautious optimism. Since Valentina's now firmly established absence, family life had steadily improved, and it no longer seemed unreasonable to picture them all coexisting in relative harmony until the next years would send one, then both of the children to college.

They moved together into the kitchen, where Julia peeled plastic wrap from various dishes and James, glad to have something to occupy him, offered drinks, clinked ice into glasses, and then retrieved Gwen's snowman construction from the fridge. It was indeed very impressive, with eyes cut from scraps of black olive, rosemary twig arms, and a tiny carrot nose. It was likely she'd spent more time on this edifice than she'd spend on a week's homework, but her academic future (or lack of it) was not James's business. An appreciative murmur went around the table. Julia moved a basket of bagels to one side and took a seat between Iris and Gwen.

"Not wanting to pit matriarch against matriarch," Nathan began, offering Iris the platter of Gwen's elaborately rolled salmon flowers, "but why bagels exactly? Pamela always makes goose on Christmas Day."

"It's an Alden family tradition." Julia pushed back her chair to retrieve the sliced lemons from the counter. She was feeling charitable, more relaxed than expected in this odd, mixed company. She took Gwen's hand and squeezed it, and Gwen squeezed back, and smiled.

"It was Iris," Philip told him, pointing apologetically at a poppy seed bagel in the basket that Julia held out. She took it and sliced it for him. "It was entirely Iris's innovation. I was often at the hospital on Christmas Day—"

"That is a total misrepresentation," Iris interrupted. "You were always at work on Christmas Day because you always offered to work Christmas Day."

Philip shrugged. "It's not our holiday, it seemed fair . . ."

"It seemed charitable to take them all bagels." Iris shrugged. "They were such a sorry bunch, nothing scheduled on the wards and these rather pathetic strands of tinsel over the nurses' station. And hospital food is just so revolting, and they did the most repulsive seasonally inspired muck. Horrid pale greasy sprouts, and slices of mystery meat with stuffing. It was an act of charity that turned into a tradition."

"They still do the mystery meat," James told her. "I've grown quite fond of it." To Philip he said, "I forgot to tell you, you know we had the quad mother?"

"Did you manage to keep them in?"

"We had to section her yesterday. She was—"

"Dad." Saskia spoke very softly, but her voice was firm. "No gross birth stories today, please. It's Christmas."

"Christmas is all about birth stories," said Nathan through a mouthful of lunch. "In a barn or whatever, with nothing but herbs as pain relief. What do frankincense and myrrh actually do? It's right up

Mom's street, it's like, the ultimate home birth." He snorted, pleased with himself. Gwen giggled.

After a few moments hunched over his phone Nathan announced, "Myrrh opens up the heart chakra."

"So says the wisdom of the Internet."

"No, so says Mom, I texted her. *'Good for making one accepting and nonjudgmental.'*"

"I'd need a hell of a lot of myrrh not to judge that utter horseshit," James told him, and then looked to Iris, regretting the obscenity, but Iris was nodding in firm agreement.

12.

"A SUCCESS ALL ROUND I'D SAY," SAID IRIS, COMING UP BE-hind Julia. She was already in her coat, and pulling on long, tangerine leather driving gloves.

"You're a lovely hostess and this was perfect, but Philip Alden's terribly tired now, so we'll take our leave. He's used some sort of minicab application—a gentleman called Stu is, so I'm told, four minutes away."

Together they peered through the doorway into the living room. James and Philip sat talking on the sofa, Saskia had sprawled in an armchair with a magazine, and Gwen lay on the floor sketching Philip's profile on a lined legal pad. Nathan was also on the floor, sitting at Saskia's feet reading the same copy of *Swann's Way* that he'd been carrying around the house for weeks, unopened until today. As they watched, Saskia's phone rang.

"Hi, Mom . . . I don't know. Dad, is there any sherry? Mom's going to be driving past on her way back from lunch; she wondered if she could come by for a glass of sherry."

"That's pretty specific," James muttered, excusing himself from Philip and standing up. From the doorway Julia called, "Of course Pamela must come for sherry." Behind her she heard a heavy breath.

"This is presumption."

"We hadn't said we'd see her today, but I suppose it's nice she feels so comfortable." Julia spoke softly to encourage her mother-in-law to do likewise.

"Oh, what tosh," said Iris in irritation, pulling at the fingers of her left glove. It came away, exhaling a rich, musky puff of Chanel No. 5. "It's an imposition. Cancel Stu, please," she commanded Philip from the doorway, as if barking orders at a court attendant. Julia watched Philip, unquestioning, reach into the inside pocket of his corduroy jacket and fumble for his phone.

"You don't have to stay."

"Oh for goodness sake, don't be so naïve, we most certainly do. It's why she's coming, to inspect us all. Philip Alden shall simply have to have an espresso and look lively."

IRIS HAD REACHED the limit of her forbearance with these strangers and to extend it was almost unendurable. But Gwen had described Pamela in vivid detail, and it would do Gwen no good to see her mother trampled like a doormat once again. It was quite enough to suffer that cheery, insipid American so conspicuously failing to make his presence inconspicuous, but to have his ex-wife arrive and wreak unchecked havoc was insufferable. She would not have the Aldens so outnumbered in their own home.

All afternoon she had found James terribly trying, with his earnest smiles and reflexive nods of agreement as he danced attendance on herself and Philip like an obliging houseboy, his urge to be hospitable hampered by an obvious anxiety to avoid seeming proprietorial. Feigned imbecility did nothing to conceal the unpalatable fact that he now had the keys to, and possession of, Daniel's house. James was so bloody sensitive, and *careful*, and several times during lunch she'd wanted to smack him. *Christ alive, man*, she'd thought, *you're screwing her upstairs every night, don't pretend you don't know where she keeps the ground coffee.*

In the last years Iris had counseled Julia to put herself about a bit—she herself had always been a believer in the therapeutic powers of sex, and the nourishing balm of male attention. Men were necessary and had been necessary to Iris, often in the plural, for much of her life. What had stung, an unexpected betrayal, had been this insistence upon cohabitation and the intermingling of lives—love, she supposed they would call it. She had always suspected Julia would be too insipid to take casual lovers; still, it would have been more tactful, and less disruptive for the rest of the family.

But at lunch she'd been kept in check by Philip Alden's cautionary frowns, which she felt across the table like the soft glow of a heat lamp. His warning glance alone was enough to lower her blood pressure, and the monitoring eye he kept on her behavior at all times relieved her of the burden of self-censorship. His silent reproof soothed her irritation, for she felt understood. I know, he assured her; I see.

SINCE PAMELA'S PHONE CALL they all sat arrested in expectation of her arrival. Saskia's magazine was in her lap. Gwen had stopped drawing and was on the floor beside Nathan, inspecting her split ends. Philip still wore his scarf and jacket. Julia, who had only just relaxed after hours of managing the afternoon's social lubrication, began to clear the debris and to gather in the colony of glasses and mugs that had taken over most surfaces. Foil chocolate wrappers and crumpled napkins decorated the spaces in between them, and beside Gwen was a square of kitchen towel piled high with tangerine peels. Nathan had recently made himself a third cream cheese bagel, a postlunch snack, and his discarded plate was also on the floor. Balanced on the arm of Saskia's chair was an empty Oreo packet. Rowan, an old school-friend of Saskia's, had come over on Christmas Eve, a tiny, angular, and white-skinned girl with severely cut black hair and impeccable manners. She'd presented Julia with a tin of amaretti biscuits, and the wrappers from these, printed with text in rose pink, had accumulated on the coffee table like a drift of flushed magnolia bells. The house looked like the celebratory aftermath of precisely what it was, a gluttonous and pleasurable family Christmas and also, to the new visitor, a bloody mess.

Julia turned out every kitchen cupboard and had not unearthed a bottle of sherry, a foregone conclusion as she had never known a bottle to be in the house. But she had hunted nonetheless, if only to show James her attempts to be hospitable. He had been nothing but charming to Iris and Philip today, which meant she did not feel she could say, *Why is your mad ex-wife descending upon my house?*

"Gwen?" she called, lightly. "Would you like to make some mulled wine for when Pamela arrives? We've got cloves and I'm sure there's some star anise somewhere. You could look up a recipe online."

Gwen mumbled something to Nathan beside her, who laughed.

"I'll help if you like," he offered, "you may not be aware of it but I am an excellent mixologist."

"You're an underage mixologist," James called, from the kitchen.

"My blends are purely in the interests of science, I assure you. Help me up, sous chef," Nathan commanded Gwen, who crossed her wrists obligingly and hauled him to his feet, and Julia's free-flowing anxiety about Pamela's impending visit was momentarily staunched by this heartwarming camaraderie between the children.

13.

PAMELA DID NOT ARRIVE UNTIL SIX, FOR "DRIVING PAST" turned out to mean that she was en route from Sussex to her hotel in Ladbroke Grove. "Glastonbury by way of Goodwin Sands," Iris was heard to mutter, refusing James's offer of a fourth cup of tea.

When the doorbell rang it was Gwen, to everyone's surprise, who sprang to her feet and rushed to open it. Pamela swept into the hall, drawing in behind her a theatrically cold wind. Iris, never anything but ramrod straight, threw back her shoulders and lifted her chin a fraction.

"I'm just so thrilled we could do this," trilled Pamela, as if answering an invitation extended months ago that had been fiendishly difficult to honor. She kissed Julia. "I just couldn't resist the opportunity to see my babies on Christmas Day. Will you send one of them out with me to help bring pressies from the car?"

A pair of Nathan's sneakers lay abandoned by the front door and Gwen slipped these on, laces untied, and trotted out after Pamela. Once introductions had been made Pamela arranged herself in an armchair and looked about with satisfaction, scanning the room until she had educed a tentative Mexican wave of returned smiles. Only Iris remained impassive, regarding Pamela as she might a stage on which an amateur theatrical production of mixed reviews was about to begin.

"Isn't this a lovely nest you have? If I miss anything from London, it's these sweet little Victorian terraces. Now, shall I make my presentations?"

"It's commendable how well prepared you are for a spontaneous visit," observed Iris, regarding the pile of gift bags and boxes that Gwen had obediently carried in behind Pamela, like a bellboy.

"Oh, everything was in the car for tomorrow in any case, but I was whizzing past and thought, why not? A Christmas sherry with you all. I'm so pleased to meet you, I've heard such wonderful things about you from James. And you"—here she addressed Philip—"of course I've read your papers on OP presentations and have so many enormous bones to pick with you, so I am utterly overjoyed we're meeting like this, I just have a hundred thoughts to share. Perhaps later I will sweep you off into a corner."

"Pick swiftly," advised Iris, "our bones are going to have to go quite soon, I'm afraid."

"No sherry, Mom, but we've been mulling wine in your honor," said Nathan, coming in from the kitchen. Gwen followed behind him carrying a tray of mugs. She was being oddly obliging, Julia thought. Perhaps later she would begin a campaign to be allowed to go to Trafalgar Square alone with her friends on New Year's Eve, or to attend the overpriced, underage driving course she'd discovered in Elstree. It was possible she'd broken something in the kitchen.

"That accounts for the gorgeous smell. I can have half a glass, I'm sure, I've eaten enough mince pies to line my stomach for a week. Or I suppose I could be devilish and have a whole one and pick up the car tomorrow."

"Why not have tea?" Iris suggested.

TO NO ONE'S GREAT SURPRISE, Pamela outstayed her tentative welcome. Iris had long since abandoned any noble thoughts of outlasting her and had called herself a taxi, without the aid of Philip's app, and the two of them had gone home. After a nod of permission from Julia, Gwen had escaped to her room where she flopped on the bed with her laptop, relieved and exhausted and glowing from a series of audacious, snatched intimacies with Nathan—his hand on her knee beneath the lunch table; their socked feet touching, fleetingly but in plain sight, as they'd all watched the Queen's speech. Alone in the kitchen they had whispered while on the stove the neglected mulled wine reduced to a sticky, overboiled syrup and they had to rescue it with a second bottle, one of James's better Pinot Noirs. There had been a sea change. The wrongness of family occasions with James, the pressure in her chest, the slight constriction of her throat during all festivities without her father—this was the sixth Christmas— were alleviated by the support and camaraderie of a boyfriend, even a secret one. And his weird mother seemed to like her.

"I really must get going," Pamela was hooting, in an ever-increasing volume that suggested she was coming farther up the stairs, away from the front door, "but you must give me the tour before I go. Show me the kids' rooms."

A light tread followed. "Right at the very top is our bedroom," she heard, "really no need to go up there; it's a mess. My practice room is here, where I teach; this is where Saskia sleeps when she stays—"

"Wonderful!" Pamela boomed. "You must be so inspired there."

"Yes." Their voices got louder as they came up half a flight of stairs and stood outside Gwen's door. "That's Gwen in there, we won't disturb her, I think she said she was going to nap, then the bathroom across the hall, and this is Nathan's." The door beside Gwen's creaked open.

"Isn't he a pig?" Pamela declared, with a hint of pride. "And everything's just giant with boys, isn't it—giant stinking shoes, and giant stinking clothes just strewn about everywhere. You really are a saint to take all this on. He said you've been doing his laundry! When he's with me of course I insist he does his own. Still. Not long before he's off and this could be the baby's room, *inshallah*."

Gwen, bewildered, stood and padded forward to listen more closely. Her mother coughed, and she heard Pamela barreling onward, "Oh no, don't blush, I am sorry, I know it's none of my business, but it would be just so invigorating to have a new little one in the family, don't you think? And it's not yet *quite* too late if you were really determined. No. *Are* you? No. I could have sworn you were just a scrap of a thing! Are you really? What a complexion. Right, on that note—on that note, lovely lady, I'll be off. Maybe I'll scoop up Saskia to come and spend a girls' night with me at the hotel, then you can reclaim your peaceful music room."

The footsteps descended once again. Gwen remained still, her heart pounding. She remembered a long-ago supper table and herself at six, nibbling at the tail of her dinosaur-shaped cheese on toast, on the single occasion she had asked her parents about siblings. Then, too, it had been at someone else's prompting—another child at school with a brand-new baby brother had warned Gwen that the same fate could just as easily befall her own slim and attentive mother. "We are perfect just us, don't you think?" Daniel had said, and Gwen had nodded, chewing steadily, and the three of them had held hands around the table. In childhood when friends had stayed over and Julia had kissed them each good night, first Gwen, and then the little girl beside her, Gwen would lie awake until long after her guest was breathing steadily, unable to sleep until she could pad downstairs alone to find and reclaim her mother. To see her kiss another child good night was a torment. Julia would look up, surprised, and explain that she had only wanted Katy to feel welcome. She would open her arms to her hot, distressed little daughter and Gwen would bury herself there, breathing away the horror of their last parting, and the memory of Julia's infidelity. She had only one mother; her mother had only her. Their devotion was balanced, and equal. Never, not once in all these last distressing, enraging, unprecedented months had she ever considered that her mother and James might have a baby. But anything was possible. Weren't there women in India having triplets at seventy-five, or whatever? She'd thought her mother too old for a boyfriend, and yet here was James. She remained by the door, winded.

Gwen picked up her laptop and sent Nathan a message. He was in the kitchen, too far away for her to hear his phone beep, but a minute later the door opened and he slipped in, closing it behind him and grinning.

"You are daring today," he said, coming toward her and putting his arms around her bony shoulders. "I thought we weren't taking undue risks."

"I'm feeling daring." And then emboldened she added, "So what are you waiting for?"

Nathan needed no further encouragement. His mother and sister had gone; he had seen his father and Julia side by side in companionable industry, emptying the dishwasher. Encouraged by this new, indoor comfort and Gwen's uncharacteristic brazenness, he pushed her backward, gently, onto the bed. She would not let him lie on top of her exactly, but he pressed beside her, one leg slung over hers, his crotch pleasingly close to her firm upper thigh. Every now and again he moved as if to readjust, and inched their bodies a little closer into alignment. And it was in this position, with one of his hands lost beneath the printed logo of her T-shirt, that Julia came in and found them.

14.

"FUCK!" JULIA SHOUTED, STARTLING ALL THREE OF THEM.
Gwen had never before heard her mother use the word and it sounded
comical, and disconcerting. Julia clapped her hands across her mouth
and looked, for a moment, as if she was about to vomit. "What the
fuck is going on in here?" But she did not stay for the answer and instead backed out, shaking her head. "I can't believe you," she kept
repeating. "I can't believe you. I don't believe this." She turned on her
heel and left. A moment later, while Gwen and Nathan were still
straightening their clothing, the front door slammed.

"Nathan?"

"Here."

James came in, surprised to see the children standing up in the
middle of Gwen's bedroom, looking at one another in awkward, complicit silence. "Hey, guys. Was that the door? What's up?"

"We've got something to tell you." Gwen threw her shoulders back
and went on, in a voice that managed to be both imperious and

confiding, "We were going to wait a bit longer but—Nathan and I are together."

James frowned. "What?"

Gwen bit her lip and looked to Nathan for reassurance but he was staring out of the window with his hands crossed behind his head, like a man before a firing squad.

"Together. Boyfriend and girlfriend. Dating."

James was staring around the room somewhat fixedly, his gaze moving from Nathan to the bookshelves of magazines and trinkets and assorted dolls' furniture, the mobile of Polaroid photographs suspended with rainbow ribbons from two reshaped coat hangers, to the homemade beaded necklaces slung over the bedpost, to the colony of clay figurines in various stages of completion, guarding the expanse of her desk like a mismatched terra-cotta army. "No. I don't even— I can't— I don't even know where to begin. This seems like a recipe for—*what?* You're not serious."

Gwen, unable to help herself, began to giggle. It was gratifying, after diverse and concerted efforts, finally to see James unsettled.

"How long has this been going on? Nathan, will you turn around, please? Does Julia know? Is this why she just left, is she okay? Was she . . . Hang on—" He pulled his phone out of his pocket. "I expect to see the two of you downstairs, at the kitchen table, in five minutes. Do not—I repeat DO NOT CLOSE THE DOOR OF THIS BED-ROOM. Five minutes. Downstairs."

WHEN THE CHILDREN DESCENDED they were hand in hand, a brief chain gang of penitents. This solidarity seemed staged. Gwen looked mutinous and defiant with lifted chin and narrowed eyes, and appeared to be gripping Nathan as if leading an uncooperative child around a supermarket. Nathan was gazing at the tiled floor. A blush crept up his neck and cheeks. They were very sorry, he said, with an unmistakable smirk in his voice. Still, he did not move to free himself from Gwen.

"We're all going out," James said, shortly. "Julia and I have discussed it. We're going to the pub and we're going to sit and talk like adults. Right now." He gave Julia a small smile of solidarity before returning to face the children looking thunderous. Beside him she dug her thumbnails into the pads of her ring fingers. *Just breathe,* James had said. *I'll talk to them.* Nathan would soon be back at boarding school Monday to Saturday. Obviously he must stay away at weekends, too, she thought, and in the holidays they could take him directly from Westminster to Heathrow. The children would not sleep another night under the same roof.

Gwen would merely have to be dispatched to a convent in the Hebrides. There were ways, she thought, to—what had James said just now?—*curb the insurrection.* He had offered castration, a chastity belt, sedation, bromide in the tea, digging a basement and locking them in it for eternity together to get on with it. *Or we could leave? Two weeks in the Caribbean? I bet Pamela would take 'em. A few days of a legume-only diet would kill the mood pretty quickly, I promise you.* He'd worked hard to calm her. Should James and Nathan move out for a month? Probably that was the best solution but—the idea of him leaving made her frantic. She had waited her whole life for him, she thought, fiercely, and if he left, he might never return. To wake up alone another morning was unthinkable—if Gwen chased him from the house, Julia could not imagine forgiving her easily. Never before had she felt so assaulted by her daughter. And never had she come so close to slipping, and telling James what she thought about his son.

Nathan had taken out his phone. "Why do we—"

"I'm not interested in one syllable from either of you until we are sitting around a table like adults, in a neutral space."

"But—"

"And I have a beer in my hand. Seriously. Just zip it, Nathan. We've been in this house all day and I need air."

"But—"

"Be quiet. You'll both do as you're told, for once. And you will leave your damn devices here and talk like civilized humans."

Nathan fell silent and Julia rose from the table, fortified. She was too angry to look at Gwen, too angry to speak to Gwen, but James had taken charge and she sagged with inward relief, leaning heavily against the strength of his resolve. He would speak for them both, until she felt able. He could be calm, where she would have raved. He was a good father. He would stop this madness in its tracks.

Nathan and Gwen relinquished their phones sulkily, but without protest. James hesitated, about to set them on the coffee table and then seemed to change his mind and slipped them into his own pocket. Coats were gathered in silence, and they all waited by the front gate while James switched on the alarm and double locked the front door.

They set off down the road in single file—Nathan toggled tight into his hoodie, followed by Gwen, then Julia and James. The pavement was deserted, but light glowed behind curtains and shutters. They walked down the terraced street, rich sand and ocher London stock beneath gnarled and naked winter-stripped wisteria. Functional, nuclear families inside home after home, Julia imagined, obedient, rosy-cheeked children bringing pride to their misty parents at the foot of sap-heavy Douglas firs. Gospel Oak, by Norman Rockwell. *I can't believe them*, Julia had said to James, moments earlier. He'd shrugged, his thumb moving gently across her knuckles and said, *Remember their ultimate aim in life is to piss us off. We don't capitulate to terrorists.* And she had found herself laughing—with disbelief at her undented happiness, at the power of James's voice to lift her heart, with gratitude that the sight of his face turned toward hers still made her throat catch, that his eyes upon her could make all the rest mute and fade into insignificance. Her daughter had launched a missile at her life and yet here was James, and so everything was okay, even when it wasn't.

The pub was closed. It was Christmas Day; their beloved, unrenovated local had bowed out of the race. Better to stay at home, its dark, etched windows advised; it would not compete with marked-down supermarket beer and glutted lassitude, and the rising screech of seasonal family tension. MERRY XMAS, read a small sign on the door in red felt tip, and then on a sloping second line the assurance, REOPEN BOXING DAY.

James swore. He caught Julia's eye, and she wondered if he was about to laugh, but when he faced the children he looked stern once again. He shooed them away, homeward.

"Back. Now."

"That was what I was trying to say," Nathan muttered, as they began to trudge back the way they'd come. "Nothing'd be open."

They had been out of the house for approximately three and a half minutes. As they turned onto their own street sloppy raindrops began to fall, landing splashily in shallow puddles from an earlier downfall.

London seemed under water; it felt like the middle of the night. Back inside they moved by unspoken consensus into the kitchen. Julia put on the kettle, as if they'd been adventuring in the cold for hours. James went to the cupboard and took out two tins of baked beans. Julia went to the bread bin. Gwen opened her mouth to request a bagel, thought better of it, and closed it again. Nathan and Gwen sat side by side at the kitchen table, waiting and watching while their parents began to orchestrate supper. Gwen had begun to find the silence unbearable, which she suspected was the intention.

"What can I do?" she asked, brightly. A new approach. Sunny and amenable.

"You've done enough," said James. He sounded almost cheerful.

Nathan said, "I think we should be allowed to put a case." Beneath the table his knee pressed reassuringly against Gwen's. "You can't sentence us without hearing the case for the defense."

James began to spoon warmed baked beans onto the plates Julia had lined up beside him. "This is a kangaroo court. I can do whatever I damn well please."

"Can I have mine—" Gwen began, wanting to ask for her beans on the side, not actually touching her toast.

"Nope." James was giving every indication of enjoying himself, but then said, in a different tone, "You've betrayed our trust. I am deeply disappointed in you both."

"But—thanks—we haven't," Nathan explained, accepting the two plates that Julia had brought to the table and setting one down in front of Gwen. Julia turned back for the others. "It's only been a few weeks, it didn't make sense to get everyone all upset if it was nothing."

"It is nothing," James told him, taking his place at the table, opposite his son. He cut into his toast with relish and said, with his mouth full, "It's nothing whatsoever. Whatever it is or was, it's done. *Finito*."

Gwen, who had been elongating and then releasing a single coil of hair, raised her head, her eyes flashing with rekindled fury. "It isn't nothing! You can't just say that—you don't know anything. You can't tell us what to do!"

Julia set down her fork with a clatter. "Don't you dare shout at James like that. This is absolutely inappropriate, Gwendolen, and I forbid it."

"Why do you even care what I do? You're such a hypocrite, you don't tell me anything about your life, you barely even talk to me anymore except to tell me to, *'be nice, be nice, be nice,'* and *'Oh, by the way, a family of total strangers are moving in, kay, thanks, and I'm going to need you to be a totally different person now,'* and we're all meant to be best friends and you don't even notice or care that everybody's miserable except you two obsessed with each other, and now something nice has actually happened for literally the first time in my life and you only care what it means for you." She was out of breath and paused. "Well, sorry if it's not convenient. Nathan's my boyfriend. You didn't tell me when you first got together and you don't tell me *any-thing* about your plans for this family and I would have thought you'd be pleased to know I have someone who cares about me while you're busy replacing me in your new fabulous life. I'm a—a *superfluous person*." She dropped her head and began to sob, her face now entirely concealed behind a mass of russet hair that had fallen forward, peril-ously close to her plate. Julia opened her mouth to reply, but closed it in stricken silence. That Gwen should feel safe, that Gwen should feel cherished: these objectives had been her life's work. Her anger began to drain from her like water from a pool.

"Can everyone please lower their voices." James was speaking in a singsong half-whisper, in the tone of one addressing much smaller children, at nap time. He picked up his remaining crust and began to mop up tomato sauce. "One at a time, please tell us what's been happening. Calmly. Nathan?"

Nathan looked to Gwen and then back to his father. "Can we please scratch everything that happened today, and can you listen as though we'd brought this to you ourselves?"

"No. Next question."

"Okay, fine. Look, we like each other, okay? And I know it's a little weird that you guys are dating and now we're dating and we all live in the same house, but we both understood the ramifications of it all beforehand and considered it worth the risk."

"You did, did you. How very mature. Well, we all live in the same house, as you so charmingly put it, because you are our offspring and we are your parents. This isn't a Noel Coward play; it's not just some unfortunate coincidence in a boardinghouse. I do not allow it, and that's the end of the story."

"We're not related, we never could be even if you guys— We were adults before you even met."

Both Julia and James began to laugh, which was enraging, and after a moment James set both his palms on the table and stood up, scraping his chair back loudly. "Enough. I've had enough hilarity for one night. Nathan, I am phoning your mother, with whom you will now stay this evening, and in the meantime, Gwen, please go upstairs. Take whatever sustenance you need for a good twelve hours, I don't want to catch sight of you again until tomorrow."

Gwen, whose usual trick of storming to her bedroom had been whisked unexpectedly from her arsenal, looked wrong-footed and gave James a scathing glance. "You're sending me to my room. Like someone from the olden days. *Fine*, I'm going. But newsflash, you're not my father. And you can't stop us seeing each other; we both live here." She, too, stood, clutching her plate in both hands as if in line at a soup kitchen. "You can't lock me in my room forever."

James already had his phone to his ear. "I will look seriously into the legality of it. Pamela? Yup. Yup. Minor change of plan. Can I deliver your son in half an hour?"

15.

"DID YOU HAVE TO TELL HER? COULDN'T YOU JUST HAVE SAID he was coming to visit?"

Taking off his coat, James paused, looking surprised. "She is his mother."

"Yes, but . . ." Julia could think of no good reason other than her own, visceral objection. Pamela's involvement was perhaps the only way to make the circumstances feel more calamitous. She could not get past the suspicion that this latest, repugnant development was due to Pamela's own unwelcome pheromones and sexually permissive influence wafting through the house. She felt an urge to burn sage leaves, or perform some other sort of occult, neopagan cleansing ritual, and then, thinking that this was perhaps precisely what Pamela herself might do, wondered if she was actually losing her grip. She thought, but did not say, *I don't like Pamela.*

"Nathan would have told her himself anyway," said James, reasonably, dropping the car keys onto the coffee table and collapsing into an armchair. "But also we have to be honest with one another.

I'd be mad if something happened on her watch that she didn't share with me."

"It wasn't 'on our watch,' we could hardly have known—"

"I'm not saying we could have stopped them, you know what I mean."

"This is nauseating," said Julia, laying her forehead on the arm of the sofa. She rejected the memory of Nathan's hand lost beneath her daughter's T-shirt, the pert denim globe of his backside aloft as he lay almost on top of her child. "I quite literally cannot believe this is happening. It cannot happen. They've chosen the one thing that will make our family life impossible. It's genius really, when you think about it. It's the perfect sabotage."

James moved to sit beside her and laid his hands on her back. The warmth of his palms seeped through her sweater to her skin. "I think it's also teenagers doing what teenagers do." She lifted her head slightly but before she could protest he continued, "But let's say you're right and there's a part of them trying to rebel and make things difficult or, what I think is more likely, looking for attention they might feel they've lost recently. It's still pretty new for them, seeing us together. That's twice the reason to show them what we're made of and to handle it like a team. We've done a lot of family stuff recently, so maybe it's time to go back to the beginning, making sure you get time alone with Gwen every weekend and I get time alone with Nathan. They're good kids."

"But that's the point, they're kids. They have no idea what a mess this could be; I don't think they even really get why it's so totally and utterly wrong, and revolting. And all those things she said—I've been selfish and I've hurt her and—"

"Stop. For right now Pamela's happy to have him and that will give them time to cool off, or pretend it never happened or whatever. They're apart during the week when he's at school, so it's only weekends we have to just say, no, obviously this is unacceptable. We'll put a stop to it and that's that. We'll figure it out, but you have not been selfish. You do nothing but think of her. There's still some mulled wine, if you want?"

Julia shook her head. "It wasn't very nice, I don't know what they put in it."

"Maybe they weren't concentrating."

"Oh, don't," said Julia, but she laughed, in disbelief. "This is actually appalling."

"Yes," agreed James. "Let's fire them and get better ones. But you know what, I'm pretty confident it will be okay. Probably the entire point was for you to see them and now the point's made."

"Loud and clear."

"Yup. Loud and clear."

FOR HIS PART, Nathan felt hopeful. He had charmed his way out of stickier scrapes than this one. He understood why everyone was angry but it would not alter the course of his behavior and now, safely across London, he had lost all traces of his own indignation and merely felt enlivened by the drama.

Gwen was not at all his usual type. Valentina, he'd known with pride, was a nine, a point docked for her high-strung madness. (His friend Edmund's scale did not even consider faces, let alone personality, merely the hardware on display from the neck down.) But Nathan had eventually become bored and exasperated by Valentina, and what security and confidence he derived from having a steady girlfriend had been undermined by their relentless rows. It had seemed passionate and romantic at first, but whatever her physical attributes, he did not want a girlfriend who was always angry. Gwen Alden was a solid eight to eight-and-a-half. She was catwalk tall and could definitely be described as willowy, and her red hair was so startling that it transcended the traditionally disparaging label "ginger" and recategorized her as "striking." She had a beautiful face. He liked her laugh, and her belief, however resentfully held, that he was an academic genius. It was worth a little heat from his father, and in any case, his mother was bound to take it in better spirits. As long as he furnished her with a few details, she usually said yes to anything.

BOXING DAY CAME the nadir. Julia sat on the end of Gwen's bed, her head bowed, her fingers interlaced in her lap.

"I've been up all night," said Julia, softly, "trying to comprehend why. I am very disappointed."

Gwen almost laughed at this grave, teacherly cliché, for she, too, had been lying awake slightly manic with nerves and a sense of guilty defiance. It would be a day of reckoning. She restrained the giggle and said, "I'm sorry." And then worried this was a concession, added primly, "I'm sorry you feel that way."

"You cannot possibly have thought this was a good idea."

"It's not an idea. I *like* him. It isn't like we planned it or anything."

"It's not appropriate."

Gwen sat up and flung the covers off. Shouting would be awkward as she still had in her retainer, but she was too cross to pause and remove it. "Who says? You can't actually control everything we do, we're adults."

"Adults! This is precisely the opposite of adult behavior. If you can't see why this is fraught with awkwardness—"

"It's not like I didn't find it *awkward* when you started going out with James. It's not like I didn't find it awkward when he took over Dad's house. That was pretty bloody *awkward*, if you ask me."

"Can you not see that's a little different?"

"No," said Gwen, stubbornly. "I can't. In any case, it's done now." To shore up her sense of dignity she removed her retainer at last, clicking it into the purple plastic case on her bedside table. She then padded over to her desk in search of her glasses, feeling vulnerable and at a disadvantage, with the world blurred.

"What's done? You mean it's over?"

"No, it's done. He's my boyfriend. There's nothing you can do." She and Nathan had never actually discussed the status of their relationship but he hadn't contradicted her when she'd made her announcement the night before, and this bolstered her confidence. And then on impulse she added, "We've been together for ages."

Julia looked startled. "How long?"

"None of your business. You don't consult me with what you do with your love life."

"Gwen, that's enough. Don't be rude." And then in a different, quieter tone, "Gwendolen, darling, what do you mean by 'love life'? How serious has this become? Many things are not my business but what happens under my roof is my concern. Are you—are you sleeping with him?"

And suddenly a conversation previously unimaginable to both of them was taking place. Gwen felt a simultaneous sense of injustice and betrayal. Here was conclusive proof of how wretchedly little Julia understood—about what was and wasn't appropriate, about life in general, and specifically about her own child who had not yet removed a single item of clothing in the presence of any boy, Nathan included, and who did not even *want* to go to bed with anyone. She might as well have asked whether Gwen had taken up skydiving. Clearly her mother had stopped paying attention some time ago. Gwen had become a stranger to her, capable of anything. Self-pity threatened, but Gwen forced herself to focus on what she had for solace. And so she swallowed the outraged, honest denial that had risen and gambled instead. "Why is our sex life anything to do with you?"

As soon as the words were out a gulf opened between them, a lake of a lie. *It's not true!* she thought, as loudly as she could, but the lie lay between them now, an expanse across which it was impossible to hear one another. Already she ached to confess, and already knew she never would. Watching her mother recede into the distance with the steady inevitability of a departing ship, she thought, hopelessly, one day it might be true. Sex was at present entirely unimaginable, but Julia had begun to cry, and then left in silence, and so it must be believable to her.

Gwen had felt known her whole life, known and cherished, and had, she realized, taken that charmed state entirely for granted. She now saw it for the flossy, muffling cocoon of naïveté and infantile solipsism it must always have been. A delusion. Only her father had entirely loved and accepted her, and he would certainly never have let Julia spend the rest of Boxing Day charging around in derangement demanding that James write a prescription for the Pill, nor allowed her to leave a frantic and humiliating message on the GP's out-of-hours answering machine after James had said his own involvement would be inappropriate. Without her father, no one saw her. Except Nathan.

part two

16.

"I'M OUTSIDE. WHAT ON EARTH IS THE DELAY?"

"I'm sorry," said Philip, words he'd spoken to Iris so often that they had become a ritual of greeting. "I need just another moment."

Iris ensured that her heavy sigh was audible before hanging up the phone, and Philip returned to the shoes he had been laboriously tying. This adventure should have begun some time ago but he had been on the computer for most of the afternoon, hunting down and then printing out an essay on Beckett to read to her. It was a habit they had developed early on in their relationship, started in imitation of Philip's mother who'd been a determined autodidact and who, in her rare moments of liberty, would take herself off to the Swiss Cottage Library. Her English had eventually been excellent but drama had always remained a hurdle, so if she took Philip to queue for returns, it would be for a play about which she had already spent snatched moments reading. Denied so very many avenues of education by gender, circumstance, and war; now, newly British, newly emancipated, she would not sacrifice a single drop of insight or pleasure by failing to under-

stand a nuance, a reference, a history. At first amused when she'd discovered what she referred to as Philip's homework, Iris had then
begun to depend upon him whenever they went to the theater.

"Oh, Philip will tell us all about it," she'd say, idly. "What do we
know about the play, Philip?" And Philip would produce his notes
from the inside pocket of his jacket, folded sheets of scrawls and cita-
tions, the fruit of an afternoon's study.

Today, it was true, he had lost track of time. It would not help to
suggest that she come in and wait in the living room while he finished putting on his shoes and then found his scarf and located his
other glasses (mysteriously absent from the coil pot Gwen had made to
house them). Instead she would sit, idling in a taxi vibrating with the
diesel engine and her increasing vexation, for as long as it took him to
emerge. She was happiest when he'd anticipated her early arrival and
was waiting for her on the pavement when she swept up, barely need-
ing to stop before they could motor away from this scene of his embarrassing isolation. The existence of this modest flat irked her.

"What were you doing?" she snapped, when he joined her in the
taxi.

"I thought you'd like Harold Bloom for the interval. On *The Lady
with the Dog.*"

"Ever since the Lessing comment I've gone off him, though perhaps it's time to make up. Thank you for the James Wood, though; I
read it this morning. Oh, and I've booked us smoked salmon, for the
interval."

"Thank you," said Philip, humbly.

"How did you like the Rosamond Lehmann?"

"I've only read the introduction so far, I will get to it, I've been
doing a little research that distracted me. Pamela Thing emailed me."

She glanced at him, sharply. "Thing's wife?"

"Ex-wife. Yes."

"I can't think of a benign reason to be e-mailing your former husband's new . . . what is she, girlfriend I suppose—girlfriend's former father-in-law."

"It's professional. She's asked me to critique a paper she's writing. We're not former, Iris."

"Oh, I know, I know. Christ, on what?"

"Orgasmic childbirth. I think she's decided I exemplify everything she hates about the—what did she call it?—medical patriarchy, and so she wants me to comment and show her the holes they'll all find when it's published so she can plug them in advance."

"Was 'holes' her word? She can't be a very rigorous academic if she can't find her own holes. Nor a very good gynecologist, now I come to think of it."

"She said something along the lines of never being able to anticipate the sly ways in which the Establishment seek to quash the revolution—"

"Oh she didn't! Does she listen to herself?"

"I assure you she did. I think I embody The Man. Because of the forceps."

"But that doesn't mean you actually have to do it," said Iris, irritated. Philip's acquiescence to the exploitation of others made her own dependence upon him less comfortable, and also less a mark of distinction somehow. "You can just say, 'No, you crackpot, I'm retired.' Also, it's perfectly obvious to anyone with half a brain that there are certain moments a girl doesn't want to be thinking about sex, and I need not tell you that childbirth is among them. Why does she think the so-called establishment should be hell-bent on depriving women of their right to orgasm during childbirth in any case? Actually don't tell me, I really couldn't care less."

"I'll send you the paper to read."

"Please don't."

"She also said something about Gwen and the boy."

Iris's ears pricked up. "What boy? Gwen's got a boyfriend? How unbearable that that busybody should know before we do. What did she say, who is he? Is he from school?"

"Not *a* boy, *the* boy, their son. Whatshisname. Nathan."

They had drawn up outside the theater, where the bright bulbs of the awning cast a gleam into oily, puddled gutters. Iris paid for the cab while Philip set about the awkward business of clambering out of it—on the one hand easier than the low-slung seats of a normal car; on the other more challenging for the larger step down to the pavement. Iris managed to stay occupied until he had succeeded and had straightened up, restored to dignity, and then slipped her arm through his. They made their way into the heat of the foyer.

"What did you mean?" she demanded, when they had settled in their seats, picking up where they had left off after various digressions and excursions for programs, bathroom visits, procuring of reading glasses in order to see their phones clearly enough to turn them off, and some inquiries to ascertain in which bar Iris had booked the interval refreshments.

"She seemed to imply that there was some sort of romance going on between Gwen and her son. It seems rather unlikely."

Iris stroked the glossy program that lay in her lap and considered.

"It's horribly likely, when you stop and think," she said, eventually. "You throw two teenagers together, curiosity and hormones flying about, and it suddenly seems obvious. They're tripping over each other, it's bound to cross their minds eventually."

"You don't think it's true? Gwen's such an innocent."

"If it hasn't happened already, we should warn them that it might, so they can head it off at the pass," Iris whispered, as the lights fell. "Despite Julia's best efforts, Gwendolen can't be expected to remain twelve forever."

17.

SÉBASTIEN BENAIM WAS AN OBSTETRIC CONSULTANT AT THE Homerton and his wife, Anne, a cardiologist at the Royal Free. Sébastien and James had worked together ten years ago when they were all new Londoners—James from Boston, the Benaims from Paris. The family lived a ten-minute walk away, on Hartland Road, a pretty terrace of ice-cream–colored blocks in whose front gardens the Camden Town revelers regularly threw bottles and cigarette boxes, or nightclub flyers in acid pinks and greens, or intermittently relieved themselves through the spear-headed railings. "If you live in Camden, you must 'ave many parties," Sébastien had told James when he'd invited him for New Year's Eve, "ozzerwise ze parties everyone else is 'aving will drive you crazy."

They arrived late and the kitchen was hot and crowded; five or six people were already dancing rather drunkenly in the darkened living room. The Benaim children, a boy and girl of seven and eight, were in their pajamas and jumping together in a corner, giggling. Julia saw

Claire, James's registrar, crouched on the floor over a laptop, controlling the music. She was a poor and impatient DJ, and two-thirds of the way through a song would become enthused about her next selection and abruptly replace mideighties singalong Madonna with harsh-edged euro electronica, or a sensual R&B anthem with the title song of a Disney movie. It was loud, and even in the kitchen people shouted at one another to make themselves heard. It was a real party, Julia thought, surprised by the stirring of pleasure and recognition within her. Not civilized canapés. Not dinner for three couples and a discussion of school policy changes and university application forms. A loud, messy, drunken, badly behaved party. The copious wine was excellent. Curls of smoke drifted in from the small back garden; a fat spliff circulating around a circle of cardiologists. The music grew louder. *I am not old*, Julia reminded herself, and found herself smiling, happy she'd dressed up, happy she'd thought to wear makeup, and to pay attention to her hair. She grinned at James, who grinned back, buoyed by the same remembered freedom. He handed her a champagne flute from the kitchen counter.

"And the best part is," he said, continuing a wordless exchange aloud, "that they're busy, they're apart, and we don't have to lay eyes on either of them till at least lunchtime tomorrow. Prosecco?"

Julia nodded and held up her glass; they were toasting their liberty as Sébastien came over to them and put an arm around each of their shoulders. After a decade, he retained a preposterously extravagant accent. "'Ow are you, James?" He slapped him heartily and turned to Julia. "I love zis man. 'E made me laugh every day. Now it is dull wizout him. 'Ow is the eye chlamydia? You did not know that James as 'chlamydia of the eye,' but 'e does, I am convinced of it. One of the best moments of my whole life was in ze operating room,"—James, too, was laughing and shaking his head, covering his eyes with both hands—"when zis man decided to operate on an *énorme* Bartholin's cyst wizout glasses." He mimed a fountain, or explosion. "And whoosh. Pus in ze eye. Even ze poor patient she was laughing at 'im. Such joy, you brought us all. It was a sacrifice, you know?" Sébastien nodded approvingly at their full glasses and excused himself, just as Claire bounced over.

Julia had met her in passing several times before, a slim, Chinese-American woman in her midthirties with short-cropped hair and a large diamond-and-ruby cocktail ring slung on a chain around her neck. This evening she was in a pair of black leather pants and high-top white sneakers, and looked, Julia thought with envy, about twenty-five. She kissed Julia and high-fived James. Julia noticed that Claire's nails were painted with a sparkly black polish Gwen would have loved. *When did I stop wearing nail polish?* Julia wondered, watching the tips of Claire's fingers flash prettily as she gestured. *Why?* The idea returned as if from another lifetime, together with a memory of admiring her own hands as they moved, claret-tipped, across the piano keys. Gwen would howl with laughter at the very thought of her mother so adorned. Can anything make a woman feel more ancient than her own teenage daughter?

"When did you guys get here? You missed Rebecca and Sam; they were going to another thing. You need to get Rebecca to tell you about the amniotic band we had the day before yesterday, I can't even. It *fell off.* On the *floor.* I'm going back, this music's terrible; I'm saving Guns n' Roses for later"—she pointed at James—"we'll get the whole disco break crew."

"What's an amniotic band?"

Claire gave Julia a dark look. "Truly—in this case, don't ask."

"I've just been hearing about eye chlamydia, I'm not sure it can be worse."

"Oh yes, but luckily your man is the world's only known sufferer. No one he's taught ever forgets glasses when they go near a Bartholin's cyst now; it's truly a cautionary tale. James is the only consultant to admit he's fallible; the others are too grand. Or too weird," she concluded, and then handed Julia the bowl of strawberries she'd been holding and returned to her station on the floor. The song changed again, and there were whoops of appreciation from somewhere in the dark depths of the room.

It was different to be at a party together. Almost immediately they were pulled apart by conversational tides but she could look across at James and recall the stranger he had been, not so long ago. She talked to his friends and felt his eyes on her and stood taller. She saw Claire say something and laugh with her whole body angled toward his, her hand for a moment on his forearm and thought, *That man chose me.* It seemed impossible good fortune. She alone would go home with James and, for tonight, there would be no children, no drama, no competition. Just the two of them, the way it had never been at the beginning. Second relationships are starved of precious, nourishing solitude, and second couples must snatch for it with jealous determination. They cannot put themselves first, but must not put themselves last. *We will,* she resolved, *try harder to be alone.*

Julia felt a hand on her waist and suddenly James was beside her. His eyes were bright. He took her wrist and led her down a corridor and into a dark spare bedroom, in which coats and bags were piled. James pushed the door closed, and pressed Julia against it.

"I missed you." His hands were moving beneath her skirt. "Don't run away with a boring cardiologist. Be with me." For a moment his mouth was at her throat, but the door behind them began to open and they sprang apart. His eyes glittered at her in the darkness.

It was Claire, apparently amused to find them there. "Just getting lip balm from my bag, don't mind me, lovebirds. Just so you know, it's almost midnight." She rummaged in the pile of coats for a moment and then was gone, closing the door rather pointedly behind her.

Alone, they remained apart, looking at one another.

"We need to behave," said Julia softly, with regret.

"I don't want to behave." James took her hand in his. "Let's go home."

From the living room they heard the sound of a countdown. Ten! Nine! Eight! Seven! This would be the year. She would learn to be assertive with her daughter, she would fight for time and space with this man whom she loved so fiercely; at half term they would send Nathan to America and leave Gwen with Iris and they would book a holiday just the two of them. Six! Five! Four! A fresh start. No more guilt. She would remember that she was allowed to be happy. Three! Two! One! Happy New Year!

ACROSS LONDON, Gwen was waiting for a night bus. She had spent the early part of the evening with Katy and two other school friends at a pizza restaurant on Haverstock Hill. At ten thirty, Katy's mother had arrived to take them all back for a sleepover and to see in twelve o'clock armed with ice cream and Maltesers, and cans of sparkling apple juice that Katy's father would later decant into champagne flutes for them, thereby mortifying Katy. Gwen, as arranged, had hidden inside the restaurant.

After the car had pulled away Gwen had tugged her hood over her face and walked down the hill to Belsize Park tube station, where she'd got the train to Waterloo, an unexpectedly exhilarating adventure. She had never before been allowed to go out on New Year's Eve. Her mother would argue she was not yet old enough now, but in the last days Julia had proven that she knew nothing about her daughter, her needs or principles, and no longer cared to pay attention. She was too busy with her own repulsive romance. And it turned out that there was a camaraderie in London on New Year's Eve, a carnival air on the Tube encouraged by the jovial announcements of the driver, and the makeup and glad rags and mounting anticipation of the passengers. Gwen could not know this would later sour into a less benign atmosphere, a bright-lit, bristling tension charged with disappointed hopes, too much alcohol, furious energy as yet unspent. In this same train there would be fights, and sobs and jeers, and possibly vomiting. But for now, while the night still held promise, all was celebratory. The mayor's drinking ban was openly flouted. A man in a rhinestone-studded denim jacket and gold sunglasses played music. In high spirits and higher hemlines, a group of girls at the other end of the carriage called out song requests and one, beneath a towering, backcombed beehive, stood up and began to gyrate around the central pole. Gwen smiled to herself, and was rewarded with a fleeting grin from a woman who sat opposite, in the midst of applying her mascara. The plan was going easily, and well. Julia, who had dropped her off and had chatted to Katy through the car window before disappearing to her own, private, exclusive and excluding plans, would never learn that Gwen was spending the evening with Nathan. Last year Gwen and Julia had shared pizzas from the same restaurant and watched

Calamity Jane till midnight. It was amazing how much her mother, who had once known everything, did not know.

Since the discovery on Christmas Day, the household had moved together through various phases. Acceptance would follow, Nathan had asserted, since they'd dwelt so exhaustively in rage and denial. He was waiting out his father's disappointment as if it was a rainstorm and he happily settled in the window of a café with a newspaper and a hot chocolate, nowhere special to be. The squall would pass and he would venture back into the pale, clean-washed sunshine. He would be forgiven—had probably been forgiven already. Gwen felt less secure. Julia's immediate fury, though it had been startling and uncharacteristic, had turned out to be the easiest to navigate. Gwen was accustomed to her mother's fierce devotion and so her mother in a fit of violent feeling was, at least, feeling violent feelings about her. In the quiet isolation of late December, that pocket of slow, padded time between Christmas and New Year when families turn in on themselves, hibernating, or festering, Julia and Gwen had been forced by sheer exposure to return to a superficial approximation of normality. Julia's temper cooled to chill disappointment. The household had grown steadily calmer, but the unaccustomed rift between mother and daughter remained in place. Gwen had no choice but to cleave tighter to Nathan, and to stand resolutely by her choice.

The bus came, bright and busy, and from it poured a steady stream of revelers. Out came the tourists in plastic rain ponchos heading for set meals at chain restaurants booked months ago, online; she pushed her way on, her height for once an advantage, and a text from Nathan pinged through. Where RU? Don't like you wandering the streets. Can I come get you somewhere? RU safe? She began to feel the rends in her cocoon slowly knitting back together. Wasn't this growing up?

Moving on, forging new bonds, and graduating into independence? If so, perhaps this desperate sadness and longing for her mother that she felt was usual, too, and would pass, in time.

On the bus, she wrote back.

Instantly he replied, Party's long. I'll meet you. Let's go just us to the river, baby, can go later to Charlie's. Bisous.

The parents did not expect them home (nor care, Gwen told herself, the taste of new, bitter cynicism on her tongue). She had said she'd stay with Katy; in her bag a pair of clean underwear, a toothbrush, sneakers for tomorrow morning, the contact lens case she'd painted with nail varnish rainbows. Nathan had told the truth: he was sleeping at Charlie's with a mixed group of fifteen other school friends, only omitting the additional information that Gwen would join him. The night would offer little privacy other than that afforded by darkness and a sleeping bag but this, already, was an improvement upon the late-night tiptoeing and furtive anxiety of home. Around them would be other teenagers with sympathy, and romantic concerns of their own.

K, she wrote back, and then almost as an afterthought, for though she'd never told him, she knew he already knew, Love U.

18.

THIS TIME, PHILIP PREPARED BY STANDING QUIETLY TO RE-call the name of James's son in advance, as well as the name of the play that he and Iris had seen together when the subject had arisen, and the name of the current book he was reading, just in case. It was not pos-sible to consider all contingencies, but with this cache he felt able to ring Iris and inform her, "I believe it's true that a romance has begun between Gwen and Nathan," with the easy, conversational flow of a late-night radio host. His memory was not getting worse, thank God. But, despite online Sudoku, it was not getting any better.

"Well I suppose it's not incest."

"Don't be ludicrous, of course it isn't."

"Aren't we relieved she's finally having a romance of any sort? Per-haps there are wiser places to look for it, but since when have teenag-ers been known for their wisdom?"

"This is a little different," Philip told her. "Imagine what will happen when they fall out."

"Well, why should they fall out? What if it all ends happily ever after and we can throw the four of them a cozy double wedding in a few years' time? One of Julia's students can play the 'Wedding March.'"

Philip sat down, heavily, in his armchair. "I don't understand why you are being facetious about this, it's your granddaughter we are discussing. It's horribly inappropriate. And it will put terrible strain on Julia's relationship with James."

"Julia's relationships are her own affair," Iris said, breezily, and he heard in the background the clamor and a thumping bass line that betrayed she was in Selfridges. "Julia and Thing threw two teenagers into one another's paths and no doubt instructed them to be nice to one another, so in a sense they're only following instructions. Meanwhile it is really about time that Gwen had a little romantic interest, even if she might have been a little more discerning. It was becoming peculiar."

"She's sixteen!"

"Oh, don't be such an old woman. Sixteen is the new thirty, according to the papers. Of course, it's none of it rational when we are meant to believe that sixty is the new thirty-five, but still."

"Those headlines are appalling. I'm content to be old. One of the privileges of being old is that I get to behave as if I'm old."

"Well, I used to write those headlines so they don't appall me in the slightest. What is the source of your information? By the way, I'm buying you a polo shirt as we speak."

"Gwen's blog. I don't need anything. I don't wear polo shirts."

"Sales. Dregs. Very nice, though, it's a sort of slub cotton. Bit see-through but it's for under things. I looked at the blog a few days ago."

"This went up today. They're arm in arm, and Julia and James are in the background with their hands to their ears in paroxysms of a very Munch-like horror. She's made a public declaration."

"I hardly think public, I'm sure we're the only people who read that thing."

"Well, I was phoning to ask about the party line, whether you think we ought to know or not to know. When we speak to her mother."

"Oh, it's always better not to know. Never know anything at all, you taught me that. See no evil, and all that. In my case it was the truth as well as the party line, until you telephoned. Ought someone to put her on the Pill?"

Alone in his dusky living room, Philip covered his eyes with his hand. "Iris. I sincerely hope it's not necessary."

"If you don't want to hear my opinions, I don't know why you always solicit them. Navy blue or black? I don't see you in black."

"Not black," Philip agreed, and rang off, exhausted.

NATHAN HAD BEEN THERE, embedded in her family like a sleeper cell, and Julia had welcomed him. She ironed his school shirts and drove him to the dentist, and had recently risked hypothermia on the sidelines of a rugby match watching as Westminster, in startling salmon pink, played a dirty and tedious game against UCS. She kept the house stocked with imported American breakfast cereals, and fruit loaf. She had tried. And then he seduced her daughter.

Since Christmas Day she had found it difficult to address him with civility. He would make polite, ingratiating conversation and she would be assailed by an image of him, conniving and predatory, pawing at Gwen like a middle-aged office roué. The laundry nauseated her; she lifted an escaped pair of his boxer shorts into the washing machine between clenched toes. Their existence was an affront. That he put them on, and took them off, in her house was appalling. She had not voiced her fantasy solution—that Nathan should move back to America to live with his mother—but on Boxing Day she had suggested to James that Nathan stay at school full time instead of coming back for weekends, thinking it seemed not only the obvious but also the most desirable solution. But James had frowned and said that he couldn't ban his son from home. They would simply have to stay strong, and keep saying no. Yet allowing them under the same roof, even two nights a week, even after a family meeting in which James had reiterated their absolute and unwavering opposition, seemed a tacit permission.

The depth of her initial distress had startled her, as had the white rage that followed it. How dare they? *How dare they?* And the relationship persisted, flourishing against the odds, and against the express wishes of all but its participants. On and on it went, from strength to strength, however much Julia demanded they stop. It was high treason to recall that Nathan had not long ago been equally devoted to Valentina, whom Gwen, with flamboyant geographic inaccuracy and conflation, had taken to calling the Demon Barber of Seville. The new allegiance had wiped out all that had come before.

Yet since that first awful discovery the children had done little to which she could reasonably object. Unprompted, they began to spend Sunday afternoons doing homework together at the dining table. Gwen developed academic aspirations, in direct contravention of her previously asserted philosophies. Julia more than once overheard Nathan meticulously explaining a concept—once subtracting vectors, another time the factors that limit photosynthesis. He introduced Gwen to the programs he watched, the podcasts he downloaded, and the two of them spent hours glued to the screen of a shared laptop or listening together with a headphone splitter, deaf to the other members of the household. What could Julia say? How could she stop them listening to a podcast? Once indolent, Gwen was now industrious; once furious with James, she was now sunny and acquiescent. Beneath the heat of Nathan's attention she flourished like a hothouse plant, and after the third weekend during which Julia had exhausted herself lying rigid, listening for forbidden nighttime visits and had heard nothing, she had been forced to admit defeat. Not aloud—she could never give the children the satisfaction. But the truth was that forbidding feelings had got them nowhere. They could forbid only their public expression.

Since James had moved in Julia had suffered her daughter's resentment and unhappiness. Now, seeing Gwen's small, private smile as she hunched over her laptop typing messages made her heart hurt in a way that was harder to define. There was a new hauteur in Gwen's address; a new, polite formality that stung, even though it was almost certainly intended to sting. Blog readers were treated to a dramatic sequence of scenes in which Gwen and Nathan stood firm against the family's disapproval and finally won them over by making pancakes, and Gwen reported that the online community was thrilled by her new love, that several fans had only expected as much and had long been rooting for the cohabiting teenagers to find one another. Julia felt far away from her daughter, excluded for the first time from her confidence, punished for daring to betray that she was a woman, and not simply a mother. Yet only six weeks had passed—six exhausting weekends—and in that short time Gwen had unfurled, had stopped scowling, had started laughing at James's jokes, and once again helped to clear the table after dinner, even if James had cooked. And so Julia began to hold her tongue. She missed her child. She missed being needed, even when that need was expressed in baleful stares and tantrums. As a parent it was impossible to foresee anything but snares and brambles along this path, and almost certainly she ought to protect Gwen from her own foolishness by continuing to forbid, by creating obstacles, by allowing herself to be the enemy. But she needed James, and wanted him, and when Gwen was occupied and contented then he and she were granted space for one another. Harmony was hard to resist, however distasteful the price.

19.

TO OVERHEAR JULIA ARGUING WITH HER DAUGHTER WAS AN exercise in restraint and took James back to the bad old days of early cohabitation. Only now did he realize how acquiescent Gwen had been of late and remembered, with an unpleasant jolt, how unappealing he found her when she wasn't getting her own way. Her wheedling, which veered from pleading to explosive rage and back to infantile beseeching again, wore on his nerves like tinnitus. And stamina was her secret weapon, for Julia would be exhausted and would run out of arguments, and seemed never to wise to this tactic. Instead, she followed her daughter down any conversational avenue she led, negotiating and reasoning and never drawing an end with a firm and final stand. "You don't need to make a case for the defense, you can just put your foot down," James would advise in their fraught postmortems, but could say nothing when she explained that with Gwen it was more complicated. From this he was to infer that a dead parent was a trump card, and his hands were tied. Rarely sober, his own father had worked selling used trucks at a lot in Dorchester. His sporadic commission had kept the Fullers narrowly solvent and when he died James had won for it no special treatment, except the further reduction of the already minuscule possibility of his going to college. His mother, a pediatrician's receptionist, had adored and cherished her only child with an intensity he recognized, but she would not for one moment have stood for the kind of backtalk Julia endured. It had all been long ago and in a land far over the sea, however, and would not, he knew, lend sufficient weight to his argument. He would have to pretend that he considered her judgments reasonable. Julia felt she owed reparations for allowing her daughter's father to die, and so Gwen continued behaving like a despot, and James had to watch as guilty Julia humbled and abased herself before her implacable little household goddess. They had their dance long choreographed; his past forays between them in an argument had ended, predictably, in both of them rounding on him, united and enflamed. Today, with Gwen deep into one of her campaigns, he hid behind his newspaper and did his best not to listen. He could not bear to hear his gentle Julia beleaguered.

"Please. Julia, *please*. You don't understand."

"I do understand and I'm sad, too, it's just bad timing. If it was any other night, of course we'd go but James booked these Rossini tickets months ago. We've got flights. I'm so sorry, darling." Julia reached to tuck a disobedient curl behind Gwen's ear but Gwen twitched away violently. She was frustrated, and increasingly desperate. This was not the first iteration of this exchange, not even the second or third, and preliminary attempts to reason with her mother had devolved to this—whining. It was fun for nobody, but it had won her bigger victories in the past. Across the room, James stifled the urge to stuff his fist into his mouth.

"But he's only here this one night! For the first time in *years*. It's Art Garfunkel, do you even understand?" Gwen flung herself down on the sofa. She glared across the room at the armchair in which James sat hidden behind his paper, and then hissed, "If it was a weekend with me in Milan and James asked you to, you'd cancel."

Julia felt a stab of pity at her daughter's wounded face and wondered, for a moment, whether this was true. She said, *sotto voce*, "That's not the case at all. You can't possibly believe that."

"It is. You put him first in everything. You guys go to boring classical music stuff all the time, you're going to that Verbier festival thing, and this is one single night. He's so old! You know he'll retire and this will literally be the last chance ever. I'll pay for it! And I'll pay you back for the other tickets, and the flights. I'll use my bat mitzvah money."

The celebrated bat mitzvah fund—one hundred and twenty-five pounds deposited three years ago in a Post Office account—was always Gwen's last resort, the straw at which she clutched for independence. It had been "used" to pay for hosting her web domain and for a great deal of the expensive art supplies she needed for the early stages of her blog; it had been drawn upon again when she had so longed for a pair of white Converse that she claimed she could not survive another day. Julia fought a momentary smile, but her resolve was buoyed by the utter impossibility of what Gwen asked. James had booked the La Scala tickets almost six months ago—in the last days of August they were to spend the weekend in Milan to see *Otello*, which had not been staged there since 1870, perhaps because it needed not one but three spectacular lead tenors. The *Otello* seats made it easy to defend her choice. To be alone in Italy with James would be a dream—long private hours, Prosecco, the heat, and the music. She would not yield it for anything. Of all the nights for Art Garfunkel to come to London this was the only one, all summer, that was out of the question.

Gwen was looking hopefully at her mother. "I'll pay you back; I *promise*. And you can go to the thingy thing concert another night."

"Dolly."

"I don't even get it, it's so pathetic. You're obsessed with us not being left alone together even for five minutes and then suddenly today I find out you've got summer plans to go to Italy for a whole weekend. So it's totally fine for us to stay here by ourselves if you get to go to the opera and Verbier, or whatever. It's like, insane double standards. So we *are* allowed, now."

"I'm afraid," boomed a disembodied voice from behind a newspaper, "that I'll be here when your mother is in Verbier, and for Milan we'll find a suitably obtrusive chaperone. The arrangements predate the current regime. Don't get too excited, kiddo."

"Maybe you could go with Nathan," Julia suggested, and felt cheapened even as she said it. To her astonishment Gwen simply gave a melancholy shrug. Then she said, softly, "Mummy, I don't want to go with Nathan. The whole point was to go together," and Julia's heart fractured, yet again.

20.

SWISS COTTAGE LIBRARY DID NOT BECOME MORE ROMANTIC IN miniature, but Gwen could think of no other way to represent the day's events. Certainly she had no desire to record the morning's argument, in which her mother had made it clear, once and for all, where her traitorous priorities lay. *Maybe you could go with Nathan,* she had suggested, not simply missing the point but readily giving up custody or care of her daughter and forgetting, erasing, a precious long-ago memory. Gwen did not usually like old people's music but when she was eleven they had gone to hear Simon and Garfunkel, and it had been a magical evening in a dark, hard year. The concert, held out-doors in Hyde Park, had been hot and dry and perfect, and the first glimpse of a possible future in which they might once again, one day, be happy. Gwen had shut her eyes tightly and tried to feel the passion her mother felt for this strange, folksy music, had tried to let the simple melodies, the unexpected rhythms of the language, move in her blood. At eleven she was already the same height as Julia but she had hunched over and drawn closer under Julia's arm and had felt safe, and hopeful. Couples stood around them interlocked, swaying, and her father wasn't there to sway and sing alongside her mother but she was there, she told herself, and after a while she had straightened her spine and stood up to her full height and put her arm, instead, around her mother. In the days that followed, Gwen taught herself the words to every song they'd heard, and learned to love them. They would be okay. They would be a family again, just the two of them. But Julia had made it clear that James was her only priority.

Her mother had needed a vessel for her love and energies, and now no longer needed to be needed. But it wasn't fair—she had lulled Gwen into believing that she would always be there. Gwen had offered up her life, her sorrows and pleasures, her preoccupations and requirements, had worked busily to keep her mother fulfilled and contented, and her being had formed around this belief, molded like ivy around a solid trunk. Now, Julia had withdrawn. Without her mother at her center she wavered. If she had seemed sturdy, it had been Julia firm beneath her.

She already had several sets of small bookshelves usually used for scenes in her mother's music room, and these just needed populating with cardboard concertinas, decorated with some fine cross-hatching to imply the microscopic titles on the folded projections of tiny spines. She set up a shoebox to be the reading room and assembled all the paraphernalia to scatter on her tiny desk and on Nathan's—mobile phones, some pens and pencils and even a lined and ring-bound notepad she had painstakingly constructed long ago for use in an imagined, flashback scene showing her grandmother at work as a journalist. All that remained to make were some textbooks to indicate homework, and the subtle nod to the real incident—the tiny paper airplane on which she had written her explosive missive and, heart pounding, sent it sailing over the wall between their carrels like a kamikaze. It was time, she'd decided, to grow up.

She wanted the blog to capture the formative events in her life, good or bad, while as much as possible sparing the humdrum, or repetitious. This was not the way her friends depicted themselves on the Internet but she had no interest in varnishing her life as they did, glamorous moments threaded one after another like an endless string of glossy and identical fake pearls. That, after all, was not brave, and was also definitely not Art. She wanted wit, or poignancy, or meaning. This was her coming-of-age story, after all, and one day when the story was over and life had acquired stability—perhaps when she was twenty-five, or twenty-six—its coherence and powerful narrative thrust would be united into a book, or possibly an animated television program, her own history reenacted by tiny clay figures in shoebox worlds. It would be an album of memories. It would be proof that she had been, and felt, and lived.

But tonight something had happened and though it was momentous, she was at a loss as to how to honor it. Her grandfather read her blog. Her traitorous mother read her blog, and in any case thought this landmark long behind her. Meanwhile, she had a more pressing and practical problem for it was very late, and she did not know what to do about the bedsheets.

ALREADY THE NIGHT'S EVENTS seemed distant. She examined her own feelings and found only deflation, and a sense of anticlimax. If she thought too long, she could summon a quiet, mawkish grief for her own innocence.

The true secret turned out to be that there was no secret. She had thought that sex would be something else, yet already could no longer articulate what that something else could have been. Instead it was what it was—the putting of parts into other, tighter parts. She had wanted to advance their intimacy, to elect Nathan as the central person in her new, adult life; she had wanted them to cleave together conclusively and could think of no more conclusive way than this. He had been loving, and gentle, and tender. He had whispered endearments, had held her face and looked into her eyes, and had shown he thought of no one and nothing but her. But when it was over she had felt weepy, and though Nathan had stroked her hair and told her he loved her and that she was beautiful, she had needed more reassurance than he could give. She had expected the intensity of his focus upon her in those few, vital moments to be the way he'd always look at her now, forever, and when his breathing had slowed and eventually his talk had gone back to normal she felt crushed. It was all meant to be different now, and wasn't.

The bleeding had been a surprise. She was not a demure and sedentary Victorian maiden. She had done school gymnastics and ridden horses; her own fingers had never encountered resistance. But there had been a great deal of blood, in disproportion to the pain, which had—a relief—been less than she'd expected. They had drawn apart and it had actually gushed from her, warm and shocking. This was not the pale spot of new womanhood. Hung outside the window in another place and time, these sheets would suggest the groom had dismembered, not deflowered, his new bride. Nathan had looked stricken, and his concern that she had not been truthful about it hurting had made it all the more embarrassing. "My poor baby," he had whispered, his hand on her heart, and his pity had made her feel pitiable.

The sheets were now stuffed into the kitchen sink and soaking in an improvised solution of washing-up liquid, peppermint hand soap, and hot water, and the contents of a sachet of something she had found in the back of a cupboard that claimed to restore net curtains to a wafting summer purity. Scrubbing had seemed to make it worse. While they soaked, she sat at the dining table in semidarkness, re-creating the watershed that had come hours before, when she had told Nathan she finally felt ready. *Maybe you could go with Nathan.* Well, maybe she would.

21.

"YOU MUST COME TO PARIS," THE E-MAIL COMMANDED, "AND
be part of the conversation. We'll bring you over. You must come." Pamela then forwarded the details of a travel agent in Stanmore named
Joan Perelman whom, she said, would be in touch in due course. Joan
was organizing a group booking for all nineteen of the conference at-
tendees and had instructions to ensure that Mr. Alden be given the
best room in the small hotel on the rue Christine. Joan would pop the
information through Philip's door.

Alone in the half-gloom of his flat Philip chuckled, then launched
a damp spluttering cough, and then, recovered, laughed again. Pamela almost certainly wished him to go to Paris not to converse with
her biennial assembly of trainee holistic midwives, but to be paraded
as some sort of animated fossil dug out of the obstetric field. He would
be both pitied and pilloried, specimen of a genus they hoped to drive
into extinction. Pamela had stepped up her campaign by offering
first Eurostar tickets, then this hotel room, and finally a small hono-
rarium, as well as the chance to attend as many of the lectures and

seminars as he pleased. He did not please. He would not have gone, even had it not felt disloyal to Julia, who was at this moment on her way over, delivering what she claimed was a spare fish pie.

At my age it would be irresponsible to commit to anything so far in advance, he wrote back, *but thank you for thinking of me.*

Philip had last been to Paris in 1974, when the Fédération Internationale de Gynécologie et d'Obstétrique had offered him a fellowship and he had spent six weeks living alone, teaching a series of courses at the Pitié-Salpêtrière Hospital. Iris and ten-year-old Daniel had stayed in London, aided by a homesick but willing Italian au pair. The final weekend of his tenure, after their long separation, Iris would join him, and two days later the au pair would deliver Daniel to Paris on her way home to Naples. Then the three Aldens would travel down to Nice for a week's holiday.

For those humid August days, he'd had his wife's sustained, unbroken attention. He alone, perhaps for the first time since they'd married. They had walked in the Jardin des Tuileries and—though Iris, unlike Philip, had not grown up in a particularly religious household—had eaten their first shellfish together, the tight, slippery mussels flavored with transgression and daring. Iris had gone further and tasted dainty snails in garlic butter, while Philip had sipped a cold beer and told her about his teaching, and she had listened. Philip read *le Monde* to her, translating Watergate coverage badly, on the hoof. On Monday morning he had a brief return to reality, a final series of administrative meetings at FIGO, while Iris had gone to meet Daniel's train, and to deliver the au pair into a second train that would take her home— forever, it turned out, for she did not return to them as she'd promised. When Philip had left the office on Monday afternoon, his wife and son had been waiting for him on a sunny street corner, and the next morning they boarded the train for Nice, where the precious bubble of happiness had miraculously held. In gold kaftan and roman sandals, Iris had been the most elegant woman on the beach. The most elegant woman, Philip thought, that he had ever seen. She would drift for idle, solitary walks along the shore, disappearing sometimes for hours, and each time as she receded into the distance he ached for her as if she was slipping from him forever, like Eurydice. This ache was at its most acute when he saw her returning. In those moments, when she was approaching but not yet close enough to hear his voice, he feared his heart might break with longing. Approaching, but not near enough. Never near enough. No, he would not go back to Paris.

"I TRIED A DIFFERENT ONE," Julia explained, shuffling the empty ice cube trays and half-crushed foil takeaway containers in Philip's freezer until she'd cleared space for the fish pie. "It's got ketchup in it, which sounds suspicious, but we had it last night and it wasn't bad, if I do say so myself, I just made a bit too much. You can put it in the oven frozen."

"Thank you, *maidele*. Whatever you make is always wonderful. Now tell me, you said you're finally going back to Verbier this year; I'm thrilled. Who is playing in the festival?"

"Everyone worth hearing, I just wish James could come. He's on call that weekend but in any case now, with everything . . ." She drifted off. "My lovely Emmeline Whitten has a master class on the Sunday morning, which is the only reason I'm still going, and we'll all have dinner that night, and I'll fly back Monday."

"I think the last time I heard Emmeline was when you took us to the Wigmore."

"She's doing so well in Moscow, Vera's pleased. I wish James could hear her. Next time she's playing nearish I'd love us to go together. It's quite hard to imagine at the moment but—anyway. Gwen made shortbread so I grabbed the last bits for us, it's very good. She's taken to baking for Nathan every Friday." She was able to say this neutrally, though everything about it was irritating.

She sat down at the kitchen table, averting her gaze from Philip's unsteady journey from kettle to sink to mug cupboard, and began to unwrap the foil parcel of biscuits. She had not known, on her way here, whether she wished to discuss Gwen and Nathan. It was all so sordid. Repellent. Worst of all was perhaps the small part of herself that found her daughter's new disposition a welcome change. No more resentment or black moods. And, Gwen continued to make clear, no more interest in spending any time with her mother. Seeing them whispering, heads together exchanging confidences, stung like a deliberate, personal rejection. It made Julia feel excluded. It made her feel very, very old. But . . . Gwen seemed happier. "It's all ongoing, you know," she told Philip now, snapping a piece of shortbread in half and handing him the larger piece, "the romance of the century. She keeps telling me I *just don't understand*. It's true. I don't. She was utterly incensed that I forbade them from carrying on with this relationship; she actually tried to lecture me on *human rights*, she gave me a horrid little speech that sounded precisely like Nathan. In any case I've stopped trying to forbid it because it wasn't getting me anywhere. I just want her to *think*. I've never denied her anything I thought would make her happy, and you know I've always tried not to say no unnecessarily; all I want is for her to think through her decisions. What happens when they break up?"

Philip sat down heavily opposite her, the wicker kitchen chair creaking ominously beneath him. "And what does she say?"

"She'll just say, 'What happens if you and *James* break up?' and then I may as well be talking to a wall because it's the same conversation over and over; she just equates the two. It's all about proving that they're just like us. Just as important as we are, just as committed, just as much entitled to be together. She's desperate to prove she doesn't need parenting anymore. I'm apparently no longer required. I've been replaced." She gave what she hoped would seem an easy, self-deprecatory laugh. "And now she's taken to calling me *Julia*, the way Nathan and Saskia call their mother Pamela, which I've always found odd in any case, so now I'm not even her Mum anymore."

"She was *very* cross about James."

"So this is a revenge attack, you mean? I thought . . ." She trailed off. "It was so much pressure, always, all those years she felt responsible for me and I wanted her to just be a child now. Carefree, a little. I thought this would be a good thing for both of us, she was meant to feel *liberated*."

"And part of her must, I'm sure. Your happiness is good for her."

"I know, you and Iris both keep telling me but do you really think so?"

Philip considered. "Certainly your unhappiness wasn't good for her. Or you. But you must remember, you're in charge, not the children. You say you don't feel you can stop them but—I suppose I don't quite understand why not. I know you find it hard, but perhaps you might try putting your foot down harder, even so?"

"She can't push me away forever." This had begun as a question, but she tried to turn it into a statement of her own confidence.

"What does James say?"

Julia shrugged. She and James had not had very satisfactory discussions on the subject, lately. As long as Nathan's schoolwork wasn't compromised and the children obeyed his basic rules—no canoodling in front of the parents, no overnight room sharing or closed bedroom doors—James seemed willing to make the best of it. He was content to catch up on patient notes in the living room while in the kitchen his son and her daughter made dinner together, and giggled, loudly. He was happy to accept that for the moment, under admittedly peculiar circumstances, Gwen was being friendly to him. Valentina had been allowed to stay over, and the thought of his son as a sexually active being did not affront or appall him. Julia had wanted his outrage to endure as hers had, and felt let down that it hadn't. He listened to her when she confided in him. He'd held her when, a few nights earlier, she'd succumbed to tears that she could not explain. She could not bring herself to admit to him that the intensity of her daughter's need had been precious in those years alone, and that she ached for it now that it was over. But she had brought this rejection upon herself, for she had reached outward for James, shattering the covenant of their solitude. She could not regret it—James had brought her back to life. Gwen was only doing what Julia herself had already done.

"Nathan's incredibly ambitious, and James is incredibly ambitious for him, which maybe explains it—he can actually put quite a lot of pressure on him I think, without meaning to. James was the first person in his family to go to university so he's quite obsessed with it, and Pamela's just as bad for all her hippy-dippy nonsense—but anyway Nathan studies very hard, and now Gwen's started to work whenever he works. She just really wants to please him. Her teachers are certainly thrilled with her, and of course that's good for her confidence, but it's hard not to feel . . . I hate that she wouldn't feel good enough as she is, for anyone. She ought not to have to contort herself to please him. I'm just holding my breath, waiting for it to implode."

Philip said, after a moment's thought, "Do you think it might implode imminently?"

"They're very settled, not that that means much with teenagers. Gwen's happy as a clam, and he was with the last one for two years. There's not much we can do, in practice. We can't lock them into their rooms after we're asleep, so we've had to just settle for stating our position and—it's nauseating, we've had to absolutely forbid them on the tacit understanding that they'll—I can't actually bear thinking about it. Don't you think she's far, far too young to be sexually active? Thank God he boards on school nights, I just wish I could convince James he should stay all term."

"I don't know, *maidele*, it does seem very young to me but a great deal has changed since my day."

"I'm utterly exhausted. When he's at home I find myself staying up later and later, as if I could somehow stay up late enough to make it impossible. I know Verbier is weeks away and it's only two nights but I can't bear the idea of leaving them. I'm longing to cancel." Julia frowned. "I miss her like, like *a limb*. But all I've ever wanted was for her to be happy, and she keeps telling me how happy she is. Endlessly."

22.

GWEN COULD NOT REMEMBER A TIME WHEN SHE'D WORKED with more deliberate, sustained exertion. Revision went by in a strange, feverish blur during which she sweated through light cotton tops like a boxer and ran dry a series of brand new ballpoint pens with the manic vigor of her practice papers. Nathan was home for the Easter holidays and she thrilled at his pride in her. Among Nathan's friends it was cool to work hard, and the competitive indifference that Gwen imbibed at her own school had backfired unexpectedly when she'd tried it on him. "I did *nothing* for my GCSE's last year," she'd once said to him, casually, and he'd looked at her oddly and said, "That was dumb. Why not? You're a more focused person than that." It was gratifying to be observed and then described as any sort of person, even if the portrait wasn't always immediately familiar or recognizable—it made her feel seen, and reminded her that he was close enough to see her. So when he told her that he knew she didn't only prioritize "clay and shit," she believed him. She did not yet know what sort of person she was becoming, and was happy to take his word for it. Inside she sometimes feared she was no sort of person at all, only a wisp, and Nathan's observations were reassuring anchors, giving solid boundaries to her self.

Now it felt good, and the AS exams would all go fine, she felt. Tests were a different proposition if you had prepared for them; when the answers were not mysterious but obvious, and merely had to be transcribed from brain to page. She sat down to dinner ravenous each evening and meanwhile she was even getting the hang of sex. They had now done it eleven times. Since Nathan was home she was barely sleeping—the parents policed them, and it was usually long after midnight before it was safe for him to sneak in undetected. Yet during the days she felt wired, inspired, and as if she'd slammed back five espressos instead of the single mocha Frappuccino with whipped cream that she allowed herself each afternoon, at their three o'clock study break.

And then she ground to a halt. On the final weekend of the holidays she found herself listless and exhausted. It was as if she had paced a perfect marathon only to be told over the loudspeaker as the finish line approached that the new goal was thirty miles, and the final leg must be sprinted. The fuel tank, once bursting, was empty. It was all she could do to get out of bed late on Saturday morning, and this she did only when Nathan sat on the floor outside her bedroom door playing an old reggae tune filled with sunshine and goodwill, on repeat. With the pillow over her head she bellowed at him to go away but he merely increased the volume. A rumor had swirled around that this year's French oral questions were about the environment— possibly vivisection, possibly carbon footprints—and Nathan was insisting she prepare the relevant vocabulary.

When she finally came down Julia was sitting at the dining table reading the newspaper, and James was making blueberry buckwheat pancakes as brain food for the final push.

"You're being an arsehole," Gwen said to Nathan, who was still whistling snatches of the song with which he'd eventually roused her. "None of you get how tired I am. You try revising hours and hours every single day and see how you'd feel."

"I did," Nathan told her, "I do. I've already done an hour of stats while you were snoring. It was awesome, I rocked it."

"Please don't bicker this morning." Julia was keen to launch the day in an atmosphere of studious calm. "And, Gwen, please don't swear."

"'Arse' isn't swearing."

James ladled more batter into the frying pan. "And yet the British way does sound more offensive. "'Ass' is somehow more innocent."

"That's because it means donkey," Gwen told him, and then laid her forehead on her crossed arms on the kitchen table and closed her eyes.

"I think 'asshole' has become the pan-Atlantic standard; 'arsehole' is for sure on the decline. It's inevitable." Here Nathan paused to spear a pancake from the stack beside his father and transfer one edge of it directly to his mouth. "With the dominance of American vernacular in the media I think 'arse' is over." Gwen burrowed her face deeper into the crook of her elbow.

Nathan had stayed up the night before doing a series of practice Physics papers and it had been four a.m. before he'd made it to bed. Despite this, he had been awake bright and early to help his girl-friend. He tried again. "Come on, baby, *allons. Effet de serre?*"

"Dunno."

"You do, you knew it yesterday. When you fart you contribute to the . . ." He gestured for someone, anyone, to complete this prompt.

"You're so close to the end, darling, and you've done so well," Julia coaxed, putting a plate down in front of her daughter, though Gwen felt she could not have been clearer that she did not want to eat. She pushed it toward Nathan.

"Just think, in a month or two they'll all be over and you'll be free. You can have a lie-in every single day this summer, you're almost there, Dolly. Can I make you something else? Do you want eggs?"

"Not hungry."

"Do you want to walk to Starbucks for an early frap?" Nathan asked. "I'll test you while we walk? I need a break from my stuff."

But Gwen shook her head and drew the hood of her sweatshirt down low over her forehead, pulling tight the toggles to cover her ears, and to shield her eyes from the lights, which this morning seemed offensively dazzling. The sweet indolence of the summer lay ahead, Nathan would no longer be away on weeknights, and they could be together every day. She had succumbed briefly to his results-obsessed propaganda and had expended needless energy tearing after the bloodless electric hare of senior school success, but in truth academic qualifications did not matter. They were all deluded. She could not summon the energy to tell them of their misconception, however.

23.

ALL AFTERNOON GWEN FOLLOWED HER MOTHER AROUND AS she packed, wearing the mournful expression of an abandoned puppy dog but, quite unlike a puppy, making no attempt to be appealing. In response to Julia's inquiries she would only offer such valuable contributions as, "Who cares what you wear with a bunch of musicians?" Her sullen unpleasantness had been increasing since breakfast, when she had told James his aftershave made her want to vomit, and had even snapped at Nathan, complaining the eggs he had scrambled with much fanfare were slimy, undercooked, and generally offensive. She was standing in the hallway while Julia dithered over whether or not to bring a coat for the festival. Julia was indecently excited about this small, solo trip.

"If you change your mind, I'm sure James will pop you round to Katy's party later. What have you planned for the rest of the weekend?"

"Weekends don't matter now it's Easter," said Gwen, who had taken deep offense at her mother's evident eagerness to go, and would not give an inch before this treacherous departure. "All days are the same. I'm tired, I don't want to see a bunch of randoms."

"Have you and Nathan got anything planned?"

"Why are you interviewing me?" Gwen whined, sitting down heavily on the stairs and slumping over her knees. "You don't need to plan playdates for me while you're away, I'm perfectly capable of taking care of myself."

If she hadn't had one foot out of the door—or had James overheard—Julia might have felt fortified to check this latest discourtesy, but instead she raised her hands in surrender. Gwen laid her head on her crossed arms, the embodiment of bleak despair. Moved despite herself, Julia stroked back her daughter's tangled hair. "No third degree, I just thought you might be doing something."

"What, like a superfun classical music festival?" Gwen mumbled into her knees, "Woohoo, par-tay."

Surely this mood couldn't be attributed to her own, brief departure, Julia thought, perplexed, and then with a thrill of disloyalty, reflected that in about half an hour this state of affairs would all become Nathan's problem. He wanted to be with her daughter? He could take her as he found her. The festival in Verbier had begun to take on the honeyed glow of a recuperative spa weekend. She was even looking forward to the drive to Heathrow.

"Mummy," Gwen looked up, suddenly plaintive. "Mummy, I don't feel very well."

Julia laid the back of her hand on her daughter's cheek. It was cool, and dry. "What's wrong, Dolly?" she asked, softly. "I'll be back before you know it. What's going on?"

Gwen shook her head, hopeless. "I don't know." She began to cry. "I feel dizzy."

Julia bent to kiss Gwen's forehead. She looked down at the mass of loose, fox-red curls escaping and unraveling into a halo of fine frizz, the bursts of psychedelic swirls and flowering creepers that Gwen had drawn in blue and red Biro across one forearm and then, above the loose cotton neck of an ancient shirt of Daniel's, she saw the blue-veined marbling of her daughter's swollen breasts. She bent down suddenly and gripped Gwen's shoulders.

"Gwendolen." Her voice was steady, as steady as an ambulance dispatcher's, as steady as due north. "Gwendolen." Behind her she heard a key scrape in the front door but she did not turn. "Gwen. Look at me. Right now. Are you pregnant?"

Gwen looked up, her pale face striped with glossy tearstains. She shrugged.

"I'M HOME!" called James from the doorway. He held many straining plastic shopping bags and had slung several others around each wrist, so that beneath their weight his hands had turned first white and then puce with temporarily arrested circulation. He edged the door open with his knee. He had determined to consider the weekend with Julia's daughter an opportunity, rather than a nuisance. Certainly he had made sure to tell Julia this was how he saw it, and he wished to make it true.

"Now," he said, slamming the door shut behind him with a violent jolt of the hip and dumping the groceries at his feet before remembering the eggs, too late, "I have big news, kiddo. And the news is this: we're making veggie pizza. Your mom's away so you get to be the queen around here."

He crouched down to investigate. To his relief, the eggs were all unbroken. Now he looked up, one hand still buried in a Waitrose carrier bag. Two stricken faces met him in silence.

"What's happened? Where's my boy? Where's Nathan?"

THIS WAS NOT THE RIGHT WAY. She should have taken a test alone, to prove that she was responsible. She should have presented the facts in a calm and considered manner, so that Julia would admire her solemn maturity and initiative. *These things happen*, Gwen imagined her mother saying, stroking her hair. *I can't believe how grown up you've been, my brave girl.* She should have gone online and found herself a doctor; should have made her own appointment to take care of it, and the magnitude of the decision and the stoic dignity with which she'd taken it would have filled both Julia and Nathan with awe. *These things happen.* She did not want to be pregnant. It was inconceivable that she could be a mother. But she knew she had not been foolish—in her head she had been courageous and responsible. She just hadn't had time to prove herself. How could you test for a pregnancy in which you didn't quite believe? Now it had all gone wrong, for her mother looked as if she hated her. They were together in the bathroom while James paced the hallway, outside.

"I don't understand," Julia kept saying. "I don't understand how this happened." She had not yet raised her eyes from the plastic window of the newly purchased pregnancy test that lay on the side of the sink, its message unequivocal. Her knuckles had whitened from her grip on the basin. And then the worst words, "How could you be so *stupid?*"

Gwen shrugged, hopelessly. Hot tears spilled down her cheeks, but she could not yet speak. She felt flushed and dizzy and slightly sick, from fear or pregnancy or possibly both. No fate, in that moment, could have felt worse than her mother's disappointment. She yearned for sympathy, for gentleness. She longed to be small, and to be taken care of.

"It wasn't on purpose," she whispered.

This had been the wrong thing to say.

"On purpose? On *purpose?* I never for one moment imagined it was anything other than, than damn *foolishness.* How long have you suspected? How many weeks—oh, God. This is a nightmare." More softly, to herself, "This is a living nightmare."

"I was going to deal with it. I was going to fix it so you didn't worry and then tell you . . ."

"But have you seen a doctor? Do you know if you even have time to *fix it?* Does Nathan know?" This last was shouted, in a crescendo of rage.

"No."

"No, what? No, you haven't seen a doctor? No, you don't know? I don't understand how you could have allowed— We trusted you. You asked me to trust you. You promised me I could trust you, and you've let me down. You've let"—Gwen had a sudden instinct to cover her ears against the next words—"you've let your father down."

Gwen felt her last hope collapse within her. She would be abandoned for this, and would never be forgiven. Now, when she needed more than ever to be restored to the full beam of her mother's love, to that deep, old intensity, they felt further apart than ever. She fell to her knees like a penitent, laid her head against the cold edge of the bath, and began to sob. *"Don't talk about Daddy!"* she begged, gasping for breath. Her shoulders heaved, and she waited for warm arms to enfold her. She longed to lay her head in her mother's lap and sob, *You used to love me—love me now.* But though she cried harder and harder nothing happened, and when she looked up Julia was shaking her head in disbelief, and there was something new in her eyes that frightened Gwen. Hatred, maybe. What happened now hardly mattered.

24.

JULIA STAYED UP VERY LATE WITH JAMES, TALKING. JUST BE-
fore midnight the evening's silence had been briefly broken by shouts
and scuffles as the pub around the corner disgorged its Friday-night
punters and by intermittent caterwauling as these liberated drinkers
carried their singing from the bar into the streets. Tonight, though
this was not always the case, it sounded spirited but good-natured, out
of sight behind the sturdy Victorian terraces. Julia and James stood
at the window, intertwined and unmoving, frozen in their bubble of
shock. The solidity of James's arm around her waist was, quite possibly, the only thing that kept her standing. Disbelief came crashing
back over her in waves, and each time it receded left a shoreline sul-
lied with debris. Strands of anger and guilt. Empty shells of self-
reproach. She felt a hundred years old.

"Maybe that's what we should have done this evening," Julia said.
"Maybe we just should have walked out and gone to the Lord South-
ampton and drunk ourselves into oblivion."

"What, take up binge-drinking? Sing our troubles away on a kara-oke machine somewhere?"

"Yes, exactly. It would have been cathartic. Or numbing. Oh"—she turned and laid her head against the broad solidity of his chest—"let's run away. Let's just go. I've got a hotel room in Verbier ready and wait-ing, right now, that I'm meant to be in. We could conceal ourselves among the violinists."

"We could pay our way across Europe giving recitals. You can play and I'll . . . dance. South of France? Tuscany?"

"We could start a vineyard."

"Let's make buffalo mozzarella."

"I think you might need buffalo to make buffalo mozzarella."

James considered. "So you'll look after the buffalo. I'll make the wine. I really think we're onto something, it will be more economical to make our own if we're going to become full-time alcoholics."

"Not alcoholics," Julia amended. "Binge-drinkers."

"Right. Tuscan binge-drinkers." James sat down on the bed and pulled her hand, gently, until she was sitting beside him. "It's a real shame about your master class, as well as everything else. I know it's not . . . This does happen, you know. I see a lot of kids at work—"

"Everyone you see at work is pregnant, it's not representative."

"True. But what I mean is . . ." He trailed off. "I don't know what I mean. I'm in shock, I think. I'm sorry, I won't quote statistics at you."

"We should have stopped all of this, the whole thing. The sex. The unprotected sex. The utter stupidity of the relationship itself. How could they be so bloody stupid? How did this actually happen?"

James could not reply to this question for in truth he blamed

Gwen, and was so angry that he did not think he could ever again be civil to her. Pamela had waged a relentless sexual health campaign with their own children since long before it had been relevant or even appropriate, and despite these assurances, James himself had given Nathan stern reminders about the importance of condoms ever since Valentina's first appearance. Each of these unsatisfactory discussions had ended with a withering dismissal of, "It's all taken care of, Father," or more tastelessly, "Dad, this ain't my first rodeo." But it had been established that they had not been using condoms, and that this current debacle was therefore entirely due to Gwen's laissez-faire attitude to taking the Pill. Nathan, James judged, had done his medic parents proud. He had taken himself off to the Royal Free for a full sexual health screening before trusting to the hormonal contraception alone, which was mature and considerate, especially given his rather limited sexual history. Nathan had been gentlemanly, principled, irreproachable. Gwen, by contrast, was a spoiled, selfish, and irresponsible little airhead. Despite tonight's earlier display, in which she had been the embodiment of abject misery and contrition and bewilderment, James thought it more than possible that she had done it on purpose. To share her mother's attention made her frantic, and with a single move she had commandeered it all, trapping Nathan in the process. Regardless of her insecurity, Gwen was a girl accustomed to her own way and now she had created such a tornado of dramatic tension around herself that it was possible she would once again get it. She had behaved indefensibly toward his beloved son. His beloved son who was staying over at Charlie's house after a gig, whose phone was still off, and who had absolutely no idea of the bedlam that awaited him at home.

He had stood outside the bathroom while the stupid girl had peed on a stick that would reaffirm what, with a little hindsight, ought to have been perfectly obvious, and by the time the three minutes of waiting had elapsed he had regained outward mastery of himself. Nathan would need his father to be calm. In any case, amid the howling and shrieking, someone had to remain clear-headed.

He saw that he had been too cautious about discipline, too careful not to undermine or challenge Julia's rule, and far too deferential to the other, absent man of the house. Once they had all recovered from this unpleasantness he would assert himself, by Julia's side, at the helm of this family. He would dispatch Gwen to a grief counselor. He would insist that they all see a family therapist. He would fix what was broken around here.

"I promised Daniel," Julia was saying, and he summoned his mind back to the present, back to her serious, pale face, "I promised I'd take care of her. I promised I'd be two parents."

"Even kids with two parents can get pregnant."

"I know, but when we talked about her life, and the support she'd need to get through his loss—he felt so guilty about leaving her, you know, she was only ten and he knew how she would suffer. Can you imagine? She was just skinny arms and legs, and this huge bushel of mad red hair, and all sunshine and energy. He said it was like throwing a beautiful, porcelain plate high in the air—you can see it flawless and unbroken as it arcs upwards and descends, right until the moment you know is coming when it hits the ground and smashes. And he was going to be the one to hurt her like that. He was so angry he'd never see her grow up. And you know, we'd talk about what she'd be, who she'd become; we'd try and imagine it together, and I promised I'd do my best to protect her and give her a good life."

James did not, in this instance, think that a father's death years ago offered sufficient excuse or explanation. He never usually acknowledged her daughter's bad behavior, but with this silence, he now judged, he had also let Daniel down. He had pragmatic feelings about Daniel. He rarely chose to think of him at all, and when he did it was as a vague, benign presence, abstract as an ancestor, and with this unthreatening distance between them the two men could and ought to be brothers in arms. He imagined Daniel's love for Julia as his own—epic and sweeping as the prairie, broad and generous as the pale sky above it. When he thought of Julia he always saw this same image—vast, open spaces; the pallor and splendor of soothing, infinite skies. He would take care of her. He would not let her be bullied by an unhinged, manipulative teenager. A teenager whose attack had wounded his son as collateral damage. He could give voice to none of this. Instead he said, "You have given her a good life. You are giving her a good life."

"Maybe, but seriously, I considered making it through secondary school without an illegitimate pregnancy as the bare minimum."

"No one, no one could love their daughter more than you love Gwen. And we will all get through this together and be fine. It's horrible, it will be horrible for both our kids, and then it will be over. We found out early, which makes everything vastly less complicated."

Julia tucked her legs up beneath her and began biting the nail of her little finger. "What exactly will they do?"

"You never had one?"

"No!" She looked scandalized. "Why, did you? I mean, did you ever get someone pregnant by accident?"

"No," James admitted. "My knowledge is purely professional. Pamela had one, just before we started dating, in fact. She was characteristically robust about it. I don't think she was entirely sure who had helped her into her condition in the first place, which would make imagining an alternative outcome more abstract. Hard to picture a baby's face if you're not sure which dude it might resemble."

"That's the bitchiest thing I've ever heard you say," said Julia, briefly cheered.

"Well, there you go. I'm allowed a slip every now and again where my ex-wife is concerned. I should call her but, Christ, I really can't deal with her tonight. And I don't want him to hear it first from her on the phone. Or she'll tell Saskia, or arrive on our doorstep or— I just don't want to handle it right now."

"So, what will they do?"

"If she's right about her last period then it's very early, she won't need a surgical abortion and can do it with mifepristone. It blocks progesterone, which then makes the uterine lining break down. Then she'll go back for misoprostol, which causes contractions, bleeding, and everything hopefully passes out after that. It's not a party, I will tell you, but it's pretty quick, they'll give her pain relief and antibiotics, and if all goes smoothly, that's it, just a checkup and then back to normal. Codeine, hot water bottle, good TV, distraction."

"Okay." She nodded, her fingernail still between her teeth. "Can you imagine, just for a moment, if our children actually had this baby together?"

"Let's not go there, it's entirely insane. You would have a grandchild related to me and Daniel. And you and I would have a shared grandchild. It's pretty fucked up. It might end up looking like both of us." He raised her palm gently to his lips. "But you're my family now. And that means any baby Gwen has, any time, with any man, is going to be our grandchild. It doesn't have to— This isn't . . . isn't anything but an accident. Whoever our kids end up marrying and having children with, you and I are going to be a team and we'll share all those grandbabies between us, and when it happens it will be awesome. We'll look after them together and enjoy them and then give them back when they cry and go back to our gardening and our vacationing and—and shuffleboard. As long as Nathan doesn't marry The Demon Barber of Seville we'll be in clover. Give it a decade, decade and a half, and we'll see what's cooking."

"I know. Thank you."

"Don't thank me." And then, to share her pain, to halve her responsibility, he offered a sacrificial lamb, an echo of the unreasonable resentment he knew she must harbor, "It's my dumb son who knocked her up."

"When can she not be pregnant again?"

"Pretty fast."

"How fast? This weekend?"

"Not that fast. A week. Ten days, maybe."

"I could literally strangle them both."

"It's a legitimate solution."

She was silent for a moment. "Can we grow tomatoes, too, and basil? And olives, for olive oil."

"Then I think we need a donkey to turn the press. Or a mule, whatever that may be; I don't know, we didn't have mules in Dorchester when I was growing up; they might be a form of female footwear. You'll wear nothing but mules when you ride the donkey to press the olives. With our buffalo we'll have an entire farm devoted to the Caprese salad." He looked at his watch. "It's two a.m., baby, let's go to bed. This will still be godawful in the morning, I guarantee."

She laughed, and his heart lifted at the sound, the promise of future recovery, the first new buds after a hard winter.

"Okay. Do you swear?"

"I swear. You'll have hours and hours of misery and stress tomorrow. Days until it's resolved. Let's go to sleep now so we can really appreciate it in daylight in all its sordid glory." He took her face between his hands and kissed her, deeply. "I love you more than anything, and I promise you we will put this right together."

25.

IT WAS IMPOSSIBLE THAT HER MOTHER HAD GONE TO SLEEP angry when Gwen so longed for her; never before had Gwen, in need, been left alone to cry. Her first thought on waking was that, despite evidence to the contrary, there must have been some mistake, half expecting to find Julia sitting quietly beside her bed, as she had so many nights in childhood. Her second realization was that it was still only four a.m., and many hours lay ahead before she could make right what yesterday had gone so very wrong. She felt feverish and queasy. She needed her mother to understand—she could not be pregnant, she was only a child, she needed to be swept up, herself a babe in arms. Her unhappiness was abject, and complete.

She lay in a mounting agony of indecision. Not once since James invaded had Gwen been up to the top floor. To enter their room was impossible. To wait, untenable. She found herself in a state of ferocious concentration, hoping her mother would sense her need and float downstairs, gather her into safety and rescue her. As a little girl she would remain in bed and shout, louder and louder, till the thud of approaching footsteps heralded relief; in later years she had realized that deliverance came faster if she flew to her parents' bedroom, though the midnight flight itself held unknown terrors. She would gather her strength and run up the stairs and throw open the door into the moon-softened darkness. On the left would be her father; on the right, her mother. Always a space between them, Gwen-sized. Julia fast asleep was all wrong, for how could she guard Gwen in her own unconsciousness? Off-duty, vulnerable, her mind who knew where? Gwen would whisper for her over and over until Julia opened her eyes, and then her arms, and made right whatever was wrong.

How soon could this be made right so that her mother might forgive her, and how would it be? She did not know what abortions entailed but found herself picturing a high-necked white cotton nightgown, strawberry jelly and melting vanilla ice cream, the mint-green paper curtains of the hospital ward on which she had eaten these after the removal of her tonsils. Julia on a camp bed, by her side. Loving, ministering, proud of her brave girl. The thing now inside her was only the size of a poppy seed, far smaller than a tonsil, and could surely be shaken loose. A speck. She felt twitchy and restless, and to think of cells colonizing and proliferating made her skin crawl. There was not a moment to lose; she must have freedom from it. She could not quite imagine Nathan's reaction but surely he would not be angry? He would support her, and they would come through it bound tightly together with the dark velvet bonds of a secret, but while her mother felt such paralyzing disappointment, Nathan remained out of focus. She couldn't breathe; she longed for absolution. One could not stay angry about a mistake the size of a poppy seed.

Upstairs she listened and, hearing only silence, knocked softly. Nothing. After a moment she pushed the door open and took a single step into what once had been her parents' bedroom. As she adjusted to the gloom she could see Julia, sound asleep, not on the expected right but in the unimagined center. Entwined with James, face-to-face, breathing one another's slow breath. A beefy bare arm slung over her delicate mother.

Gwen stared, arrested by curiosity, and revulsion. What betrayal had filled the last waking moments before this easy, slumbering union? *I'm sorry about my daughter,* or perhaps, *Never mind, nothing matters as long as we have each other.* Sleep had softened her mother's face to girlish smoothness as she lay in her lover's arms; her brow was open, her hand resting upon James's bare chest. She did not look like a woman worried for her only child. She looked contented. She looked as Gwen had never known her.

Gwen backed away and closed the door, softly. On the landing she stood very still for a long time. She feared she might be sick. What truths had lain hidden in plain sight: she was alone. *Fuck you,* she thought, and then whispered it louder, to steady herself. She was drowning; she must evaporate her terror with burning rage.

Fuck you.

You didn't choose me.

You don't get to decide.

A SERIES OF THUDS and scrapings brought Julia downstairs early the next morning. The night before, James had steadied and calmed her, and they had already taken decisive action. Falling asleep she'd remembered Claire, James's former registrar, young and approachable and direct, with an easy manner that Gwen would appreciate. She had asked James to e-mail her and they'd received an instant reply, though it was almost three a.m.—Claire was on nights. She would go home to sleep and would then make herself available for a checkup, a scan, a chat, a cup of tea. Julia descended the stairs aching to put her arms around her daughter who must—now that anger no longer occluded her vision she understood—feel so lost and frightened. Julia longed to tell her she'd taken steps to help. But overnight, Gwen had made radical alterations of her own.

Apparently unaided, Gwen had wrestled the mattress off Nathan's single bed, deconstructed the slatted base, and reassembled it in her own room. What had once been Nathan's room now resembled a university study, their pair of pine desks back to back on opposite walls. Gwen's room, the larger of the two, now contained nothing but an improvised double bed. Julia entered to find Gwen in a burst of furious energy, pulling taut a fitted sheet to unite the two single mattresses. She was red-faced and slightly damp with sweat, and did not look up as Julia came in.

"What are you doing?"

Gwen did not answer. She was on all fours, straining to tuck the sheet beneath the corner. Then she succeeded and sat back on her heels, satisfied.

"What the hell are you doing?"

"Moving a mattress."

"You moved the mattress. And a divan."

"Yup."

Julia sat on the edge of the newly enlarged bed. "Can you stop, please? I need to talk to you. I've made an appointment with James's friend—"

"—Nearly done, one sec."

"Gwen, stop right now."

"*What?*"

"What the hell are you doing?"

"I'm *nesting*," spat Gwen, with heavy irony. "Can you stand up, please, I want to put the duvet down."

Julia stood up, casting around for something on which to fix, and feeling faintly hysterical. "You've lost your mind. This is not your house, Gwendolen. Darling, I know you're upset but you can't just— Help me, please, you will not believe this," she told James, who had just appeared in the doorway with a tray, and three cups of tea. He peered in, looking bewildered. "What's going on in here?"

"Gwen moved the beds. Herself. She's apparently taken up weight-lifting."

"Did you have permission to do that?" James asked, and was ignored. He went to set his tray down on Gwen's desk, but Gwen's desk was no longer there. He cast around for another surface and then finally set the tray on the floor.

"She could have hurt herself, couldn't she? They're heavy. Please tell her. Gwen, sit down, you're upsetting me."

"Moving heavy furniture alone is not smart," James agreed. "But also, and more to the point, there's no damn way in hell that you are sharing a room with my son. Are you out of your damn mind with this? And now? *Today?* Seriously?"

Gwen was shaking a pillow into a pillowcase and began to snap it violently, like a terrier breaking the neck of a small animal. Her teeth were gritted.

"Gwen," Julia pleaded, "please stop. Just sit down, darling. We need to talk. It's going to be okay."

Gwen set down the pillow and began punching it violently into shape. "I am not an idiot and I actually don't need to ask permission to share a room with the father of my baby. I'm fine, there's nothing wrong with me, I'm perfectly capable of moving a bed, I'm not a fuck-ing *child*, and obviously we'll have to share a room when the baby comes so we can do nights together and you are not the only adults in this fucking house, you're not the only relationship that *counts* around here, and I don't have to ask permission to move things around in my own room. Why are you even in here?" She wiped away angry tears with the back of her hand.

"What are you talking about? Father of what baby?"

"You don't control me! You don't get to decide every single thing that happens!"

"Come on." James rested a hand on Julia's shoulder. "I don't know what the hell's happening but this is not productive right now. We'll be downstairs when you're ready to explain yourself like a civilized adult," he went on, and Gwen wondered how he could still be stand-ing there stolidly in her doorway, how his heart could continue to beat under the annihilating pressure of her hate for him. He had taken everything from her that counted, but what little remained to her, she would keep.

LATE ON SATURDAY MORNING Nathan came back from Charlie's house to find his family waiting for him in the kitchen. His father and Julia were pale-faced and grave, and before he'd had a chance to make a much-needed cup of sweet, strong coffee and address his ravenous hunger they imparted unimaginable news about his girlfriend—at that moment flushed and weeping noisily in the corner. Nathan made an odd, involuntary noise in response. A hoarse bark of a laugh; a sin-gle, mirthless staccato of irritated disbelief. He felt nothing except a surge of impatience that with their histrionics they were disturbing the warm afterglow of a perfect evening. The last big night out, they'd all decided, till summer. He was looking forward to fried eggs on toast, and then a long, hot shower to wash away the grime of the bar, and the two cigarettes he had accidentally smoked on the walk home. But everybody was now looking at him, expecting a reaction. In the corner Gwen's sobs grew louder and she surged forward and fell upon his neck, her face blotched and swollen, snorting raggedly, as if she had been crying for hours and was only now clearing and loosening rolls of mucus from the back of her throat. He was alarmed and briefly repulsed by this transformation but he folded his arms around her narrow back to reassure her. It was only when over her shoulder he noticed his father's expression that his stomach twisted, and tightened. This was not Gwen's solitary tragedy. Hot tears of panic began to rise and he held her tighter, for his own comfort.

He did not have time to speak to her. Almost immediately she was whisked away by her mother to see a woman who would talk to her about "options" and the noise and drama departed, together with his unrecognizable beloved. The kitchen was silent and sun filled. His father spoke softly. This must be a godawful shock. But Claire was calm and a pragmatist, James explained, and would inject a little reality into the situation. It would soon be resolved. Nathan felt his panic recede and a numbing wash of disbelief rise in its place. *A drowsy numbness*, he thought, *where do I know that phrase, or perhaps I've coined it myself? Worth remembering—though "numbness" is a bit clunking.* His head throbbed. Gwen herself had only suspected since yesterday, James went on, and it was not enough time for anything but stubborn, reflexive posturing. She could not mean what she said, and in fact last night she had clearly wanted the opposite. Nathan must have so many questions—(Nathan did not)—but he was not to listen to or be terrified by any of the girl's wild assertions. A nightmare episode, uncomfortable, frightening, perhaps a wakeup call that one was not as mature as one believed. Nathan should know that James loved him and wasn't mad, even though it was a goddamn stupid needless screwup. Things would change around here. Time to knuckle down, refocus, reestablish priorities. Nathan must be so angry.

Nathan, who wasn't, pressed his temples. James fried him eggs and buttered him toast. Nathan said, "Okay," meekly, and began his breakfast.

"It's just about attention, it's nothing to do with you," James continued, battering the heel of the loaf into the narrow slot of the toaster with unnecessary force, "and we'll figure it out." Nathan took this statement at face value, and as all the explanation required. He had no wish to think deeper, or further. He had taken up the reassuring, containing phrase "nightmare episode" as an accurate description of the terrible five minutes during which his girlfriend had been wailing beside the refrigerator. That had been intense, but now he wished to burrow into his hood and sleep. It was a further unpleasant jolt to learn that before he slept he would have to help his father carry a divan and a mattress back to his own bedroom—the temporary theft of his single bed had been if anything a greater shock, and with it an attempt upon his autonomy and very *manhood*, he'd felt—but Gwen was obviously in distress, and would need careful handling until the nightmare episode was over. After the sheets had been restored he muttered, "Keats!" rather sorrowfully to his father, and then fell into a dreamless slumber, without pausing to remove jeans, or sweatshirt. James kissed his brow, reiterated softly that he loved him, and departed.

Nathan had surprised himself with his devotion to Gwen, for he had believed himself sincerely in love with Valentina and had since learned something deeper. With Gwen he was able to be himself, or at least, whichever version of himself felt truest at the time. She loved him without limits or conditions, and without apparent judgment. As he was, so she took him. Schooled by his friends to be quick and judgmental and to seize gleefully upon the slips of others, he was humbled by Gwen's simple, earnest loyalty. In their private spaces, she had made it safe for him to be sometimes wrong, or undecided. With Gwen it became less frightening to be fallible, because she resolutely refused to believe him so. If he were in trouble, he would not doubt her steadfastness. This weekend she was not rational, but his father assured him it was an episode, so he would stick by her until she had recovered. It was about attention, James had said, and once she's well and had truly traumatized Julia, there was no damn way she'd go through with any baby. Well, Nathan remembered what it felt like to be sidelined in a parental drama and was anxious to believe this explanation. No one his age could be pregnant. He was not such a statistic— he went to private school, for God's sake.

NATHAN AWOKE IN THE AFTERNOON to the return of the women, and of fear. By dinnertime Gwen was vomiting copiously and pitiably, as if the revelation of her condition had unleashed her symptoms like hounds uncaged. She did not have anything resembling a glow about her but instead after only a few hours had begun to look haggard and almost feral, like something, he thought, swept in off the moors. Claire's celebrated pragmatism had had no discernible effect. During the brief moments she was not on her knees in the bathroom Gwen lurched from a soft-voiced, reasonable calm, stating her position with the deliberate, even tones of a well-trained customer service agent, and a moment later would be unhinged by an imperceptible provocation, wild-eyed and snarling at James and her mother like Bertha Rochester. For Nathan she had only words of love, and of contrition, but through all of Saturday evening and most of Sunday they were alone for only fleeting snatches.

In the end it was decided that when term began the next morning he would go to back to boarding, as planned. Regret could be stoked and fostered into a full-time activity but it was not a very constructive one and, as the stalemate continued, it became clear that there wasn't much Nathan could actually *do*. The baby about whom they all raved and ranted would be—an unimaginable hypothetical—his baby. And yet when mother and daughter clashed, eyes flashing, hands on hips, or more bewilderingly, crying softly in one another's arms, no oxygen remained. The tears and slammed doors, the ragged apologies and immediate retractions: Nathan had no place in these scenes. Neither Gwen nor Julia thought to ask him what he wanted. Instead he retreated behind his father. It became harder and harder to believe that it would all, as James continued to promise with grim determination, be okay. Gwen had lost her mind and so far showed no signs of recovering it. He missed his mother, and longed to be at home.

26.

"WELL OBVIOUSLY SHE'LL HAVE TO GET RID OF IT," SAID IRIS equably, just as Julia had known she would. She waited for the rest of the address while her mother-in-law clicked sweetener tablets into her teacup. Julia felt almost giddy with relief to be in Iris's living room, awaiting judgment and a brisk shot of fortitude. In her mother-in-law's presence there was nothing that did not seem obvious or manageable. It was healing to be spoken to in the imperative.

Philip had been the one to tell Iris the news, and had therefore taken the unrestrained brunt of her wrath and disappointment. It was with Philip that Iris had also wept, once, briefly and in silence. Nonetheless, Iris did not understand the extended lamentations. She saw merely an unpleasant, regrettable expedient they would all hasten to forget once it was over. A young woman's future hung in the balance. On one side an education, choice, independence. On the other Iris saw the scale loaded with all the heavy, dark weight of the past. Biology as destiny: it no longer had to be. If that maddening child had any grasp of her generation's privilege, she might have been more respectful of the sovereign miracle of contraception. She ought, Iris thought furiously, to have cherished it. Worshipped it. The Pill was golden liberty, deliverance from both the baby and the scalpel, and this needless mess was due entirely to Gwendolen's own stupidity and ingratitude. Never mind. It was not too late.

"She's got herself into a horribly foolish situation but all that matters now is that she be forbidden from doing something far stupider. If you don't like the place that Thing's pal found, then that ex-wife of his will know the right women's clinic, surely. God's teeth, what I wouldn't give for a cigarette right now." Iris took a prim sip of tea. "If that girl undoes my Allen Carr, she'll really learn what trouble looks like."

Julia had not moved to speak, and so Iris continued, "Look. Mistakes happen. This is truly one of Gwendolen's more spectacular balls-ups, I will give you that, but it can't possibly be allowed to dictate the rest of her life. You are her mother—no more fluffy Fabian philosophies and all that utter guff you thought would be so healing. *Trust the child.* I've always known it was a nonsense but I now see in serious circumstances it's positively dangerous. We've watched and we've said nothing till now, but really, Julia, there must be limits. Teenagers have no impulse control, it's a neurological fact. What on earth does she know about anything? It's not at all the same as letting her choose her own bedtime or have marshmallows for dinner. You must save her from herself now, and you simply cannot allow this madness to proceed." Iris gave a short, mirthless laugh. "Julia? God help us, you're not suffering a sudden bout of Catholicism?"

Julia came to life. "No! How can you even— No, of course not, you know I don't think there's any other sensible course, it's— She's just being so, so *intransigent.* Every time we talk she ends up screaming. She is absolutely deaf to sense."

"Then you must be louder," said Iris, stoutly. "Time is ticking."

"Believe me, I'm well aware. I spent half the night writing her a letter, and I left it on her pillow yesterday and she came down looking sort of grave and pious and told me very calmly that she knew I only wanted the best for her but that she wasn't going to change her mind. Nathan was in tears this morning, he's frantic, Saskia apparently e-mailed her and even Pamela's spoken to her, not that she has any influence, but she's at least full of fire and statistics, and Gwen put the phone down on her. I don't know what to do, I can't *reach* her. I don't know how to make her see what she's doing to her future. And to my future, not that she seems particularly concerned about that. I can't actually force her, can I? Can I? You can't force someone. What if she really did regret it for the rest of her life? It would be unimaginable. But this—this is unimaginable. It's all unimaginable. I'd give anything to rewind, I'm longing to make it all just go away."

Iris set her teacup and saucer down on a large, hardcover copy of Le Corbusier's *The Modulor*, which sat at the top of a stack on a gold silk ottoman beside her. She began to speak more slowly, as if to a person of limited understanding. "The 'someone' in question is a child, and not a particularly mature or clear-headed one. Your language is problematic. Of course one can't *force someone* but one ought to direct one's minor children and take responsibility for their lives, it's a mother's job. If you want to discuss lifelong regret, I suggest you try imagining this: all her little girlfriends lining up in mortar boards to collect their degrees, or shouldering backpacks to binge-drink on Vietnamese beaches, or throwing their first dinner parties after a day in some jolly little graduate scheme, and I urge you to picture alongside it our young Gwendolen alone, for you and I both know she will be alone—

these boys don't stick around for five minutes—*alone* with a scream-ing toddler at her knee, hanging up laundry."

Julia nodded and said nothing, and Iris began to look mutinous. She had begun with her usual affectation of serenity but Julia was vexing her. "Well?"

"I know," said Julia, quietly. "It would be a tragedy."

"Well then for God's sake, stave it off! If you're all so worried about lifelong regret for this hypothetical infant then no wonder she feels she ought to keep it, you might as well start putting it down for schools. Not that it will be going to private school, of course, having grown up in ignorance and penury."

"I can't actually drag her there by the hair! What am I meant to do? I've made the appointment and I'll try to find a way to get her there. There's only a few weeks left before it's too late. Oh, God. I should never have let this happen in the first place and then we wouldn't be here. I feel culpable. I've made an appointment to talk to a family therapist next week. I know we should have separated them, but the idea of James moving out again——"

"No self-flagellation please, thank you very much; this is entirely Gwendolen's fault. But you can fix it."

"And Nathan's," said Julia, ignoring the second assertion. In the last days she had longed more than ever to dispatch James's mon-strous, con artist, sex offender of a son to a life of hard labor in the colonies, or even to the lesser sentence of a life burying eggshells and peeing on compost heaps under his mother's permanent charge in Boston. She wished, with clear precision, to murder him. The vivid violence of her imagination shocked her. She saw house fires and gas leaks. She saw him jaunty and carefree, mown down into a cartoon two dimensions by a speeding bus. She was too angry with her daughter to allow herself safely to feel or even approach it; Nathan, therefore, received the full force of her fury. Fury was more bearable than sorrow.

"I will apportion him precisely twenty-three percent of the blame. Nathan wasn't the one, after all, who 'forgot' to take the Pill." Iris left her hands frozen where they had risen on either side of her face, fingers held in drooping peace signs around the stinging, crucial word.

"I can't deal with accusations of deliberate idiocy right now. I do know what it looks like."

"For the moment why it happened is irrelevant; now we find ourselves here. Listen to me. Do you know a single person in our milieu, a single girl of our acquaintance lucky enough to be from a privileged, educated north London family of means who has had a baby under these circumstances? Don't be so arrogant as to assume we're the only ones; it's statistically impossible that no one we know has had a daughter run into a bit of trouble. But they don't go leaving letters around like the tooth fairy, they *deal with it*, Julia. The parents deal with it. And the girls chalk it up to experience and go on to university and careers and marriages and there's *no harm done*."

Composed until this moment, Julia suddenly covered her face and began to sob. "I've lost her. I don't know how to get her back."

"Oh, darling." Iris's expression remained stern but her voice softened. She sighed. She felt less equipped to deal with Julia's grief; it was moving beyond her remit. "Listen to me. You're very happy, in case you'd lost sight of it amid all this mess. You're happy for the first time since . . ." She abandoned this sentence, and began to readjust the gold watch that hung loosely on her left wrist, rotating it, checking and then rechecking the clasp. This was one of her forbidden paths of thought, leading only into snares and brambles. Back up, back out. Yet it was indisputable that Julia was in many ways better suited to this large, affable American than she had been to Iris's beloved son, and she was stung with sudden furious envy for Daniel. Daniel had been fiery and impetuous and brilliant—her captivating, flame-haired boy. Julia was unchallenging, far too passive for him, and they had argued, and she had not stood up to him as he'd needed. Her wilting would further aggravate him and they would then limp on for days in unresolved, unignorable tension while little Gwen, attuned and vibrating with every mounting bar of pressure, would prance between them like a court jester, exhausting herself in her efforts to effect a reconciliation. Daniel should have married someone with a bit of spice. Instead he'd chosen this pale flower and she had gone about looking harried. Julia had softened and unfurled. Yes—Iris had talked herself free of danger—it was no insult to Daniel to concede that she and anodyne Thing were a better fit. She drew in a deep breath and looked down at her hands. On the left a grape-colored chip of ruby set in ornately engraved eight-carat plate that had once been Philip's mother's—the thin, scuffed gold of her wedding band now retired to her right ring finger, where Philip also wore his.

"My darling girl, I do know." Here she paused, certain that Philip Alden would caution her not to sermonize. "You won't lose her, the two of you are part of one another, which is precisely why this must hurt so much. And you and Thing have enough on your plates. In not very long you'll be carefree together, and you'll be starting an entirely different sort of life. You cannot allow Gwendolen to sabotage everything and destroy her own life in the process. Believe me, that would do your relationship with her no good either."

Julia wiped her cheeks, and nodded.

Enough, thought Iris, suddenly overcome with irritation and unwilling to mourn a catastrophe while it could still be headed off at the pass. All this ululating and rending of collars was simply wasted energy. "Anyway. Your plans are your own business and are for you and Thing to discuss once the nest is actually empty. In the meantime"— she looked steadily at Julia—"before the children go forth, you must forbid them from multiplying. Deal with it."

27.

"WHAT ABOUT UP HERE?" NATHAN OFFERED, POINTING TO-
ward a patch of balding grass beneath a giant sycamore. It was less
crowded than the larger clearing they had just passed, in which he'd
spotted a group of local teenagers he half knew and urgently wished
to avoid. A damp chill remained in the air, but an unexpected wash
of pale April sunshine had drawn hopeful crowds to the Heath. Nathan's parents had given him a series of coaching sessions prior to this
outing, and he had set out determined to act upon them.

"Ugh. You're *so* lucky you get to escape to school. I wish I could
escape from Mum and— Julia and James. They're probably desperate
to get rid of me anyway. I'm so sick of crying and being yelled at and
groveling and then crying again, it's not exactly relaxing."

"I don't think the throwing up is majorly helpful. Maybe you
should consider quitting that."

"Okay, I'll think about giving up, but it's just been so much *fun*. I
feel human again today, though."

"I'm glad," he said, with feeling. It had been dreadful to watch her heave, with the surreal guilt and awe that his own ejaculation could have such terrible power.

They sat down on the seam of shadow that fell across the grass, Nathan in the sun, Gwen in the full shade. She had showered and put in her contact lenses and looked pretty and fresh faced again, in a pair of heart-shaped cerise Lolita sunglasses and a denim jacket on which she'd long ago embroidered a seam of prancing, rainbow-tailed unicorns. She had been cheerful since they'd been alone together. Sucking intermittently on an orange lollipop, she looked the picture of youthful innocence. Here was someone he recognized.

"I'm sorry this has all got so crazy," she said, after a while. The lolly clicked against her teeth as she removed it to speak. "I just get so frustrated that they don't get it. And I know I'm superhormonal so it seems like I don't know what I mean because I keep crying but I do, I just express myself badly. It's like, insanely clear in my head. They're both so rigid, it's like they refuse to see that people can take different paths from them. From them? From theirs? Anyway. I think"—she paused to tuck the sweet back into one cheek—"I think sometimes it can be very hard for parents to see signs that their babies have become adults."

Nathan saw the truth in this statement, and also its dishonesty. Their parents were not upset because their children were growing up but because they had done something infantile. He had never felt less like an adult. This was most acute when he spoke on the phone with his mother, longing for the stifling warmth and reassurance of her soft arms around him. Last night he'd dreamed he had been entrusted with a minute baby in a jam jar. The jar had smashed, and the baby lay gasping and suffocating at his feet like a tiny landed minnow.

Gwen turned to him to speak again and he took the lollipop from her hand, crunched it between his molars and then grinned at her, handing back the remaining shard on its paper stick. She liked these small, exclusive familiarities, he knew, liked sharing his spoon, or his toothbrush, enjoyed the ostentatious intimacy of licking a swelling drop of ice cream from his wrist, or passing chewing gum mouth to mouth. Or carrying his child, he thought, and found himself shaking his head involuntarily, as if the thought could be dislodged like water from his ears. He desperately needed her to listen.

"Tell me honestly what you want." Gwen began to peel at the damp stick with a fingernail. "I go mental when *they* ask because they're so judgmental and it's none of their business, but it's different just us. This is our decision."

"Okay," began Nathan, slowly. "Well, right now we're talking about, like, a grain of rice."

Spoken by James or Julia, this would have tripped Gwen into a spasm of white rage, but alone with Nathan, she did not feel defensive. Nathan was not a threat. To compare it to a grain of rice did not reduce it to the insignificance of a grain of rice. Her chin lifted a fraction.

"But it's actually more like a grape by now than a grain of rice. So okay, what if you did cast the deciding vote? What if it was your body?" He noticed her hands slipped beneath her jacket to her lower belly, still muscled, still firm. It was unimaginable that beneath the sleek concavity of her navel could be anything so sinister and alien. Then her hand moved from her own stomach to his, demonstrating, inviting.

He lay down on his back, though the hard ground was cold beneath him. It was easier to speak freely if he shut her out, and instead watched the crimson capillaries of his closed eyelids. "We've talked about it. I think to have it would be a major-league mistake. I can't make you do anything." This was the dutiful line, and he discharged it with feeling. "But I think it would be a huge mistake. We're way too young. It's a nightmare. Neither of us has finished school, and I'd want any son of mine to have everything I have. We've been insanely privileged, really. And I'd want to provide my kids with what I've had, you know, educationally, and travel; I've lived in two countries already . . ." Here he tapered off because, apart from having a vague awareness that his parents had argued over his own monstrously expensive school fees, he was at a loss to articulate the innumerable ways in which he felt ill-equipped for parenthood. It came down only to this— he didn't want it. He *could* do it, he felt. If there were nuclear war, or the aliens came and it fell upon him to repopulate the earth with his bevy of flaxen-haired warrior-women, he would step up. But unless he found himself in those circumstances, where in any case he would have awesome weapons and iron-hard biceps and a life-and-death battle against evil forces, and the cameras never showed screaming infants but instead dwelt on the necessary and heroic adrenaline-charged trysts amid the rubble; unless it would be like that, he did not want children. Not now, maybe never. Panic like a trapped sparrow fluttered in his chest.

"I know." She nodded in enthusiastic agreement, as if warming to an established theme. "I know, totally. And we could have waited and got married first and been all organized and— But I mean, this happened now, so plans change."

It had not escaped Nathan's notice that she had begun to speak as if their lives together were inevitable, already planned and committed. Just weeks before, he remembered her saying something about a possible barbecue, if they were still together by summer. At the time he had been touched, and happy she saw their relationship continuing. He was at his best with a girlfriend, fortified by the knowledge that there was one person who would dependably choose him first. But now the conditional tense had been entirely abandoned. He had, apparently without noticing, acquired a wife. Still, they could not talk sensibly if she was defensive. "I never knew you wanted kids so young," he said, carefully.

"I guess I hadn't thought about it until this happened"—she had flopped onto her back beside him but sat up again, speaking urgently—"and maybe some parts aren't ideal but it just feels right, it's like my whole life is clear suddenly, and makes sense. I know I probably sound crazy but it's like it was meant to happen. This is *everything.*"

He gave a dry chuckle, frowning and pinching the bridge of his nose, a position in which he looked, for a moment, exactly like his father. He sniffed. His eyes were stinging in the sun and watering, inexplicably. "This was meant to happen, you think?"

"I know I sound insane. And even a few days ago I would have said it's the worst luck in the world but yes, really really *really* I think this is my good luck. I have never felt more certain of anything in my life, I was meant to have this little grape, I'm its mother already. I feel it. It wasn't what I planned but now it's happened." She beat a small fist above her heart, tightly clenched. "I feel it, this is who I'm meant to live for. I'm not against it or anything; if you'd asked me before, I would have said I'd totally have an abortion and feel relieved and we'd plan our lives all neatly and go to university first, blah, blah, blah, but I don't think things happen like you plan, do they? And this way I'll take, like, six months or a year out now, and then go back to everything and go to uni a year late and just start my job one year later. It will be like, my gap year."

"I don't think having a kid is much like a gap year. It's not like, I don't know, counting starfish on some eco mission in the Philippines. It's not hiking the Inca trail."

"But I would never want to hike the Inca trail. Don't look at me like that, you're making me laugh and I'm being totally serious. I'm not that type, I'm a homebody. Compared to most of the country we're rich, really, and obviously I'll get a job part time or whatever, but I know my mum will help look after it once it's here, because she'll want me to go back to school. They were probably going to have a baby themselves." She lifted her chin, defiant, and an indecipherable expression crossed her face. Her eyes flashed. "Now they won't have to."

Nathan glanced at her oddly. "Isn't your mother, like, fifty?"

"No!" Gwen looked wary. "She's forty-seven."

"I mean, it now seems fairly obvious the men of the Fuller family have supersperm"—here Nathan paused, dusting lint or perhaps falling confetti from his imaginary epaulettes—"but I don't think even supersperm can do much with forty-seven. Why do you think they'd even want another kid anyway? In five years my dad will be *sixty*. There's no way. They're just getting rid of us and starting their new phase or whatever, it would be craziness. My dad goes on about whisking your mom off into the sunset to hear Scriabin or Messiaen or whatever. He can't wait to be done with school fees." Nathan reverted to their own case. "And what if taking the Pill has like, fried it in there?"

"They might have done. They *might*." Tears threatened.

"Okay, okay, if you say so, they might."

"They won't anymore!" She stroked his arm and her voice softened. "We make such a good team. We've grown up more than our friends already; think about Katy or Charlie or anyone. We've had to."

Nathan had no other way to get through to her, and could not raise his voice. She shifted slightly, and her shadow fell across his face so that after the dazzling glare of the sunshine he could see again, and with this fleeting clarity of vision he spoke, as frankly as he dared. "I'm not ready for a baby. I'm not ready to be a father. I, I just don't want to. Please don't—I *can't*."

"I think you're ready. I think you'll be amazing." She lay down beside him again and inched closer, curled on her side, one leg slung over his, her hand resting lightly on his chest. After a moment he heard her breath change and realized, startled, that she had fallen heavily asleep.

When on the warpath both his parents were formidable in their own way, but his father's love for him was vast, he knew, and could conquer cities. James would always protect him. He had not felt able to present Gwen with some home truths, as his father had instructed, nor to threaten, as his mother had commanded, but at least all the adults were in agreement and he had only to survive down this topsy-turvy rabbit hole a little longer; parents were parents and ultimately she would not be allowed to go through with it. Surely there was no need for his throat to tighten like this; no need for the tears that threatened, again, again.

The sun had moved and bright stripes now fell across Gwen's face. As carefully as he could, he maneuvered himself from beneath her hand and sat up, leaning forward so that the shadow of his back would protect her pale, unaccustomed skin. For the sake of the imaginary film crew he dropped his head into his hands, an exquisite picture of broken, masculine despair.

28.

"PLEASE DON'T EVEN JOKE ABOUT DELIVERIES. THIS OBVIOUSLY cannot happen."

"Well, obviously not," Pamela snapped, her voice made tinny by the speakerphone. "Someone has to knock some sense into her. I can't believe Nathan was such a bloody wet blanket about it, I told him what to say."

James and Pamela had been speaking every day for the last terrible fortnight, so she was well aware that there had been no change. Gwen had moved beyond the reach of all reason, as if beneath a dome of thick glass through which nothing, no sound, no sense, could penetrate. She had the blank-eyed conviction of the religious zealot, and the zealot's placid, maddening pity for those who didn't see the light. She was having the baby, she could do it, she'd been reading about it on the Internet, she had an instinct, a second sense; they just needed to have faith. James found it hard to look at her. How was it possible that one spoiled, angry teenager had wrested control of all their lives?

"Anyway," Pamela went on, "speaking of deliveries, you delivered our boy back to school. He sounds like a different child; you'd think he was at Disneyland. It's heartbreaking. My beloved little boy. I'm driving on the freeway in the sunshine and I was feeling such lightness thinking, yes, he's going to be okay, my baby's going to be himself again, but now I'm questioning the wisdom of his absence. He should be processing, he's deeply in denial. It's dangerous. He should be fighting to prevent it before it's too late, that's the key here, isn't it? You can't do anything from a place of denial. For God's sake, he can be home a few weeks and then go back to boarding once it's dealt with; he's the only one with any influence; he's got to tell her as many times as it takes that she's being a bloody moron. I don't know what went wrong when they spoke on the Heath, I couldn't have prepped him any better but when I spoke to him just now he sounded manic and was wittering on about spending his gap year volunteering in a South African clinic. It's out of sight and utterly totally bizarrely out of mind."

"Gotcha."

"That's what Gwen said. Ha, ha. Anyway, so you see. I did mention that by the time this supposed gap year rolls around he'll have a six-month-old and won't be gapping anywhere, but it didn't seem to register. Total denial." In the background James could hear the voice of the satellite navigation commanding Pamela to keep left ahead. "But between us, I will say I hated making every word of that speech to him. I don't want to be Mean Mummy, the voice of doom and responsibility, but I was trying to scare him. Surely she'll listen to him if he's insistent enough, if he collapses when they talk face-to-face, then he must e-mail her from school like I've instructed. That is, assuming she can read. I've written him a draft. I want my baby traveling the world, carefree, with girlfriends in Argentina and Italy and Australia and Japan, learning his heart, expanding his horizons. I always tell him, if you call all your girlfriends 'Darling' it will save you the trouble of keeping their names straight. You know something, he's having that bloody gap year if it kills me, whatever I said to him. If she wants it so much, she can look after it. What was the point of— Wait, what? One second, the road's— I need to read the signs. The satnav's saying North-South and the road's saying East-West. Okay, right. What was I saying? Oh, yes. I wanted him to fly. I did not envisage him trapped in the suburbs with a sulky little teen bride and a bawling bundle. It's not what I wanted for his *soul*."

"I hope you didn't make teen bride jokes with Nathan. We've had enough dumb moves."

"Are you kidding? I told him I'd disown him for his stupidity. Luckily it hadn't crossed his mind, he sounded suitably horrified. Why the bloody bollocks is there an exit here? One second. I'm going to call you back, I've gone wrong."

SOMETHING HAD GONE WRONG for Pamela lately, and not simply with her navigation. Her very identity was in conflict.

Her office at the clinic was a parlor. No hierarchical furniture arrangements, no barriers of desks or intimidating swivel chairs that spoke of diplomas and educational advantages and a disconnection from the common lives of those she sought to help. Instead, soft, womanish furniture—soft sofas, pairs of matching, soft egalitarian armchairs. And in this safe, cushioned space women cried and cried about men. About what had been done to them. About what had been sown in them by men. Biology itself dictated who was taking possession of whom; that was the oldest metaphor, the oldest reality. It was there in the syntax—women were never the subject, only the object, subject to a man. And yet two brains make a sequence of decisions; two bodies unite and two people should face the consequences. With the women in her office Pamela sympathized, and raged, and helped. The men must be made to take equal responsibility. They must.

But—when she thought of Nathan, when she considered her sweet son, his puff-chested naïveté, his ebullience, his grin, she felt that something essential had been stolen from him that he had simply been too innocent to guard. Gwen, predatory and conniving beyond her years, had entrapped him. Some women did, we were not all passive, not all united in benign and supportive sisterhood, after all. Seeking revenge upon her mother, or a means to get her claws irretractably into Nathan (for he was manifestly out of her league, only available because of this accident of circumstance; of this Pamela felt quite certain), or perhaps just wanting a warm, responsive living dolly to cuddle, she had attacked—*mugged* was the best word—had mugged Pamela's little boy. It was almost as if— She toyed with the word that had risen spontaneously to the surface. No, all right, she conceded, defensive against herself, it wasn't quite like that. But something like it. Certainly a violation.

She had not gone wrong. She found her exit and after leaving the slip road redialed James, who answered immediately and said, "Look, maybe he should be around but you can't imagine how godawful it's been in the house with Julia and that girl at each other's throats; I just wanted him out of it. The boy deserves some peace and quiet to study now."

Pamela whistled through her teeth. Ahead she saw a drive-thru Dunkin' Donuts and realized with a flash of grateful recognition that a large iced coffee would elevate this journey from tedious to transcendent. She slowed and turned, her mood already transformed.

"What a trip. Do you remember when he begged for that Japanese fighting fish? And then he forgot to clean it out and it suffocated. I retract what I said, I actually think it's a gift that he's away during the week and he can breathe. Charlie came into his room while we were on the phone and he sounded so happy to be with his friends again. They're good boys, with all their high fives and weird Masonic hand-shakes."

"I asked the other day if he'd told Charlie about the baby and he looked at me like I'd lost my mind and I thought, you know what? Let him have his denial. If we can't change her mind in the next few weeks, he won't have much longer to be a kid."

"Oh, Jamesy," Pamela breathed, back in the seductive tone she assumed when she felt he was no longer opposing her. He could picture her quite clearly leaning forward, steepling her fingers and offering beyond them the musky darkness of a substantial cleavage, and an outrageous pout of her lips. In fact, she was idling at the mouth of the Dunkin' Donuts takeout lane, reading the menu with greedy plea-sure. "He'd still be a baby. He'd just be a baby with a baby. Which is precisely why you cannot let it happen. We're depending on you now; all these random people are your bloody responsibility. Please give your son a kick up the arse and get him to fucking deal with it."

29.

PHILIP HAD BEEN DISAPPOINTED IN JULIA BEFORE, SADDENED that in her guilty indulgence she succumbed to Gwendolen's rages. Gwen had been sent to a progressive school at which the delayed gratifications of discipline and academic success were sacrificed in favor of immediate comfort and coziness, and which placed primary emphasis on the value of imaginative self-expression, time that elsewhere might have been devoted to the studying of parts of speech or long division. Even so, Gwen had never been made to go to lessons, nor to do what little homework she had, nor to help her mother around the house. She had not been taught, or helped, to see her mother as a differentiated individual, for both Julia and Gwen found pleasure in the obsessive and intricate fulfilling of Gwen's needs, and this shared interest bound them. She had never been told, "no." Ever since Daniel's final diagnosis, Julia had devoted her life to smoothing away tiny quotidian discomforts like the ultimate, inexhaustible celebrity fixer, toiling to compensate for that one, huge, unrelenting sorrow. But giving Gwen what she wanted did not mean it was what she needed. "Babies protest if one confiscates the steak knife they've grabbed," Iris had observed, during one of their lengthy analyses, "it doesn't mean one lets them play with weapons." Philip agreed and had always agreed—Julia ought to have confiscated the knife long ago, and had the foresight and strength and conviction to withstand the howls. To parent well, sometimes one makes one's children unhappy, yet Julia had never had any ambition for her daughter's future besides a nonspecific "happiness." *She doesn't have to be an astrophysicist; all I want is for her to be happy.* She spoke of it as though such a state somehow precluded hard work, or discipline, or focus. He and Iris discussed it interminably. Weren't there happy astrophysicists? But Philip had always dissuaded Iris when she announced her intentions of wading in, and for that he, too, now felt complicit. They should have spoken. He should have braved Julia's unhappiness by speaking out—he himself was guilty of the same indulgence.

IT WAS PASSOVER and Passover was somehow unavoidable, even for so lax and assimilated a family. James's suggestion that they "pass on Passover" this year was tempting but was as unrealistic as canceling Christmas. And so they were assembling at Iris's house for the first time, aping normality, just a fortnight after the bombshell. Iris would almost be choked by the commands she wished to issue, by the speeches she longed to give, and Philip alone would hear them all, over and over on a loop inside his head. Julia had already warned them both—*it's not the place to attack her; if we want her to see sense, then ganging up will backfire; if this really has to happen, then let's just have a nice family evening*—but restraint was not Iris's forte. She would need an outlet, and there was no such edict in place against attacking Philip.

"You can spare me the sanctimony," Iris told him sharply when he arrived, though he hadn't spoken. She signaled toward the kitchen with the paper-wrapped bunch of crimson tulips he'd presented. "Go through. If you hush me again, I shall go wild. I'll be *shtum*; as instructed, just don't repeat it. Don't even think it."

It would not help for him to say, "I didn't say anything." She had heard his thoughts. Together, they had exhausted every iteration of every argument. So much of their map was covered in this old terrain—familiar pitfalls and ravines into which they fell and then revolved together, uselessly. They were trapped in their old roles and their own selves.

Gwen appeared behind her grandmother holding a bowl of cashews, which she was posting into her mouth with the regular swipe of a metronome. Her lovely hazel eyes were blackened with too much makeup, her freckles partially erased with something powdery and pale. "Grandpa," she said, smiling uncertainly from beneath her lashes, and wiped a salty hand on her jeans before coming forward to embrace him with her free arm. "Cashew?"

"Not just yet, thank you. How are you, *maidele*?"

"Fine. A bit . . . have to keep eating or I feel sick." She colored.

Philip watched Iris drift upstairs without obvious purpose, repelled away from their granddaughter like a slow, elegant magnet. Keeping Iris silent would be impossible if Gwen kept referring to her pregnancy, even obliquely. Gwen barely seemed abashed. She seemed almost jaunty. He felt an urgent longing to go home.

In the kitchen he found James laying the table. As they exchanged greetings Philip held out his hand for a bunch of cutlery, to help.

"No, it's almost done, thanks. How are you?"

Philip lowered himself into the chair he hoped Iris would permit him to occupy for the evening. She had strong ideas about seating plans and might well, though it was only family, have a configuration for this dinner scrawled on the back of a notecard. She was not above asking people to move, if they'd installed themselves somewhere that displeased her. "Fine, thank you. How have you all been?"

James gave Philip a long look. "Put it this way. Blood. Frogs. Pestilence. Cattle disease. Whatever. It all sounds better than twenty-four hours in our house. I must tell you, I'm ashamed. I feel I must apologize to you for my son's part in all this. You and Iris must have been very shocked."

"Yes," said Philip, simply. "But you have no need to apologize."

"Well, I'm deeply sorry nonetheless. And now we must set it all aside this evening to contemplate the Exodus, so I'm told. I've been deputized as bartender; can I get you something? I intend to drink heavily; I advise you to join me."

"Nathan's not here this evening?"

"No, we decided . . . He's studying at his friend's house for the night. I felt . . . Do you know where the corkscrew is? I just felt he needed . . ." James seemed unable to complete any of these sentences. It seemed likely that Nathan was avoiding Gwen, or all of them, and Philip found it hard to blame him. He, too, had dreaded this evening. He began the arduous process of standing from his seat and abandoned it with relief when James said, "Here it is. There's only red, for the seder."

"Red," Philip said. "Thank you."

Philip did know where Giles had kept the corkscrew, as well as the several other places between which it migrated in the time since Iris had reclaimed sole stewardship of this house, none of which were where he himself had filed it when he'd lived here, on the shelf beside the bottles. Giles and Iris had shared a distain for his regime and though it had been many years since Giles had moved to Provence, much of the disarray he'd introduced still remained.

Giles had died shortly after moving to France full time, and the two states—being dead and residing in a French farmhouse—had fused in the family lexicon so that between Philip, Daniel, and Julia, one had become a euphemism for the other. It was not kind. Philip had in fact been friends with Giles, and Daniel had also been on cordial terms with him, but the phrase had nonetheless evolved, and stuck. Philip could only hope that, as a man who'd loved the reassuring intimacy of a private joke, Giles would have been forgiving. Daniel had spoken of moving to France himself in the last months of his illness, and had studied his father's countenance, insisting, with his eyes, upon a small returned smile. Cool, insouciant, hiding his fear to spare them. His brave boy. *It's an obscenity that he is gone and I'm still here.* With effort, Philip recalled himself to the kitchen, and to James.

Philip liked James. James was likeable. He put Julia at ease and made her laugh. This year she had become beautiful again, recalling the fragile, striking girl she had been when he'd first known her, where for years she had begun to look—it was Iris's uncharitable word, though he had had to admit a truth to it—slightly haggard. Now she looked young again, and luminous. James exuded a sort of Viking strength and vigor and, searching for a description, Philip found his first true use for the term "in rude health." He understood, choosing to steer his thoughts firmly away from his own son's swift waning and diminishing, why Julia would be drawn to such a man.

Now, under extraordinary circumstances, James was proving himself over and over, tested in his kindness, his generosity, his understanding. He had found a clinic, he'd spoken to the psychologist in his department, he'd been the one to source online videos for Gwen to watch, to help her understand the realities of teenage motherhood. Not once, Julia said, had he raised his voice. He was kind to Gwen, and liked her. He understood that gentle steadiness was their only hope for persuasion. He was taking care of all of them. Still. Daniel.

"Pamela told me that she dispatched her travel agent to hunt you down. I'm sorry about that, she's not very good at taking no for an answer. I don't think the assembly will be for you, if that's okay to say. It's not for me, anyhow."

"Yes, she sent along a great deal of unusual literature. I'm afraid Joan, the woman she sent, was rather misled to believe that I was simply a nervous traveler in need of a little coaxing so she was terribly embarrassed once she realized. I tried to reassure her that I was interested to hear the details nonetheless. Apparently"—he began to laugh—"Joan's had terrible trouble finding a source of dairy-free croissants for the breakfasts. It's made the hotel manager very cross."

"I think hearing about any of it would make me mad, too. Julia's just upstairs, by the way, fixing some sort of formatting issue on Iris's laptop." James set a glass down before Philip, but at that moment everyone came in together, Iris shooing Julia and Gwen before her and demanding, "Can we sit down now?" as if it had been someone else occupied upstairs for the last half an hour.

They sat, and raced through a perfunctory Haggadah reading led by Philip, prompted intermittently by Julia. Iris had forgotten the horseradish and they were forced to settle for the closest thing in the refrigerator, a squeezy bottle of yellow American mustard. It was then discovered that she did not have a shank bone either, but after scrabbling in the cupboard Iris presented Philip with an organic lamb-flavored stock cube, wrapped in shiny purple foil. She had not cooked, but instead had bought lime-marinated chicken wings and red quinoa studded with tart currants, premade, in the Selfridges Food Hall. Philip had two helpings of salad, which he did not prepare for himself at home, so felt duty bound to consume for its phytonutrients when it was served to him elsewhere (and for the same reason, he had taken a punishingly large piece of parsley during the *Karpas*). Work had seemed a neutral topic and he enjoyed a quiet discussion with James about a VBAC uterine rupture earlier in the day, called to a halt when Gwen, overhearing, said it was gross and could they stop, please, and he had then realized his own insensitivity. More than once he noticed James and Julia holding hands, beneath the table. By contrast, Julia and Gwen did not speak to one another directly, except for a brief, bitter exchange overheard as they were ladling out soup together. He sensed Iris's mounting incredulity that Julia, while clearly seething, would not allow anyone to acknowledge the pregnant teenage elephant dominating the room. The evening had a hallucinatory edge—conversation was polite, brittle, utterly empty. Between Julia and Gwen hummed invisible electric wires of resentment, studiously ignored by everyone else. It was painfully, ludicrously English, and he wondered how James could stand it. James's praise for everything on the table irritated Iris, he noticed, though she demanded this same excessive flattery from her own family. Later James helped to clear the plates, and Philip observed Iris's disapproval of this, too, watching her dismiss it as both unseemly and overfamiliar. His son had compromised her granddaughter—he was implicated, and culpable, and entirely unwelcome at her dinner table. Philip wished sometimes to be liberated from his understanding of Iris—when they were in company together her feelings sometimes crowded his out; spoken in her rich and strident voice, they were frequently louder inside his head than his own mild thoughts and observations. He was tired.

30.

THE ANNOUNCEMENT, LATER IN THE EVENING, CAME AS A surprise.

"We are all family here, after all," said Iris, looking with undisguised irony from Julia to James, who paused, arrested in the act of reaching for another macaroon. Her eyes slid over Gwen, who was sitting primly, hands folded in her lap, and came to rest finally on Julia again, who was refilling Philip's water glass.

"As everyone's assembled I would like to say something important. I've decided I'm selling the house."

"You always say that, Granny."

"There's no need for you to move just yet, is there?" Julia asked.

"It's not a question of need. I'm moving. I've got a good buyer, a developer. She's the right person."

"What do you mean, you've found someone already? When?"

"As it happens we exchanged this morning. She's happy not to dawdle, which was exactly what I asked for. There's really very little to do, if I'd known how easy it would be, I would have done it years ago. I want options, and I want to be in a position to—who knows what the future holds."

Nobody spoke. Philip, Julia saw, looked stricken. He said nothing, but was now gazing down at his hands, their joints stiff and swollen, though he would rarely admit they bothered him. She felt an urge to defend him but could think of nothing to say that would not diminish or shame him. He did not move or look up. Eventually Gwen said, "But, Granny, I really don't think it's a good idea for you to move; everyone loves your house, and you're so close to us." More quietly, "And it's where Dad grew up. Don't sell it. I think you should think more about it."

"Where will you go?" James asked.

"I've found a flat in St. John's Wood. Well, off the Finchley Road, in actual fact. Really, I don't know why you are all gawping at me; you can't have thought I'd stay in this enormous house forever and I'm not waiting until I'm wheeled out of it. I want to be able to walk to Regent's Park. I want to be closer to town. I liked Giles's flat in Bayswater before he gave it up; it was convenient, and I want to have a management committee to deal with the roof and the hallway carpets. I want the financial freedom to be able to— I don't intend to spend my seventies enslaved to the running of a house, I have far better things to do."

"But it's your seventies, Iris, not your nineties."

"Regardless," said Iris, primly.

Beside her Philip still had not spoken. It seemed he'd known as little as anyone else. Surely this house was his, too? How could Iris just sell it without his consent? And why? Strolling through Regent's Park was not a convincing argument when she currently lived on Hampstead Heath. Gwen had not understood what it meant to exchange contracts, Julia saw with exasperation, and it would have to be broken to her that her grandmother's house was all but gone, and further discussion pointless. Gwen needed support and stability to face the choices ahead, not further upheaval and insecurity. At that moment, Gwen scraped her chair back.

"I'm *desperate* for the loo," she announced unnecessarily, and then trotted out into the hall, one hand cupped against an invisible bump.

Iris tutted. "What a mercy she reminded us all she's pregnant, we've been talking about something else for all of twelve seconds. How remiss of us."

Julia caught James's eye and began, despite herself, to laugh. James shook his head; he, too, was fighting a smile. Just as Julia felt that giggles might overwhelm her Gwen returned and James straightened his face and stood up, abruptly. "It's been a great night, thank you. *Le shana haba'ah be* Finchley Road. And it's getting late. Philip, shall I give you a ride back?"

Julia and Iris looked up at him in surprise. Gwen stood in the doorway yawning, widely.

"That would be lovely, thank you," said Philip. He had not joined in the laughter. He leaned heavily on the table and rose, slowly, to his feet.

WHEN THEY WERE ALONE, back in their own kitchen, James asked Julia, "Did you know she was doing that? Philip seemed stunned, in the car."

"I don't understand; surely it's half his. She can't just sell without asking him. He bought it before they even married, I think."

"It must be in her name."

"But whoever's name it's in, doesn't common courtesy require you to at least ask your former husband about selling the family home? Your best friend, supposedly? She's been there"—she began to estimate—"Giles lived there with her for a few years after he sold his flat, I think, before he moved to France." She allowed herself a small smile here, at the phrase, but did not pause to explain and, in any case, in this instance she was referring to his actual move to France. "And before then all those years with Philip. Daniel was born in that house. What an awful thing to announce just like that. It's classic Iris. You know that for ages we didn't even know if they ever actually got divorced? They made it impossible to ask. And then in the end it turned out that the divorce came through exactly around the time she and Giles were breaking up anyway. It was all part of their act, you know, how unusually civil it all was. Oops! We almost forgot to divorce."

"It's not very civil to make unilateral decisions."

"No."

At that moment the phone rang. "It's Granny," Gwen shouted, from upstairs. "She wants you, Mum."

Julia picked up the kitchen phone.

"You needn't have looked at me like I'd grown a second head this evening," Iris snapped, without preliminaries.

"I'm sorry, I was just a bit surprised."

"Well, lots of things are surprising. I was surprised to discover that my sixteen-year-old granddaughter thinks it's reasonable to have a baby, but I've adapted," said Iris, shortly. "Now I'm equipped for bribery and corruption—art college, a gap year, whatever her little heart desires if only she abandons this insanity. And if she does have the bloody thing, it won't have to be dragged up by its bootstraps, not that I will tell her that at present."

"Oh, Iris, surely that's not—"

"I have several reasons, none of which I owe it to you to explain. It's my house, to do with as I wish."

"Of course, I know that. But I really hope it won't be necessary—"

"So you say, and yet the days pass and nothing changes. I dearly hope I'm wrong. Thank you for coming this evening," Iris finished, stiffly. This formality was intended to be wounding. "Tell Gwendolen I'll call her over the weekend. I sincerely hope this family therapist person knows her onions." She rang off and Julia shrugged, in response to James's look of inquiry. Her mother-in-law's self-righteousness, her generosity, her ominous prophesies—Julia could not face discussing any of them.

31.

THE GABLED REDBRICK MANSIONS OF FITZJOHN'S AVENUE WERE
built in the late nineteenth century for the great and the good of
Hampstead—spreading gothic piles with grand staircases at their
hearts, down which the bustled daughters of shipowners and silk
magnates and wine merchants could sweep toward waiting carriages.
Now, the great and the good of Hampstead trudge up these stairs to
try to understand their own unhappiness, for these palaces have been
carved into a warren of magnolia consulting rooms for Freudians and
Jungians and Kleinians and, in the case of number 88, for three In-
dependents, two marriage guidance counselors, and one Dr. Rhoda
Frankel, clinical psychologist, family therapist, Wesleyan graduate,
and grandmother, she'd said on the phone, of seven. Her voice was
warm, her accent broad Long Island, and upon learning that Julia's
sixteen-year-old daughter had recently been impregnated by a newly
acquired de facto stepson, Dr. Frankel had not offered a noncommit-
tal, therapeutic "mmm" but instead whistled through her teeth and

said, "Well, *that*'s not easy." Her photograph on the Internet was of a bright-eyed woman in her middle sixties, broad chested, with a sharply cut bob of caramel hair that fell neatly either side of a pair of cherry-red plastic-framed glasses. She was all in navy, except for a long chain of complicated, interlocking Lucite squares of neon green slung round her neck. Julia had looked into the eyes of this facsimile while on the phone to the original and, speaking as calmly as she could manage, yearned to collapse and weep like a baby in Dr. Frankel's comfortably substantial arms.

Julia sat beside Gwen in the waiting room on a low, sagging buttercup-yellow sofa before a glass coffee table tattooed with fingerprints, its stacks of curling *National Geographic*s long neglected now that passing patients instead hid their faces in their phones, busily online, resolutely pretending to be elsewhere. A spider plant cascaded dustily from a hanging basket in the window, above a vibrant aspidistra that was, on closer inspection, plastic. Gwen sat with her hands retracted into her sleeves and clamped between denim thighs. Her brows were knitted into a frown, her lips pushed out, her eyes fixed on a point somewhere in her lap. Her posture, her expression, her every movement conveyed, megaphone loud, that she had come on sufferance. *You are detestable*, Julia thought, *and you have ruined and continue to ruin my life; I should have had cats instead.* She noted with an anxious pang that Gwen looked woefully drawn and pallid—almost gray.

Julia found she was unable to break from the constant repetitions of her own case. The prosecution, or was she the defense? In planning this session she had appointed Dr. Frankel as their savior but was gripped by a new fear that the kindly American woman was to be her judge; that they were to receive not arbitration but a verdict, and sentence. Gwen had gone back into their shared and precious past and had set fire to every room. *She's too young,* she rehearsed, *she has her whole life ahead of her.* And, without knowing for what she pleaded she returned to it over and over. *I fought with every breath to be two parents for you. Why are you so angry?* And—*Please. Please. Please.*

AS SHE HAD BEEN in her photograph online, Dr. Frankel was all in navy blue, stouter than her image, her hair the same resolutely expensive caramel, her crimson glasses replaced with frameless ovals resting on the very end of her nose. She greeted them warmly by name, "Gwen, Julia, do come in," and gestured to a pair of narrow biscuit-colored armchairs. She herself squeezed into an upright wooden chair opposite them, a ring-bound notebook on her crossed legs, an expectant smile for them as they settled. Gwen surprised Julia by arranging herself bolt upright, her hands neatly on her knees, an expression of anticipation on her face. Her head was cocked slightly to one side, as if listening for instructions. Dr. Frankel turned to her.

"I'm sure you know, Gwen, that Mom and I had a brief chat on the phone when we set up this meeting, and so she's had a chance to tell me a little bit about what she feels has been happening, but I'm really interested to hear from you. I take it for granted that each of us has a different perspective, right?" Julia thought she saw Gwen offer the ghost of a nod. "And I'm here to listen, and maybe to help everyone else find a way to listen, too, in a way that might feel easier than when you're at home together. I'd like to hear why you're here, and what you hope to achieve. How did you make the decision to come today?"

"My mum wanted me to come."

"Okay."

There was a long silence. Julia's hope wavered.

"I understand. So it wasn't your plan to be here."

Gwen shook her head.

"So then I'm thinking"—Dr. Frankel leaned back and considered a point above their heads for a moment—"I'm thinking then that it was quite a decision you made to show up, in that case." Her gaze returned to Gwen. "After all, you're here now. Our moms ask us to do a lot of things, and would you agree it's fair to say, as teenagers, we don't always do them?"

"I came today because you asked me to." Gwen then turned to address Dr. Frankel. "I came because she asked me to because it would show that I don't just *not do* stuff . . ." She blinked several times and cleared her throat but lapsed once again into silence.

Julia had not yet given her prepared speech. There had been so much she'd wanted to say in this hour—to Gwen, to Dr. Frankel, perhaps also to herself. But something passed across Gwen's face that made her suddenly ask, "Would you prefer to talk to Dr. Frankel alone? I can wait outside?"

Gwen glanced up and met her mother's eyes for a moment. She nodded.

Julia stood. "Okay," she said, brightly. To Dr. Frankel, in her thoughts she whispered, *She's a baby*, and then one final time, *Please*. She slipped out.

UP FITZJOHN'S AVENUE on a late-spring afternoon, beneath the heavy spreading sycamores and horse chestnuts, several academies are spaced at regular intervals; this is where north London's most privileged three-year-olds learn to read and write, are taught computer code and Mandarin in striped winter caps, or, in summer, beneath ribboned straw hats. Today the little girls were in deep blue gingham dresses, woolen cardigans, and navy elastic purse belts; the boys, in miniature blazers and gray tailored trousers. Many emerged skipping, as yet unencumbered by their parents' weighty expectations. The pavements thronged with mothers and nannies. Where Gwen and Julia crossed, two black Range Rovers and a black Jeep were double-parked, badly, the traffic crawling up the hill behind this presidential convoy in their variously armored vehicles. And babies were every-where. In buggies and in slings, or toddling on reins attached to tiny backpacks, greeting older siblings at the school gates. Julia averted her eyes from this sea of tiny creatures, but as they walked she reached for Gwen's arm. This school uniform was royal blue. At primary school Gwen's had been red, almost, but not quite, as bright as her hair.

THEY WERE TOILING UP the hill toward the art supply shop. Gwen had not known if her mother would agree to this extension of their outing, but she did not feel ready to go straight home, where nowa-days they could never be alone. It had been Dr. Frankel who'd sug-gested (in desperation, Gwen felt, after several other conversational dead ends) that mother and daughter spend more time together on activities that made them happy, and there was nowhere that brought Gwen as much joy as this paradise of pristine dyes and clay, and the promise of future projects. She did not know with any certainty which activities made her mother happy. Maybe playing the piano? A knot tightened in her stomach. Until recently, she had always believed that

Julia's happiness lay simply in spending time with her, regardless of what they did—certainly that was what she'd always said. But in the last few days, Julia could barely look at her.

The remainder of the therapy session had not been an enormous success. Initially she'd felt her mother's presence hampered her ability to defend herself with any eloquence, but after Julia had gone Gwen felt a sudden tender homesickness, and a longing to rush out to the waiting room and beg forgiveness for dismissing her. She hadn't wanted Julia herself to go away, only Julia's disapproval and disappointment. After that, guilt had stifled her and made her feel hot and snappish, and she had shut down the rest of Dr. Frankel's valiant approaches. She had not deserved the professional kindness palpable in that room.

Now mother and daughter walked up the hill in silence. As they crossed Prince Arthur Road, Julia reached out for her and they walked the rest of the way arm in arm, and though neither spoke, Gwen began to feel a slight easing of the pressure in her chest. She shuffled a little, shortening her gait to keep pace. On the threshold of the shop they separated. Gwen held the door open, shy, chivalrous. They made their way through Painting and Drawing, over to the temple's inner sanctum, Casting and Modeling.

"So what are we looking for?"

Gwen shrugged. "Dunno. Just browsing." She frowned over a package of "skin tones" polymer clay with professional interest. She had been mixing her own flesh tones for years—this overpriced multipack was for amateurs. But next to it stood a tray of wire-tipped modeling tools with sleek wooden handles, and on one of these she pounced, turning it over and over between her fingers as if rolling a cigar. It was sixteen pounds, an enormous sum. But it was double ended and one tip, the needle, would be useful every day. Future promise lay in all these wares, the world a bit less lonely when she could sculpt and share it. She fished in the pocket of her cardigan for her purse.

"Mum."

"Yes?"

"Do you still hate me?"

Julia looked stricken and Gwen felt fractionally heartened. Hope unfurled and blossomed when her mother reached to stroke her cheek.

"I could never hate you, my darling; you're the most precious thing in my world. You know that."

Gwen nodded uncertainly, the cuticle of her little finger between her front teeth. After a moment she fingered a packet of frog-green modeling clay. "I'm going to use this to make that massive green cactus thing in her office. I mean, that was so weird. It was like this giant looming *thing*."

Julia smiled. "It was rather phallic."

Gwen began to giggle. "And it had massive spikes!"

"I wonder what a Freudian would make of that."

Laughter overtook them both, drawing looks of disapproval from the checkout girl. Julia covered her mouth, then turned away. A sob rose in her chest and she swallowed it down. Enough. For healing and for sanity, all that would have to end. She wiped her eyes, took a breath, and turned back, resolute. Gwen's giggles petered out, uncertain.

Julia took Gwen's hand between her own. She raised it to her lips and kissed her daughter's dry knuckles, above the mulberry-colored hearts and black stars that Gwen had idly inked upon the back of each finger.

"My darling, what do you really want? What does your gut tell you?"

Gwen looked down at her mother and blinked, steadily. She said, no longer confrontational, but as calmly as she knew how, "I have to keep my baby," and her all-powerful condemning possessive made possible no other answer. Julia put her arms around her hunched, gangling little girl.

part three

32.

IRIS SWEPT GWEN AND KATY UPSTAIRS INTO HER BEDROOM, where the beveled-glass doors of the empty, lilac-papered wardrobes gaped open and the windows were now uncurtained. Bonfire heaps of clothing lay on the bed, on the floor, on the armchair, and on one bedside table stood a tower of small white boxes ominously printed in red with the words MOTH KILLER. Each pile had been labeled with torn sheets of lined paper on which Iris had written queries and imperatives such as "Charity?" "Keep!" "Do Not Throw!" "Maybe for summer?" "Gwendolen?" in her tense, listing copperplate.

"You may take anything except from that chair; those I still wear. And if you would like anything from that heap by the wall, then please show me first; there are a few pieces for your mother; the trousers would be far too short for you in any case. I can't wait to see the back of it all. I feel freer and freer as this exercise advances, I ought to have moved years ago." She swept her arms out wide, a conductor acknowledging her orchestra. "Anything you don't want just pop into that empty box over there to take to Norwood, with a few sachets of the moth murderer. I'm scrupulous but it would be mortifying to infect the charity shop."

Gwen looked over at the cartons uncertainly. On each was printed a red bull's-eye and a rigid insect, various legs radiating in odd directions as it suffered electrocution or rigor mortis. "I don't think I should touch moth-murdering stuff, Granny, it might be toxic."

"As you wish," said Iris, tightly. She turned to Katy. "The world seems filled with gestational hazards these days. When I was pregnant with Gwen's father I was desperate to go to Vietnam and everyone was terribly difficult about it, worrying about stress and helicopters and gas, and nonsense like that. I'd never actually *been* a foreign correspondent; in truth I don't really know what came over me but I was suddenly longing to go and it was still early days but it was clear that that was where the action was, especially after the Gulf of Tonkin. Of course the paper wouldn't have it. I told them, my husband is my obstetrician and he says there's no reason why not, women have babies in Vietnam, one's *brain* still functions after all, but then they gave me my column and that suited me far better in any case. And Philip Alden was awfully good about my wanting to go but of course men are always happier to have one stay at home, whatever they say."

Katy tucked her hair behind her ears, smiling in admiration and with an evident fear that she might be required to respond intelligently about Vietnam, or pregnancy, or men. "Yes," she said, dark eyes blinking. "Gosh. You were so brave."

"Women must be brave, Katy darling, if we are to achieve anything at all. Cowardice and skinlessness are the enemies of female success. If one cares at all what others think, one's done for. In any case, there will be crumpets in the bread bin when you pause. Assuming," this to Gwen, "that your mother hasn't done another wonderfully officious sweep around my kitchen and packed the bread bin. When you have a cache call me up."

Alone in the bedroom, the girls exchanged incredulous glances. Iris had always had exquisite taste, even in the days in which she and Philip had been supporting his parents as well as managing their own mortgage, and she had kept almost everything. Already Gwen could see two BIBA dresses, one in burgundy, the other lilac jersey, and, from a still earlier era, a yellow poplin blouse with an oversized Peter Pan collar. A vision of her future self arose—she could become stylish and eclectic and enviable, and could sashay to school next year in lace and silks. By then she would have an unimaginable new life, and a new, more sophisticated wardrobe seemed only fitting.

They began clearing the bed. Ruthlessly they discarded cotton shirts and office slacks. Then Gwen unearthed a boxy sweater in pale peach mohair and moments later Katy held up a slippery fuchsia blouse which Gwen, who did not wear pink, said she should keep.

"So how long will you be able to wear normal clothes?" Katy asked, folding the blouse with care. Gwen had confided in her only a week ago, swearing her to secrecy, and they had talked exclusively and exhaustively of the pregnancy ever since.

"Dunno, forever probably, because I'm so insanely tall. I don't want to tell anyone at school till the end of term. My mum will tell the teachers then, and start planning next year and stuff."

"Is there anything at all yet? Like, a minibump?"

Gwen lifted up her sweater and Katy peered speculatively.

"Nothing, you're still superskinny. It's just so crazy. I think it will feel more real once you *look* pregnant. Is Nathan getting excited?"

"It's a bit early for all that," said Gwen, suddenly vexed. She pulled down her sweater and returned her attention to the bed. This was a provocation from Katy, she felt, who was well aware that excitement had been thin on the ground in the Alden-Fuller household. In any case, how could anyone be expected to get excited about something more than half a year away? She dropped a belt into a pile of rejects.

"I'll take that if you don't like it."

Gwen handed her the belt, and then returned in silence to her own heap. Katy's questions always pertained to Nathan—how did he feel, what did he want, would he "stand by" her—closed-minded Katy had instantly reverted to the language of another century. Gwen had had to explain that pregnancy happened to two people, it was not for a woman to be "stood by" or otherwise, and that she and Nathan were in total accord. This last may have been a slight exaggeration for he had so far resisted her attempts to bring him round to the idea of fatherhood, even in the abstract. The last few times they'd talked he'd grown panicked, twice had cried, and each time, to comfort and convince him, she assumed a depth of conviction she did not feel. But unlike the parents he never seemed angry, nor did he seem to blame her. Something had befallen them both, and he said he believed she was trying to make the best of it, even if his best and hers were not (yet?) in concert. He was still her boyfriend. Relations between them improved when she realized that all he wanted was to discuss it as little as possible; if she adhered to that stipulation, everything continued between them, if not exactly, then almost as before. That morning she had taken time away from her own work to bake raspberry and white chocolate muffins that might fuel his; he had eaten three and lifted her heart by declaring them (and herself, she inferred, by proxy) "awesome, thanks." When he was home he no longer chided her nor even seemed to notice if she played with her phone or doodled blog designs on the corners of her notes and this, conversely, encouraged her to focus in order to win back his notice. At first his disengagement had unsteadied her but she knew him, and knew how it would be. He would be incredible, once it became necessary for him to be incredible. The male instinct was to deal with what lay immediately ahead; he had exams and university decisions and these were all-consuming. Nine months of pregnancy would take them to Christmas; it was now only May. Katy had sworn secrecy and support and undying friendship, but today she was filled with irrelevant, childish questions, and Gwen had begun to wish she had not told her.

"It is actually ages, isn't it? I guess you found out majorly early." Katy was twirling a glossy lock of dark hair round and round the end of her nose, thinking. Then she ventured, "Aren't you scared? You must be, a bit."

"I'm really not. I'm just excited to meet my baby."

An opportunity offered, and rejected. Katy recognized the lie, for behind her eyes Gwen saw a willing empathy shut down; instead, disappointment that she, long-trusted, wasn't to be trusted now. Katy would have said, "I *know*," she would have stroked Gwen's hair and said again, stoutly, *You'll be wonderful, you're doing the right thing. It's natural to have wobbles, it doesn't mean you're making the wrong choice.* No one else would offer this reassurance. But how could Gwen confess that she struggled to focus upon what would inevitably follow this pregnancy? It was there in her peripheral vision, but when she turned her head it slipped away like a phantom and her mind would skip elsewhere, distracted, relieved. Far easier to daydream about how her classmates might react upon finding out, about how she might look by late summer, a neat, startling bump, a badge of distinction; a commanding unequivocal sign of adult womanhood. It was the pregnancy for which she had fought. What must come next—a baby, motherhood—was hazier, and harder to comprehend. Ludicrous, even. But to admit fear was to admit doubt, and if she admitted her doubts aloud, she knew, her outward conviction might crumble.

Katy held up a polka-dotted handkerchief, a peace offering. "This is megacute; maybe you could put this on the baby's head, like a bandana. It's all just so crazy. You have to tell me everything. I want to know every single thing."

"Then stop talking so seriously about everything," said Gwen crossly. But then she relented and said, "Obviously I'll tell you everything. But you'll see, so you'll know it all anyway."

"I told you I'll come every day on my way home, I'll be, like, the fun auntie. And I want to come with you when you have scans, and help you buy things and get ready and everything."

"I feel sick again, I'm sitting down. You can hold stuff up and show me." Gwen sank heavily into the armchair, on top of an untouched pile of coats. It helped to imagine a future with Katy always there, involved. With her friend by her side it would be far less frightening to do whatever needed doing.

They worked on, exclaiming intermittently about gems found and horrors unearthed. At the back of a wardrobe Gwen spotted a small, scratched leather suitcase and she humped this onto the duvet. Katy was holding up a pair of white silk trousers when Iris herself appeared and took these from her reverentially. She wore a misty-eyed expression, as if an old lover's photograph had slipped from the pages of a battered paperback.

"I bought those on holiday in Nice one summer. I'll keep them, I might wear those again. Ah, I have heard the mermaids singing, each to each, though they're not flannel, thank God, they're Pierre Cardin.

Where on earth did you find that case? You've no reason to concern yourself with that," she snapped, laying down the trousers, but Gwen, who considered her grandmother's presence to be sufficient permission, had already clicked open the thick brass buckle. The lid of the suitcase flopped back to reveal its torn and faded paisley-print lining, and six neat stacks of pressed and folded baby clothes.

"Granny!" Gwen breathed. "Were those Dad's? Oh, *please* can I have them?"

"Absolutely not," said Iris, firmly, but was met by imploring looks from both girls, and a quivering lower lip from her granddaughter.

"No. Oh—*fine*. But I'd like to be clear that this does not constitute endorsement. Katy, I have not yet heard your opinion on the matter but I shall tell you for the record that I believe continuing with this pregnancy to be an act of self-sabotaging imbecility on my granddaughter's behalf, as she well knows. You may keep them if you insist. Lord knows what's in there. Your father's baby clothes, a baby blanket, and if I recall, an elaborately hideous collection of rather itchy cardigans knitted by Philip Alden's mother, who had, as you will soon see, a great deal too much time on her hands." She turned to go. "I sincerely hope if they do anything, they drive home a little reality. Those are clothes for a human, not a plaything. I am displeased."

It was Katy who a moment later was wiping away tears and this decided Gwen's own course of emotional action, till then uncertain. She had many precious artifacts, but it had been so long since she'd unearthed something new of her father's. A lump had risen in her own throat, but when she saw Katy crying she said firmly, "Don't be silly." Her father as an infant had not yet been her father; these were adorable but did not represent a person she could reasonably miss. She put her arm around her friend and realized, with a pounding heart, that it was possibly her first spontaneously maternal gesture.

Katy nodded and sniffed, wiping invisible mascara smears from beneath each eye with her ring fingers. "I'm sorry. It's just, it's so nice. You might have pictures of your Dad in some of these little outfits, and I just thought that when your baby comes you can take the same pictures, and—and that's really special. Oh, no, Gwen, please don't cry, I'm so sorry, please don't cry. They're beautiful. They're happy, as you said."

They sat for a moment with their arms around each other. Gwen reached out reverentially to stroke a tiny playsuit in smocked white cotton, uneven mother-of-pearl buttons down its front. It was utterly unthinkable that a human was at that moment gestating within her, and would one day grow to fit these garments. Her throat constricted. She did not want to picture plump limbs within these tiny sleeves, nor the hot monkey cling of a tiny body. She wiped her nose inelegantly on her sleeve and said, "I have to tell my mum, like, now, she'll be so shocked that there's stuff she hasn't seen, she's going to freak. And look at these, they're so gorgeous. I hope she's okay, she gets upset about my dad, you know. If she comes straight over when I text her and she's supersad, do you mind hanging out with my granny just for a bit? Just for like, ten minutes?"

Katy said that of course she wouldn't mind, Gwen's granny was fantastic, but that she would soon have to go in any case. Actually now, in fact. This had become urgently, pressingly true ever since Katy had seen those tiny, yellowing clothes, museum faded, inert, as lifeless as the man who'd once worn them. She was desperate to get on the Tube back to Totteridge where her own father, full-bellied and balding and a hale and hearty forty-five, would be there to give her a hug and to promise her, Scouts' honor, that he wouldn't die. Gwen's suitcase of Gothic, desiccating sleep suits, like the dead husks of abandoned snakeskins, was intensely distressing.

"It's a sign," Katy said firmly, retrieving her own sweater from beneath a pile of pillows. "Even if your granny didn't want you to, your dad meant you to find them; even though he passed away he's looking over you and the baby."

Gwen said, "Mmm," not very convincingly. She loathed such specific and improbable states as "looking over," which evoked a nosy neighbor peering over a picket fence. She also disliked "a sign," and particularly "passed away," the latter because she felt it sounded somehow passive and a little foolish, as if her father had accidentally missed an exit on the motorway when, if anything, to die was to take the ultimate definitive action. And she did not like to have the pregnancy connected to her father. She had tried to tell herself he would be proud of her for choosing a hard, brave path but still, it seemed unlikely he'd go so far as to send gift baskets from on high. The only person who understood the delicate vocabulary of her bereavement was her mother. Gwen needed urgently to speak to Julia. The girls parted, with equal relief. As soon as she could hear Katy downstairs taking polite leave of Iris, Gwen picked up her phone.

It rang, and rang. Gwen hung up and immediately called back. Where was her mother? And why couldn't she sense, as of old, that she was needed? Gwen threw her phone onto the bed. The endless steady nausea was insupportable. Without Katy she no longer had the motivation to continue, and she felt hot, and teary, and possibly in need of a nap. She would take her treasures home, and she would wash them and iron them herself, and keep them in her room and she wouldn't allow her treacherous mother even to look at them. They were precious, and she could not let them frighten her with intimations of a flesh-and-blood reality to come. Julia did not deserve such relics. She was building a new life, and Gwen must do the same.

33.

"THIS IS NO GOOD, YOU KNOW. BY THE TIME WE REACH THE front it will have started," Iris complained, shifting irritably from one foot to the other and peering around the group in front of them, searching for the source of the delay. She was with Philip at the O2 Centre cinema on Finchley Road, waiting in line to buy their tickets for a documentary he was keen to see, about whales. "Wales?" Iris had asked, puzzled, and Philip had clarified. On the assumption that an independently made wildlife documentary was unlikely to cause a box office stampede they had not booked in advance, but when they arrived the line snaked disconsolately around a Pac-Man configuration of security barriers. Iris glanced again at her watch.

"I don't think it matters a great deal if we miss five minutes. We know the gist."

"You know the gist. Until five minutes ago I thought it was about scaling Snowdon."

"If you prefer, we could go downstairs to one of the places for some supper?"

Iris wrinkled her nose in distaste, as if he had suggested they forage for their dinner in the shopping center dustbins. "Can't we go somewhere civilized every now and again? Coming to the pictures here is one thing but it's not exactly a culinary destination. In any case, I've utterly lost my appetite. This morning has quite literally sickened me. I feel ill."

"Gwen seems—"

"Gwen is behaving like the stubborn infant that she is, and the most heartbreaking part is that she's so pleased with herself, and all the while she's careening toward a cliff; you should have seen her cooing over those baby clothes. She's overjoyed to be the center of attention and what she doesn't realize is that she's simply ensuring in about seven months she will never be the center of attention again. And that friend of hers is sweet enough but utterly air-headed and childish."

"Well, they're children, so if they're a little childish, you'll have to let them off."

"I'd feel more comfortable if she had some contemporaries with a brain cell between them. Peer pressure ought to be what changes her mind. If she had some friends with a little ambition she would have made entirely different choices. If Julia had sent her to a decent school—"

"She's got a wonderful mother. And a kind stepfather. And us."

"She'll need more than just us."

They shuffled forward, the queue diminished by several faint-hearted patrons abandoning their positions, rather than any real progress at the tills. Iris tutted and moved her handbag from one shoulder to the other. "Really, you would have thought the elderly ought not to have to stand around like this. That someone might let them— Oh, thank you so much. Yes, thank you. That's very kind. Come on," she commanded, striding forward, "Thank you, yes. Thanks. Now's the time to say if we're seeing this or not. Quick. Marine life, or we could give up and call it a night. Perhaps we should call it a night."

"We're almost there."

"I know, but I think I'm too depressed for fish. There are not one but *three* obstetric practitioners in Gwen's immediate family circle; I cannot understand how this was allowed to happen. How was it not put right, having happened? It's derangement. It's a tragedy. How am I expected to care about whales?" She had become grandly theatrical, which was a bad sign. But they had reached the front of the line, and the moment had come to decide.

"I know. I do—we can give it a miss if you'd like."

"I'm very tired," said Iris, which was true, but an uncharacteristic admission of fallibility. She stepped aside, back into the cheery mezzanine of the shopping center. Philip followed her, apologizing to a number of other patrons who had ceded their places to them.

They rode the escalators in silence. Then Iris said, hotly, as if he had contradicted her, "It's a *travesty*. Gwen doesn't deserve—she's an innocent. She's an innocent and she has no idea, absolutely not the faintest idea, what's about to happen to her life. She thinks she'll have a dolly and all this gratifying attention she's commanded will go on and on, and instead her life is going to be torn limb from limb by ravening—I was going to offer anyway but if she nips it in the bud, then I've told Julia I'll put her through art school. Tuition, accommodation, extra for blackmail, whatever it takes." She stepped off at the bottom of the escalator and with an irritable gesture offered Philip a hand to disembark, which was accepted without comment. "Are you walking or am I driving you?"

"You're driving me if you wouldn't mind. Of course it's a very generous idea, if they'd like it."

"They're a bunch of ostriches, and I'm including the so-called adults in this situation. Mass inertia. Needless. *Needless.* And if she really goes through with this entirely dishonorable kamikaze maneuver, I'm going to hire and subvention a nanny myself." Iris began to hunt in her handbag for her car keys and Philip felt suddenly relieved to be going home. The whales could wait. He was weary, and Iris was in a dangerous temper.

"Do you remember that Italian au pair?" he asked, hoping to draw her back from the brink. It was sometimes possible to soften her, with care. "May I hold your umbrella? You'll have a hand free. She was a nice girl. It was very helpful having someone."

"Gioia. She was a bloody idiot," said Iris, shortly. She had located the keys and set off at a clip into the dark parking lot. Philip strained to keep up, his knees singing in protest as he marched stiffly behind her, the umbrella angled forward to shield Iris from the drizzle. A moment later she drew to an abrupt halt.

"Where is the bloody car?"

"Over there, I think. She was only homesick, wasn't she? Daniel liked her, which was what mattered. She was good with him."

"She left me high and dry, five minutes before I was due to join you in Paris for the weekend. Can you hold that thing a little higher; it's starting again. She was a selfish little girl. Ah, I see it there, thank goodness for the beeper thing. Giles had to bring Daniel out on his way to Bargemon."

"Giles had to—what?" Philip slowed. He struggled to recall a summer, a weekend many years ago, a story from their canon of cherished stories. We were happy: here is Exhibit A. He lowered the umbrella, which was hurting his wrist. "She brought him to us in Paris on her way to Naples. Gioia."

"She was meant to, yes."

"I don't understand."

"Oh, darling, it just didn't line up." Iris glanced at him, impatient or possibly wary. She seized the umbrella and held it rigidly upright in both hands. "There was a coach that left from London and she was absolutely adamant about making her parents' wedding anniversary or some nonsense. It all ended on bad terms because she was a fool and I was cross and then I was absolutely in a fix. I couldn't leave the boy to travel by himself on the ferry."

"Well, of course not but— I don't entirely understand. You left him with Giles, is that what you're saying? When you came to Paris?"

Iris had begun to walk again but Philip didn't move, and she was forced to turn around to address him. She had begun to look indignant. "Yes, Philip, there's no need to sound so outraged; that's what I did. On balance it was expedient. You and I had had that awful row before you left and then you'd written a sweet letter about the two days you'd planned for us and I didn't think I ought to let you down. It's raining; can we talk about this in the car? Well, come and stand under this bloody umbrella then. Oh, *really*. Things were feeling a little unsteady. And it wasn't even a change of anyone's plans at all in the end; Giles just drove a slightly longer route to Bargemon; he was coming to France anyway. I couldn't exactly leave Daniel with the au pair when there was no au pair to leave him with. Look, I didn't want to cancel, and Giles offered to help me out of a fix and that was that. Why do you look so cross? He took his charge very seriously, I assure you; they had a wonderful time. Daniel told me all about it."

Philip rubbed his eyes, slowly, and did not look up. "You lied to me."

Iris could think of no appropriate answer, for she and Giles had both lied to Philip a hundred times over the years, mostly about sex at parties or on assignments or for weekends in the Cotswolds, or late nights at work. She had always assumed Philip had taken for granted these many small deceptions. Calculating now, she realized that this revelation dated her affair with Giles long before it might otherwise have been suspected. Certainly years before the official record.

"You and Giles lied to me," Philip repeated.

"It was only— This is madness, you and Giles were great friends later on. Please get under the thing."

"You made my son lie to me."

"Well, darling, there were other little white lies flying around in those days." She halted, suddenly uncertain. This was dangerously close to heresy in the sealed, private world they'd spun; she was in high winds, and playing precariously near to the cliff edge. The enchantment had kept them safe for almost five decades, a flexible, devoted love and companionship, enfolded in a cloak of tacit understanding. She fell silent. The rules were the rules.

Philip said again, "You made Daniel lie to me. He was a little boy. You put a lie between me and my son."

"We had such a wonderful time that holiday, the three of us," Iris said, weakly. Philip's voice had broken as he spoke this last, awful, and surely disproportionate accusation; she felt a tickle of panic that he had so misunderstood. "He adored you, how can you think that anything could come between you."

"Iris." There was a pause as he removed his glasses, streaked and beaded with raindrops, flashing amber and saffron in the reflected light of slow-passing headlights.

"Better you had stayed with Giles," he said, quietly. "Better some truth, finally, so there would be no, no *wound* between me and my son. Better anything than distance with my son, than a lie between us. He must have been so bewildered and you colluded with him, you and Giles, and made his father into a— I don't know, I don't know, I don't understand. And Daniel isn't here. He isn't here for me to tell him not to worry." He took several steps backward, unsteadily, away from her.

"We'll talk more in the car; come on," said Iris, turning decisively. "Darling, this is madness, he was a child, he'd forgotten it by the time he'd had a crepe and seen a little of Paris." She felt perilously close to a full-blown row, something that had not happened, she realized, since the day they'd finally signed their divorce papers. Or perhaps not since the day he had shouted at her for shouting at Julia for wearing black to Daniel's funeral. In any case, she couldn't stand to see him standing in this downpour, could not bear the way the rain had plastered his fine, white hair to his scalp, the way fat drops slipped down his cheeks like tears. Without glasses he looked vulnerable, and very old. How could Philip Alden be so old? He should not be out in this weather, at this time. She put her head down and strode the few remaining steps to draw him with her into the car. She turned on the engine, the heater, the heated seats. The first thing was to get him warm and dry, and then she could explain. But he had not followed her.

34.

IT DID NOT SEEM FAIR TO INVOLVE JAMES IN HER MOTHER-IN-law's unexpected packing but James presumed himself involved, and Julia was grateful. Whatever mattered to Julia was drawn without question into the inner circle of James's concern, a way of his she'd noticed and admired, early on. In any case, without his and Nathan's assistance the team would comprise only tiny, slender Julia herself, arthritic and unsteady Philip, and a queasy and evermore distractible Gwen, who at present did everything with irritating, self-satisfied lassitude. No doubt she would find several opportunities throughout the day to remind them that she couldn't lift heavy objects because she was pregnant, she couldn't join them for too many coffees or cups of tea because she was pregnant, she couldn't leave them a moment's peace to forget she was pregnant, because she was pregnant. For lightening the load and the atmosphere they needed James, even if no one else in the family would admit it.

The furniture would go with professional movers the following day, which was the formal date of sale, but there remained the *stuff*: velvet cushions the removal men were not permitted to touch; framed prints and pictures; three drawers of splitting Kodak photograph packets spilling muddled, slippery negatives; a great deal of musty, unused but beautifully pressed table linen; a white archive box of ancient telephones, from a black, midnineties cordless all the way back to an avocado Bakelite rotary, which enchanted Gwen. Supermarket bags of unidentifiable wires and chargers for items long discarded. Shadeless lamps in which expired bulbs wore a gray fuzz cap of static dust. A printer. A scanner. A cumbersome fax machine of sickly oat-colored plastic with which Iris could not be enjoined to part, though it transpired that she only exchanged faxes with Philip, whom she also e-mailed, texted, and instant messaged. Box files containing hundreds of sallow, fading newspapers in which Iris had a byline. And books, and books, and books. Iris had supposedly been sorting and packing (certainly she had made frequent reference to her toils) and yet the house looked discouragingly unaltered. It had been the Alden family home in one configuration or another for decades. Julia had known of her mother-in-law's intentions for barely a fortnight, and this final exodus was supposed to be accomplished in a day.

"They'll do it all tomorrow if we add a few more hours to the booking," Julia ventured for the final time. She, James, Nathan, and Gwen had arrived early as planned, armed with tape dispensers and scissors and marker pens, but she still nurtured the wild hope that Iris would permit the professional movers to do it all, and they could instead go to South End Green for eggs Benedict and cappuccinos. The man on the phone had quoted for the lot. They were thorough, he told her, she needn't lift a finger. His boys even packed the toilet paper off the holder, don't you worry, love. Iris was having none of it. Boxes and bubble wrap had already been delivered.

"Darling, I won't have unknown gentlemen fishing around in my possessions," trilled Gwen. Everyone laughed except James, who would not, Julia knew, have dared even to smile at Iris's expense. Instead he rolled up his sleeves and began to construct the flat-packed cardboard boxes that were leaning in the hallway.

"Well, I won't," Iris said, with an elegant and unapologetic shrug. She had dressed for the occasion in black slacks and a narrow-ribbed black cashmere sweater with a high turtleneck, unseen since the early years of their acquaintance. Unfamiliar enameled bangles in cobalt and emerald clinked on her knobbed, narrow wrists—clearly this move had unearthed some long-lost, once-loved treasures. "It would be ghastly to have them poking about. They'd manhandle everything and mix it all up and break things. I'd really much rather the family did it." She kissed Julia, embraced Gwen, and gave James a dry and unprecedented peck on the cheek. Julia felt briefly touched, until she remembered that Iris must also realize that James's presence was essential. "Is Philip here yet?" she asked, prompted to remember the sweetest and most ludicrous manual laborer among them.

Iris kicked off neat, black pumps and stalked back to the kitchen. Julia and Gwen followed her. "Philip Alden's not here at present. Shall we start upstairs? Or here? Shall I make us some tea?"

Gwen sagged into a kitchen chair. "It's *so* hot," she said, which was true for no one except herself. "I'm roasting." She pulled her sweater over her head and fanned herself. Julia averted her eyes in irritation. On the phone earlier Iris had made an unforgivable joke about giving Gwen the heaviest trunks to lift.

Iris nodded. "Very well. Why don't you label boxes for us; that's a good, nonstrenuous task. But you'll need to ask me as you go along, because the most important thing is to mark clearly the name of the room it's headed for, or it will all end up in the hallway there and be nightmarish. The rest of us can start in the bedroom, I've prepared piles. I'm rather pleased with my winnowing; there's a vast heap of *objets* to go to Norwood."

"Shouldn't the writing be Philip's job? Maybe Gwen can fold things. He's been terribly elusive, by the way, is he alright? He's not answering my calls."

"I'm sure he's right as rain. I didn't want to trouble him with all this; he's not coming. He can't lift anything anyway; he'd have been less than useless and got under our feet. And he hates me throwing anything away. We'd only have rowed."

Julia started to say that she was sure Philip would nonetheless want to be included, but something in her mother-in-law's expression cautioned her, and she stopped.

"I don't see that it should take all that long if we're efficient. If you'll all come up with me, perhaps someone could dismantle the computer, and then we'll start at the top."

"I can do the computer, Granny."

Gwen set off, and in the hall could be heard to inform Nathan that they were all to begin at the top of the house. Julia began to tidy the kitchen, which was strewn on all surfaces with piles of bills and letters beneath yellow sticky notes. On the kitchen table was a stack of hardbacks in various conditions, *Lucky Jim, Women in Love, The Rainbow, Anna Karenina, Les Fleurs du Mal.* Julia ran her fingers over their spines.

"Giles's. They're all first or early editions. I thought I'd give them to Camilla." Camilla was Giles's daughter, a journalist who lived in Brighton and kept urban chickens in an egg-shaped fiberglass hutch in her tiny backyard.

"That's thoughtful."

"She's got most of his others, they ought all to be together. He left his collection here, moldering in my office when he moved to France—oh, don't be so childish, when he *actually* moved to France. I kept saying he ought to take them; after all, why own them if you don't look at them? But he insisted I be custodian, and then he filled that house with cheap paperbacks instead. Typical Giles," she finished, fondly.

"Shall we post these or is she coming up soon?"

"Just pop them aside, I don't think we ought to trust them to Royal Mail, not that I wouldn't willingly see Lawrence dispatched into oblivion. We'll carry them loose." These last were the ominous words Iris had spoken about a great many possessions. Julia imagined a column of hundreds of people moving like a line of toiling ants from Parliament Hill to the new flat, each ferrying one teaspoon or a single mug.

"How much is actually packed?"

"Oh, there's barely anything left, I've worked and worked. Look, I'll show you." Iris tripped lightly across the kitchen and flung open the pantry door to reveal a tower of neatly taped brown boxes. Julia felt a wave of relief.

"Shall I start taking these out? James found a parking space right outside. It might be good to get things out of the house."

"That would be lovely, darling, and now I must go and supervise; God knows what the children are doing with my belongings. I'll send

Thing to help you with your labors." Iris then swept out, and Julia surveyed the contents of the pantry. P.A.'S BOOKS, was scrawled across the top of one box. P.A.'S CLOTHES. P.A.'S MED. TEXTBKS. P.A.'S TENNIS R. AND SPORTSWR. P.A.'S PAPERS. And on the side of each the words, SECOND BEDROOM. SECOND BEDROOM. SECOND BEDROOM.

35

A BRIEF MOMENT OF RESPITE. JAMES AT WORK, THE DELIN-
quent, enervating, relentless children at school, and Julia alone in the
house, alone with her own thoughts and alone, finally, with her piano.
No students until four p.m. A few days ago James had come home
with some Nigel Hess sheet music for her, a piece he adored, but she
had not yet taken it from its bag. Of late, her free hours had been
spent envisaging various calamitous paths Gwen's life might take as
a teenage mother, and plotting every possible contingency. Now, turning the pages in silence, she felt her blood slow. Time contracted and
folded in upon itself; in this stillness worry lifted, fractionally. This
was the reason for James's gift—to coax her back to a pleasure she
had been too guilty and frantic to permit herself. It would last, she
knew, only as long as the concerto. But here on this bright, silent afternoon, here was meditation and repair.

By the end of the year she would be a grandmother. A grandmother! Only in the last days had she forced herself to envisage it, as
it felt right and necessary to confront what lay ahead. Gwen had made

her decision and from now on, Julia resolved, would have no cause to doubt her support. She would bury her fear, and her anxiety. She no longer discussed alternatives. She and James had made a conscious decision to alter their language, and to help one another come to terms with what lay ahead. They would try not to call it "a disaster," "a nightmare," "an accident" (at least not too often) but to say, instead, "a baby." For that was what the nightmare would become. Another person in their family by Christmas.

There had been years in which the longing for another child had consumed her. She had tormented Daniel with it until eventually he'd decreed that for their marriage they must draw a line, must formalize their contentment with their funny, mischievous little Gwen, and Julia had wept silently and had assented, continuing, in secret, to chart her ovulation, to take her temperature, to hope against hope. All that spilled and needless grief for an imagined, unknown soul, and all the while wasting precious, jeweled seconds with the real little girl around whom her whole world turned. Wailing for a paper cut on her fingertip while a fat, vermillion clot slid closer and closer to her heart.

And then James, and happiness, so many years later. Loneliness ended. She had surfaced from the submersion of parenthood and filled her lungs. Who could bear to begin all that again? She had found passion and peace and a future with a man she loved, this time not for the children he would give her but deeply and purely for his own soul. James was all she wanted, and more than she'd ever dreamed.

She watched her own hands moving lightly on the keys. Green veins visible through fragile pale skin, a broken blood vessel between the third and forth knuckle of her right hand. Nails cut short for the piano. They would soon be the hands of a grandmother. The whole household would be beginning all over again, like it or not. James had swept into her life and made her feel young and hopeful, and in an instant Gwen had once again reminded her she was ancient. She turned the music back to the first page and began to play.

The phone ringing came as an otherworldly intrusion, and she answered only to make it stop. There was a scrabbling sound and then Iris, panting and shrill: "Julia! Thank God."

Julia roused herself unwillingly from the treacle depths of the second movement—the pure, sweeping romance, its grand and unapologetic sentiment. When she raised the handset her own damp cheek surprised her; she had not known she had been crying.

"Are you alright?"

"No, I am absolutely not alright. I am the opposite of alright. I am absolutely— This is intolerable, and your concealment is unforgivable, after all our confidences—"

"Iris, hold on, what are you talking about?"

"He's seeing somebody!"

"What?"

"He's met someone. He's got a secret good-time girl, and I don't know who the hell you think you're protecting by playing ignorant but I know everything. I've just driven past him on Hampstead High Street having coffee with some ghastly, trashy, dumpy blonde and holding hands."

It was as if she'd had a whiskey and a Valium on a night flight, and was now being shaken urgently awake in order to pilot the plane. Julia blinked and tried to focus. Her eyes moved forward through the music, still listening. She closed the pages and looked down.

"Was it Valentina? He's back at school; he shouldn't be anywhere near the High Street. Please don't tell me—"

"What? Who in God's name is Valentina? Why didn't you tell me?"

"Nathan's ex-girlfriend. Italian. Fake blonde. Bit trashy, as you say. But they can't have been holding hands, were they? Seriously?"

"Whose— What the hell are you talking about? Philip Alden's on the High Street with a woman. And don't tell me you don't know, I've no doubt you've all been cozy as ever whilst I've been sent to Coventry for something trivial from the Stone Age. Who is she?"

"Philip? I don't know anything, honestly, I've no idea—and we've not seen him at all, he's all but disappeared on me. He's in touch with Gwen; I know they e-mail, that's it. The first time I'd seen him in ages was the other day and I suppose he was being a bit mysterious but I was so distracted and we only talked about Gwen . . . I did see someone dropping him off, but—"

"Blonde?" Iris demanded, "Moplike corkscrews of yellow sheep's wool? Outrageous, greasy dark roots? Fat? Clad in *jeans*?" This last spat like poison, as if jeans on such a person were tantamount to an SS uniform.

"I didn't see her legs, she was driving. But yes, curly blonde hair. I don't know who she is, I assumed she was a neighbor giving him a lift."

"Well, they looked very neighborly indeed just now. Very neighborly. My God, the man's a quick worker. Although for all I know it's been *years*—"

"You sound upset. Come round, where are you?"

"I am not upset!" Iris roared, "I am incredulous. I am at home—ha! How ludicrous. It's a travesty to use that word to describe this sterile, anonymous green-carpeted brassy wasteland of a building. I am in the spare room of my spare new abode. I'm in Room 101 of my sanitized, elevator-enhanced, elderly-friendly, Finchley-Road-accessible, joyless, white-walled jumbo-sized coffin. I'm in a box, surrounded by boxes. I'm *filed*."

"Come over, get a taxi. Come."

"I'd like you to tell me why in God's name I am living in this purgatorial block if he doesn't need me to? Why, may I ask you, am I here? Why, if not to care for Philip Alden in his dotage, did I sell my beloved house with all its very *challenging stairs*?" Iris shrieked, with climactic hysteria. Julia struggled with this series of questions and the nested series of revelations embedded within them. Iris had only ever mentioned wanting financial freedom to enable Gwen's future; Julia had not understood that Philip's, too, had been planned for and secured, had possibly weighed more heavily on Iris's conscience even than her granddaughter's. Yet several things now made sense—the urgency with which she'd sold her house, though James and Julia had expressed every intention of taking care of Gwen and Nathan's needs themselves; the odd location of the new flat. Gwen's pregnancy seemed only the impetus for executing a plan long brewing. Had Iris actually expected him to move in with her again? Through the phone Julia could hear a musical scale of crashes, as if objects had fallen, or been hurled.

"Come over," Julia said again, gently. "I'll put the kettle on."

"There's no need to speak to me like an invalid. And he stopped using his cards so I've not had the faintest idea where he's been or what he's been doing and until I clapped eyes on him just now I've been beside myself that he was starving in a gutter. He's not even been to Sainsbury's. It would have been considerate for someone to tell me that I no longer needed to expend endless time and energy worrying about him. Now I see I went above and beyond to even give it a second thought."

"What cards?"

"Bank cards," said Iris impatiently. "I'd hardly take an interest in his library cards."

"But how do you see his—"

"Well, we have a joint account, obviously," and then before Julia had a chance to absorb this startling disclosure about a couple who had been separated since time immemorial, went on, "and now there's all that money from the house just sitting in it that he hasn't touched while he makes some sort of *moral stand,* and he's probably still got his thermostat on *fifteen,* for God's sake, while he entertains his lady friend, and I live in an old people's home that he won't come to. It's quite hilarious."

"But Iris, you don't really hate that flat, do you?"

"I do," snapped Iris, tight and decisive. "I hate it. I loathe and detest it and now it's where I live and that's the end of it. More fool me for feeling responsible for a doddering old imbecile feigning interest and dependence. Perhaps I shall move to France. Camilla never goes; she's always offering the house. I'm coming round. May I?"

Julia had never before known Iris to ask permission for anything, and it moved her. "Of course, come right now. I'm sure it's nothing. I'm sure he was just with a friend."

36.

JOAN PERELMAN WAS A SCORPIO, A PART-TIME TRAVEL AGENT
and full-time widow who lived, worked, and bred miniature Schnau-
zers in a semidetached pebbledashed house in Stanmore, airy and
spotless (despite the proliferating puppies), the mortgage of which she
had recently and triumphantly finished paying off. She was sixty-six,
had been only fifty when her Steve had died, and had been alone and
lonely since then though she would never have admitted it, not even
to the girls in her Thursday book club, perhaps not even to herself.
Her two sons (journalist and doctor, Aquarius and Pisces), matching
pair of fire-sign daughter-in-laws, and five grandchildren all lived in
Israel, and while she was glad they were settled, and happy for them
that they were all together, it did make life in London very quiet.

She had been e-mailing Mr. Philip Alden, MRCP, MD, FRCOS,
FRCOG, intermittently for several months. He was supposed to be a
speaker at an assembly for trainee holistic midwives in Paris organized by a British woman named Pamela Fuller who lived in Boston
and who, though demanding, had given her a great deal of business

over the years. Joan had made the travel arrangements for the last three of these retreats and so when Pamela had asked her to pin down an elusive participant, she'd hopped in the car armed with some encouraging soft-lit beauty shots of the Left Bank and a spa menu, as well as the material for the conference itself. She would coax him to commit, if Pamela so wished it.

It had been, as Joan had confided in her friend Cathy in the changing rooms after Hip Hop Hips, a whirlwind. Of course he was quite a bit older, but he had such a beautiful face, and clear, sad eyes that shone with humor and wisdom, and after setting her straight about the conference, which he had done almost immediately, he nonetheless offered her a coffee. This he made on the stove and then carried through on a precariously clattering tray. He had poured her coffee, offered her UHT milk, the sight of which had touched and saddened her, and had asked, with ever such a naughty twinkle in his eye, for her to tell him all about what he'd be missing. "Tell me about the"— he'd reached for the top two brochures—"tell me about the 'bilingual past-life regression refresher.'" And so she had told him about having to find a simultaneous translator for the evening meditation master classes, and somehow she had then moved to other topics, and he had listened to her prattle about her son and his family visiting next week (staying with the *machatonim*, sadly, not with Joan) and her grandson's upcoming football party and the gift she'd chosen (a kit to make a robot out of a soda can; she didn't believe in video games though that was what he'd asked for), and Philip had asked all the right questions and said, how hard to have them all so faraway. And then he'd told her about his son, Daniel, who'd died of cancer and she'd cried, and said sorry, it was awful of her to cry over a stranger's story but she'd just been so sad for him and here she was complaining that she had to fly to see her boys, sorry, sorry, and he'd said, solemnly and, as if he meant it—thank you. Then she had told him about Daisy, who was due to whelp in less than a month, and he had taken such tender interest that Joan had relived the conversation over and over in the days that followed.

And it seemed that Philip had remembered, too, for out of the blue he had phoned her weeks later, on a rainy evening in May, to ask about the dog. Moved to daring she'd asked, would he like to come for tea tomorrow to meet Daisy? And in case he'd got the wrong idea had added, stupidly, that she'd love to hear his medical opinion. He'd been reading up, he told her, when she was defrosting a spinach lasagna for supper and he was still, miraculously, in her kitchen. It would be an honor to be at the delivery. Since that day he had barely left her side. A week later Joan was due in Pinner for her grandson's eleventh birthday and it already seemed right, by then, that Philip should join her. He met the boys, he attended the birthday party, he helped with the 7-Up can robot assembly. It had been a short time, it was true, but they knew all they needed to know about each other. Unexpectedly, wonderfully, all consumingly, it was love.

37.

GWEN'S EXAM WEEKS PASSED WITHOUT INCIDENT, WHICH WAS
in itself remarkable, under the circumstances. If pressed, she would
reply that the day's module had gone "okay," or "fine," or in the case
of an art history paper, "alright, I think," and no more would be
forthcoming. Each evening she sat down ravenous to supper, did an
extremely brief spell of French vocabulary on the sofa, and then retired to the bath where she would lie for an hour, occasionally memo-
rizing history dates but more often listening to a meditation track
that she had recently downloaded from the Internet. Julia would walk
past the bathroom and hear snatches of, "allow your mind to empty
like the waves receding," or more oddly, "you can know anything you
wish, if you simply wait in stillness for wisdom to enter." Keeping up
the Easter revision intensity for these final few days seemed a more
sensible approach than waiting in stillness for wisdom to enter the
cooling silted waters of a bathtub, but Julia recalled the tears and
nightly hysteria of the GCSEs the year before and passed no comment. Gwen's morning sickness had been violent but unexpectedly

brief and had passed entirely, as had her fatigue. She no longer had any symptoms at all and, she would boast to anyone who'd listen, she felt entirely herself again and could forget about it for days at a time. Nonetheless she took herself to bed each night at nine p.m. "to be responsible," and James and Julia had a series of improbably lovely evenings alone, curled together on the sofa, as it had never before been. And might never be again, Julia thought, with an ache in her throat. Gwen might be able to set aside her pregnancy while she finished off the year, but it could not be ignored much longer. She was ten weeks pregnant—in some ways very early; in others, late.

WHILE GWEN apparently grew calmer, Nathan grew increasingly desperate. His own exams would not begin until the day hers ended and, for him, everything was still to play for. Oxford had asked for two As and two Bs. He told Gwen that he did not have time to call her from school and she did not protest; she, too, was under pressure. Without the sound of her voice, it became surprisingly easy to pretend that nothing at home had changed. He was working every waking hour, and for efficiency's sake had increased these waking hours first to eighteen, then nineteen, then, finally, to twenty a day. When his eyes closed over his books he drank coffee or took caffeine tablets, and then stayed longer at his desk to make effective use of the jittering insomnia. Charlie gave him eye drops, and these helped with the burning and dryness. He would have all summer to recover.

There was nothing he had ever wanted as much as he wanted straight As, now. He would forgo all sleep, all pleasure; he would work until his hands seized and his brain bled. When term began it had been a relief to go back to the easy, studious camaraderie of his boardinghouse but it wouldn't have mattered. He could revise polynomials at the back of the 24 bus. He would have walked the streets reading about gene expression. He could have memorized the properties of transition metals at the foot of Eros at the heart of Piccadilly Circus while around him the pubs emptied, and the crowds flooded out of the theaters on the last Friday night before Christmas. He feared life closing down around him but he would fight his way free and Oxford would harbor him, offer safety, redemption. He was the embodiment of single-mindedness. He was indefatigable. He would succeed. He would fly.

38.

NATHAN'S EXAMS HAD FINALLY BEGUN THAT MORNING AND since then James had carried his phone around the house, mooning and checking his watch and sighing with impatience like a love-struck teenager. He was anxious to hear about this afternoon's Mechanics. Physics had gone very well, he told her without looking up, frowning as he typed his reply; the question they'd expected about Friction had come up and Nathan had aced it. It was his apparent confidence in the morning's module that had prompted this unwelcome discussion about next year. Julia continued to zest a lemon in silence, the sharp scent rising in her nostrils. She did not feel charmed, or generous, or celebratory, though she was in the midst of making a cake that she hoped would substitute for all those feelings. Gwen's own exams finished that afternoon.

They had made it through her AS fortnight with preternatural calm and harmony, but her daughter still had a year of school before she could be in Nathan's privileged position, considering universities, making plans, and what the hell did her future hold in any case, and how would she manage any of it if Nathan didn't stay in London? Julia would do whatever it took to prevent Gwen's own dreams from evaporating, but she did not intend to be left holding the baby while Nathan swanned off to Oxford, scot-free. It seemed obvious that he must live at home next year to help with his child, so obvious, in fact, that she had barely thought it needed discussion. He would still have the choice of many medical schools, several of which ranked among the best in the country.

The night before returning to Westminster, Nathan had announced over dinner with a faint but discernible touch of sorrow that he would no longer be applying to faraway Harvard, as if they would all be surprised and moved, and full of praise for a grand and unexpected sacrifice. Julia had only managed to say, "I see," and had asked to be handed the asparagus. Harvard? After Christmas her daughter would barely be able to go to the corner shops. For Julia and James, too, the future to which they'd looked forward had become hazy with uncertainty—music festivals interrupted for feeds and tantrums; the new piano in a Lewes cottage vying for space with a shattered rainbow of plastic tat. Yet for Nathan, Oxford remained the plan, and there had arisen this slim, prickling weal of irritation on the previously unspoiled surface of Julia and James's intimacy. They had approached it, circled and retreated without resolution. "He might not get the grades," James would offer, which really meant, *Peace, please, I love you, we've made it this far, we are united, please let's not fight.* And he might not get the grades, Julia knew, but the truth was that he almost certainly would. It was conditional on his earning two As and two Bs, and his teachers had long predicted five As. And then what would happen? Whatever James might insist, it was too far to commute. He would have to turn it down. Julia found herself praying that he would miss his marks and so would not have to make a sacrifice for which he would almost certainly punish Gwen.

She considered Oxford. Its Brideshead splendor and indolence, the low *click-thock* of croquet mallet, the self-conscious delight of sub fusc and black tie and tail coats, emerald lawns and muddy riverbanks, of simply messing around in punts; of cobbled streets and echoing cloisters, wide open quadrangles and covered markets, of squeaking bicycles, of dusty, leather-scented library corners where light streamed in through high windows onto the bowed and privileged heads below. Nathan would soon be handed the key on a velvet ribbon, and in autumn would disappear into that enclosed and enchanted garden. And for Gwen, a life of schoolgirl motherhood. Oxford would never have been Gwen's world, she knew, but still, she had her own dreams. They'd walked around the animation department of the Leeds College of Art one half term and Julia had not been able to tear her gaze from Gwen's face. Her hungry eyes had taken in the banks of drafting tables, the modeling studio, the long rows of huge-screened iMacs. She'd turned to her mother with an expression of joyful disbelief and Julia had felt an unexpected pain at her daughter's impatience. *Don't grow up so fast,* she'd thought, *not yet.* Gwen had shown her around instinctively—here is where they do traditional frame-by-frame work, these puppets are for stop-frame animation, this must be the recording studio for voices, here's for 3-D, computer-generated work. Her little girl wanted to join this band of serious young people with their dyed hair, their septum piercings and eyebrow rings, their checked flannel shirts and army boots, their intense frowns over joystick and mouse and pencil and clay. And Julia had felt stricken, understanding for the first time that her daughter longed to leave her, and that it would happen soon, and Julia's world, without its center, would quietly and catastrophically collapse. Gwen would take with her everything of meaning. It had been shortly after that visit to Leeds that she had agreed to a date with James.

No. There was no question that Nathan must live at home. He would have responsibilities, unimaginable though it was, and his second choice was not exactly a tragedy. Medicine at Imperial was not to be sneezed at. As Iris would say, you don't exactly sit shiva for Medicine at Imperial. He didn't get to have the sex, the girlfriend, the intellect, the freedom and then, the crowning triumph, the Houdini act that spirited him away into a limestone paradise of books and beauty in that sweet city, with its gleaming infant-free spires. He couldn't have everything.

"I don't know what you want me to say."

"I want you to talk to me. I want to understand why you're so against it. I want us to make plans—"

"But your plans involve your son sixty miles away from my daughter. And from *his* son or daughter, more to the point. For five years."

"Oxford terms are only eight weeks long and he'll come back every weekend, Gwen's high school terms will be way longer than that."

"If we can get her back to school."

"She has to; it shouldn't be a negotiation. And she'll have a huge amount of support during the week; she's never going to be alone. I've told you I'm going to be there for this baby. I'm going to do whatever I can to free them, no one's life should be derailed, you and I are here, and we can do it. And the other day Pamela was saying she could maybe also arrange to come over for two weeks of each term, if it helped—"

"What do you mean? *Our* life will be derailed! Our life is going to be totally derailed—I don't even recognize what's ahead of us . . .

I'm almost fifty, James; it's too much to even think about starting all over again with an infant in the house. I don't know how it was for you and Pamela, maybe you had babies who slept through the night and never cried and sterilized their own bottles, but I certainly didn't; I remember being so tired I felt jet-lagged, *all the time*, and I never imagined— Of course we'll be there but you can't just decide you'll do it *for* him, and it's not as if we're talking about success or failure here; medical school is medical school and he should be grateful—" Julia halted quickly, though not before noticing that James had raised his eyebrows. She tried again. "He should still be happy and excited about next year wherever he goes. I'm just saying, to get a medical degree from a great university is a triumph under any circumstances. He can go to UCL or Imperial, and most kids don't have that much choice even when they don't have a young baby. There's no reason to go so far away." The idea of Pamela descending upon them was too alarming, so this she ignored entirely.

"So far away? Julia, it's sixty-two miles, it's barely up the road." James pointed behind him, toward the front door, toward Golders Green, toward junction eight of the M40, toward the rosy gold horizon over which his golden son was to set sail. She knew what he valued— he had been to Harvard for both his degrees, and before Harvard Medical School, nauseating Pamela had read Natural Sciences at Christ's College, Cambridge. They were speaking more often these days and she could imagine their discussions—why ought their son to turn down a world-class institution when they could manage his temporary absence? Even for a good London college, it would be symbolic self-sacrifice. James could keep the baby cared for, the household mollified and managed, and would of course do it with better grace, better humor, and a great deal more competence than his teenage son.

She understood it, in principle. It was atavistic. To launch your child into the world toward success and freedom, wasn't it this for which every parent strove, lifelong? If an impediment lay in Nathan's path, James would raze it to the ground like a bulldozer, but in this case the impediment was her own child and she would not allow Gwen to be flattened for an indulged, overprivileged little so-and-so. She took a deep breath and began her explanation again, from the beginning, and saw him grit his teeth with unaccustomed irritation. But then her phone rang and she sprang for it. It would be Gwen, reporting on the final exam. Those, at least, seemed to have gone without incident. James checked his own phone.

"Hi, my darling, how was it?"

"Mummy," the voice on the other end was muffled and warped by digital interference. It sounded as if Gwen was underground, or perhaps under water. "Mummy, can you come?"

"I can't hear you very well, my darling, where are you? What happened? It's only one module, my love, I'm sure it will be okay."

"I'm in the loos. Mummy, please come." Julia heard a shuddering sob. "I'm bleeding."

39.

WHEN NATHAN TIPTOED IN, GWEN WAS IN HER PAJAMAS ON
the sofa, her hair in two thick braids, her knees drawn up, a hot water
bottle cradled in her arms. Behind her glasses her face was very white,
her eyes fixed on the flickering television. She had the cuticle of her
right thumb between her teeth, and did not appear to hear or sense
him entering. The room was stuffy, the only light in the room the
screen and a reading lamp casting a yellow glow on the far wall.

Nathan hovered in the doorway, uncertain. He spoke her name
softly, as though waking her from sleep, and she looked up and gave
him a wan smile.

"You didn't have to come back."

He sat down beside her, very gingerly. He did not know whether
she was in pain, nor what to say if she was. What had been done to
her, in the bright white sterility of the hospital? What had been taken?

"I mean, it's lovely that you did. But you've got two exams tomorrow." Her voice was husky, as if her throat was very dry.

"You're more important," he said, fiercely. His father had said the same on the phone: exams tomorrow. But how could they possibly think he'd care about exams today? How could he stay in his boardinghouse tonight? His father's voice—filled with warmth and pity and a promise of his own reassuring solid presence, at that moment just out of reach, across London—had brought on such a violent lurch of homesickness that he could not have stayed in school another moment. As soon as he stepped out into Victoria Street, arm aloft, purposeful, he felt better. At first in the taxi he felt himself racing against the clock, in a panic to reach the heroine for the climactic scene in which he would be tested and would comfort her, and triumph. Nothing of these last, strange weeks had felt real—around him weird storms had raged, but when he kept his head down life remained unaltered, the threat too far ahead to fear, too abstract to comprehend. Now he felt electrified. Telling the driver "as fast as you can" was manly and exhilarating. This was reality. But then nearstasis in the red neon and clamor and spewing traffic of Edgware Road, and the film crew departed and left him alone, and he was no longer needed to perform. The adrenaline seeped away and left him shaking. No one was picking up the phone. He tried his mother, over and over, but it was midafternoon in Boston and she would be in clinic, inaccessible for hours. Then he had screwed shut his eyes and bitten the soft flesh between his thumb and index finger to try and punish himself into control; he had not been able to answer when the cab driver turned and asked him if he was alright. He did not understand the source of all this sorrow, only its magnitude, and that it had engulfed him.

He had expected hysteria at home, he realized; he had feared blood, or a confrontation of female biology. This muted calm was disconcerting and made his role unclear. She already had a hot water bottle, and beside her on the coffee table lay a still life of sickroom requirements: a plate of biscuits, a cup of tea, a glass of water, a packet of chocolate buttons, a box of painkillers, a small packet of tissues, a weekly celebrity magazine. He had come home intending to nurse her, an evening of his own hard penance so he could go back to school having altered something. But her requirements had been met.

"Are you okay?" he asked, foolishly. He leaned over to kiss her and she inclined her head toward him so he ended up catching her paternally on her hairline.

"I'm okay. Your dad got me an appointment with his friend tomorrow morning. Not that Claire person, someone else. It's nice of him, usually I'd have to wait longer. It'll be more comfortable after that, apparently."

"Does it hurt?"

She shook her head. "They said I could take Paracetamol, but then when we got back your dad gave me— He said I didn't have to be hurting when he had something stronger that's okay to take. So he gave me something . . . American," she finished. This speech had taken effort; she sank back onto the sofa, wearied by it.

"Lucky, Dad never gives me his good drugs. But I mean, *you're* okay. You're safe?"

"Yes. S'just one of those things. Wasn't meant to be, or whatever."

"But how can it just be—" His voice broke and he took Gwen's white hand and raised it to his lips. He could not quite find her in the dark hollows of her eyes. It had begun to dawn on him what had not seemed real or possible before this loss—that he had almost had a child. A son, maybe. A moment later he found himself weeping. Gwen shifted to her knees and held his head tightly against her breast. "How can it just be *gone*, just like that? That was our *baby*."

"It's okay," she whispered, "everything's okay." Her hand stroked his hair, but the more she soothed, the harder he wept. He did not want to stop. Nothing was okay. He had lost something in which he had never believed.

UPSTAIRS, GWEN SANK INTO BED. She had ordered Nathan back to school, back to his necessary responsibilities and the unaltered reality of exams. It had been a relief when his father drove him away and the house was silent again. When James returned she could vaguely hear his voice and her mother's mingled, soft and low in the kitchen, and for once she did not feel an angry impulse to eavesdrop, did not fear secrets or treachery. She knew they were speaking of her, and speaking tenderly. She did not deserve it.

Her mother had changed the sheets and refilled her hot water bottle and this Gwen clutched to the dull ache in her abdomen—though in truth the pain was not bad, no worse than period cramps. After a moment James knocked and came in, with two tablets and a glass of water.

"In case you wanted something in the night. You could take one now and one after two a.m., if you wake."

"Will it help me sleep?"

He nodded.

"It's not actually hurting that much. But can I take it anyway?"

"Just tonight, sure. One at a time, though. Gwen"—he paused in the doorway and ran a hand through his hair, gathering the front in his fist, a mannerism she recognized in Nathan—"I'm so very sorry. I'm on call tonight but you know I won't leave this house unless I really have to. If you need anything in the night—"

"I know. Thanks."

"Good night. Your mother will come in in a minute."

"Wait!" She heard her own voice calling him back, and seconds later he returned and was at her bedside.

"Can I ask—" She had no vocabulary for her question but her hand was suddenly between James's, clasped tightly and shaken on each emphatic syllable.

"You did not make this happen, you hear me? *It is not possible.* It's not coffee or what you ate or what you didn't eat or a heavy box you lifted or anything within your control. This happens in one in five pregnancies, even at your age, and people don't talk about it and I have no idea why; it would spare a lot of women a lot of needless, toxic guilt. I would not bullshit you. I need you to hear me, okay?"

He would not look away, she knew, until she nodded.

The door closed, and she took a deep, unsteady breath. James had not understood. She had done this, not with her body but with her mind. She had wished away a baby. Overjoyed at the end of the fatigue and nausea, she hadn't known that for days she had been celebrating death within her. She had longed for liberation and in answer a violent, unexpected liberation had come.

Beneath her hot spread hands her abdomen was flat and unremarkable. In, out. She sank back into her pillow exhausted, washed into unconsciousness on a tide of Tramadol, and a rising steady surge of dark relief.

40.

LONG AGO ON A DIFFERENT FLOOR OF THAT SAME HOSPITAL, Julia had cradled newborn Gwen and known her body's work: to shield this child from harm, lifelong. The cord between them severed but her daughter pulsed in her veins and swelled her heart. Life, she promised her, would be a thing of beauty—no less was due to such unblemished perfection.

The arrogance! Vigilance could not keep her child beyond the reach of germs or falls or playground bullies, nor from allergies or fights with friends or the teachers who found her unfocused, or petulant, who couldn't see her unique brilliance and charm. Julia had failed so often, and then could only suffer for Gwen, suffer with Gwen, and try in the aftermath of each small calamity to make amends. And then Daniel had died and huge wet fawn eyes had looked up at Julia and pierced her, and she had read in their bewilderment, *How could you let this happen?*

Far taller than all her classmates, awkward and angular and exuding toxic sadness, for that first year Gwen had repelled the other girls.

At the school gates they passed her by in flocks, tiny sparrows twittering, avoiding the unsettling spectacle of her bent, trudging form. In her hands an egg of Silly Putty constantly molded and remolded, on her back a grubby purple rucksack and in it the world's weight. She was not open or appealing but heavy browed, frowning, angry, impossible to befriend. Julia picked her up each afternoon with a lead weight in her stomach. She couldn't make it better. Instead, she compensated.

Now such an adult misfortune, a complex, adult sorrow. It was obscene and unbearable to feel relief, seeing Gwen's face pale against the pale sheets, her daughter meek and bewildered, curled fetal beneath a winter duvet on long summer days. For her child's lost innocence, Julia wept. Such knowing, now, as no grown woman ought to know!

WITHIN A WEEK Gwen relinquished the daytime hours in bed, still rising very late but then managing to stay awake, clothed, communicative, till bedtime. She came to the supermarket with Julia, and to the post office. She waited in the car while Julia ran in to the dry cleaners. While Julia taught she lay on the sofa with magazines or her laptop or sat at the kitchen table, modeling a large, elaborate replica of the Hampstead Ladies' Bathing Pond. She clung close and Julia was grateful. So often in the last months she had been forced to stifle the instinct to reach out and draw her nearer; now Gwen sought the touch and care that Julia had so long craved. She had her only on loan, she knew, just until Nathan came home. But for the meanwhile it was a return to a rhythm as familiar as a heartbeat, mother and daughter together except when brief circumstance parted them and one waited patiently, before a seamless return to one another. For the first week James stayed late at the hospital or did paperwork discreetly upstairs, and each evening Gwen worked on her models while Julia made dinner. At Gwen's suggestion they spring-cleaned. They sorted out Gwen's clothes. They cleared the drawers beneath her bed to make place for a proper archive of her models. They tidied the spice rack, the utensil drawer, the bookshelves of Julia's crowded little music room. They made easy order from small chaos. Her child had returned, prodigal, temporary, beloved, and Julia treasured each moment she was granted like a jewel.

For the Ponds, they packed as they always had. Towels, books, a pack of cards, warm clothes and a fleecy blanket for the moments just after an icy immersion. A picnic of peanut butter sandwiches, carrot sticks, a bag of grapes, two red apples. The same lunch she and Gwen had favored for this outing many summers ago. The weather had turned cloudy but this was England, and to wait for clear blue skies might be to wait forever.

Safe from exhausting dissecting male eyes, the Ladies' Pond offers tranquil safety almost impossible to capture elsewhere. Gwen had brought an old, black swimsuit from long-ago school lessons and in this she sat, comfortably cross-legged. Around them women relaxed. Stomach muscles released, shoulders hunched—flattering angles and postures abandoned. Freed. Gwen rolled onto her stomach on the towel and sprawled, facedown, forehead resting on her rolled-up T-shirt. A brief flicker of sun lit the grass, was gone again, but hinted at return. Julia unpacked sandwiches, balled up foil, struggled briefly to unscrew Gwen's requested bottle of Coke.

Gwen said, mumbling into the earth, "Can I ask you something?"

"Of course."

Gwen raised herself to her elbows and began to pluck grass blades. "So, Katy's the only person who knows . . . who knew I was pregnant, and Nathan's teachers know 'cause he was still at school and stuff and so James told them but no one else, and I've been thinking about what to do about my followers. Online, I mean. I always said it would be everything that happened in my life, not just the bits I wanted to show off, but it just feels a bit weird."

Julia recoiled at the thought but said, carefully, "It seems very exposing . . . What do you want to do?"

"I don't think I want to say anything. I mean, what would I do? Because I was planning this big reveal, you know, like with a little bump and an announcement in those little old-school wooden baby blocks, you know? Telling everyone that way about the baby. I just wanted to wait"—she gave a sideways glance toward her mother and then looked down again—"just till you guys were a bit more used to it, and more . . . excited, and then tell everyone first on the blog, with this little stork and balloons and stuff."

Julia's eyes filled. To think that Gwen had longed not only for acceptance but also enthusiasm. It would not have come, and then what? She wanted to reach out to stroke her daughter's cheek, her hair, but Gwen went on, "But now it's like, I'd have to explain that I was pregnant and now I'm not pregnant at the same time and it just feels . . . I dunno. Wrong."

"Some things are very painful to share, very private. And maybe it's too soon to even know how you feel yet. It's okay to protect yourself and keep some things off the Internet. Then later you get to decide who you tell, if you want to, and who you don't."

"You don't think it's dishonest not to put it up?"

"I don't," said Julia, firmly. "I think it's brave."

Gwen looked relieved. She rolled over and sat up, and reached for a sandwich. "Okay. Then next I'm going to do the one of us here, because the pond's going really well; I've almost finished it, and then the one after can be when Nathan finishes finally, and we can do something fun instead of me like, dying on the sofa." Here she rolled her eyes, and Julia had a glimpse of how it would be when Nathan returned—the miscarriage dismissed, cast off as embarrassing, or too much of a downer. "I've been planning loads of amazing stuff. I'll meet him at Westminster so I could model that, but afterwards we're going to Covent Garden. D'you know you can check which street performers are going to be there? So I thought I'd plan out a few that would be amazing, and then there's this American sweet shop that Katy found so we'll go there as a surprise and buy stuff he likes from home, and then there's this bubble tea place that's just opened, and then James is really into this barbecue idea which sounds cool if that's what Nathan wants. But basically, I'll organize the whole afternoon and then the best thing I'll model." She peeled apart her remaining corner of sandwich and laid a carrot stick onto the slice with peanut butter on it, rolling this into a cigar. She frowned. "It's been a bit weird that he's basically not been here for anything. We've talked on the phone but not really about what happened because he has people in his room a lot, and also he was studying and it seemed unfair to bring it up when he has to concentrate. But he keeps saying how he wished he could take care of me." She bit the end off her rolled sandwich and said, her mouth full, "I've been thinking, and I think we'll have a baby when I'm twenty-five. Or twenty-four." Impossible not to see the flicker of challenge in her eyes. A test. Julia resolved not to fail.

"You'll see what feels right," she said, neutrally.

Gwen bit her lip. "But it won't be this baby."

"No, my darling."

"It's like, another baby doesn't just make it okay about this baby, or make it like it never happened. You don't think . . ." She paused. "You don't think James is just saying it to make me feel better, that there was nothing we could do. If there was something that was my fault, I'd want to know." They had covered this ground more than once before, and each time Gwen's guilt seemed fractionally eased.

"I don't. He's very straight. But if you wanted to talk to Claire again, I'm sure she'd see you."

"No, it's okay. It was a girl, I think. I'm so sure it was a girl. Do you believe mothers have instincts about these things?"

"I knew you were a girl."

Gwen nodded, relieved to have her instincts affirmed, pleased, also, to have to been recognized so early as herself. She wiped her hands on the grass and stood up, inelegantly. She was going to swim, she announced, and it was clear from her tone that she wished to go alone. Julia took out a book, but did not open it. She watched Gwen climbing down into the slippery green of the pond, watched her daughter's long form move off through the murky water. A woman's body now. A separate being, thinking her own closed, unguessable thoughts. She felt a sudden ache of longing for Gwen's own babyhood. It took so little to call it back, the private rapture of her new daughter's warm weight, slack and loose-jointed and slung, milk-drunk across Julia's shoulder. Gwen in her arms had exuded an opiate. The tiny breaths against her neck, the sudden startles and then stillness and silence, the soft, urgent moans of baby dreams. Her finger gripped like a lifeline, unblinking gray eyes locked with her own in an exchange of silent promises. What would she give to start all over again, to be handed her infant daughter afresh, to file away each moment like a treasure, to do it right? She thought about the child her daughter had almost carried, and allowed the tears to come. She would listen harder. She would watch more closely. Next time she would be there to catch Gwen even before she slipped.

41.

ON THE MORNING OF NATHAN'S FINAL EXAM GWEN WASHED
and straightened her hair. He had not been home for more than two
weeks and the last time they had seen one another had been just after
she'd returned from the hospital when she had been curled on the
sofa, barely responsive. She had been startled and touched by his dev-
astation then, and it had shown her the right way to respond. Like a
good army wife she had used her little strength to soothe him and
patch him up and send him back into battle. When they'd spoken
since she'd done her best to sound cheerful, and to listen when he
talked about school. It became easier and easier to sound okay, for she
had begun to feel okay, but there was still a conversation missing;
she had comforted him, but missed her own comforting. She wanted
back the concern he'd shown that first night. She wanted praise for
her bravery, and coddling for her trauma. And she wanted to remind
him as much as possible of her old self. His last day at Westminster
was a milestone; she had needed him, and now she could tell him so

and they could be together. They could reassemble their bedroom (surely now the parents would allow it) and they would feel close again, and united. He would begin to fathom the leaden weight of all she felt, the dull guilt and the piercing flashes of disbelief. Nathan's love and admiration for her courage would lift the last sorrow from her shoulders like a cloak; he would be gallant, attentive, and she would shrug loose, would emerge poised and damaged, wiser and more beautiful, and walk free into the candlelight and music of the rest of her life. She could start to forget all she had learned about loneliness. In the darkness their fingertips would touch, and it would not be despair but safety and connection.

IN ST. JAMES'S PARK the grass had just been cut, and the warm air was filled with drowsy summer. Passing crowds of tourists stayed dutifully to the paths, studying their maps and phones and invariably in search of either the Mall and onward to Buckingham Palace, or Birdcage Walk and the Houses of Parliament. The Westminster boys lay on the freshly clipped lawns, blithe and privileged in charcoal suits and new freedom, playing a lazy, seated game of catch with a tight-crumpled ball of white paper that had once been an A-level exam sheet.

From his inside pocket Charlie drew a bottle of vodka and a packet of cigarettes while from the same hiding place in his own wrinkled jacket Nathan produced his hip flask. The sight of it made Gwen smile to herself.

A dark-haired boy loped over to join them and dropped his rucksack in the middle of the circle. This was Edmund, who sat next to

Nathan in Pure Maths. Edmund had long ago dated Valentina, briefly, which made him an object of interest. She studied his face for signs that he'd been branded in some manner by the Demon Barber.

"Champers?"

"Have you got? You star!"

"Gift from the olds. I've even got glasses." Edmund unzipped his rucksack and began to flick plastic cups into their laps.

"Mixers?" asked Charlie.

"It's champagne, you muppet."

"For the vodka."

"Nope. Mixers are for pussies."

"I'll go to the newsagent," Gwen offered, seeing a way to participate whilst also getting away from his friends, for a moment. She stood up, squinting in the sunshine. Her sunglasses were in her bag but she now worried they were babyish; when she bought them she'd thought the heart-shaped lenses quirky and original, here she felt uncertain.

"Top girl. Orange juice, cranberry juice, soda."

Gwen looked at Nathan, waiting.

"What?"

"Wallet?"

"No cash? Here." He handed her a twenty-pound note. "Buy yourself something pretty." His voice was hard and public, straining for cool and distance. He couldn't help it. Later he would coo and nuzzle her, overcompensating, anxious for reassurance that she would not hold him to the distance he himself had made.

The shops were farther than she'd remembered. She decided to spend the rest of Nathan's money on food, something that his friends would not have considered, and so bought cheese-and-onion crisps, Jaffa Cakes, and three large bags of Wine Gums. The drinks were heavy, and the thin plastic bags were splitting by the time she was halfway back across the field. She managed to fit one bottle into her own bag, but the others had to be tucked awkwardly into the crook of each arm, and her return progress was cumbrous and slightly sweaty in the rising heat of the afternoon. Every few yards she had to stop and readjust her burdens.

There were ten or twelve teenagers cross-legged in a circle by the time she returned, mostly boys, as well as two girls she didn't recognize, one of whom had her stockinged feet in, or near to, Charlie's crotch. The champagne and vodka bottles were empty, and a large Malibu was circulating.

"You can't mix Malibu and cranberry juice!" snorted Nathan, when he saw her. "What were you thinking, woman?"

"It was vodka when I left."

"Water into wine. Vodka into Malibu. Transubstantiation." He widened his eyes. "It's a miracle."

"Transubstantiation's not water into wine, Fuller." Beside him Edmund began to guffaw with tipsy laughter. "Such a fucking Jew."

Shocked, Gwen dropped the bottles rather heavily in the center of the circle, but Nathan had only punched his friend rather lazily in the bicep and grinned. "Well, what is it, then? It'd be fucking impressive. Imagine turning Evian into Cab Sauv."

"S'when the communion wafer becomes the Body of Christ." Edmund tossed his heavy hair from his eyes and tore into one of Gwen's bags of kettle chips, without acknowledgment. "You take the host." He laid a large crisp on his own extended tongue in illustration.

Nathan hooked his arm around Gwen's neck and pulled her closer, his exhalations loud and heavy against her ear. She was pleased by this display of possession and desire, and somewhat less pleased by the smell of his breath and the slightly glazed look in his eyes. He had grown sloppy, and his laughter came in loud, forced shouts. The group was raucous with freedom but Nathan seemed further gone than the others, his head lolling, occasionally pulling her to him and plunging a rather clumsy tongue slightly too deep into her mouth.

The afternoon settled. The boys played a brief game of football but soon gave up in the heat, balled their obsolete school jackets, and stretched back in the grass. Gwen lay down dutifully beside Nathan, who rolled over and began to kiss her, messily and ostentatiously, until Charlie threw a Wine Gum at them and to Gwen's relief he stopped. She sat up again. By now she'd hoped to be alone with Nathan, perhaps somewhere in this park, walking, talking, holding hands, shaking their heads in awe at the extraordinary bond they shared.

Today marked a momentous transition, and counting down toward it had steadied her in some of her darkest moments. She had pictured that first moment in which the huge oak doors creaked open. She'd imagined Nathan swinging her around with joy at his liberation, not only from school but from all the academic constraints that had hampered his ability to take care of her. Today, Nathan would assume the mantle of his responsibilities, solemn as a graduation gown. She would see him come back to her, and see her once again. It had already begun when, on the walk here he had hung back from the others, had pulled her for a moment down a quiet stable mews, cobbled, blue plaqued, and she had recognized in him the old fresh urgency, undiminished. Though she now found even the idea of sexual contact repellent, almost intolerable, her heart had leapt. Teenagers have always been forced to take these quiet public corners and make them private, temporarily, and here, with Nathan's heavy breath and roaming hands, was proof that they were once again normal teenagers. The daylight and his waiting friends ensured she was safe to sigh, and pull him tighter, and imitate his frustration. She found herself rising above the scene. She saw her red head bent close toward his dark one. They could have been parents, bound together inextricably, and eternally. Can you believe it? Those two down there, kissing—forever united. Look at them!

AT HALF PAST FOUR the group began to stir. There was a general agreement that they should go back to Yard and meet those who had been in afternoon exams and then move the celebrations to a pub behind Victoria Street, or perhaps to Marina's house, in Vincent Square. Gwen tugged on Nathan's sleeve and whispered, "Now we can go to Covent Garden." It was already much later than she'd hoped. They would have to rush if they were to make it to the Taiwanese bubble tea place, before heading home in time for James's barbecue.

"Come and meet Dom and the others from Geography, *ma petite.*"

She shook her head. "We're meant to do something just the two of us."

"I tell you what." Nathan stepped back unsteadily and slung an arm around Charlie's shoulders. "This is what's going to happen. You go and do what you need to do in Covent Garden. She needs to go shopping," he whispered to Charlie, confidentially, "and then you come back and meet us in the pub. We'll be in the pub, and you can come back and meet us."

"Or at Marina's," added one of the girls, unexpectedly. She was a few feet away; though they had seemed busy gathering their belongings, collecting crisp packets, brushing grass from their clothing, everyone was in earshot.

Gwen shook her head again. "I'm going." Her voice came out louder than she'd intended. "I'm not coming back again. I'm going home."

"Okay, baby, have fun. I'll be home in . . . soon. I've just got very business— I've got very important business to attend to, which is the business of celebrating."

She set off across the lawn and he loped a few steps to catch up with her.

"Are you pissed, baby?" he asked, in a different, private voice. She didn't care. Respect concealed from his friends had no value. Shouldn't he want to be alone with her?

"No," she snapped, "you're pissed."

"Both can be true, in very different ways," he said, sorrowfully, "the American way and the British. I prefer the English way, in this case. I'm pissed in the British sense; you're absolutely right and I highly, highly, highly, highly recommend it. Don't be pissed with me."

"You said we'd talk after the exams. You said we'd hang out, and we'd talk about everything—"

"Fuck, seriously?" He bent down and began bundling his jacket into his school bag. "Not *now*. I am not thinking about *that* today. It's literally the last thing I want to think about, I've just finished my exams. S'the end of my exams. S's my big day."

"I spent the last day of my exams in hospital. And P.S., it's all I think about. All the time. It's not like, a *choice*, I can't just decide, 'Oh, I don't want to think about this today.'"

"Well then you should get over it," he said shortly, standing up again.

She stared at him and he nodded vigorously, in agreement with himself.

"Seriously. Get over it! Come get drunk, come toast the end of my exams. You missed it for yourself because of the thing, so come toast the end of your exams, too! We should be celebrating the fact that you can drink; drinking's awesome. Not drinking is just . . . a waste. Come toast the fact that we had a fucking lucky escape, we got like a, a get-out-of-jail-free card, baby; we should be toasting. Cheers!" He raised an invisible glass to her, squinting slightly.

Perhaps he sensed that he had gone too far here as he then lurched forward and tried to kiss her with sloppy tenderness, but Gwen jerked herself free and began to run across the lawn, lowering her head and succumbing, finally, to her sobs. When she reached the path she turned to see that Nathan had lit a cigarette, and with this dangling from his lower lip was bouncing a football from knee to knee with a maddening, surprising coordination. She did not wait, in case he didn't look up. *A lucky escape.* She hated him, and herself.

42.

TODAY NATHAN WOULD COME BACK FOR THE LONG SUMMER holidays. It had been a blessed relief to be without him, but Gwen had been so excited earlier, racing up and down to model outfits, carefully painting too much garish color on her pale face. For Gwen, and for James, Julia gathered her strength and went to welcome the children in the hallway when she heard the key.

It was Gwen alone, and she had been crying.

"Where've you been? What's wrong? What happened, Dolly?"

"Everything's fucking stupid!"

"What's stupid? Where's Nathan?"

"Who cares? I literally hate him. I hate my life. Stop asking me questions."

Julia waited while Gwen kicked off her sneakers on the doorstep, in the immediate path of anyone who might want to come in or out.

"You don't have to stand there looking at me like there's something wrong with me!" Even Gwen did not sound convinced by this complaint. She tried again. "There's nothing wrong with me, *I'm fine*; stop looking at me like I'm a fucking invalid!"

"Enough, now. I won't be spoken to like this. I don't know what's happened but you can't just come in here and instantly take it out on me. Where's Nathan? Why didn't he come home with you?"

"Nothing's happened," Gwen whined, extending this last word over several seconds, and pitches. She was pulling her shoes back on.

"Where are you going?"

"It's literally none of your business! I'm going around the corner to make a phone call with some privacy, okay?"

After the front door slammed, Julia paused. Then she threw it open and called after her daughter.

"Wha-at?"

"Bring back some ice cream, Dolly, something nice that you really fancy."

Gwen grunted noncommittally, and then the gate swung shut behind her. Julia gave a small moan of anxiety. She should have spoken her conviction aloud in time to do something about it: it was a terrible idea for Nathan to come home for the summer.

IN THE KITCHEN, singing to Bon Jovi beneath a pair of Nathan's green, padded headphones, James had missed the shouting. Nathan had requested a barbecue for his first night of freedom, and James was making barbecue sauce. Saskia had just arrived from Boston and was sequestered upstairs with her friend Rowan, who was spending the night.

"Why didn't he come back with her?" he asked when Julia lifted an earphone to update him.

"I don't know. I think they've had an argument; she's in the most revolting mood. She'll be back any minute."

"God save us. Where's that apricot jelly?"

"We can't still have that, it was from Christmas."

"This'll blow your mind, I promise you. What did they fight about?"

Julia sank down into a chair. "I have no idea but she seems really rattled, and now she's marched off again. I think she knows Saskia's here with Rowan and probably wanted to phone Katy and compose herself a bit. It might have been quite uncomfortable being around all Nathan's school friends, and I imagine she feels quite guilty and ambivalent about celebrating anything. She's so tired. And the last day of her exams—that was not a good day."

James had found the remains of the apricot jam, as well as another unopened jar Julia didn't recognize that read FIGUE in elaborate curlicues, and he was dumping their contents into a stainless steel bowl along with the entire squeeze bottle of ketchup. "She's wiped out, she needs time. We'll just take it very easy for the summer," he said, squirting, "and make sure you guys get lots of time alone together. Mom-and-daughter time."

Julia rose and put her arms around him, peering around his shoulder into the contents of his bowl. "Thank you. That looks terrible," she said, her chin moving against the solid curve of his bicep. He grinned. "It's going to be awesome, just you wait. It's Nathan's all-time favorite. They've done it, you know. I'm so damn proud. They've been unbelievable little mensches for the last few weeks, both of them; it's a huge night tonight. We got these kids through . . . through a war zone. Think what they've been contending with, both of them; it's unimaginable. I really think she'll turn a corner now, you'll see.

She's not had any space. Do you think I should make guacamole? The avocados are like bullets, I'd have to try and microwave them or something. Gwen likes hot dogs, right? I got ballpark hot dogs and relish. Next time we go to Boston I have to take you to a ballgame, you'll love it. Actually you'll hate it but I'll love it. You'll love it when it's over, maybe." He ducked to kiss her behind her ear.

The day Nathan's exam timetable had been published James had swapped his clinic in order to be free to prepare this banquet. Along with the frankfurters, barbecued chicken, and grilled peppers he had made some sort of Cuban-style sweet corn with feta and mayonnaise, and had come back from Queen's Crescent with a watermelon the size of a small house pet. It felt far too soon to be celebrating anything but when consulted Gwen agreed it was still a good idea, and had even offered to bake Nathan an end-of-school cake—online she'd found a recipe for some elaborate confection that spilled out jelly beans. Gwen was surely the child more deserving of treats, but Julia had been happy, at least, that she was once again planning creative activities. In any case, given Gwen's mood the cake now seemed rather unlikely. What little enthusiasm Julia had for the evening had evaporated. James had a great deal for which he ought to be grateful—his daughter was visiting from college, his son had finished senior school. She had a child enraged, beneath whose eyes bloomed mauve stains of exhaustion. It had only been, after all, a few weeks. Revelry was not her uppermost concern.

BY NINE P.M. Nathan still had not come home or called, and Julia persuaded James to eat. Gwen had taken herself to bed, the first time that Julia had seen her be openly rude to Saskia, who had tried and failed to convince her to have dinner with them. Gwen had responded with an unpleasant comment about James's cooking, had clattered around preparing herself Marmite toast, leaving butter, loaf, Marmite jar, and a good many crumbs all over the counter, and had then clumped upstairs with her plate, looking thunderous.

"I'm going to sleep," she told Julia, who had followed her upstairs, anxious. "There's nothing to talk about, life is shit. I'm literally eating this toast and going to sleep in four seconds. See you tomorrow," she relented, and allowed herself, stiffly, to be hugged. Julia held her daughter's bird-narrow frame for as long as she was permitted, and then returned to James and the girls. Her heart remained upstairs. The evening would be easier if Saskia had not brought home a stranger.

Rowan had arrived in a crisp white shirt with a sharply pointed collar, black tailored trousers that ended high above her ankles and were held up by black, snakeskin suspenders and a pair of polished black wingtips, very small. Her pallor was accentuated by comically oversized black-framed glasses, and pinned to one of the suspenders was an Art Deco crystal brooch, shaped like a Scottie dog. When they'd met at Christmas, Gwen had gazed down in open distrust at this severely attired pixie-person, and her scowl had hardened when Saskia said, "Rowan's supercreative; she makes loads of stuff, like you," in a misguided attempt to find common ground. That had been her last visit. Julia hoped Gwen would sleep in, and that Rowan would leave early in the morning. Home should be a sanctuary, not Piccadilly Circus. Saskia's belongings were already strewn around her music room.

They ate from their laps in their square scrap of back garden. In his earlier enthusiasm James had grilled two packets of hot dogs, and a cold stack of these, alongside a lukewarm mound of baked potatoes and a tray of now slightly wrinkling corn cobs, lay on a card table around his centerpiece, a heaped platter of barbecued chicken wings.

"At what point do we get worried about him?" James asked, though he had clearly begun to worry some time ago.

"I don't think he'll come back tonight, Dad." Saskia frowned at her phone. She was sitting next to Rowan, cross-legged in the center of a sun-lounger, hunched over and typing furiously. "I think he's pretty wasted."

"What did he say? I'm glad he's communicating with someone, at least."

"He's somewhere with Charlie. It's got a million spelling mistakes and then, '*Tell Dad seed tortilla*,' and then a zillion emojis."

"Seed tortilla?"

"'See you tomorrow,' maybe."

Rowan cocked her head, birdlike. "God. I still think of your little brother as an actual child. It's insane to think of him old enough to drink, and now he's finished school! Supercrazy."

And he was nearly a father, thought Julia. *Supercrazy.*

The girls both stood and announced that they were going out, and would come home quietly at an unspecified time. Neither offered to help clear away dinner. Julia regarded Saskia, who looked rather blowsy and dishevelled beside her sharp little friend. Her hair had grown too long, and though she had gained weight at college she had not bought clothes to accommodate it. Buttons strained. Julia dismissed the urge to tighten Saskia's bra straps, and to tie back her hair.

Rowan, by contrast, had made an effort. She was severe-looking and not pretty, but had polished herself into a striking presence.

James pressed several ten-pound notes into Saskia's hand, which were accepted without comment, and then the girls disappeared.

"What can I say? My people cater for emergencies." James gave a resigned look at the groaning card table.

"I would have taken some of it to Philip tomorrow but I'm not sure he needs my deliveries anymore. I must say, as bizarre as it all is, it is nice to think of him being taken care of. Strange. I never thought it would be Iris I'd have to worry about."

"You don't have to worry about Iris, do you? She's been taking care of herself just fine since, what was his name?"

"Giles."

"Right. Since Giles moved to France." James gave her a cheeky grin, proud to have absorbed this family vernacular, and Julia shrugged off the ungenerous part of her that considered his use of it unseemly.

"She hasn't really been *alone* alone; she's had Philip on the other end of the phone. And text. And e-mail. And fax machine. Even when Giles was in the picture they were always in touch."

"Well she couldn't expect him to be at her beck and call forever if they weren't in a relationship any longer. What was he getting out of it?" James asked, reasonably, and Julia fell silent, considering. Iris and Philip had seemed immoveable as a mountain range yet, unexpectedly, Philip had moved. What had seemed hewn from granite had shivered to pieces like glass.

"I was thinking, I probably should have figured he'd want to spend tonight with his friends. Your old dad's barbecued wings aren't the most rock-and-roll way to mark your high school graduation. If that damn kid is not coming back, I'm opening another beer. Would you like one?"

Julia shook her head. Her plate had been sitting on her knee and she moved it to the grass. James went inside, returning with his beer and a roll of plastic wrap, and began to cover the chicken. "I should have figured. I mean, when you think of the last few weeks—the kid needs a break."

"Gwen needs a break."

An edge in her voice made James stop. "Of course she does. There's no competition. We're never going to play that game, baby, let's not start. There's only one team here." He dragged his chair over and sat and faced her, looking serious. "It's been awful and they both need a break. Thankfully it's not Gwen's style to go out drinking like a frat boy, and my son—every now and again he gets the urge to behave like the dumb teenage boy that he is."

"But she has been longing for time alone with him. You've seen, she's been so generous with him, she's made a monumental effort not to disturb him while he was working. Now he's free he should have understood that. She's been counting the days. It's not just party time now that exams are over; these aren't normal circumstances." Unable to stop herself she added, "He has responsibilities."

James stood up again. For a moment she thought he looked pained, but then he picked up a wrapped dish in each hand and headed back into the kitchen. "They're not normal circumstances. You're right, and it's my fault; I should have drawn his attention to it."

"It's not your fault in any way."

"Come on."

"Come on what?"

"Come on, let's not fight the kids' fights."

She fell silent. He was right, of course, but Gwen's destructive temper was contagious, and Julia felt an urge to keep pushing. Instead she took his beer from the table and blew a low note across the mouth of the bottle, like a ship's horn. "Okay," she said, after a moment, decisive. "I'm sorry. I've caught Gwen's mood. Give me the frankfurters. Will you bring the ketchup back out?"

43.

"WE NEED THIS," JAMES ANNOUNCED THE NEXT MORNING, battling a knapsack into the boot of the car.

Nathan mumbled something and James came around to the back window.

"What?"

"I said, *like a hole in the head.*"

"That hole in your head is called a hangover, my boy. I offered intravenous fluids, you said no, my next best offer is a walk on the beach. You can get two hours' quality sleep in the car. Righty ho, then," he added, in an execrable British accent. Nathan closed his eyes.

A day in Sussex seemed an ambitious plan, but James was insistent. It was the weekend, Saskia was with them, the weather was beautiful, and now was the time to begin a slow piecing back together. He was taking them all to Camber Sands. "This family needs airing," he'd told Julia early that morning, and with that, at least, she was inclined to agree. But she was fairly sure that Gwen and Nathan had not yet spoken to each other, and Gwen's reproachful glances over breakfast had been painful to witness. A London day trip might have been more sensible.

From the passenger seat, Julia turned to smile encouragingly at the children but received no response. Nathan and Gwen, sullen and uncooperative, were looking anywhere but at each other. Saskia shifted and laid her head on Gwen's shoulder.

"Sleepy," she mumbled. "Ro and I sat up talking for ages when we came home." She leaned across Gwen to address her brother. "What time was it you got in?"

"Dunno. Three, maybe?"

"Right, but then he made us sit up with him and make him scrambled eggs and listen to his drunken rambling. You were going on and on about the Egg McMuffin being your personal madeleine."

Between them Gwen scowled, and then leaned forward between the seats and turned up the volume of the radio. Finally James climbed into the driver's seat and announced that they were ready.

For the first hour they drove in silence. The road glinted in the sunshine and Nathan grudgingly yielded his sunglasses to his father so he could see to drive, and then threw his head back and covered his eyes in the crook of his arm. Saskia hummed intermittently to the radio, and Julia watched her own daughter's face in the rearview mirror and worried, and worried. She should have told James to take his own kids to the beach, and she and Gwen should have spent the day alone. This was too much for her, with Nathan in a temper and vacant, saccharine Saskia, whom they had not seen for months and who had once again become a semistranger.

At Maidstone, James swung the car into a service station. "McDonalds. Sas gave me the idea, I absolutely insist. Your challenge, should you choose to accept it, is to compile the most unhealthy combination of items you can think of. Someone get me the fish thing with fries, nuggets, and a chocolate milk shake." He turned and winked at Nathan. "Next best thing to intravenous fluids." Julia wondered why he seemed to find his son's excessive drinking to be amusing rather than reprehensible. Nathan slipped wordlessly from the car.

But McDonald's turned out to be an excellent idea. Back on the road with steaming paper bags, the children revived. Gwen spoke, voluntarily, to say that her cheeseburger was "the best." Nathan, finishing his second Big Mac, observed that fat and salt combined had magical restorative properties, and began to call out musical suggestions to his father. Saskia dipped a chicken nugget in Gwen's ketchup and nudged her gently with an elbow.

After a while Gwen said, "I so should have got a milk shake," and Julia was surprised to see Nathan take his from between his knees and offer it to her. James, who had been lifting his own from the cup holder to hand over his shoulder, glanced briefly at Julia and smiled; Julia gave a tiny shrug and sipped her black coffee in silence. They drove on through Kent and south, to East Sussex.

They were not the only people drawn to the water. The line for the car park stretched back more than a mile and so Julia, keen to preserve the fragile good tempers, did not object when James said they should go ahead. They took what they could carry and began to make their way along the road toward the shore, Gwen and Nathan lagging behind. Julia found herself walking with Saskia. She did not have the energy for someone else's daughter. She had been dreading Saskia's arrival in the house—another personality, more needs, emotional, practical, dietary. Last night, seeing Saskia and Rowan together, she had been riven with envy at their carelessness, their intimacy. Lucky, lighthearted, untraumatized. Katy had been to visit only once, carrying a small white orchid in Marks & Spencer cellophane and looking utterly petrified. Gwen did not seem to answer her phone anymore, except Nathan's calls.

Julia's mind was upon the reconciliation taking place behind them; it took effort to turn her attention to the girl and think of a conversation she might begin. She settled on their location, the weather, the white-streaked purple bells of sea bindweed flourishing along the path. All this, so close to London—they should remember it year-round and come more often—and all the while thinking, *Has that little shit apologized? Has he let her speak, will he give her a chance to tell him everything she suffered, and what it means to her?* As they mounted the dunes she paused for a moment, craning backward, and spotted Gwen's red hair, still a way off.

Saskia began to screw her toe into the fine sand. "It's been weird to be so far away with all this stuff happening to my family. I've been worried about my brother and Gwen and everyone and, I dunno, it's just easier to be here. Now I know that like, even though this supersad thing happened, it's all going to be okay."

Julia was startled; a moment ago they had been discussing the dune grass, and whether or not the beach would have a changing room. She and Saskia had never before had a conversation with any content.

"Is that your sense now? It's going to be okay?"

Saskia nodded. "Definitely. I just can't even imagine what she went through, you know? And on top of everything there must have been this guilt that she'd let you guys down by getting pregnant in the first place, and she was agonizing and agonizing and then out of nowhere comes this massive stark reminder that we don't actually get to decide a lot of the time. Like, we're not in control at all. You don't think of someone having a miscarriage at sixteen. My mom says it's actually no less common than any other time, and it's just one of those things. But that doesn't make it any easier when it's actually happening to *you* and not to all those other people. I just feel better being here with you guys so I can see them. And yeah, so I think they'll be okay. A sad thing happened that was no one's fault, and they love each other. And that's it."

This was the longest speech Julia had ever heard Saskia make and she was struck by the girl's compassion. Now, something eased within her, remembering she liked James's daughter. Saskia would be kind to Gwen.

"They love each other," Saskia said again, watching Gwen and Nathan approach across the car park. She spoke with admiration. Their arms were around one another and Nathan had taken Gwen's bag so she had nothing to carry. They were talking intently, not smiling, but not arguing. Gwen's palm was pressed to Nathan's chest. Julia turned away. Teenage relationships were always roller coasters, but how had the whole family ended up trapped with them on the ride?

The beach was crowded, utterly unlike her last visit when she and James had come alone and walked for miles along wide empty stretches of blond sand, met only by the odd dog walker and a few determined enthusiasts flying kites in the stiff winter wind. Today the heat had drawn hundreds of families, gathered in untidy sprawls behind candy-striped windbreaks, and in sinking plastic chairs. There were not enough umbrellas—tender English flesh was laid out everywhere like the aftermath of a massacre, gently roasting in the unaccustomed heat. Julia and Saskia unrolled towels, and Julia had read a chapter of her novel by the time Gwen and Nathan approached, fingers interlaced. Intermittently, Julia's eye was drawn to the baby at the center of a large family group nearby. Naked but for a watermelon-pink sunhat, she was banging a tube of sunscreen onto the towel beneath her, pausing only when her mother spooned mashed banana into her mouth. Watching recalled to Julia the passionate, consuming Stockholm syndrome; the beautiful tyranny of early motherhood. She wondered how Gwen felt to see the slideshow exhibition of new parenthood enacted beside them throughout the afternoon—the endless soothing, changing, feeding—but Gwen showed no signs of having noticed.

44.

"IT'S JUST SO NICE TO MEET YOU." JOAN'S LOOSE NEST OF blonde curls bounced as she nodded. Over the crook of her arm was a pink paper bag, from which white creamy shredded paper overflowed. In her other hand was a bunch of tall sunflowers, which she pressed shyly into Julia's hands.

"Thank you so much, they're beautiful. Come in," said Julia, brightly and irrelevantly, since they were already in. For Philip she had resolved to make this new woman feel welcome, but could not shake the fear that she had entered accidentally into an illicit affair. "If she tells you to call her 'Granny,'" Iris had told Gwen, "I'm calling the lawyers." Iris had visited only that morning and her presence still hung in the air, like woodsmoke. Julia wondered if Philip could smell Chanel No. 5 and lingering, imperious disdain. But Philip, holding a coat and a small, mint-green ostrich-leather handbag with a long gold chain, had barely taken his eyes from Joan. His hair had been swept up and forward, in a rather stylish cut. He was, Julia realized, startled, wearing jeans.

Footsteps thundered above them and Nathan appeared, striding into the hall with a hand already extended to shake Philip's, as if about to welcome him into a glass-walled corner office for an interview. Gwen padded down after him, drawing with her a scent of nail polish and acetone. The fingernails of one hand were painted green, with white polka dots; Nathan, too, Julia noticed, had a single green thumbnail. Julia made introductions, and they made their way to the kitchen, where James was making a pot of tea and unwrapping a banana bread from the market. He wiped his hands and came forward to greet them.

"How is it to be free, at long last?" Philip asked Nathan. He was still holding Joan's light mackintosh, which he smoothed every now and again, a patient, attentive valet. Julia took it from him and hung it over a chair, along with the handbag. Joan fussed and protested and said she mustn't worry, but then began to move kitchen chairs around so that Philip might have one with arms.

"Supercalifragilisticexpialidocious," Nathan told him. Gwen came to sit beside him and from the pocket of his jeans he produced her bottles of nail polish, one green, one white, and set them before her. "Delivered. You remain unsmudged. I never intend to do any exams again. I'm not going to medical school, I've told my father already. I'm going to become a crab fisherman in Thailand."

"When my boys were doing A levels it was a nightmare," said Joan, accepting the mug of tea that James handed her before sliding it immediately toward Philip. "But then it's all over before it's begun, and suddenly that's it, before you know it. And all these doctors in the family, you'll sail through." She looked from James to Philip, and back to Nathan. "Isn't it a funny thing, all these obstetricians in the family? Both your parents and Phil."

Iris would die, thought Julia, turning away to hide her smile. She would spontaneously combust. Philip Alden. Phil.

"On a good day Obs and Gynae is the best job in the world," James told her. "On a bad day I wish I was a plumber."

"Will you deliver babies, like your parents?"

"No," said Nathan, rather too firmly. "I'm going to do oncology."

"Oh, isn't that wonderful, we need young men like you." Joan pressed a hand to her heart. "My Steve had lung. And your Daniel had liver, Phil said." She turned to Julia, who nodded, though her eyes flew to Gwen, who did not take kindly to discussions of her father's cancer, certainly not to such abbreviated, familiar references to it. But Gwen was at the sink rinsing strawberries and either hadn't heard or hadn't minded.

"What a mensch." Joan looked around for affirmation and found it in Gwen, who was looking at Nathan with an irritating pride. Nathan himself looked down modestly at his hands. He rubbed a finger over his green-painted thumbnail and it smeared. Gwen giggled and dispatched him upstairs for polish remover and cotton balls.

"Where will he study next year?" Joan took Philip's hand across the table and squeezed it. "Josh, that's my eldest, was at Guys and St. Thomas's and he made some lovely friends, though they did work him very hard. I must say, I know it's not what matters but it's nice for the parents that all the medicine's best in London, isn't it. He did six months of cleft palates in Guatemala, but mostly he was just down in Lambeth and even that feels far away when it's your eldest and you're used to having them upstairs. Aaron went to Birmingham. Has he decided?"

"He's got a place at Oxford," James told her, while at the same time Gwen said, "He might stay in London."

"My goodness, isn't that something?" Joan blinked and nodded several times and looked rather uncertainly from Gwen to James.

James said nothing but stood and moved to the head of the table where he began to slice the banana cake rather formally, as if carving a side of roast beef. Gwen began to run her finger round and round the edge of her empty plate. There was no longer any reason for Nathan to stay in London; Gwen's convenient misfortune had liberated him. He would go to New College, Oxford, and Gwen, with one more year of school to go, would pine.

James distributed slices of cake and then left for the hospital, apologizing to Joan, who apologized in return for having taken him away from his patients for even this long. After he'd gone Joan gave Philip a small querying glance, received a nod, and then turned to Gwen. She was still holding a paper bag on her lap and this she handed over, hurriedly.

"I hope it's alright, but this is just a very little something, I had a pattern and I just thought, something cozy. Good for snuggling on the sofa."

The gift turned out to be a white knitted blanket with a perfect rainbow cabled into its center. "It's gorgeous," Gwen breathed. "This is amazing, I can't believe you can do this! Thank you *so much*." She hugged Joan, who flushed, looking pleased.

"Oh, it's only practice it needs. I can teach you if you'd like; you'd pick up cable in no time. Phil told me that you liked rainbows, so."

"I do, and I love knitting, I just haven't had that much practice. I do mostly polymer clay, and a tiny bit of oils. But knitting's cool 'cause you can do it while you do other stuff, like watching TV or whatever.

I've been sitting at home a lot for the last few weeks; I could have knitted myself, like, a whole house."

Joan's expression softened. "You know, when I first married I had baby fever, and I thought it would be easy-peasy. I got pregnant straightaway and at eight weeks I had a mis." Julia froze, horrified. Gwen was looking down at the folded blanket on the table, unmoving, and it was impossible to see her face. "The hardest time of my life, till then. And back then no one talked about it, we were just meant to get on with it, pull your socks up, try for another, make it right that way. I don't know why anyone thinks that's the answer; it isn't. Or isn't for everyone. I didn't want to try again so we didn't, not for two more years. I was scared that maybe my body couldn't do it and it would all happen the same way. And I was very sad for a time. So sad. But then I started to get better and then all those years later when I lost my Steve all I could think was, 'We had those precious years together first, just the two of us, just to be married.' And I've got my boys, and that time we had, back then I wouldn't have chosen it for all the world I was so desperate to have a family, but they were beautiful years. We got to know each other. We grew up. I can't wish it differently." She ran her fingers idly over each colored arc of the rainbow, in turn. "I like rainbows, too, you know. They're hopeful. My first Schnauzer dam was called Rainbow because she had these lovely stripy markings, not really what you'd want in a pure Schnauzer, very odd; that's why I got her in the end; the breeder said no one would take a funny-looking scrap like that so she was left on the shelf, but in the Poodle crosses it just came out beautifully. And what a temperament. Twelve, she lived to. She was my precious girl, she saved me, after Steve. She saved me."

Julia was cringing, waiting for some unforgivable rudeness, and felt a rush of anger when Gwen raised her head and she saw a tear slip down her face. But Gwen was looking at Joan intently. She said, "We had Mole, and he saved me, too."

"They just know, don't they, dogs," Joan agreed, and she and Gwen smiled at each other.

45.

A, A, B, C, C. OXFORD WOULD NOT TAKE HIM. IMPERIAL WOULD not take him. It was University College London, another world-class institution, and it was unimaginable, the end of the world. Controlled while on the line to Nathan's housemaster, James had put down the phone, paused, and then slammed his palm into the doorframe, leaving a fine spiderweb of cracks beneath the heel of his hand. The next minutes were a blur, from which Julia could only recall the gist of her own soothing, reasonable words—she had talked about perspective, about difficult circumstances, about a sense of achievement, personal fulfillment, and who you actually were as a human being mattering more than historic names—but only moments later found herself screaming that he should think himself bloody lucky his child was being educated at all when her own child's life had come close to ruin; somehow James was roaring that she wanted Nathan to fail just because Gwen made destructive choices; her outraged denial of this indefensible accusation had been loud, but had not been convincing to either of them.

She hadn't wanted Nathan to fail. But Gwen had suffered, and Nathan's impermeable cheer, his impending success, the new stage he was impatient to begin had all filled her with envy. He seemed shatterproof, and she could not quite let go of its unfairness. It was Gwen's strength and affliction to feel to the quick even a glancing blow, while Nathan had been so effectively in denial about its existence that the loss of his child made no lasting impression. And now to grieve for something so petty—how could James truly think a university so important? It was ludicrous. What message did James's own disappointment convey to his child about what mattered in life? She would have liked a little less emphasis placed on the boy's curriculum vitae, a little more placed on his character. No. Julia could not pity Nathan. She could not even like him, even in these last weeks when his devotion to Gwen had apparently returned, and redoubled.

James and Julia went to bed in a frosty silence, unaccustomed and distressing to both of them. They had never before raised their voices in anger and it was only now, after the smashing of that precious, celebrated myth (we are a couple who always speak with gentleness, we are a couple who sleep each night face to face, we are a couple unlike other couples) that each had realized the wonder of it. After all, they had weathered more treacherous storms. As parents they made very different choices, true, but James had proven himself wise and generous to his marrow, a better man even than she'd known. And Julia's gratitude, above all else, had never left her. She had expected to live the rest of her life without love and had found James, and had never before lost sight of that revelation. But tonight she had abandoned her gratitude when James had seemed to forget his own. He made it clear he blamed Gwen. An act of sabotage. Had he really said that? Not quite, but almost.

. . .

IN THE MIDDLE OF THE NIGHT, she woke to find that they had moved together in sleep and were entwined, arms and legs wrapped tightly around one another, the sheets kicked off and entangled at their feet. James was sleepily kissing her face, her eyelids, her mouth, and she had begun to cry and to whisper frantic words of love and of apology before it began to dawn that what had roused them both was furious shouting, somewhere in the house. They froze, pressed tightly chest to chest, breath held as if sharing a narrow hiding place. Against her cheek Julia felt James furrow his brow as he listened. He dropped his forehead against her collarbone, and rolled over with an exhausted groan. Julia fumbled on the floor for her dressing gown and followed James downstairs. As she passed her practice room the door opened and Saskia emerged, sleep-tousled and squinting, mumbling something indistinct.

"It's fine, go back to sleep," Julia whispered, and Saskia nodded wordlessly and closed her eyes and the door again.

It was three o'clock in the morning and on the ground floor of the house both of their children were screaming, voluble and operatic. Over James's shoulder Julia looked down and saw Gwen at the foot of the stairs, dressed in tartan brushed cotton pajama shorts and a faded Rainbow Brite T-shirt. She had worn this at seven or eight years old and called it back into service as an ironic retro item, though it seemed to Julia that she had been seven or eight only yesterday and there was nothing ironic about a child in child's clothing, however much midriff it now exposed. Gwen's hair was electric, huge and wild around her pale face and she was pacing back and forth in the narrow hall as if barring the front door, a scrawny and gesticulating Cerberus.

"You can't! You can't say that, you can't, you can't just rewrite everything." Gwen's thick glasses slipped to the end of her nose on a slick of tears and sweat, and she was forced to pause and push them back up with her forefinger. "It's not fair!"

"Hey. Keep your voices down. What's wrong with you? Where've you been, Nathan? I've been calling you, come here, I've been worried. We needed to talk today."

Neither teenager gave any evidence they could hear James speaking. Nathan lurched into view from the kitchen and began to repeat that Gwen was insane, out of her mind, impossible to reason with. His voice was loud, slurred with alcohol and outrage, and he had the hood of his sweatshirt tightened low over his brow so that his face was in shadow and he looked as if he were about to commit a mugging, or an act of light vandalism. Gwen, who had begun to hyperventilate, was gulping back strangled hiccups of rage between each choked word of accusation.

James rushed to pull his son into a tight bear hug as Julia went to embrace her daughter. Gwen did not succumb easily, her long limbs stiff and flailing, her narrow shoulders heaving with jagged, desperate breaths.

"Shh. Breathe, Dolly. What is going on?" Julia pushed back the few damp curls that had stuck to Gwen's sweating brow just as James, in less compassionate tones, turned and demanded, "What the hell is going on down here? Why are you shouting at him?" He had one arm thrown over Nathan's shoulder, his hand upon his son's chest, upon his notionally broken heart. Nathan's eyes were pink-rimmed and blood-shot. Crying? Drugs, maybe? Julia did not feel particularly sympathetic to either cause. She glared at James.

"Ask her," Nathan said bitterly, pointing, "she's having a psychotic break. She's actually psychotic. I haven't done anything wrong. My life is officially over now, thank you, thank you very much; you can't actually keep me chained in this house anymore; I'm not a hostage, I'm allowed time off for good fucking behavior. And I'm allowed to say that the reason my life is over is—"

"Your life is not over, you got amazing grades—"

"Oh yeah, they're really amazing. They're amazing for a retard. Amazing for a school like yours where everyone does Goat Milking and General Studies and fucking *Art*, amazing for you with your accidental, 'Oh, I only care about rainbows and glitter and oops! I get As.'"

"Art is just as important as what you do!"

Nathan turned unsteadily on his heel and set off toward the front door; Gwen shrieked with incoherent rage, shaking Julia off and chasing him. "Stop walking away from me! Come back! COME BACK!"

"Enough," hissed James, springing forward to bar Nathan's exit. Gwen and Nathan paused and looked at him. "Nathan, I want to talk to you, properly. But this is not the way, and you are not walking out of this house again tonight, do you understand? You both sort your asses out like civilized adults."

Nathan, who had been looking slightly queasy and fleetingly contrite, raised his face in a sneer. "Oh, because we never heard you and Mom yelling, never. It was nothing but raindrops on roses and whiskers on kittens in our house growing up. One endless picnic. Like the fucking Waltons."

James looked thunderous. "Stop. Cursing. Both of you. You will behave like human beings in this house, and like the adults you claim to be. I don't care if you are sixteen or sixty, this is unacceptable. We need to sit down and talk; I promise you, we just need to—"

"What are you even talking about? Nothing's going to be okay, and by the way, you can't promise me shit because my life is over already, because she has chopped my balls off. Literally one by one, my balls have been chopped off, she's torn them off with her teeth like a Rottweiler. 'It is all rather unexpected and disappointing, Fuller,'" he quoted, shaking his head sorrowfully and stroking the air beneath his chin as if pulling on a beard, "'so unexpected and disappointing but *under the circumstances*' . . . I knew it was a mistake that you told Markham; now he's all like, 'Under the circumstances it's lucky you're not in a ditch.' 'Under the circumstances it's lucky you're not a crack addict eating from the trash under Waterloo Bridge.' 'Under the circumstances we'd have been happy if you'd dropped out of school and got a job licking the toilets clean at McDonald's; we'd have been jolly proud of you *under the circumstances.*'"

Gwen gave a gasp, outrage mingled with disbelief. "You're such a snob! And there aren't any circumstances! Your circumstances are literally exactly how they were before; it's made no difference whatsoever, your life never changed even one percent. We've all been walking on eggshells for you pretending that any of this actually matters, like your *school exams* were the most important thing in the world; do you even know how stupid that is? Do you know anything about the real world at all? Newsflash—no one cares at all about your A levels, literally no one. And you never let me talk about the fact that we lost our baby; you don't care, you've just had everyone pretend that the whole thing never even happened, like *our baby* never even happened; it's the stupidest thing I've ever heard, it's the most selfish— and now you're blaming me and—and you're the most immature, disgusting—" She broke off, weeping extravagantly. Julia tried to put an arm around her again, to guide her back upstairs, and was once more abruptly pushed off.

Nathan spread his hands and gestured around, gathering looks of sympathy from an imagined crowd of supporters, though only Gwen and Julia were facing in his direction, neither inclined to solicitude. Julia stepped forward. "Go to bed," she ordered, attempting the same commanding air that James had achieved moments earlier. "Enough. We will talk as a family in the morning. I'm sorry you feel you've had a hard day, Nathan. I know you don't want to hear it right now but I think in time you'll come to be very proud of yourself. You've had a shock, but now it's three o'clock in the morning. Go to bed. Now, please."

"I was under the impression this was a free country." Nathan was not looking at her but instead continued his slurred address to the invisible audience in the galleries. "I was under the impression people could air their dirty laundry in the privacy of their own homes. This is my home, isn't it? I was under the impression it was good to talk about our feelings. To *express*."

"Yeah, Julia," said Gwen, which startled Julia and came as an unexpectedly painful betrayal, "it's actually none of your business. It's not like I tried to get involved when you guys were screaming at each other earlier."

"We weren't screaming," Julia protested, as Nathan began a rather hollow, mirthless laugh. "Pots and kettles all over the place. 'S'like living in a kitchen cupboard. We're all mad here," he added, smiling in a way that suggested that the spectators in the dress circle had appreciated this reference, "I'm mad, you're mad. They're Hare and Hatter, baby. Visit either you like, they're both mad."

"They were screaming," Gwen told him. "They were, while you were out. When they couldn't get hold of you and they were worrying and then they phoned the school, they were screaming their heads off at each other for ages."

"Love's young dream. The lesson in all of this, baby, is that there's no such thing as perfect anything, it's all just PR bullshit, 's'what I've been saying to you all along if you recall, and you didn't want to hear it. I get called cynical so often that people forget to call me right, which I also am, but cynical's just sensible. There, that's my bumper sticker contribution. Cynical's sensible, and it's all sunshine and roses until you start fighting and then next stage is, '*It's not you, it's us, Mommy and Daddy still love you both very much.*'S'amazing how everyone reverts to cliché. Here's a cliché: Life's a bitch. Life's a bitch, and then you die. Everyone knows I'm right; we're all dancing on the *Titanic* and no one will admit the Emperor's got his cock out. Now please come here." Nathan opened his arms and Julia was astonished to see Gwen move into them, grateful, and without hesitation. She had hunched over automatically, so that he might put his arms over her shoulders. Moments ago Gwen had been almost unhinged with righteous fury; now she had buried her face against his neck and was stroking his hair and murmuring, inaudibly.

Julia thought she caught the words, "going to be . . ." and, "I hate . . ." but could not hear and so did not know what Gwen hated. Julia, with sharp clarity, hated Nathan. Still too inebriated to modulate his voice, Nathan began to whisper loudly and ardently into the fox-red cloud of Gwen's hair that he loved her, that he was sorry about the baby, their poor baby, that he hadn't meant it, that he had never been so unhappy. "I don't understand," he kept saying, "I don't understand." Julia watched his hands roaming up and down her daughter's narrow, bent back, the sharp shoulder blades, the knobbed spine visible beneath faded cotton, his gestures both one of reassurance and perhaps preliminary sexual advance. Julia looked away in disgust. She heard footsteps on the stairs and saw James heading upstairs. He gave a grim little smile and gestured to Julia to give up, to join him; together they retired to their bedroom, feeling fragile and somehow brutalized.

In the living room, Gwen and Nathan were still crying and kissing, kissing and crying, cupping each other's faces in desperation, drawing each other in as if they were reuniting or perhaps parting before an uncertain future on the chill, gray platform of a wartime train station.

46.

"NOT GOOD," SAID JULIA, IN RESPONSE TO HER MOTHER-IN-law's inquiry. An exhalation could be heard through the phone. Without warning Iris had taken herself to France; her displeasure came through with a Gallic-hinted shrug, the imagined aroma of lavender, and pastis. Julia stepped out of the elevator from the underground car park and battled to release the chain of a tethered supermarket cart, one-handed. "You can't even begin to imagine how horrible it was yesterday. It was as if everyone finally lost their minds, once and for all. I said such awful things and James looked so hurt and I still couldn't stop myself. The only thing I'm longing to say and can't is that I hate his son, and I want him out of my house. And Gwen's absolutely insistent that everything will be fine once Nathan gets over yesterday, and it won't be; I saw his face. He'll never forgive her—not for Oxford, not for getting pregnant. And not for her results. Which by the way, I am bloody proud of." Julia bit her lip and stared glassily into her empty cart. "Though not as proud as I am of how courageous she's been recently. Unlike James, I have not raised my daughter to believe that grades reflect the value of a person."

She had come to lean on James so completely that thinking of it gave her vertigo, yet now it was James's son about whom she needed counsel and, almost without realizing, she had begun to withdraw from the safety of their private, holy confessional. She took her fears to Iris, leaving with James the banalities, the palliatives, the careful and protective white lies so essential to a new family. We are all fine. It's fine. Your son is a fine, upstanding citizen who I'm so fond of. Of course he needs to blow off steam. A small, unnerving gulf had opened, a crack in the earth between them two inches wide, a mile deep. She had come to the supermarket for fruit and eggs, and tuna steaks for this evening's dinner, and to rant in guaranteed, luxurious privacy. She did not care about fruit or eggs or tuna. She was wandering up and down the aisles of Waitrose looking blankly at product after product, and off-loading her anxiety onto Iris. Iris, whom she longed to visit in Parliament Hill, whose face she longed to see. Iris, who no longer lived in Parliament Hill, who made fresh starts with such dignity, who had taken the sorrow she refused to acknowledge to the far side of the Channel.

It had been many years since Julia had been to Giles's house in Bargemon. Gwen had been eight, engrossed by her crochet kit, utterly uninterested in Giles's attempts to teach her tennis or Julia's to take her down to the ponds to visit the squat, fat, interesting toads. Gwen had sat cross-legged by the swimming pool making pink-and-purple coasters shaped like four-petaled flowers, her tongue clamped between her teeth with stern concentration. She would do nothing else. It had been uncomfortably like having their own little sweatshop,

Daniel had observed, staffed with one extremely diligent child laborer. When she'd run out of fuchsia they'd expected the coaster craze to fizzle but instead she had begged and pleaded, hopping from foot to foot, and Julia had driven her the hour and half back into Nice to find a haberdashery.

The house, Iris had assured her, had barely changed since that summer. It was rather quiet, perhaps, but several people in the village remembered her. Julia pictured her mother-in-law outside on the highest of the terraces, sitting at a terra-cotta–tiled table beneath the shade of an ancient fig tree. Iris herself was a blank in this image. It was high summer, and possibly 40 degrees, but surely she wasn't in anything as undignified as a bathing suit? Loose white linen, possibly, and a broad straw hat. Would she always be chic, even in complete, unbroken solitude? Then Iris brought her back into the fluorescent chill of Waitrose by saying, "Well, you do have rather different child-rearing approaches, put it that way. It's tricky to bring two sets of values together so late in the day, but I must say I don't think Thing has it entirely wrong—"

"And that's fine, but what about raising children to be kind, or to be thoughtful, or to take responsibility for their actions, or to trust their own intuition? I don't understand—he puts such value on generosity in his own behavior and with his kids he has this blind spot; the most important thing above everything is pedaling away on this hamster wheel. He can't think that's what matters most in life, and yet he does. It's just so, so *narrow*. A degree doesn't make you happy."

"Hamsters don't pedal. I agree that one can be equally miserable with an Oxford degree as without, but you do see why he's disappointed when it was such a close thing. And I do think the ex-wife has some fairly substantial expectations for the boy, too."

Julia was glaring into a chiller cabinet at an array of Cheddars and Wensleydales and Red Leicesters. Did they need cheese? She couldn't remember. She threw several blocks into the cart, then replaced one. When she reached the end of the aisle she hesitated and returned for it, dragging her cart backward. "I couldn't care less what loony Pamela thinks. I can't see how the pregnant women of Boston have coped today when she's spent every waking hour phoning either Nathan or James. Or me, to ask for Nathan or James. And meanwhile James is finally having to confront the reality that Nathan—shock horror—isn't necessarily a genius. What's to say he would have got anything different anyway; maybe he didn't mess up and these are the marks he deserves? Till yesterday James was genuinely resolute that the last months wouldn't have to cost Nathan anything, as long as we all worked hard enough, as if we could manage it away so beautifully that no one would even have to break their stride, but now he needs to give his son a kick up the backside and get him to stop behaving like such a bloody child, and to come home, stop drinking, get a bit of perspective. None of this will matter remotely in the long run—Oxford, not-Oxford, who cares? He's in a ludicrously privileged position. And he can't just leave Gwen in this awful limbo that she won't even admit she's in; he has to tell her if it's over. Enough's enough. I'd like to see them all prioritize some *values*, not just marks."

"Have you and Thing talked this morning?"

"About what? What is there to say? I feel as if we're speaking different languages. But I do know his son can't behave like this and live under my roof."

"It isn't just your roof."

"Exactly," said Julia, ignoring what she suspected had been Iris's point. "It's Gwen's childhood home. She has a right to feel safe, and looked after, and secure. If they break up—"

"Listen, darling." Ice clinked in a glass and Julia felt a stab of envy, picturing pale Provençal sunshine, chilled rosé under a sheen of condensation, Bleu de Bresse weeping on a board of olive wood, *magret de canard*, the air heavy with ripe figs and citronella smoke, a hot and honeyed escape from muddy reality. Iris had been made unhappy by a change of circumstances and had thrown back her shoulders and booked a ticket to France. She would give no straight or definitive answer about her return. She had wanted to sell her house, so she'd sold her house. She had wanted to go to France, and a few weeks later had taken up residence in Bargemon. She made apparently effortless fresh starts. Julia flung several cartons of fat-free yogurt into her cart with unnecessary force. "I'm so glad you phoned me," Iris went on, "you need to get this off your chest, and I must say it's rather a relief not to hear you Pollyanna-ing around the place, but now you're going to hear me say the opposite of what I usually tell you. It's all very well to be expressive and let things out in a relationship and everything else, but this time you simply can't do it. You must call me or at a push Philip Alden, if he can find the time between filling Viagra prescriptions and manicuring poodles to answer the telephone, but for God's sake don't say any of this at home. He'll never forgive you. You feel aggrieved by his child and he feels aggrieved by yours, so please stop talking about them. I agree that you are very different sorts of parents but the beauty of your position is that you don't have to bother finding common ground because you don't have to parent together, so none of it matters in the slightest. Just leave one another to get on with it. Your efforts now need to be directed back toward your own business."

Julia wheeled slowly through the biscuit aisle, then reversed to snatch a treacherous roll of Marie biscuits. Philip was bringing Joan for tea. "We're supposed to be going out for dinner tomorrow night. James insisted."

"Don't you go out for dinner all the time?"

"I can't even think . . . We've not been out the two of us since before everything happened. Months ago. We're actually meant to be going to Milan for the weekend in a few weeks—James has those Rossini tickets—but I can't even think about that just yet."

"Listen to yourself, anyone would think you had survived a nuclear holocaust. *Everything happened,* as you so coyly put it, and it was horrid, but we need a firm return to real life now, please. I'm desperately relieved to hear you're getting a weekend away soon. Listen to me. Put on something attractive, get your hair done, go out tomorrow, for the love of God. All this micromanaging of the almost-adult is unhealthy for absolutely everyone. Why don't you book a hotel for the night?"

"We *can't.*"

"I don't see why not, but then what do I know. Listen, enjoy tomorrow evening. I must go, I've decided to lunch every day in the square, I can't lurk in this house just because—I can't just *sit here.* Come and visit."

She was gone, and Julia, too, was alone again, wheeling her cart toward the tills and unpacking onto the conveyer belt her various acquisitions, having forgotten almost everything for which she'd come.

47.

GWEN SLEPT INTERMITTENTLY ALL AFTERNOON, STIRRING ONLY briefly when her mother came in from shopping and sat beside her silently for a time, stroking her hair. When she next woke she was alone and it was cooler—the sky through the window, a bank of dense bruise-dark cloud. There were voices downstairs and she knew without hesitation that Nathan was in the house.

The ground had shifted. When they had eventually gone to bed last night he'd seemed full of a determined, unfocused, angry passion, had pulled her to him urgently but it had been without affection or even much awareness of her. Afterward he had turned his back to her in brooding silence, and later must have crept out while she lay sleeping for she'd woken alone, and a new, sick sense of foreboding had kept her cocooned beneath the muffling safety of the covers. His absence filled the room that morning. It squatted lead-heavy on her chest, and she had the sudden understanding that they could have weathered his physical removal to Oxford, and that if he had won the place she'd so feared, she would have cost him nothing, and might still have been

his girlfriend. Now he was going nowhere, but in his bitter disappointment he was moving beyond her reach.

She had planned to change. She had wanted to brush her hair. She
had wanted to paint her nails, and find her push-up bra, and paint
black kohl over the red rims of her bloodshot eyes. Instead she padded
downstairs where she knew he'd be, herself unaltered.

Gwen entered the living room to find Saskia's friend Rowan sitting neatly on top of Saskia's closed suitcase, cross-legged, like a pixie.
She wore a white vest and black denim dungarees, small, very round
mirrored sunglasses, and burgundy lipstick on a very white face.

"It's a travesty," Rowan was saying. "Hi, Gwen, cute bracelet. A
week is a travesty. I'm going to climb into this suitcase and come
with you. I'm going to slip into your pocket."

"Come with me!" Saskia said, and Rowan sprang to her feet so the
two could embrace, rocking from side to side in one another's arms
savoring their maudlin, pantomime sadness. Nathan was lounging in
an armchair and as Gwen entered he did not look up, but instead
smiled toward his sister with her friend, indulgent, paternal. Behind
her James came in with the car keys.

"I'm so sorry, guys, but I have to take Miss Saskia. The time has
come."

Rowan stuck out her lower lip in protest. "Boo," she said, "boo, boo.
Let her stay! We say let her stay forever."

"Believe me, if I could, I would. Take it up with the college; they
claim they need her back."

"Transfer to Magdalen," Rowan said, finally removing the mirrored sunglasses and letting them fall. They were, Gwen now saw, on
a long chain of black-and-gold links that hung around her neck.
"Come back with me; you know it's the only sensible thing to do."

"Magdalen? Only losers go to Oxford; all the cool kids are going to UCL." Nathan swept back his hair. To hear him, Gwen thought, you would never know that he had cried for most of last night.

James picked up the suitcase. "I'm taking this and we're going in five minutes. Four minutes. Who's coming with me?"

Nathan raised his hand. "I'm coming. Rowan? You in?"

"I hadn't really thought about it. I'd love to but I don't have a means of getting home again."

"I can be your means," said James, pausing to set down the suitcase he held. "I'll drop you home. But if you're coming, we're all leaving now, now. Gwen?" he asked, squeezing her shoulder. Gwen shook her head. The presence of the others dropped a cloak of public silence and propriety over her; Nathan's inaccessibility beyond it was insupportable. He still had not looked at her. When they were next alone, he would say things she did not want to hear.

Outside James began to toot the car horn and Nathan jogged out after the others. After a moment Saskia returned. Gwen swallowed, thickly. Saskia's loss severed yet another fine wire of connection with Nathan and left her perilous.

Saskia took Gwen's face between her hands, squeezing her cheeks, shaking Gwen gently from side to side. "Please don't let my brother be a dick."

"I don't know how I can stop him." A tear slipped down each cheek.

"Oh no, don't be sad, I'm sorry. You're still my sister; please don't cry. You are, I mean it, that's the amazing thing. You'll always be my sister whatever happens. Always."

Gwen nodded, tightly. It was not true, of course. Saskia was Nathan's sister. Gwen had nobody.

. . .

"I THOUGHT I'D BE ABLE to talk to him on the way home this evening but then Rowan came to Heathrow with us, so I had to drop her back. I had to listen to him pretend to be fine instead."

"Well, where is he now?" asked Pamela. She sounded faintly accusing, as though James might have mislaid their son like a dry cleaning ticket or a bunch of keys.

"Asleep, it's two a.m."

"Are you at work? Why are you awake?"

"Yes," James lied, closing the kitchen door behind him and lowering his voice. "On call, my house officer rang. Shoulder dystocia and postpartum hemorrhage and— I can't talk about it twice," said James, who had not, in fact, even talked about it once, and was a poor liar. He was not on call, and the prolonged dystocia had been first thing this morning, an unpleasant enough birth that he felt guilty using it now as an excuse. The mother had been morbidly obese and suffering gestational diabetes and he ought to have insisted on a section, but she had cried and pleaded and James, overtired after yesterday's emotional scenes, had not had the energy to resist her. She had tried to push, and the newborn had suffered brachial plexus damage. James did not, now, feel good about this decision.

The truth was that he couldn't sleep, had longed for someone to talk to, and had no wish to wake Julia as he did not trust himself to remain civil. She had accused him of having no sense of perspective, of snobbery, of inhabiting an elite and rarefied plane while discarding "what really matters." Hadn't she heard anything he'd confided about his background? About his own childhood? Did she really think that names and labels were what mattered to him? To accuse him of snobbery was risible—and the hypocrisy had taken his breath away. All he had ever taught his son was the value of hard work, of discipline, of aspiration. It was far more indulgent to raise a child to think that academic education was an irrelevance as long as their self-esteem was thriving, or whatever the hell it was she believed. What really matters? What horseshit. Meanwhile, along the way, Julia had lobbed a series of adjectives at his son for which, twenty-four hours later, he was still struggling to forgive her. *Selfish. Immature. Self-absorbed. Inconsiderate.* All these on a day when Nathan had needed not condemnation but comfort, a day when the memory of Gwen's monumental selfishness was heightened, its consequences livid and raw. Julia accused Nathan of disrespect, of behaving badly toward Gwen. Well, Nathan had his whole life ahead and it was understandable if he did not want to remain in a joyless and precociously serious minimarriage with an infantile, spoiled little girl who whined with hectoring neediness. James found himself grieving the Oxford loss afresh. As well as everything else it would have granted Nathan total liberty from Gwen.

He'd walked away expecting any minute that Julia would calm down, follow him upstairs and apologize, and when she hadn't he had grown angrier and more resentful. Pamela, who loved Nathan as he did, would understand.

"Was the baby okay?"

"What baby?"

"Shoulder dystocia? Never mind, never mind. Nathan sounds terrible. Should I come, do you think?"

"No," said James, reflexively, but then thought for a moment. "Maybe, actually. I think we should sit down with him. I still can't believe it. Mr. Markham is shocked; we've talked twice today. When did you speak to Nathan?"

"Darling, I've spoken to him twenty-five times today; it's precisely why I'm worried. He barely called all summer and now it's like the Batphone. I popped to one of Beth's deliveries this morning and when I switched my phone on I had eleven missed calls. I think I should come. It's only three weeks till the Paris conference in any case; I could come and just stay through. Are you okay? You sound very cross."

"You make it sound as if I haven't been taking care of him."

"Jamesy, I don't know what's afoot with you, but I said absolutely no such thing. I said the boy phones his mother."

"Julia called him vindictive for blaming Gwen. I don't see who else we should blame."

"Julia's delusional," said Pamela, shortly.

"We had a crazy fight yesterday," James admitted.

"I'm amazed you have the energy to fight with everything else going on. You know, I feel I ought to do something nice for Gwen. She's one of the most spoiled little girls I've ever met and I am absolutely consumed with loathing. For my own sanity I need karmic balance. I should give her a gift."

James, long familiar with Pamela's complex and contradictory theology of giving, said nothing. He had many times been on the receiving end of these presents of karmic redress, and they were usually tied in a stinging ribbon of acid.

"Listen, for God's sake, if you really think it's over between them, don't let him have break-up sex with her; she'll get pregnant again, I promise you. Don't laugh, I'm absolutely serious, she will. She's a conniving little so-and-so who will have to readjust to the idea that she's not the center of the universe," Pamela concluded, apparently abandoning all thoughts of good karma. "Enough flinging herself around like Ophelia and then pulling that bloody exam rabbit out of the hat. *Her* life's on track. She made her bed."

"Yes. But look what it cost Nathan to lie in it. What I don't understand," James went on, feeling a guilty rush of disloyalty and relief, "is how it can be possible to put such a premium on children's happiness and self-fulfillment or whatever, with no understanding that encouraging academic success teaches precisely the delayed gratification that is essential to later happiness in the real, adult world. Happiness isn't having your needs met instantly, like an infant. Fulfillment in later life is effort rewarded. In work, in relationships, in marriages . . ." Here he trailed off, thinking it unwise to pursue a discussion of marital fulfillment with his ex-wife.

"You can't eat happiness," said Pamela, shortly. Her pragmatism had always been robust, if incongruous. "A joyous adolescence playing with Play-Doh won't pay the gas bills later on. And more to the point, someone somewhere will say no to the girl, and then what will happen? She'll fall apart."

"Julia thinks I'm pushy. She called me a snob."

"Take it as a compliment. Has Nathan said anything to you about America?"

James opened the fridge and stared blankly into its depths. "He's missed the applications, no? I thought we'd agreed not."

"That was mid-debacle, if you recall, when the shackles of imminent teenage parenthood awaited him in London. He could start spring semester; it wouldn't take much, quick SATs, personal statement. Wentworth will write him a reference, and with that he'd be a shoo-in everywhere. What are you chewing? It's loud. Even Harvard's still not out of the question."

"Chicken from yesterday, I'm starving. My God, that would be incredible. It would have blown my mother's mind, two grandkids at college. A son and a grandson at Harvard! That's what she busted her ass for, to get me out of Dorchester, to teach me—"

"Take a little credit, you got yourself out. You won the scholarships. And," she conceded, seizing an opportunity to criticize Julia obliquely, "your mother taught you the value of hard work. We can sort it out, you know; there are enough Ivy League schools. I'll come to London, and we'll powwow."

Someone else was awake in the house. James heard footsteps and the floorboards above his head creaked as one of the children padded across the landing to the bathroom.

"I'd better go."

"Good luck. I'm really not sure I'd eat yesterday's chicken at the Free, you know," said Pamela, confusing James until he remembered he'd said he was at work. "It's bad enough on day one. Consider a few days a week of veganism. Or even just Meatless Mondays. You'll feel better, I promise. I'll e-mail when I've booked flights. Kiss, kiss. *Ciao, ciao.*"

48.

JULIA AND JAMES HAD COME TO AN UNEASY TRUCE. RESENTING, fearing, longing for the extra hour away from Gwen, Julia thought they should save time and drive, but on James's insistence they had instead walked in late summer dusk across the bottom of the Heath, keeping pace in a silence that might have been lingering animosity, or new shyness. They went to the Bull and Last for smoked salmon, warm soda bread, and sharp, strong gin and tonics; for space, for fresh air, and above all else for respite from the house, which hummed with steady and claustrophobic tension. Julia had steeled herself for protest, and had been unprepared for Gwen simply saying, "Okay, Mummy," in a small, dull voice, and then subsiding back onto the sofa with a look of such blank and eloquent wretchedness that Julia had immediately opened her mouth to say that she wouldn't go. The next moment she'd caught sight of James's grave, tired face and had bitten her tongue.

"I know, I know, we need to talk about the children," she'd said earlier, when he told her he'd made a reservation, and he'd looked hurt and said, softly, "We need to *not* talk about the children." He was right, but knowing it hadn't eased her conscience as the front door closed behind them.

How good it would be to walk away. What a relief, not to see that flushed and tear-greased pleading resentful face. What soothing music the silence would be, free from Gwen's petulant, disconsolate voice; what restorative paradise away from all the weeping. To be alone with James. Julia ached to stay, and longed to flee.

She must not forget that Gwen had chosen this relationship with Nathan. Yet who would choose this? A hurt and angry little girl couldn't know what she had fought for, and those who understood should have tried harder to stop her. *It's my fault*, but then again, *Gwen had stamped her feet and demanded adulthood.* And on and on, tramping the same tight and tedious circuit over old, worn ground, the same regrets unending, unresolved.

Julia refused a starter and then, barely settled at the table, they almost rowed. James said irritably that they may as well get a take-away and a taxi home if she had only allowed twenty minutes for the meal; they'd better start back now, in fact; it had been a wonderful evening and, after all, they'd exceeded their yearly allowance of fun. He looked cross and flushed, and he was in the right once again. She noticed that he had shaved and put on a favored, dry-clean-only white shirt. He had come home that afternoon with a bunch of creamy white and violet-streaked Lisianthus, now in a vase on the piano. She said, quickly, it had only been that she wasn't that hungry but of course there was no rush, she'd have a green salad to be companionable if he was getting two courses, and she watched him decide to believe her, electing to avoid the fight. "And maybe some olives first?" she added as the waitress moved to leave them, returning her small notepad to the pocket of her apron. When their drinks came Julia raised her glass and said, "To us," and saw relief in James's face. Across the table his aftershave reached her, lime and faint, spiced wood smoke. She began to feel lighter, threw her shoulders back, pushed the candle aside, and reached for his hands.

"In this family we are the original couple," James told her, clinking his highball glass against hers again. Beneath the table his knees closed around her own and squeezed, gently. "We need to remember how we all got here. It's us. Everything else can be figured out."

"The original couple? You mean, like in the garden?"

"Right. You'd better Adam and Eve it."

"I don't know this is Paradise, at the moment." She intended to say this playfully but it had sounded bitter and she arrested her own train of thought before she could pursue the analogy any further. She did not want either of them hunting for serpents. "London's rubbing off on you, very impressive," she added quickly, changing the subject.

James rattled through his brief Cockney lexicon—"apples and pears," "Sherbet Dab," "septic tank" (this one, meaning "an American," was new to her)—and concluded with a demand for another butchers at the drinks menu. Another pitfall dodged, and she relaxed again. Their food came. Julia found that she was ravenous, and took pleasure in a meal for the first time in months.

She had no conversation, could think of nothing to say except to express over and over her disloyal relief and gratitude that they were not at home. Whenever she attempted to speak it was this that rose to her lips: thank God we're away. But each felt the other's child had done theirs damage and so had fallen naturally onto the enemy team. James was her best friend, yet could no longer receive such confidences. How she longed for the release: *I can't bear it any longer;*

Gwen's passive misery is suffocating me, I've worried myself sick about her, lifelong, I am tired.

For a while they ate in silence, until James clattered down his knife and fork, dropped his head back, and said, addressing the ceiling, "God, it's good to get away with you, I'm sick of those fucking children. We need to do this more often, seriously. For God's sake, let's go to Milan for longer; let's make it a week. I need you. I miss you. I know they've needed us but it's relentless and never-ending—they're like, they're like *vampires*."

Julia's eyes filled. "I miss you, too. I can't bear this. I know, you're right, I feel bled dry." That was the way back—not my child to blame, not your child. A safe, bland plural. *The children.* She risked a question, though she feared the answer: "Do you ever feel like we're being punished for being people? Instead of parents? I kept telling myself it was for Gwen, too, that it would be good for her to have a man in the house, have a father figure and a family and—but it was because I wanted it so much. I wanted you so much. You came along and changed everything and I was just drunk on it. I was thinking like a person, instead of like a parent. I let myself want."

"You should want," he said, fiercely. "Christ, Julia, you *are* a person."

"We could have waited, maybe this was all because we rushed them. We could have moved in together once they'd all left home and it was just us—why didn't we wait?"

James had been shaking his head, disagreeing before she'd even finished. "Life is so damn short. I didn't want to *date* you, I wanted to make a life with you. This life, the life we have. Every day I didn't wake up next to you was wasted." He seized her hand. "With you I'm who I'm meant to be—you teach me how to be. Your honesty, your gentleness, your generosity—I've never known anyone who loves like you do; you give with your whole self. It's humbling, and you do it so quietly, and utterly without guile. You know, when I first met Philip, before he even told me you taught piano or suggested I take lessons, he had already told me a story about you. He said that you'd been dropping by with meals for more than ten years and not once had you ever said you'd cooked for him, always that you'd made too much by accident and he was doing you a favor. 'She's terrible at judging quantities, my daughter-in-law,' that's what he said, and he said it with such love and I remember thinking, now there's a woman with *grace*. And I was right. And I found you and in every way you're more beautiful than I ever could have imagined and somehow, impossibly, it turns out that I'm fifty-five when I'm sure last week I was twenty-two, and I'm not waiting around . . . and yes, I could have moved out when we found out about the kids—we could have said okay, we tried, we'll go back to our apartment and I'll come for dinner every Tuesday and Friday or whatever and keep the kids apart that way and when they leave home I'll move back in, but we made a commitment to be a family. And don't forget we said that was an important lesson for them, too; you don't just quit when things get hard. We live together now, we work through our shit as a family. If we'd waited, we would still be waiting." For a moment James closed his eyes. "You know what, I actually can't pursue it. We did the right thing for us, and in any case what's done is done. I'm sorry, baby, can we just not? I cannot think about them any longer, not for one damn second. Can we just get this"—he glanced down at the dessert menu—"can we just get this Ferrero Rocher ice cream, and focus on that instead? I'm having a Sauternes."

In the early days, Julia remembered, they had planned for family harmony and anticipated it with patient conviction—the initial disruption and eventually a grudging, more settled, united normality. Love invites magical thinking. But how did we believe such a fairy tale? We had no alternative better than wild, empty hope as we careened toward a cliff edge. Yet—*I wanted. I want.*

She kissed his rough knuckles, where they still held her own hand. It pleased him when she showed her commitment to this evening, and so she asked for a rhubarb crumble that she did not want and saw his brow clear, as she'd known, or hoped, it would. She then excused herself. In the bathroom she checked her messages, where a text from Gwen said with unsophisticated yet devastating efficacy, I hope you're having fun, I love you, Mummy. Unwilling to be manipulated and manipulated nonetheless, Julia buried her phone back in her bag and returned stiffly to James. When he asked whether she wanted to see what was on at the Everyman Cinema she shook her head and said she was sorry but she was really a little tired. It had been a very long week. "It's been wonderful," she told him, stroking his clean-shaven cheek. "Really." She pretended not to see the look of disappointment on his face, and when he asked for the bill she did not protest.

IT HAD NOT BEEN their most successful dinner but it had not ended in a row, and at present that was the best for which either of them could hope. James and Julia walked home hand in hand, in an easier silence.

As they passed Parliament Fields the floodlights were on, and what appeared to be a women's athletic club had colonized the grassy slope and field. Four runners in striped club Lycra crouched in the starting blocks while the rest zipped themselves in and out of tracksuits, tightened fluorescent shoelaces, touched toes, stretched impressive, geometric calf muscles. The gun fired, and James and Julia paused, leaning on the railings to watch as young legs pounded the baked rust of the track and young arms pumped with savage determination. A hush had fallen among the spectators.

Nearest to them sat a dark-browed girl with tight black curls, waiting alone, knees pulled up beneath her chin, skinny arms wrapped around them, her face tense with concentration as she watched her teammates, or rivals, hurdling below. She reached up to retie her ponytail and something in the gesture was so familiar, the stern contracted eyebrows, the spread-palmed, businesslike gathering in of unruly corkscrews, that Julia caught her breath. James made to move, but Julia put out a hand to stop him. She wanted to see *this* girl run.

Between races there were long breaks; the coaches began an intense discussion by the far bend, heads together over a clipboard; no one moved to right the hurdles that had fallen. After a while James pushed himself back from the railings and said, "I don't know how long middle-aged men are meant to watch teenage girls doing calisthenics in tiny shorts, you know, if they're not actually racing. I'm starting to feel a little creepy," and Julia dragged herself away. As they left, the black-haired girl remained apart from the others, bending to stretch the back of her legs, pulling her nose toward her own shins with fierce, quick little bounces. As they reached the footbridge, they heard the starting gun.

THE SHOPS OF QUEEN'S CRESCENT stay open late, offering a charade of purpose to the gangs of teenagers who patrol it. The chicken shop serves chips and battered sausages till the small hours; with the

radio tuned to the muezzin, the halal butchers do intermittent business until midnight, two brothers beneath the buzzing fluorescent
light strips behind a display of lamb shoulders and blood-dark livers
glossy as polished glass. Next door the greengrocers play the cricket
coverage with equal reverence, their narrow doorway flanked by ply-
wood steps heaped with taro, okra, yams, jackfruit, as well as plastic
buckets filled with less exotic fare—red peppers, granny smiths, pale
tomatoes—on sale, along with booze and cigarettes, straight through
till morning. To this strip of scrappy, eclectic commercial enterprise
come local kids to meet and mate, retiring to its darker side streets for
interludes of tender privacy.

When they turned off the Malden Road, James halted. He took
Julia's elbow, slowing her, turning her, pulling her back toward him.
"There's no rush," he murmured, into her hair. "Home's not going
anywhere."

She leaned into him. They stood unmoving and she felt his warmth
against her, her own blood heat, her own breath slow and deepen.
This, after all, was what mattered. Tonight had all been for this fleeting, vital union, the current of energy restored between them, the
body reminded. He and she.

Over her shoulder, James caught a movement in the shadows on the
other side of Malden Road. On the far corner of Queen's Crescent two
teenagers embraced—a boy in a hooded sweatshirt, his hands lost beneath the denim jacket of the slight, black-haired girl he was kissing.
The boy's hands locked beneath the girl's backside; he lifted her up,
mouths still pressed together, and with her neat legs wrapped around
his hips he backed up several steps against the wall, almost disappearing into the darkness. Small white hands roamed up and down his
bent shoulders, coming to rest on either side of his face. James caught

a glimpse of the boy's sweatshirt and jerked his head to the left, almost pushing Julia over. He reached out instantly for her hand.

"Come," he said, urgently, "let's go home." He began to stride on but his eyes had clouded, and as Julia followed she turned to where his gaze had been just a moment before. She saw what he had wanted to conceal—Nathan, grinding in a horrible, porn-inspired hip rotation against an equally feverish little Rowan. Before James could stop her Julia stepped forward instinctively, into the road. A car swerved to avoid her with an angry flashing of headlights and a fist held to the horn.

Nathan glanced up, and the color drained from his face. He whispered something to Rowan, who buried her face in his neck, shaking her head with what might have been laughter. Julia stumbled back onto the pavement and began to walk, and then run, toward the house. At their gate James caught up with her and reached for her arm. She shook him off violently and did not turn, but once she reached their front door she hesitated and then stepped back. For a moment she stood with hands on hips, trying to recover her breath.

"Julia."

She looked past him, vaguely, down the street. "I can't go in. I have no idea what to say to her." Her voice was flat, expressionless. "You will have to talk to—your son. Obviously he has to move out. Obviously he has to go."

49.

HER LITTLE GIRL WAS CURLED INTO A COMMA, HER THUMB slack in her mouth, index finger resting lightly on the bridge of her nose. In sleep she frowned, brows drawn low together, the other fist clenched on the pillow beside her. The room was hot and stuffy, the windows closed against the cool, clear summer night. Gwen had kicked off the covers and her long, pale, freckled legs were pulled up to her chest, defensive. So much passionate feeling, even in unconsciousness. Her fierce red hair was loose, spread behind her huge and untamed, like Boudicca, Julia thought, stroking back the bright curls that had fallen over Gwen's hot forehead. A young warrior, tensed for battle as she dreamed. In sleep, she drew Julia backward in time. Even as a new mother Julia had ached with longing for the infant that still lay in her arms, living over and over in her mind's eye the moment Gwen would crawl, then walk, then release her hand on the first day of nursery school and one day pack a bag and shatter her heart. She had held six-week-old Gwen to her chest and lowered her head and sobbed; when Daniel had tried to help, to take the baby from her, she had clutched Gwen jealously and could only cry, *"She's so perfect,"* meaning, *Please God, let this last.* This time, too, would pass in a heartbeat, and tomorrow or the next day her daughter would be eighteen, or twenty, or twenty-five, no longer in need. No longer hers.

On the bedside table Gwen had laid out a scene, lit up now by a silver wash of moonlight. She had used the inside of a shoebox as well as its top; the scene spilled out on two levels. On top of the box everyone had gathered. It was a party, or a parade, and behind them was a cardboard backdrop of balloons and glitter and fireworks. Iris, in sunglasses, wielded a huge, outsized croissant. Philip and Joan were arm in arm, four black-and-white woolly dogs frolicking ahead of them on pink cotton leashes. Saskia had a string bag filled with tiny books over one shoulder and a ring-bound notebook in her hands; she danced to the unheard music that filled her ears through miniature headphones. Nathan, ahead of her, wore a white coat and a broad grin and had a stethoscope plugged into his ears, its head held against the obscenely inflated chest of a blonde in a bikini—unlike the family she was cardboard, and in only two dimensions. And farthest away, in the far corner James and Julia embraced, their gazes locked.

Below, inside the shoebox itself was white, and at first glance it appeared empty. Julia bent to look. Gwen had made a new version of herself for this scene, a tenth of the size of everyone else, the little body only roughly hewn in modeling clay. Her face was hidden in her hands. In that huge blank space she looked desolate. By her feet a tiny scrap of paper, a tiny pencil, "I'm sorry" scrawled, doll-size, and above her the parade continued, unaware. Julia touched the minute sculpture and found the clay still soft. Within her something broke, barely perceptible, a snap like a dry twig underfoot.

Gwen had cast a pillow to the floor and Julia sat down and pulled this into her lap, holding it to her chest beneath crossed arms. She leaned back against the side of the bed.

When she opened her eyes it had begun to grow light outside, first oyster gray then faded tulip pink. Pale London sunshine, chill and morning-damp. The birds began, first the low fluting call of a wood pigeon, and then the twittering gossip of brown sparrows assembled outside in the cherry tree. She heard the diesel rumbling of the 24 bus on the Malden Road; outside, the creak and crash of a nearby front gate. Across London Philip would already have risen, moving softly so as not to wake Joan, creeping downstairs to retrieve the newspaper and to prepare the precarious cup of tea that brought him happiness to take to her each morning. An hour ahead on her pine-green French hillside, Iris would be waking to another day of thick golden sunshine and empty silence broken only by the frogs and crickets, and the chug and hiss of sprinklers beneath her window. She would make coffee on the stove, heating milk, laying a cup and saucer on a tray, a teaspoon, a small warmed jug. Later she would sit in the village square beneath the plane trees and study a production she would see when she re-turned to London. Erect and dignified, in her white linen and her loneliness.

And downstairs, James. Julia could hear him moving around the kitchen, though it was barely dawn. She wondered if he had slept. He had come in as angry as she had been—she'd seen his face, and barely recognized it. Angry with Nathan, angrier with Gwen, raging with Julia for having witnessed his son behaving with such callous immaturity. She had caught him out being imperfect, and knew from experience that for each to bear witness to the other's child's foolishness became quickly unforgivable.

But hours had passed and James would already be calm. He would have poured himself a glass of wine and talked himself around. Julia had all but banned his son from the house; to carry on James would decide to forget she had spoken that banishment. His door must always be open to his boy—no other way for him was possible.

Their love had seemed enduring and immutable, huge and sturdy as an ancient redwood, and was in the end, she saw, so easily felled. No matter how broad the trunk, each light fall of the axe deepens the wound and now, though it still appeared to stand, its roots were severed. Just a single stroke and the whole vast tree would crack and topple. She would not bear its slow precarious decay. For in the half-shadows of Queen's Crescent she had seen James's expression and had understood, as she had never before allowed herself to believe, that he hated Gwen. She realized with a sharp contraction of pain that he hated Gwen as she herself hated Nathan, for he had nurtured such wild, unrealistic hopes for his son, only to see them dashed to pieces against the solid enduring bulk of Gwen's foolishness. James hated her daughter. The thought fell into her consciousness with the steady clarity of a stone dropped in still water and settled there, black and solid. She had seen his hostility, and could not unsee it. By now he would have hidden it, packed it tidily away again beneath the right words and an appearance of limitless tender understanding. But she would raise her daughter only with love, and for that, she now understood, she must raise her daughter alone.

She would not be needed long. Three years, maybe four, while Gwen made her painful, inelegant transition into womanhood and strode, or tiptoed, or limped back out into the world. Gwen would leave and Julia would be—where? But she could not think of it. That sorrow was inevitable and didn't, couldn't alter her course now. Julia took a breath and stood. Then she went downstairs to break her own heart. Wasn't this, after all, a mother's love? And if she could not know it yet, one day, Gwen would learn.

part four

. . . .

50.

"I JUST WANTED TO SAY ENJOY, DARLING."

It was Iris. In the foyer of the Everyman, Julia wedged the phone between ear and shoulder and continued to hunt for her ticket in the recesses of her battered bag. As usual her mother-in-law had caught her at a moment of minor panic; Julia stepped aside to allow other, more organized cinema-goers ahead of her. Out came pens, dry cleaning tickets, loose Polo mints, car keys, and then a block of fresh fudge wrapped in striped waxed paper, a miniature pot of clotted cream and another of strawberry jam. There, beneath this odd collection, was the ticket. Julia had come from an early supper at a nearby gastropub with the new Dr. and Mrs. Alden, who had just returned from a weekend in Cornwall. It was in Joan's nature to package up and distribute to loved ones what she herself had barely had time to enjoy or even experience—in another bag Julia also carried a pair of luminous green and sapphire sea-glass coasters, a tea towel printed with a recipe for cheese and onion pasties, and a white cardboard box tied with pink curling ribbon containing scones. "They've gone hard since this morning," Joan had fussed, dithering while she presented them, as if she might decide at the last minute to take the unsatisfactory cakes back again. "You must promise you'll do them in the oven a little." Over fish and chips ("so we can pretend we're still at the seaside") Joan recounted their adventures in Tintagel, where the purchase of these souvenirs, as well as innumerable others for her sons, daughters-in-law, and assorted grandchildren, seemed happily to have occupied the visit. She and Philip were full of praise for the weather and the coast, and Joan was only sorry they'd had to leave the dogs, who would have loved the beach. By way of atonement Daisy had joined them for dinner, gently head-butting Philip's shins in gratitude for each scrap he delivered, tenderly, beneath the table. He had caught a little sun, Julia had noticed.

"Thank you. I'm late already; I don't know how I always do this." Julia switched her phone from beneath her left ear to her right and offered her ticket to the usher.

"Go, go," Iris commanded. "I'm envious, I must say I'm rather theater-starved out here. A feistier Desdemona than Verdi's, no? There was meant to be a wonderful revival in Milan last summer, but of course the Met's the Met. These live link-up things are so clever, though I do wish people didn't feel they had to munch their way through it like ruminants; it's still opera even at the cinema. Oh, and listen, if you speak to Gwendolen, tell her that Katy left some sort of fuchsia straw fedora number in their room; I only spotted it when I got back from dropping them at the train."

"I'll text her, I've been instructed not to ring."

"Quite right. And it's not important, no doubt she can pick up something equally hideous in Italy. It feels like it's made of polythene, or polyester or polystyrene—I don't know, something flammable. They're absolutely fine by the way, though Gwendolen's done something ghastly with her hair, did you know?"

"She sent me a picture last week, I wasn't sure if it was that bad in real life."

"Worse. Sort of carroty-blonde, and patchy. Never mind; it will perhaps fend off the Italians. Enjoy, darling. All those tenors. How bad can it be?"

Julia switched off her phone and went in. She was directed to a wide leather armchair in the back row and she set down her glass of wine to curl into the cushions, pulling her knees up beneath her. She had Pinot Noir and Rossini. What more could she want? Some company, perhaps. The seat beside hers was empty. But Anne had canceled at the last moment and Gwen could never be dragged to opera even had she been in London. In any case it was time, Julia had long known, to get used to doing things on her own.

She spotted him just before the house lights fell. At the front, sharing a burgundy velvet sofa and a small bowl of popcorn with Claire, his former registrar. Claire's cropped hair had grown long and heavy down her back, and she was laughing as she reached forward into the bowl. Her other hand wasn't visible, but might have been on James's knee.

It had been a year. It was, Julia told herself, only to be expected. Yet still she found she was fumbling on the floor for her jacket and her gifts from Joan, hearing loose change and unknown possessions spill from her handbag as she leaned forward. Claire was young and wore leather trousers, and had been unquestioningly attentive and compassionate and efficient when they had needed her on a very dark morning last spring. Julia would go home. She would not listen to the Rossini, which she now realized would have been a mistake. Under cover of darkness she left, knocking her wine over into her vacated seat and whispering a hurried apology to the usher without pausing to explain. She would not sit alone, watching them from the shadows.

James caught her wrist in the lobby.

"Julia."

"Hello."

"You're leaving." This sounded like an accusation, and she flushed.

"I didn't think you'd seen me."

"I hadn't, Claire did."

"How is Claire?"

"What? Oh, good, she's good, she's moved to the Homerton. How are you?"

Julia assured him she was fine, without elaborating. She did not say, *I have plans to become someone else.* After months of prevarication she had made an appointment at the salon for the following morning—she intended to shear her hair off, blunt and neat and high above her shoulders, and to color it the true blonde for which Iris and her hairdresser had always lobbied. It was happening tomorrow. Tomorrow she would become her new self: sharper, better defined, more definitive. Today, by accident, she still resembled the person she had always been. But she had no way to explain any of this and instead said, "Anne was meant to be— She had to work, in the end. How are you? How is Nathan?"

"He's good. Great. Loving it. Rowing, the whole deal. I'll see him next week, I'm stopping on my way to California." He seemed to hesitate and then rushed on: "I've been offered a job at UCSF, I'm going to talk to some people, check out some apartments, get a feel . . . it's a research post again. Better weather. Much better Chinese food, you know, which is definitely something to consider." He had been speaking very quickly but now seemed to catch himself and slowed. His hair on one side stood on end where he'd held it briefly in his fist. He added, softly, "Time for a change, maybe."

Julia pulled her jacket tighter. From the auditorium came the sounds of the orchestra tuning, loud and discordant, a sweltering afternoon in Lincoln Center beamed live into this mild north London summer evening. Any minute the overture would begin, and she would no longer be able to ensure her composure.

"Do send my best to Claire and—and, I'm happy for you both."

He frowned. "Thanks."

She began to walk away, but after only a few steps he called after her, "I'm— We're just friends, really."

She turned back to see his face change almost instantly, from embarrassment to hesitation, or perhaps it was a trace of defiance. "I've been lonely."

She said again, more softly, "I'm happy for you."

"Stop saying that," he said, irritably. He was wearing a pair of dark trousers she recognized, and a shirt that she did not. Behind him a woman's laughing face magnified, chiseled by falling photographic sunlight and shadows on a huge framed playbill; a documentary he and she had seen together here, last year, in a former lifetime. The espresso machine behind the counter buzzed and thrummed. Julia began to search for her keys and James stepped forward, as if to bar her way. "Where are you going now?"

"Home."

"How's Gwen?"

"Shouldn't you get back in?"

He waved away this suggestion, dismissing it. "Where's she going in September?"

"Leeds, in the end. She's Interrailing with Katy at the moment. Last heard of somewhere between Bargemon and Dubrovnik."

"Quiet without them, no?"

"Yes. And less laundry."

"And less laundry," he agreed, holding her gaze. It was Julia, after a heartbeat, who looked away. In the mirrored wall beside them the lobby extended, doubled, and she became aware of their reflections, a slight, pale woman, face upturned; a tall man with new threads of silver in his fair hair, thumbs hooked into his pockets, his shoulders raised in a tense shrug. She shifted slightly to avoid the sight of these two, awkward strangers.

James said nothing further and yet made no move to return to the darkened cinema, from which was now clearly audible the galloping opening bars of the overture, eliding almost immediately into the plangent lovesick strains of hope and longing that would follow. Soon the foreshadowing of bloodshed, between bars of pomp and flourish. True love vanquished. Foolish, needless death. James glanced back toward the closed doors of the auditorium and Julia dared to look at him, studying his profile for signs of—what? He had not changed. Here was the face for which she searched in every crowd, scanning, hoping. All her life she would know its contours as her own. She had no right to wish him anything but happiness.

She said, "I can hear Jago, I think."

"So what? You already made me miss the whole thing once in

Milan." And then seeing she looked stricken he sobered. "That wasn't funny, I'm sorry. I'm nervous."

"Nothing makes you nervous."

"That's not true. Unlicensed fireworks make me nervous. Pigeons. You."

It was her turn now to smile. In the cinema behind them Otello was disembarking, welcomed by the grateful Doge as a son of Venice. Love, hoped Otello, would crown all his achievements in battle. His audience in Belsize Park knew better.

"It sounds so optimistic. Rossini has a way of making impending heartbreak sound so cheerful. Poor Otello."

"Poor Desdemona," James countered.

"Victims of their own flawed characters."

"You think? Or of circumstance."

"One leads to the other."

"I think," James said, softly, "that you're being very hard on them."

Without warning the couple in the mirror moved toward one another; she closed her eyes to feel his arms enfold her, one hand warm at the nape of her neck, his forehead resting lightly, for a moment, against her own. Her lungs filled with the scent of him; spice and citrus and skin. Against her cheek she felt his fist close, momentarily, in the falling mass of her hair. Then he released her and was gone. For as long as she could, she held her breath. She remained until the doors of the cinema closed behind him.

On Haverstock Hill she waited for the lights to change. Dusk was falling, London muted and softened by the thickening darkness. She would go home. Back to prim tidiness and silence, to objects untouched since she alone had touched them. Back to still, close air. But tonight, before the words she now knew that she would write to him, she could hope. That their two fragile human hearts continued to beat each hour she knew to be a miracle. A car slowed to let her cross and she nodded her thanks and found, when she reached the far side, that she was smiling. She had seen him. He might still love her; either way she would love him all her life. She felt her chest expand and fill. Tonight, she would open the French windows. She would sit in the garden. She would listen, after all, to the Rossini.